BLACK BIRD

A NOVEL

MICHAEL FIEGEL

Skyhorse Publishing

First Edition

This is a work of fiction. Names, places, characters, and incidents are either the products of the author's imagination or are used fictitiously.

Skyhorse Publishing books may be purchased in bulk at special discounts for sales promotion, corporate gifts, fund-raising, or educational purposes. Special editions can also be created to specifications. For details, contact the Special Sales Department, Skyhorse Publishing, 307 West 36th Street, 11th Floor, New York, NY 10018 or info@skyhorsepublishing.com.

Skyhorse® and Skyhorse Publishing® are registered trademarks of Skyhorse Publishing, Inc.®, a Delaware corporation.

Visit our website at www.skyhorsepublishing.com.

10 9 8 7 6 5 4 3 2 1

Library of Congress Cataloging-in-Publication Data is available on file.

Cover design by Erin Seaward-Hiatt

Print ISBN: 978-1-5107-2355-9
Ebook ISBN: 978-1-5107-2356-6

Printed in the United States of America.

For Damien

MANFRED. I disdain'd to mingle with

    A herd, though to be leader—and of wolves.

    The lion is alone, and so am I.

ABBOT. And why not live and act with other men?

MANFRED. Because my nature was averse from life;

    And yet not cruel; for I would not make,

    But find a desolation.

                      —Byron, "Manfred," 1817

IAD

Of Fate, Free Will, & Anaphylactic Hypersensitivity

09/08/2008

I see her while waiting in line at one of those cookie-cutter burger joints, the ubiquitous sort with sticky plastic chairs, sticky plastic floors, and bathrooms you wouldn't wash a dog in. And of course there's the smell, the sweet reek of grease-steeped everything: burgers, fries, shakes, employees—one big drippy clot of wrong. Necessarily this includes me as well, but then life occasionally demands sacrifice, and I would sacrifice many things for french fries. And have.

But I digress.

I am patiently waiting my turn when a gaggle of tweenage girls squall in through the door, dragging a wave of piss-hot air into the lobby. I wrinkle my nose and clench my teeth but there is no avoiding them—they are instantly everywhere, like maggots on a rotting corpse. They seem to move as one mass, each dressed in a matching red bathing suit, a damp towel wrapped around slender shoulders or a slightly too-plump waist. Hideous fat toes wriggle from within a mass of green and pink sandals, slippery with wet; a scant few wear sneakers instead, water from their legs dampening what socks are present, saturating the canvas and ruining the floor with kidney-shaped prints rank with chlorine.

I nearly dismiss them all in this one lump sum, but then I catch a glimpse of bare feet and follow them up too-thin legs, past hand-me-down shorts, and on to their owner.

And there she is.

She is the second-shortest of her group, perhaps eight years old, with matte blue-gray eyes—steely, scared, and sad—peering through thin curtains of pooldamp blonde hair, half of it smashed crudely behind her ears, licking her neck. Ripening bruises purple her thin, pale arms, giving her the appearance of a fallen nestling, thin and floppy, not even worth a cat's time. Or a trapped bird, stuck in a house, banging against the windows, not dead yet but dying to get out.

The girls jockey for position as they queue for soft serve and french fries, doing their part to contribute to the obesity epidemic. But she just sets herself in place, sliding in without a word or an elbow, neither first nor last. On the surface she looks just like them but I can clearly see she is not. What they are is a neighborhood swim team or club of some sort, and she is not a team person. She is "take your sister with you." And she is "but Mom." And she is "no more buts, you take your little sister with you or so help me." And she is ignored, here and everywhere, yet content in her moments, and in this moment she is simply and wholly in line for an ice cream cone, just as I am in line for my dinner, and I know her.

I *know* her.

A void opens near the counter, and I instinctively step forward, filling the space to keep things whole. While I patiently wait my turn, I am as always trying to monitor my surroundings, watching for threats, but my attention keeps getting drawn back to this noisy horde of girls, their pudgy fingers fumbling with fistfuls of paper and silver, unable to decide what they want.

I have already decided.

The cool air sends chills down my sweat-soaked spine, raising gooseflesh in anticipation of something that has not fully hit me yet. The back of my mind is still putting it together, spinning, measuring, cutting as I watch the girl, alone in this crowd just like me. She does not want to be here. She wants to be *else*: somewhere else, someone else. She seeks focus, calm amidst the storm, and finds it by staring at the coins in her tiny palm. She fails to notice me watching her, sees nothing at all but the coins, the coins, the coins she got from daddy.

She drops them when I take her.

• • •

"He's not so tall," was my first thought.

It seems odd to think that now, because back then everything seemed tall, surrounding. Even him, at first glance. But somehow I could tell it was an act, a lie. Beneath the trappings, the posturing, he was just average: average height, average build, a body built from more flight than fight. Average looks too, although I think I thought he was just a little bit handsome back then, even if he was clearly headed towards the low end of the spectrum as middle age dug its claws in. Gray hair hung like feathers in his face, peppered with bits of black where the dye didn't wash out; it was the longest he'd ever worn it and the longest he ever would. His eyes were brown and warm that day, flecked with just enough green to pry the word "hazel" from witnesses' lips. Intentional, as was everything: the scuffed black boots, the thrift store trench, the dirty baseball cap, even the months-old beard, scratchy and uncomfortable and completely atypical for him.

He wasn't someone you would notice on the street, or on a subway, or in line for fast food. He was a nobody. And that, of course, is why he was what he was.

Some people claim we are in total control of our lives. They say we have the power to change our present and our future just by making a series of small choices from the menu of life, slowly building up the story of who we are, and who we wish to be.

Others say our lives are predetermined, that we're simply living out a set of instructions like a character in a video game. Just a bunch of pixels pretending to have free will, controlled by a bit of code that determines everything: hunger, thirst, fear, and fury.

When I was eight years old, I was abducted from a fast food restaurant by a man who took me, in all likelihood, because of a small splotch of mayonnaise on his hamburger. And so I believe in neither free will nor predetermination.

I believe in condiments.

• • •

The conversation before me ends, another customer served, so I step forward to place my order. Described literally, it is as follows: a large box of greasy starch sticks steeped in sugar and salt; a sandwich containing four ounces of low-grade, rancid beef scraped out of a drain, seared for ninety seconds before being placed into an unnaturally soft sesame seed roll (plain, absolutely no mayo); and a small cup containing a tiny amount of sugar-free cola-flavored syrup, a large quantity of ice, and some fizzy water for good measure. Large fries, plain burger, small Diet Coke. Simple.

"You want the combo, then?" The countersheep speaks in a thick, indeterminate accent. I swallow hard, silently wishing he had chosen a different career path. "If you get the combo you can get a large drink for less—"

"The large is bigger than my bladder. No one should consume so much liquid at one sitting."

"But it—"

"I do not want the combo." Luck is being pressed here, instead of buttons.

"Okay . . ." He breaks off into mumbles, and before he can even think to ask me about dessert, I toss some cash on the counter. He seems confused that I have given him exact change, but eventually he hits the right buttons to make the drawer splat out, then turns to assemble my order.

I sneak a glance at the little barefoot girl, still in line. Her friends are off in a distant corner of the lobby, laughs mingling with piped-in hip-hop, a whitewash of spine-grating irritation. She looks so alone, yet not unhappy.

To his credit, and my honest surprise, the countersheep shoves a tray of food into my elbows, derailing my thoughts. Shocked by his efficiency, I wordlessly step aside to let the next person order but find no one behind me. My little white dove is two places back, and her friends are enjoying their ice cream. This is not a difficult decision.

I turn and stoop to her level, mentally daring the people in front of her to defy my wishes.

"Come over here," I say. "This line is shorter."

She looks startled, confused, but nods dully and steps up to the counter, eyes barely high enough to see over the top. She reaches up to drop a handful of coins, the last few sticking to her moist palm for a half-second before peeling away to join the rest.

My good deed for the decade done, I walk to the so-called self-service station, because they no longer see fit to give me napkins, straws, and condiments at the counter. I collect what I need, squirt some ketchup into a cup, and put it all on the tray, just so. But just as I turn to head for my usual corner booth, I get that feeling in my gut that something is not right, so I set the tray back down and unwrap my sandwich. And of course, of fucking course, it's not plain at all. It's wrong. It has pickles and cheese and onions and horrible, filthy mayonnaise all over it.

I spin, furious, and bring the tray back to the counter, only to discover to my chagrin that the barefoot girl is still there. The sheep looms over her from behind the counter, clearly being anything but helpful.

"No shoes, no service," he says. And then he reaches out, puts his hand on the counter and—I cannot believe he actually does this—he pushes her coins off the edge. I am aghast at the pointless brutality of his action, and yet for some reason I'm unsurprised by it.

"Can I help you?" he asks, looking me in the eye as coolly as if the coin thing hadn't just happened. And though they still dance underfoot, I too forget the coins for the moment. As they say, in the event of a loss of cabin pressure, you put your own oxygen mask on first.

"I cannot eat this," I say, slamming the tray down. "It has mayo on it. I said no mayo."

And at this point he should take it back, apologize, and make a new one. That's how this works. Instead, he for some reason decides it's not worth his time to play nice.

"Can't you just *scrip* it off?" His accent seems thicker, and it takes me a moment to interpret. I don't know how to respond. The suggestion I just scrape mayo off anything is appalling. But his dismissive tone is what pushes me towards the edge. What about "the customer is always right?" The doting sycophancy that was company policy for so long? Fuck, right now I'd settle for mere civility.

Deep breath. Hold it. Exhale.

"I can't just scrape it off. I am allergic to eggs."

"There's no *icks* on our burgers."

"No, but there is mayo," I say, unfolding the burger to demonstrate. "Which contains eggs."

"There's no *icks* on there, dude."

I'm frothing at this point.

"*Eggs*, you dumb fuck. Eggs. Not *icks*. Speak the fucking language. Any language. Just pick one. English, Spanish, fucking Esperanto. Just make sense, you piece of shit."

"Would you like me to get the manager?" he asks.

People are beginning to watch. The grill cooks are staring out from under the heat lamp. About the only person who *hasn't* noticed is the manager.

"No," I say. "I simply need you to grasp this one simple fucking concept: I cannot eat eggs, and mayonnaise contains eggs. In fact, it's nothing but eggs. Eggs and oil. And therefore it cannot be consumed by me."

Something hits me in the shin. I look down to find the girl on hands and knees, picking up her scattered coins. She peers up at me and tries to smile. Tries.

"Sorry," she says. Voice like rain, like feathers, a soft mumble. "I just wanted ice cream—"

"No," interrupts the countersheep, who has no place in this moment. The rest of his flock back in the kitchen are egging him on, laughing. And he feeds off it, pushes his luck over the edge. "No shoes. No service. No ice *crim* and no *icks*. Now you both need to leave."

The girl starts to cry. I look up and around, scanning the room to see if anyone cares. No. Not friends, not family, not strangers. No one.

Well, almost.

"Go," the countersheep says. "Go or I will call the police."

I cannot help but smile.

"Oh, please," I say. "Please do."

• • •

"Close your eyes," he said.

A whisper, meant just for me.

The gun was for them.

• • •

My ears ring, my eyes tear, my nostrils burn, yet all my senses seem clear, never clearer, as I look back down at her, my smile genuine for once.

"Open your eyes," I say. But she cannot hear me clearly, fists pressed against her ears, trying to rub away the noise. I kneel and take her chin in my free hand as she blinks tears down a face spattered in red. I retrieve a napkin from the floor, lick one of the cleaner corners, and gently wipe her cheek. Some of it comes off, but some things will never be clean again.

What am I doing? Run, I think. Always run. But I cannot leave her here. Not now. Standing, I reach down blindly, searching about until I finally connect with her hand, a sudden jolt as her fingers close around my thumb. Her hand is cold and wet and her hair smells like chlorine. I can nearly taste it, and forever after she will be that smell to me: clean and caustic. Deadly.

I try to pull her along, but she cannot or will not stand on her own, so I bend over and grab her up in one motion as we head for the door. She struggles and slips, the coins tumbling from her hands as she leans her head against my neck, surprisingly warm tears creasing my salty back.

And for a moment, a tiny one, all is right with a world full of wrong.

● ● ●

Hell, I thought. Either I was in it, or he was dragging me there. I cried, of course. I always cried easily, especially then. The more I rubbed my ears, the worse the ringing got, and the more I rubbed my eyes, the worse they hurt. I put my head against his shoulder and crammed my eyes closed tight as I could, thinking that maybe I would wake up and it would all be gone. Or maybe just me. But the steel wool of his beard, scouring my face away layer by layer, made sure I knew there was no hiding from this.

And then I slipped, and I was suddenly afraid of him leaving me behind there in that sudden mass grave. I grabbed for his shoulder with my free hand, the other still holding the last of my father's coins. But I couldn't hold both at once. I would have to let go of something.

So I let go.

I still dream about how the coins hit the floor behind us and began to dance in the blood, circles in circles. Heads I win, tails I lose.

To this day, I wonder which way that last coin fell.

I Scream, You Scream,
We All Scream

09/08/2008

Twenty-four rounds, twelve injured, maybe nine dead. Or something like that; I neglected to take a head count on the way out the door, having been in something of a rush to get into the car and on the road. I am certain about the heroes who pulled their phones out and the little shits behind the counter. As for the others? I can get the numbers later on the news.

I never did like guns, in part because of the uncertainty. Is someone alive? Dead? Is the wound fatal or not? Too confusing. In all the chaos, I am impressed I remembered to save a few rounds: always one for myself, as there are worse things than death, and an extra for my guest, because there are worse things a little girl can encounter, too. I know some by name.

She is very quiet in the back seat, or so I assume. Right now she could be singing the national anthem and it would not get past the ringing in my ears—every time I do something like this, it gets a little worse, takes longer to go away. Another reason I hate guns: they're loud. This is to say nothing of the mess they cause. People spatter a bit at close range, and my coat is filthy with blowback: blood and other bits I would rather not think about too much, including the sticky goo they pass off as a soft drink. Luckily, my little captive audience of one has avoided most of it, but there are things in her hair she does not need to see.

When we get home, first thing that happens is I get rid of the mess.

Assuming we make it home.

The key to any successful escape is focusing on where you are going and where your pursuers are coming from; everything else is mere distraction. The cat pounces, the bird flies away. There is no time for thought, just instinct. Just reflex. Fly home. If pursued, fly to a new home. Just fly.

Flying blind is unwise, so I turn my scanner on to listen for signs that police are in pursuit of a vehicle heading west on 66 at seventy miles per hour. They are not. In large part, this is because I know how to blend in. For starters, I am driving a common car; this month I have a Camry, of which there are over ten million on the road. Also, obeying the unwritten rules of the road goes a long way. Unwritten being the key—technically the speed limit is fifty-five miles per hour here, but at nearly nine at night, fifteen over the limit means barely keeping up with the flow of traffic.

I know the getaway was clean—I have been eating at that place every other day for a few weeks now, so I knew the layout, where to park, and so on. But really, my odds of escape have less to do with my own ability, and more to do with the ineptitude of others. The police are probably still outside the restaurant, positioning snipers and negotiating with a ghost. If the cameras were even recording, all they have is maybe ten or fifteen seconds that shows nothing useful. What I look like now, I never will again. All the bystanders outside saw as we fled was a white man in a baseball cap, carrying a child from danger. I will barely even register in short-term memory. Eyewitnesses? I shot two with phones and the rest ate the floor; anything they have to say is going to be mixed and contradictory. It always is.

"What did he look like?"

"Tall, but on the average side."

"Hair?"

"Light black. Is that gray? Gray, maybe. I don't know."

"What color was his car?"

"Darkish."

"What kind?"

"Average? Mid-size maybe?"

"Domestic or foreign?"

"Him, or the car?"

In the first few hours, they will try to track the phones I took, a chirping, 3G breadcrumb trail for them to follow with their IMSI catchers, but that would only be possible if I was stupid enough to not pop the batteries and destroy the SIMs. Over the next few days, they will scour the scene for forensic evidence, spent cartridges, and stray hairs. They will search their databases and find no match, because I do not exist there. Over the next few weeks, they will look for patterns, but I will not do what I just did ever again. I will not revisit the scene of the crime, no matter what. I am not in this for fame, or infamy. This is what I do. And so I will probably get away. As I have before. And, hopefully, will again.

Still, a healthy paranoia keeps me checking mirrors for flashing lights, which is how I notice her watching me in the rear view, jagged arcs down her cheeks, dark smears interrupting the current where her hands have tried to wipe it away. Everything is just gray on gray in the evening light, but every time a car passes there is a moment when everything is all lit up in red, like a warning. A vivid reminder that while they might not be looking for me, they will be looking for her. She is a liability. A ticking bomb full of baby teeth.

We exit at 234 and I migrate south. There is a long light at Lomond, and with two minutes of silence to fill I peek in the mirror. Words, words. Say something. To think this all started over . . .

"Ice cream," I say, a bit too loudly. Her expression does not change. I try again, turning in my seat, halving the distance between our eyes. "You wanted ice cream. Right?"

I expect nothing, am shocked to get a nod and a sniffle. Something to work with.

It only takes a few minutes to get to the mall, where I begin looking for a dark spot, quickly finding one beside a van that looks like it has been in the same place for days. Safe bet it will still be there for another fifteen minutes. All I need.

I slip the car into park and turn off the engine. Consider. The ice cream kiosk is in the center of the mall and we are at one end. I am clean enough, sans trenchcoat, but the girl is not, and despite the fact there are likely more than a few teens in this mall whose makeup looks like bleeding, she would draw unwanted attention. I will have to leave her.

"Stay here," I say. "Just lie down. I will be right back with your ice cream. What kind do you want?"

She declines to answer.

"You have to tell me what you want. Or no ice cream." I jangle my keys. I generally dislike idle threats, but they work so well on children.

"Plain," she says as the key hits the ignition.

"Plain? You mean vanilla? There are thirty flavors and you want vanilla?"

She nods. Briefly I consider arguing the point further, but instead I get out, lock the door, and head inside. She wants vanilla, she gets vanilla. Not that it matters anyway. When I get back, she will probably be gone. And that is probably for the best.

● ● ●

Why did I stay? I have no idea. Not even after all this time. I had every reason to run. He was a stranger, and strangers were bad. Not the kind my parents had warned me about, either, with a van full of candy and puppies. A murderer. How many had he killed? The man at the counter, a few others for sure. Maybe my sister's friends. Maybe my sister. Maybe me, soon.

I should've run away, found a guard or a policeman or a mother. Anyone, really. Even another stranger. How could they have been any worse than him? Whoever I found, they could've saved me and arrested him and then I'd be safe.

But if he was going to kill me, why was he buying me ice cream?

Funny . . . you know, I think it was the ice cream. Blood, tears, noise, and despite all that, all I could think about was dessert.

I should've asked for sprinkles.

• • •

For a moment, when I return, I think she is gone; she is well hidden in the shadows. Only her reflection on the window betrays her. I am admittedly a bit shocked, but only just; I did, after all, buy two cones. I like to be prepared for any eventuality, including the unlikeliest.

Somehow I manage to fumble a key in the lock, open the door, and slide in without tipping the cones. She hardly reacts except to reach up and feebly take her ice cream from my hand. And now she has her vanilla, and I have my orange sherbet, which I can safely eat without dying since it is egg-free. The list of things I am unable to eat is almost as long as the list of people I have killed. Likely longer.

I turn on the light and watch her little pink tongue carve icy little troughs, trying to think of words. Sentences. Conversation. For a few minutes, there is nothing but licking and the little panting gasps between licks as we catch our breaths.

"Do you have a name?" I try.

She does not answer. This will not do.

"Listen," I say. "I realize you are scared. I am a stranger. But we have to be able to talk. And seeing as I just bought you an ice cream, I think you owe me a little cooperation."

She stops licking.

"Tell me your name," I say.

Words half-emerge through a glob of vanilla ice cream.

"Swallow first. Talking with your mouth full is rude."

"Christian," she says at last, meekly. It comes out like a sigh, like a dying breath.

"Odd name for a girl," I say, wondering if she is lying. No, why would she? Not yet, at least. "Are you? Or are your parents just *American Psycho* fans?"

Blank stare.

"Have you gone to church? Drank blood? Rubbed ashes on your forehead? Told a man in a closet that you felt guilty about being alive?"

A long pause. "No."

"Good. Religion is best avoided. The world is bad enough without imagining some sky person made it that way on purpose. Now, what else? How old are you?"

"Eight," she says.

"Good. And are you . . ." Conversation, not interrogation. "How about you ask *me* a question now. Go ahead. Ask me anything."

She thinks for a long while, but I do not prompt.

"What's *your* name?" she asks, eventually. Victory. Braver than I thought.

"I am nobody important. Nobody and everyman. Alpha and omega. I am the egg-allergic man. I am the walrus. Goo goo achoo."

I mime a sneeze, make a face, and she smirks. "You're crazy."

"So they say." They. *They* do, in fact.

"Did you go crazy from eating eggs?" she asks.

"No. Eating eggs would just make me very sick."

"Would you die?"

I wonder for a moment if she is just curious, somehow worried, or plotting my demise. That would be a hell of a way to go.

"I might die. I have some medicine just in case, though." I tap the glove compartment, but that is hardly the only place I keep it. I believe in redundancy.

"Any more questions? Other than those involving my death?"

She nods her head and begins to speak, but I quickly add, "Or my name."

She frowns and gives a little shrug. I sigh.

"Look, names do not matter past hello, and we are well beyond that already."

"Then why did you want to know my name?" she asks, licking her cone.

Ice cream has mingled with the blood on her cheeks. I do not point this out as it would certainly horrify her, and I do not wish to lose ground recently gained. I just devour the remainder of my sherbet, start the car, and pull out of our spot. I swing directly towards the street, cutting a wide swath across empty parking spaces, spreading a few puddles as we cross insignificant, impotent yellow lines. Thinking, hesitating, second-guessing myself.

When we reach the street, I stop to wait for a gap in the traffic. I peek into the mirror, and of course she is watching me. Waiting. I lower my eyes, close them, and decide.

"Edison North," I say to the dashboard. "My name is Edison North."

Then I pull into traffic and leave the past behind.

I open my eyes a few blocks later.

In Hot Water

09/08/2008

Most people are ignorant on purpose. They studiously avoid seeing things right under their noses: climate change, the beggar at the off-ramp, children being abused. This attitude is not without merit. Knowing about something is useless unless you can do something about it.

For example, take Man-Portable Air Defense Systems, shoulder-fired rockets that can travel at twice the speed of sound. Some call them the second greatest worry outside of suitcase nukes; the folks on TWA 800 would probably have ranked them higher. They are easily concealed and incredibly easy to operate—any moron can use one. And there are a lot of morons around.

As I type this, there are about a thousand unaccounted-for MANPADS loose in the world, according to my sources. Does knowing that fact do any good, if there is nothing anyone can do about it? Or would it be better to not know and thus not worry about it?

In keeping with this philosophy, my neighbors choose not to notice me, just as I choose not to notice that the woman next door sells pot, or that the guy upstairs beats his wife and kids. So nobody notices when I carry a small girl into my apartment. Or rather, they do, and then they tune it out and go back to licking their own asses. Humanity is a vestigial tail on the ass-end of the universe, wasteful and shitty. I live in the litter box.

This month, home is a two-bedroom shithole in a low-income complex thirty miles or so west of Washington, DC, in a town called Manassas where people are still fighting the War of Northern Aggression. Manassas is close enough to the capital for "work," but far enough away that there are far fewer security and traffic cameras around. Being a tri-state area (if you count DC), there is a wide variety of license plates to steal. Escape routes are plentiful, too. I am nine hours from Canada, within ten of a few dozen major cities. There are three major airports and an extensive light rail system, not to mention plenty of coastline just a few hours away, and—in a pinch—the Appalachian Trail. I think things are safe for now, but the more options, the better.

My guest probably wants to run, but right now she is more focused on "fright" than "fight or flight." I feel it in the way she clutches my shoulder on the walk from the nearby mini-mall where I parked. I see it in her eyes, reflected in my television the moment I lock the door. All those stories are circling in her head. Never talk to strangers. Never take candy from strangers. Never accept rides from strangers. And I am a stranger, and of course I am going to kill her.

But first, a shower.

I set the girl down, dump my trench on the back of the couch, and pull off my shirt and holster. The shirt goes atop a pile in the corner, the gun goes on top of the fridge—out of reach of a small child—the two confiscated phones go in the trash. Throughout, she remains rooted beside the door, eyes darting from the shotgun over the window, to the tangle of wires on the kitchen table, to the faint scars that crisscross my back and chest. I would be scared of me, too.

I take a few steps forward and settle on my haunches, bringing my eyes down to her level. She drops her gaze, but I catch her chin and force her face up.

"I am going to say this once, so listen," I say. "I am not going to murder you. I did not go through all of this effort to drag a young girl thirty miles only to hide her body under the sofa. There are no bodies under there. You can look for yourself. See if you can find the remote. If you do, you can watch Nickelodeon. You watch that?"

She nods, more vigorously this time.

"Good. So, rules. There are three things I do not want you to do. I am not going to tell you what will happen if you disobey. I am just going to ask you not to. Understand?"

She nods again. She has the nodding down pat.

"First, do not leave the apartment. There is food in the fridge. There is television. There is nothing outside you need. There are dangerous people out there. I acknowledge the irony in this statement, but trust me, they are terrible. I live here *because* this is a bad neighborhood.

"Second, do not use the phone. Any phone. There are at least six of them. If they ring, you ignore them. No calls, no answers, no texting. You need entertainment, you watch television. Phones are for work only. Later, I will let you go online. You know what that means?"

No reaction. Perhaps she has no idea. Twenty-five percent of the country has not gone on the Internet once. This is why television gets tech wrong about as often as they get crime wrong. Probably she knows, though. I just have no interest in caring right now.

"The third thing is no noise. Outside, you will hear shouting, music, dogs—but I am quiet and my neighbors know that. If there is noise they will ask questions I do not want to answer. So, to recap: no outside, no phone, no noise. Understood?"

She nods.

"Good. I am going to take a shower. You are on your own."

The apartment is smallish. It is exactly ten steps from the front door to the bathroom and my office, six more to the back of the main bedroom. Enough space for her to be alone if she needs to be, close enough where I can keep an eye and/or ear on her. For now it is important that we build trust. This is why I close the bathroom door behind me, leaving her alone. Well, half the reason. The other half is so I can be alone with my reflection. I have questions:

Why did you do it?
Why there?
Why her?

What does this accomplish?

What does she *think about this?*

There are no answers, not there before the mirror, and not under the hot water as I scrub myself clean for what seems an hour, wash everything down the drain, the water pinking and then clearing and pinking again as I open some old scabs. The blood reminds me that I need to don a new mask, so I grab the razor and get to work, nicking my face in the process and adding to the mess.

Hair dye? Red or brown? I might also leave it natural, cut it short, and let the gray show. Either or. The specifics are far less important than the fact that there is some sort of change.

Change. Lots is coming, and someone is going to send the hounds to flush her out. As soon as I finish what I came here to do, we are gone.

We?

The hard water hurts my eyes, stings like acid, but I shove my head under the spray anyway and dial myself a hotter temperature, the water tank groaning as I bleed it dry.

What the hell is wrong with you?

Why is she still here?

What the hell is wrong with her?

The hot water goes before answers come, so I clamber out and towel off. Through the door, I can hear the television, faintly. Good. That should keep her occupied while I write.

Some people keep diaries. Some have dream journals, madly scrawling images and words when they wake at three in the morning, looking for meaning in the chaos. Others piece their days together with yellow sticky notes, ideas and thoughts on the fridge. I have my chronicles.

I am not one of those psychopaths who writes down everything that happens to him, if indeed there are such people outside of Hollywood. My bookshelves are not filled with spiral notebooks full of literal psychobabble. I have a reliable laptop with Microsoft Word installed, and that is more than enough. I catalog the interesting bits, the stuff worth remembering, things out of the ordinary. Things that seem to matter at the time.

To who, I am really not sure. Me, I suppose. Perhaps a *me* I am yet unaware of, some future me I am not willing to acknowledge yet. A me who starts to forget and wants to remember.

I have not had much to write about lately. There is a limit to how interesting life can be, and even the best life has to offer is mostly mediocre. The earth is twenty-five thousand miles around, and in their lifetime, the average person walks about three times that amount. But they spend all of it walking to the bathroom, to and from the car, crawling into bed. Beer and sex, sports and sleep. Walking the dog. These things are all that most people want in life.

I want more, but I know better than to hope. Hope in one hand and defecate in the other, I know which one fills up first. I know firsthand. It was all too recently, with not much to do, not much to say, for stretches of time which—as I write this now—seem impossible to comprehend. Years. But now I find myself suddenly bothering with a little girl.

Why? All I am sure of right now is this: I suddenly have a lot more to write about.

• • •

Back then I didn't know what it was he did every night, clacking away on his elderly laptop for hours and hours. Maybe I thought he was talking with someone online. And he was, sort of. Just not online. Everything he wrote, it was all just him. For him. With himself. And each night he'd peer into the depths of his soul, then drag himself out just before the abyss could look back. His chronicles kept him right on the brink, but I'm still not sure which way they were pushing. We never discussed them; I never even dared to knock on the door when he was typing.

He'd taken his time that night, leaving the TV to babysit me (a reality I was familiar with). His cable box only went into the low sixties before flipping around to the blue nothing of channel AUX, and that night there was nothing I wanted to watch anyway. All that seemed to be on were shows like *Prison Break* and *CSI: Miami* reruns, full of carjackings and kidnappings—far from reality TV but all too real to me. Very current events. I had fallen half-asleep as channels dripped by, listening to the white noise as dialog popped in and out, forming random sentences. Like a lullaby. *When the bough breaks . . .*

When he reached down and shook me, I woke right up, though, and barely managed to hold a scream in. Thoughts of escape must have run through my mind, but I knew it was too late; if there was to have been any getting away at all, it would have been earlier, in the car, alone. Why hadn't I run? Stupid. Stupid girl.

When people talk about "fight or flight," they always seem to leave out the third one, which is "frozen in terror." Play dead. Lots of animals do it. Don't move, and maybe they'll get bored and go away. Problem is, that doesn't work with people.

• • •

"Get up," I say. "You need to get clean." She is still dotted with blood, most of it in her hair, and I am not about to ruin my flannel sheets.

"Hey." Still no answer. Fine, I decide. We can do this the hard way. I grab the ugliest blanket from the back of the couch and drape it over her, then— hesitating for a moment—reach underneath and pull her shorts down over her legs and feet. The next bit is especially awkward; were she wearing a shirt this would be easier for both of us, but as it is she has on just the swimsuit, so I close my eyes, reach quickly underneath and up to her shoulders, and fumble it off, sliding it down with the blanket and dumping the whole mess into an increasingly large pile of laundry that will require a setting somewhere between "heavy duty" and "crime scene."

When I reach back to scoop her up, she unfreezes, whimpering as I carry her towards the bathroom, my eyes tracing cobwebs along the ceiling. Then I realize that if I want her clean I will have to see her, and that is not something I am ready to deal with right now. If ever.

I divert to the bedroom; I decide I can overlook a little blood on my pillows. I tuck her shivering and naked under the sheets and turn out the light, but even in the dark I can feel her eyes open as I make my way to the door. She expected the worst, possibly could have handled that, but has no idea how to react to this. I am not sure I do, either. I pause in the doorway and address the floor.

"I know you have heard stories about bad men who take little girls and do bad things. I am many things, but I am not that."

She is silent; softly, barely breathing.

"I am going to sleep on the couch. This door locks from the inside. There is no key that I am aware of, so you are safe. Try to sleep. We have a lot to discuss in the morning."

She says nothing, so I lock the door and pull it shut on the way out. For the briefest of moments, I consider saying "sweet dreams," but she is not that naïve.

And I know better.

Breaking Fast

09/09/2008

Pizza. Breakfast of champions.

My guest wakes up halfway through my third slice, which means I am almost finished eating, possibly for the day. Breakfast is not just the most important meal of the day, it is occasionally my only meal. I never know when I might be spending a few hours in a crawlspace, so it is never wise to leave the house on an empty stomach, even if all I have to eat is three-day-old pizza. A dish best served cold, of course—after the second day, reheating pizza just makes it worse, so eating it straight from the fridge offers the minimum amount of suffering possible.

"Morning," I say as she wanders into the room, dressed in one of my flannel shirts. She looks like she has been awake most of the night—I know for a fact she was up to use the bathroom, as I sleep lightly. I also know she slept at least some; she snores.

"Your clothes are in the wash," I say. "Take a bath. Or a shower. Are you old enough?"

She nods.

"There are semi-clean towels and shampoo in the bathroom. Use conditioner. The water is hard and your hair will be like onion straws otherwise. By the time you get done your clothes will be dry, and we can talk."

She nods again but just stands there.

"Go. Unfilth." Only then does she turn and leave. I sincerely hope this is not how things are going to go or I may have to kill her after all.

I bite, chew thoughtfully as the water splashes into the tub, too hot, too cold, just right. Then that forever moment between faucet and showerhead, as water changes course and the pipes shudder in the walls, and then spray hits the curtain. Swallow.

Why is she here? I had thought about it all night long, dreamt about it, and still had no answer. She was an impulse buy, the candy in the checkout line, the magazine, the pack of cigarette lighters—two for ninety-nine cents, what a bargain. If you had never seen it, you would never miss it, but now that you have it, you have to put it somewhere. Perhaps in a kitchen drawer, behind the rubber bands and half-dead batteries. The et cetera of life.

The microwave trills, telling me her clothing is dry. There are no laundry hookups inside the apartment, so I spend an uneventful few minutes betwixt home and the Laundromat in the mini-mall, briefly checking on the car on the way back. It has not been stolen, although I do discover that some inconsiderate asshole has parked his goldfinch-yellow Camaro across two spots, one of them adjacent to mine. I slip underneath and use a pocket knife to cut through everything not made of metal or hard plastic. I will have to wash this shirt again, but it will be worth it even if I never see the outcome.

By the time I get back, she is out of the shower and into my robe, as well as the last slice of pizza. Apparently she is getting the hang of this situation better than I.

"Your clothes," I say, dumping her things in a pile on the couch. As I cross the room towards her—too quickly, perhaps—I see the food catch in her throat, in that little V where my blue robe splits, but she chokes it down. I sit across from her, pour myself a glass of tepid water from a filterless Brita pitcher. With her there, I am more acutely aware of how messy my table is.

"Why are you here?" I ask. She is silent, so I add, "Why did I take you? Why are you here? First thing jumps in your head."

It takes a while for a kernel to pop. Then: "Money?"

"Okay. Sure. How much are you worth?"

She stares into her lap, fingers rasping across the crust of pizza on her plate. She is acting her age, and I am losing patience with her.

"Listen, you are a bright girl. I am going to talk to you like an adult. If you do not understand something, you ask me. Else I will assume you are ignoring me, and I will get upset. Do you understand me?"

She nods.

"Say it."

"Yes."

"Okay, how much are you worth? A hundred? A thousand?" I grab a crumpled twenty dollar bill from the table and wave it. "Pick a number."

"Twenty?"

"Wrong," I say, flicking the bill onto the floor. "You are worthless. I am not interested in money, at present. But at least we know how little you value yourself. Try again."

She scratches her leg with her foot, shrugs, opens her mouth, closes it.

"Sex?" I say. She blushes. "Do you know about that? Where babies come from?"

She nods, subtly.

"We already discussed that. While there is a distressingly large portion of the population that is evidently interested in small children, I am not among them. I do not do that."

"What do you do?" she asks, unprompted. Progress.

"What do you mean by that? I eat, I drink." I sip some water. "I want to impress upon you the need for detail. It will save your life. Now, ask again."

A pause while she parses, then: "What is your job?"

"I am a serial mass murderer." It is the closest term I can think of; I have no résumé. Domestic terrorist is too narrow in scope, and the point is not terror, per se. "I kill people. Lots at a time. I am sure you have watched shows where people get paid to kill other people. Hit men. Anyway, that is . . . kind of what I do. Sometimes on purpose, sometimes as a side effect."

"Why?" she asks.

They wonder why children kill each other. This is why. They are not old enough to think anything is "wrong," have not had time to "learn" that it is "bad." In some states you cannot even be tried for murder if you are under eight. That murder is bad is a matter of opinion, and it is an opinion I do not share with society. Is it murder when a hawk eats a mouse? It is just as premeditated, just as purposeful.

"Why not?" I answer. "There are plenty of reasons. Some people are doing things that should be stopped. Some need to be moved out of the way. Some deserve it, frankly."

"So you kill bad people?"

"I could not care less about good or bad. Too messy. I hate cleaning up messes."

She glances around the filthy apartment, quite damningly.

"Yes, I know. This is . . . This is a . . . tool shed. Those are meant to be messy. I am like a gardener, and the garden is, I guess everything. Out there in the world." As I speak, I arrange the detritus on my table into neat rows, thinking this will help her understand, at her age. There's so much to work with: bottlecaps, potato chips, stray pepperoni. My table is *filthy*.

"Okay, so there are good and bad plants in a garden. Weeds are bad, right? There are also good bugs, like bees and worms, and bad ones. I take out the pests and the weeds so the garden can grow. I even prune the good plants, sometimes, to make the whole garden better. My job is not good, or bad, though—just necessary. And it sometimes gets messy."

I wipe everything but the paper to the floor, then hold up my hands, stained with newsprint. I then proceed to point at various front page stories.

"Humans are animals. You know that, right? Biology? Filthy, messy animals. They make a mess whenever their zoo gets crowded. America, Iraq, Afghanistan. Africa. Israel. Georgia. It has always been this way. Do you know about the Crusades?"

She looks confused. I am going too fast. Need to take a step back. I stand up to get some water, and she flinches a bit as I brush past her, but not as much as before. She is like a wild bird in a box, gradually struggling less and less until finally you get it eating out of your hand.

Of course, the bird eventually dies either way. Best to not get attached.

"What grade are you in?" I ask. "First?"

"Third."

"Third. Did you learn about the Crusades?"

She shakes her head.

"The Crusades were basically white people against brown people. One god against . . . I guess the same god. Same war being fought right now, over the same tiny rectangle of land. Jews, Christians, Muslims, Canaanites. Everyone claims their god promised it to them. So they have been killing each other for it ever since, well, ever. In the Middle Ages it was a specific set of wars, the Crusades, fought under the banner of your namesake. They even sent children, some younger than you. All killed or enslaved. You can imagine what they did to the girls your age. Boys, too. All in the name of a benevolent god. Good torturer, bad cop, this god.

"But it never stopped. The wars continue. And there is plenty of room for children in the ranks, too. The Moro Islamic Liberation Front runs ten-year-old girls through military training. The Ugandan Lord's Resistance Army is a third children. Half the Afghani army is . . ."

I am losing her again. Ranting, rambling. Deep breath, pull it back. Wrap it up.

"The point is, imaginary gods and pointless causes have killed more people than I ever will. At least my causes are tangible, even if I happen to be the only one who believes them. My reasons. That brings us back to your question, which was . . ."

"Why?" Long pause, but shorter than before. Improvement.

"Why. Indeed. Let me tell you a story." I close my eyes. The memory is vivid as ever. I can smell the exhaust. Burnt oil and asphalt.

"My car broke down one day while I was on a job. I was a bit more than twice your age. No one really had mobile phones then, so in ninety degree heat, I had to walk to a pay phone. You know what that is? Big glass box? Nearest one was several miles away, and when I got there of fu— of course the phone was out of order, like they all are now. I looked across the street, and there was another phone, but between me and it were six lanes of traffic, whizzing by.

"For a minute, I felt like a cog in . . . No, you have no idea what a cog is. I felt like . . . a tiny little worm inside of a big monster, a giant ugly bird.

Stuck inside a big belly that just wanted to grind me up and liquefy me. I was nothing. And there was nothing I could do but stand there and get chewed up and digested and eventually turned into shit. Like everyone else.

"But then I reached out and I pushed the button to cross the street. And everything stopped. Traffic stopped. The monster stopped. The world stopped. Because of *me*."

I jab at the table to emphasize the point, realize I am too close, staring into her eyes from just a few feet away, and so I sit back. I have not let myself get this deep into it in a long time—no use reciting doctrine to a mirror—and I have lacked an audience. Of course she cannot understand. She is a child.

"Traffic, religion, war, society, politics—all of it is alive. And anything that lives can be killed if you push the right buttons. Not just me, you. We might be trapped in its bowels, but it can be hurt from within. You can choke it as it swallows you, you can tear up its guts while it grinds away at you. And you can bite it in the ass on the way out. The beast has a mouth, but so do you and I."

I grab the remainder of her pizza crust from the floor and stuff it in my mouth, expanding my cheeks and nearly choking myself. She smiles, and I note that although her mouth is still half-full of baby teeth, the permanent ones she has are clean, straight and strong. Perfectly suited to crushing, slashing, cutting. Designed for killing, as she might be. Not yet, of course. But some day, with some effort . . .

I'm willing to teach, I realize. But only time will tell if she is willing to learn.

I Live in This Hole

10/15/2008

The weeks fly past like stray bullets when one is on vacation, which I am.
Have been for months, unless you count the lull before, which makes
it years. The "incident" at the restaurant (inasmuch as I hesitate to use that
word) was not work. It was . . .

I will just leave it at "was" and move on.

My vacation has not been entirely self-imposed. I get paid for what I do,
and I am at the mercy of those who pay. I could "work" now if I wanted—and
I have in the past—but that is a lot harder to arrange and the pay unpredictable. Some others use downtime to hone their skills: practice at the range,
torture for fun and/or profit, serial kill. I sit tight and suffer through reruns,
alternately bored out of my mind and cursed with ideas. Doubts, sometimes.
More so recently.

Having a guest keeps me occupied, but things are strained. There have
been some minor victories—she seems to be over the fear that I will try to
kill her, and I am over the ridiculous worry that she will walk in on me in the
bathroom—but nothing else of note.

We talk a lot, or at least I do, and I keep little from her, for it has been
a long time since I had anyone who found me interesting enough to listen

to. Her mind is a sponge, but the thing about sponges is you need to let them dry out once in a while or they begin to harbor unhealthy things. We both need a break. But there is nowhere to go, no need for either of us to leave the house other than my brief forays to the Laundromat. Thirty-some days, ninety-some meals, a dozen take-out menus, hours of games and television and movies. Everything can be delivered now, either by phone or courtesy of my upstairs neighbor's poorly secured wifi. America is a wretched dystopia and I am glad the worst of it can be avoided, but even I have limits.

It is just when this routine is starting to stagnate that the call comes in. Brief, a series of digits, and then silence. Sometimes we still do that bit on paper, but now it is mostly burner phones, cheap and disposable. Keeping Radio Shack in business. I disable the phone I got the call on, pick up another, call back. They speak, I listen. I say yes.

"I have to go out," I say as I walk through the living room to get my things; it does not take long, since I leave most of the essentials in a bug-out bag by the front door.

"Don't you only go out at night?" she asks.

"I am not a vampire."

She is not so sure.

"I will be gone all day," I add. "I have things to do and get. I have a job, in a few weeks."

"Can I come?"

I give her a look. Seriously?

"Fine," she says. She looks disappointed. Perhaps I need to lengthen the leash. But not today. Today is a solo flight; she stays in the nest.

"If you behave, when *Twilight* comes out—"

"Really? We can go see it?"

"*If.* Be good. No phone. Watch television or play games. But no multiplayer games. I do not like the language those kids use."

With that, I grab my trench and walk out the door, convinced, as I always am, that when I return she will be gone.

• • •

In hindsight it's easy to recognize that it had only been about a month since he took me, barely any time at all. But standing there in too-big socks and an itchy thrift store nightgown, strange clothes in a strange place, it suddenly felt much longer. Time seems so big when you're little. Days last for weeks. A month seems like forever. And it had been about that long since I had been alone for more than the length of a shower.

Alone. I could leave. I could run.

Or could I? What if it was a test? "Be good," he'd said. Running away wasn't very good. What if he was standing outside, waiting for me to open the door so he could shoot me in the head? What if there was a camera in the TV? An alarm on the door?

And even if he wouldn't do any of that, maybe someone else would. If he was a liar, he was trying to trick me and it would be fine if I ran, but if he was telling the truth then there were terrible people right outside the door. I knew for sure there was at least one monster upstairs. I heard his kids crying every night. They seemed about my age.

I couldn't run. But if I didn't, I might never get the chance again.

All the emotion, everything I'd bottled up for the past month, came out there and then. Fear and frustration. I cried, as I did so often back then, though as I remember it, not long enough. Tears are pointless if there's no one around to see them. I learned that long before I met Edison. I quickly got into sniffling and then boredom. What should I do? What would he want me to do?

"Be good," he'd said.

In my previous life, "good" meant being quiet, staying out of the way, and doing chores. I'd already been doing the first two here, with him. Maybe it was time to do the third.

For sure, the place needed it.

The kitchen was a mess as ever, sockbottoms sticking on food-stained tiles. The sink was the worst, full of sweet-and-sour mold and eternally full of dishes. Clearly it needed to be washed, but there was no detergent to be found, so I explored below-sink, fascinated by how different it all was from my old home. Our cupboards had been perpetually on the verge of empty, but Edison's were full of stuff: kerosene, ammonia, moth balls, aluminum foil, drain cleaner. Random, useless things, to me at least. The bathroom was also a bust at first—iodine and peroxide might be good for cuts but wouldn't help with the dishes—until I remembered the shampoo, which sudsed up nicely, the smell of White Rain quickly overpowering the gagging reek of mold.

There was no dish rack to speak of, so I washed, rinsed, dried, and stored as I went, walking on top of the counter to reach the higher cupboards as I tried to make some sense of it all. Canning jars were stored beside light bulbs, duct tape alongside lighter fluid. Vinegar and corn starch were stored in the same place as charcoal and propane, behind jars of salt, flour, baking soda, and—of all things—anise, vanilla, and almond extracts (which he'd forbidden me to touch for some reason).

The fridge made no sense either. There were the predictable boxes from several different pizza delivery places, but beyond that it defied all logic. Whipped cream, herring snacks, off-brand diet cola, condiments, expired eggs. The freezer was more mysterious, filled with things I'd never seen him use, like vodka, first-aid ice packs, and several unlabeled metal canisters I knew better than to tamper with. There was also a carton of vanilla ice cream, which I ate half of, once I found a clean spoon.

Through it all I kept looking over my shoulder and I couldn't figure out why at first. I realized after an hour or so that it was because I kept expecting to get punished for getting into things I had no business getting into. It felt strange to not be yelled at. It didn't feel like home.

At least, not the one I was used to.

My mother had worked at a diner. She didn't make a lot of money, so she worked at night sometimes, too, dressed up extra fancy, and of course now I know what that was. Those were the nights my father would get especially drunk, and when Mom came home they would argue. They didn't try to hide the yelling, and sometimes not the hitting, but it didn't bother me much. I saw worse on TV. Mom mostly slept in my room on those nights, for some reason preferring me to my older siblings. Maybe just trying to limit the damage to one room of the house. We'd lie there afterward on wet pillows with matching bruises, and she'd whisper how it would all be better tomorrow, and we'd both fall asleep like that. At the time I thought the whispers were for my benefit, but really they were just for her.

My father didn't make a lot of money either, which I guess is why they fought, struggling to fill five mouths besides their own. He couldn't fix his own problems, so he worked extra long hours at a garage, fixing other people's. Then he'd stop off at the bar on the way home to forget his own. I almost preferred him drunk—it seemed more honest. Sober, he always looked at me strangely. Not like *that*, though. I mean, in retrospect there were plenty of awkward moments between bathroom and bedroom, and it makes me wonder about my sisters . . . but he never touched me. From what I figure, he never touched my mom either, not after I was born. Maybe that's what the weird looks were. Disappointment. After my brother died, a few years before I was born, they tried again and again for another boy, for what my father apparently saw as perfection, failing in each of five attempts to tie X to Y.

I was the last mistake he'd ever make.

We weren't poor really, I guess, but there was never quite enough. The recession had hit us hard. So in addition to their incomes we lived on the cast-off kindnesses of others: a noisy old PC, used clothing, leftovers. There were days, weeks when we didn't spend a single cent, licking the teeth of friends and neighbors, but it kept us alive. Bills got paid, clothes got bought, and no one went hungry. Going out for ice cream was a big deal, but no one starved.

I even had friends—though mostly I shared my sisters'—and I had a puppy until I left the front door open, and I had books and dolls and a jump rope and sugar and spice and all that. In short, I had a typical, lonely life that was sinking from lower middle into upper lower class as the economy got worse. And there was nothing we could do about it. It's no wonder they didn't try harder to find me. No news, no search parties, no Amber Alert. Nothing.

At home, I was always underfoot, and always getting yelled at, and never alone. Here I was alone, and it was quiet, and I didn't feel unwanted. Maybe it was for the best I did get taken, I thought. Maybe they were doing better without me. And, come to think of it, I without them.

Once the kitchen had exhausted its mysteries, there wasn't much left to explore. The desk in the hall was just a mound of paper and empty takeout containers, and the living room was already known to me, little more than a couch, a table, a TV, and stacks of games, DVDs, and books, all of which I'd been devouring over the past few weeks. I swept the rug, fluffed a few pillows, and called it a day. The bathroom was as clean as it was going to get, and the bedroom had been relatively organized since he'd given it over to me. That left just one room.

For all the times he'd snuck in and out, always careful to shut the door behind him without offering me so much as a peek, he'd never once explicitly told me not to go inside his office.

Was it where he kept his dirty stuff? I doubted it; I don't think he ever owned dirty stuff. *Joy of Cooking*, maybe; *Joy of Sex*, no. Maybe weapons? Or maybe he had cash in there, piles of stolen moneybags with cartoon dollar signs. Was there something he didn't want me seeing? Maybe he was testing me? Maybe he'd see me going in, maybe he'd be recording me, and when he got home he'd kill me for going in there.

Ultimately, logic slapped fear aside. Opening a door he'd never told me to keep shut would certainly not lead to anything worse than a scolding, and I'd gotten worse in the not-too-distant past. The door was open before the other half of my brain could argue, and I was inside looking around before it occurred to me that it hadn't been locked.

I was immediately disappointed. One half of the room was filled with tall stacks of empty boxes. The other half held a small desk, a wooden chair, a desk lamp, and an antique laptop, tethered to the wall by power cords and gray cables. Beside it, a pad of yellow paper, jagged strip across the top where he'd torn the last one off. No dead bodies, no weapons, no drugs. Nothing but a boring screensaver and, after I bumped into the desk, a login prompt on the laptop. It didn't even occur to me to mess with it; its mere dullness was security enough. I turned in disgust and shut the door behind me.

I'd been abducted by the most boring murderer in the world.

I played games for a while after that, eventually falling asleep on the living room floor. I woke up hours later on the bed to the sound of angry mumbling, drifting about in half-sleep until finally the door opened and someone came in, surrounded by a smell like gasoline. Someone had been, was still saying something. Probably him, maybe me.

"Huh?" I mumbled. I peered up at a stranger named Edison, not entirely sure I wasn't still dreaming. He had gotten a close-cropped hair-cut—nearly military—matching a clean-shaven face. Everything dyed red, now, the color of blood. Different clothes, clean. His eyes looked different, too, and now I know it was because of the blue cosmetic lenses he'd put in to complete the change. Every day with him was going to be like Hal-loween.

But there was more. Something intangible had changed. He seemed more coarse, patience worn thin from his time out among the natives. Something in his voice cut through the fog even as I struggled to fall back asleep—it was a tone of acceptance. I was no longer a rent-to-own; he had purchased me outright.

I mumbled again, and he repeated himself for the third time. This time I heard him clearly.

"I said, never put foil next to the drain cleaner."

For some reason this made perfect sense as I dozed off again. It made even more sense a few years later when I learned why. But at the time his statement was just a mystery, like counting sheep backwards, nonsensical yet purposeful. With that in mind I fell asleep, dreaming of whipped cream and gasoline, wondering idly—just before I drifted off for good—why there were eggs in the fridge if they could kill him.

I think he thanked me for cleaning before he shut the door, but it's probably just wishful thinking.

Words of the Prophet

11/04/2008

I have only just reached the Ballston station when the last call comes in, instructing me to take the next Red Line towards Metro Center. I only have a few seconds to wait—excellent timing. The idea of spending any amount of time in such close proximity to this number of people makes certain things in the back of my head run screaming for the shadows of my unconscious. So when the car arrives, and the door slides open, I immediately step across the threshold, eager to get this over. Just me, my briefcase, and a bundle of high explosive. Of the three of us, only one will be getting back off.

I had not thought it possible for the Metro to be more irritating than it has been this past week, yet it is; I would chew off my own skin if I thought it would ease the pain. It is not that it is crowded, but rather the nature of the crowd, a tangle of freaks swaying back and forth in the belly of a motion-sick beast. I somehow manage to find a seat, and as I settle in for what will hopefully be a short, uneventful ride, I cannot help but take inventory of the zoo. They are all of them animals, albeit animals who can vote. It may as well be an ark, and a redundant one at that, because there are more than two of each kind on board.

The woman closest to me is clearly one of the cows. Not because she is overweight—she is, but that describes most of the passengers—but more her docile, laconic nature. She exists to serve. Good breeding stock, someone might say: broad hips, large breasts. White stockings, white dress. A nurse, perhaps. Or a wet nurse. Do they still have those?

Beside her is one of the many pigs. Short, bewhiskered, round. Brown and gray all over, head to toe. Face in his phone, one of the new iPhone 3Gs, no doubt wallowing in some Internet mire. He chortles, tries to show the screen to the blonde-haired mare next to him, but she ignores him, staring blankly at her own device, vast, vacant blue eyes, an uncaring goddess of nothing. She knows she is better than him. He knows it, too. We all do.

This being DC, there is plenty of cold blood on board as well. The snakes are most plentiful, pearly white teeth practically dripping with venom. Lobbyists, mostly. Lawyers too. Brown and blue and gray, their scales the only differentiator. You get the occasional intern or junior congressperson mixed in, but they are easy to spot by the flag pins and the Blackberries and the foolish optimism that has not quite been crushed out of them yet.

There are whales, there are dogs, there are rats-a-plenty. There are insects and cephalopods and slime molds. And filling in the cracks and crevices is a vast assortment of lesser beings that fall outside of the animal kingdom entirely, not even worth my notice, only relevant to me in that they are occupying space that might be put to better use. Wasting my oxygen.

In years past I might have also complained about the noise, the incessant chatter, but the only sound is that of the Metro rambling along, occasionally asking passengers to make room for others to crowd aboard. That, and the children, of course. But the crying does not bother me. Children are built to cry—it is their purpose to remind us that life hurts. The problem is their uncaring parents, faces buried in magazines and mobile phone screens. They should be forcibly spayed like dogs with a rusty knife so they can no longer spawn. Or, failing that, should be killed in whatever manner might be most expedient. I wonder if my little guest had horrible parents, too. Probably. I did.

As terrible as my childhood was, things used to be better, or at least more innocent-seeming. I remember streets safe enough to walk down at night, sidewalks covered in chalk instead of urine and shit, lawns peppered with divots from tackle football rather than blued with cancer-causing chemicals. When children played outside, and a president actually resigned from office (eventually) when faced with possible impeachment for his misdeeds. It was still a time when there was more to be afraid of, yet for all that, people were less afraid. And more human.

When I was the same age as my current house guest, I lived in Maryland for a time, and there were twin girls who lived two doors down about the same age. For some reason they would play hopscotch in our driveway— possibly because it drove my father mad, possibly just because our driveway was the only one both consistently empty and relatively flat. Every weekend, one or both of them would be out there with their cherry cola hair, freckles, and blue jeans, drawing squares and throwing stones. And this would last for a few minutes or an hour and then my father would come out with the hose and chase them off before rinsing the driveway clean.

I never even considered I might make friends with them. Such a word was not part of my vocabulary. At the time, we only lived in any one place for a few months, and then my father would "transfer," and we would hop to another neighborhood or another state. I had even begun tracing the journey on a US map, my own little grid of Metro stops, stretching from the Carolinas north to central Pennsylvania. Red and blue and green. Then one day I came home to find my father holding the map. He asked me what I was thinking. Then he asked me again, with his belt. He asked me that a lot, that night. Over and over. And later, when he had finished asking, he watched as I fed the map into the fireplace, blood on the flagstones and tears in my eyes.

We moved a week later, and I forgot about the map, and the fireplace, and the girls. And a lot of other things. But I did not forget the pain. I make a conscious effort to remember that. It keeps me alive.

And now here I am, what . . . thirty-six years later, and of all the things I should be thinking of at a time like this, it is those girls. No doubt because of the new girl. She looks nothing like them, is nothing like them, but my brain has made a connection anyhow. And I think I know why.

I am wondering how long it will take to forget her, too, once I leave her behind.

But there is something else, too. Something in the back of my head, lost temporarily behind memories of chalk. It lingers there until the Metro woman chirps about the doors closing, then leaps into my conscious mind as the car starts moving: I have missed my stop.

I double check the map on the wall, compare it to the one in my head, but I already know. I am sure. I have ridden this line multiple times over the past month. Practice runs. That station was Courthouse, and I was supposed to get off there. And the next station, Rosslyn, is three minutes away. For a normal person, on a normal day, during a normal commute, this would not really matter. I happen to know, however, that something bad is going to happen to this train in a few minutes. And I would really rather not be on board when that happens.

My pulse quickens, my face flushes, my ears grow hot. Useless chemical reactions. Where am I supposed to run? Nowhere. Not for two-and-a-half minutes. I consciously force myself back into more useful patterns of thinking. For starters, I stand up and leave my briefcase under the seat, where no one will notice it, then begin to make my way down the length of the car. No sense rushing—the doors are not going to open any faster, and I know I have at least two minutes until hell literally breaks loose. I'm just not entirely sure how far beyond two, so I may as well get some more bodies between me and the case.

There are plenty of bodies, too. Disgusting sweat boxes. I have little choice but to slip along between them, feeling their stink, tainting myself. It feels like watching evolution in reverse as I go. Suits giving way to jeans and T-shirts, party hats and placards. Crowds heading to the Mall, to celebrate or protest. Dogs and cats and sheep. Mediocre, all of them. Impotent and repugnant.

But despite loathing them, I want to laugh. Because I know the one thing they all want to know, deep down. I know when they will die. They have filled their days with nothing and spent their nights lying awake wondering how much longer they had. And I know the answer: not very long. This is what separates us, no matter how close my flesh gets to theirs. I am an actor, they are the acted-upon. I will act, they will react. Not consciously, of course. Perhaps it's better to say that they will be part of a reaction. Chemical in nature.

I do this not because of any hidden agenda—certainly this act alone is too small to make a difference, too weak a specimen to incite a true reaction from society other than the most localized swelling and mild discomfort. If there is an end to this, I do not care. I am simply a means to an end and happy to be it. I do this because I am locked in their cage, and it will be a more comfortable prison without them. They are trapped by their mediocrity, by their failure to strive for something more, and I will free them, and be free of them at the same time. Win-win.

Or, if I fail to get off the Metro in time, lose-lose. I will know in a few seconds.

The car slows and shudders to a halt, and I quickly step down through the door and onto the platform, first one out the door. I have done this a dozen times in a half-dozen countries. Step off the train with the crowd, blend in, and I am gone, and they will not catch me, as long as I am smart enough to never go back, never do it that exact way again. And they can check hours of videotape, they can ask witnesses for testimony, they can bring dogs, but they cannot stop me, because they do not know who to look for. Sure, they can find *someone*. They need someone to be responsible. But that will not be me. Not today.

I maintain that perspective for about fifteen seconds. And then reality sets in. Because I just so happen to be the only person to exit a crowded Metro car at one of the biggest and busiest stations in the city less than a minute before everyone aboard dies a horrible fiery explosive chemical death somewhere near the Potomac.

I wish I could but I cannot pin this one on fate or some invisible sky wizard. The lack of a crowd is because of the calendar—they are debarking further down the line (or at least they think they are). And the missed stop is simply my own stupidity—or senility or absent-mindedness. Weeks of preparation wasted. And over what? No, not what. Who.

Why did you take her?

My expression, pace, gait, none of this changes. Internally, though, my mind is awhirl, instincts jumping, noting the position of each guard, each passerby who might remember my face. I note each camera, avoiding each lens even though I know most of them are disabled, not even recording. I do my best, overall, to act normal, just wander on through and try to look like I am simply on my way home from work. Which I am.

The escalators in this station are among the largest in the country, perhaps the world, and it takes a full three minutes to ride to the surface; the elevator is faster, but would still take a full minute, and if something happens and the power cuts out, I would be trapped. Escalators it is.

Fortunately, as the crowd is almost nonexistent, I can jog up at a steady pace without having to push anyone aside, trying to balance speed with a desire to not look as if I am running for my life. As I ascend, I cannot avoid the mental clock ticking in my head, counting seconds since the Metro pulled away from the station. Not sure how much time is left.

I get to thirty-five before the end comes.

Lights flicker, but the escalator keeps moving as the sound hits with a dull, distant thump, an extra murmur in my chest. Other necks turn and look downward, curious, concerned. But not me. Not me. I am concerned only with what lies up and ahead. I forget the girl. I forget myself. I forget everything but this: run.

Always run.

The Law of Inertia

11/05/2008

L ife is full of punctuation: periods to mark endings, question marks, the occasional exclamation point that this day has turned out to be. But I like the commas best. The little pauses that come between whatever *is* just was and whatever *is* is next. Calms between storms. But no one can prolong the inevitable forever. At some point, the clouds will give way to rain. And it is about to rain here. Hard.

I try to start my car before I do anything else. Strictly speaking, it is not *my* car, but I have had a key for months. The car does not seem happy about this arrangement, and neither am I, but life sucks. I need a car and I need to be moving before my comma collapses. I have to leave. No. We.

We have to leave.

Right.

After a few more tries, the car starts at last, and I step back out, listening to it mutter. It should be able to keep itself alive for ten minutes. It should be able to remain unstolen for ten minutes. But just in case, I'd better try for five instead. It will be a new record for me.

I rush inside the apartment, grabbing important things along the way, reconsidering what I am about to do right up until I actually do it. Most of what I need is in the back, so I start with the bedroom, which is thankfully open so I don't have to kick the door in. Not that I am trying to be quiet; she needs to wake up, now. I go right to the closet and pull out some things, tossing them roughly on the bed.

"Put those on," I say as she groans. "Now."

She rubs bleary eyes as she slowly sits up, bare feet pushing the blankets down as she wiggles upright. I silently curse her inability to wake up on a dime—for me there is no lengthy "waking up," only a brief transition between sleeping and awake. Anyway, I have no idea how she sleeps while the man upstairs beats his children with the furniture.

By the time she is more-or-less fully awake, I have gotten a shirt and pants pulled over her remarkably warm torso. She would show up great on infrared tonight. I consider shoes, but this is taking too long. We have to move, and keep moving. I go right for the vest.

"It's too heavy," she mumbles. "I can't move."

"Kevlar," I say. "Bulletproof." Resistant, I mean, but there's no time for semantics. She is clearly frightened, feeding off my emotion, only fatigue keeping her just this side of panic. I sense tears are coming. I do not have time for that.

"What time is it?" I ask her. I know exactly what time it is—five after midnight, just about nine hours since things literally blew up—but I need to get her mind off what she thinks is happening. She scrambles over the bed to find the alarm clock, which has gotten knocked over. While she looks, I take a moment to peek between the blinds. There is nobody there; they have not found me. But I know all too well that there is a word tacked onto the end of every statement like that: yet. It's safest to assume they are chasing and you should be running. If you always run like someone is at your heels, you'll be well ahead before they get close. The theory has kept me alive so far.

"It's broken," she says. "It broke." She holds up the alarm clock, face blank. The cord has come right out of the wall, and I never bothered with batteries. This is among the least of my worries, anyway; the clock is not coming with us. Not much is.

"Not important. I need you to look at me. Can you help me?"

She nods.

"Come here. I need you to go into the front room and stand by the door. You stand there and wait for me. And if anyone knocks, you say nothing; you just come get me. Do you understand? Okay, now go."

It is time to burn.

It never takes long to do this, so I wait until she is out of the room before I crack open the box in the closet and start cleaning up. No lights; this is always easier to do in the dark. No matter how hard I try, I get attached to things: pieces of clothing, jackets, nice shoes, a book. If I see it, a part of me wants to take it, but with the lights out, all I see are blobs of gray and vanilla, easier to disremember. It is never entirely painless but it gets easier each time.

This is the eighth time, I think.

It only takes a minute or so before fumes are seeping into my sinuses, making me dizzy. When I hear her start coughing, too, I know for sure that it is time to go. I add my laptop to the backpack full of essentials—hers is staying behind, being comparatively unimportant and certain to die in the fire—and walk to the door, handing her the pack.

"Go," I say as I shove her through and out, down the alley. "Just go. To the white car." It is quite obvious which I mean; its parking lights flutter as the engine struggles to stay awake, like her. She toddles off uncertainly as I turn and prepare for surgery, pulling on latex gloves topped by leather—not because I fear leaving the wrong sort of evidence, but because I don't need blood on my hands just before a long road trip. Not a mistake you make twice.

I lock my door from outside, take two steps back and kick, boot catching just above the deadbolt. Twice more, and the frame gives and the door pops inward. I kick the frame again for good measure to make sure it looks like a break-in, brush a few paint chips off my jeans, and reach inside for the shotgun. Then I turn and take the stairs three at a time.

It feels like flying.

• • •

Could I kill people? I wondered as I hopped in the back of the car, smelling the exhaust and pine, already sniffling. Could I do what Edison does? What he was probably doing, right then?

It was easier than it probably seems to think about it like that. Edison wasn't my first exposure to the concept. Just a year or so earlier, a kid at a nearby school set a record for domestic mass murder. It had been all over the news, and even though it was clear on the other side of the state—and thus, to my young mind, in a different universe—people talked like it was just down the block. At least for a few days. People forget fast; Edison got that right, and a lot more.

But could I do it?

Experts (Edison would no doubt put that in "finger quotes") say that mass murderers and serial killers share a number of things in common.

First: they are typically young, lower-middle-class white males who have easy access to weapons. That covers a good chunk of the voting population, but not me. So strike one, I guess.

Next: they often aspire to greatness, yet see their hopes and dreams dashed by other people or society. Halfway true for me. I never aspired to greatness. Ball one?

What else: unemployed, lonely, family problems, work problems. Couple of hits in there, but nothing solid. Meanwhile, Edison was hitting home run after home run.

But really, how many does that cover? It could be your boss, or your husband, or your father. Or you, maybe. If mass murderers and serial killers are just like everyone else, what separates the fallen from the ready to fall? The Internet says there are maybe a hundred serial killers roaming around at any given time, but why isn't it a thousand, or a million? I think it's the same reason there's only one president, nine Supreme Court justices, and a hundred senators. The same reason you aren't your boss, or the pope, or the king of Spain. The position's already been filled.

But what about the non-serial sort, the people who just blow up one day? What keeps a person from snapping and killing a few dozen random strangers? What's the deciding factor? Brain malfunction? A tumor pressing on the rage button? Maybe a hormonal imbalance? Exposure to a heavy metal as a child. Lead? Cadmium? Metallica? Maybe an abusive father, or a mom who didn't hug hard enough?

If you ask me, there's no such thing as a magic bullet explanation. There's just retrospect, and guesses, averages and composite profiles. And, in some cases, mayonnaise.

● ● ●

I knock heavily on my upstairs neighbor's door. He opens it a few seconds later without asking who it was. A shame; I had such a good answer. I watch his face for a moment as he looks at me, scans me head to toe. The short red hair, the clothes, the scruffy barely-there shadow of a beard. He could be looking in a mirror. But for the double-barreled shotgun.

"What th—"

And then double-ought disintegrates the bottom of his face, and the resemblance ends. He falls, messily twitching as I enter and shut the door. It is the exact same layout as my place so I need no light, just to count paces in the dark as I aim for the screaming in the back, moving cleanly, no time to waste. The clock started running when I booted in my door, accelerated tenfold once I pulled the trigger.

Reek of stale beer. Snack food strata underfoot. The carpet needs a vacuum.

Eight steps and I'm at the bedroom door. Locked, of course, but that hardly matters. It opens with a kick, nearly falls off the hinge. What you get renting from slumlords.

"Shut up," I say to the screamers. I remove my coat, taking care to keep the shotgun pointed in their general direction. Mom, son, daughter, all crying, all three with matching black eyes that confirm what I've been hearing through the ceiling for the past few months. She has a phone in hand and I have no doubt what number she's dialed, but they will not be here in time, so I let her cling to her security blanket and turn towards her son, the loudest.

"Daddy?" he says, an easy mistake in the dark. I let the shotgun tell him no. Then I reload as the other two whimper; at least it's quieter than screaming.

"Thank you," I say, tossing my coat in a heap at the foot of the bed.

"I'm sorry, I'm sorry," sobs the mother, not knowing what she has to be sorry about. "Please, don't kill us. Take the money." She points somewhere behind me, at the closet no doubt; without bothering to look, I shoot her next. That sets the daughter off again, but I kneel down beside and shush her as I pick up the fallen phone and end the call—they've heard enough. The girl is the same age as my own (my own?), and for a moment I consider . . . but no. I am not starting a boarding school.

"Listen," I say, "I would love to explain this to you. Why, how, et cetera. But to be honest I just do not have the time. The condensed version is this: life sucks, and I am doing you a favor."

And I do, with my last shell.

I move for the door, thinking too late that the money would be helpful. There is no time to go back, though. No room for second guesses. Instead, I head straight over to the cooling, stinking corpse in the living room, drop the empty shotgun and leather gloves, throw the phone into the drywall, and close the door behind me.

When I reach the car, the windows are only half-thawed, but I cannot afford to wait for clarity. I just hop in and throw the car in reverse, just as the apartment suddenly ceases to be apartment-like, bursting into fast, chemical flame, magnesium and oxidizer and other bad, bad things from my kitchen chemistry lab, from the magic box in the closet. Given the proper fuel, a fire will double in size every thirty seconds, so by the time anyone who matters gets here, most of the unit will be too far gone to do anything about, and the rest will be well on its way. Plenty of flame to destroy everything I left behind. And everyone.

How many this time? I'll probably never know. Perhaps a dozen, two if they were all home. Not much time to get out. Perhaps a few seconds.

Sometimes you just can't run fast enough.

As always, eventually there will be rubble, and they will dig, but I've long since learned to cover my tracks, not just with fake ID but with fake evidence. And there is plenty within the ash for them to sift through, helpfully dropped in what will be the top layer of strata: a scrap of dirty trenchcoat, fitting a description of that worn by a recent bombing suspect, traces of bomb-making materials matching those used on the subway. Not to mention the shotgun and shells, and the pair of now-bloody gloves—all of which my deceased neighbor unknowingly paid for a month ago, after I signed up for a credit card in his name. People should really learn to shred their mail.

A horrible tragedy, a murder-suicide after a terrorist action. An easy suspect, matching the description. They want an answer, so they'll take the bait. They always do; everyone knows mass murderers always kill themselves last, just like serial killers always return to the scene of the crime to gloat, and the police always get their man. *Law & Order* served up hot and fresh every sixty minutes, less commercials. Always and always.

Except for exceptions.

• • •

It must have been an hour before I stopped randomly sobbing for no reason and focused on shivering. The heater was not working hard enough, and I could feel my body gradually numbing itself to sleep despite the too-loud radio shouting election results, intercut with news about the subway bombing. Edison occasionally shouted back, in between angry rants. Fatigue was clearly starting to affect him. On more than one occasion, I think we nearly drove off a bridge into an abyss. The kind that looks back at you all the way down.

"Hey," he said. "Chir . . . Chrs . . . Chin. Hey you."

His words came slowly, heavy and labored, his mouth dry, his voice raspy and blown out. I didn't answer. His behavior was frightening me. I hadn't seen him like this before, pushed to the end of his limits, physically and perhaps mentally. He probably hadn't slept in nearly a week.

"Nexit is . . ." he mumbled, watching signs flicker into visibility. Talking half to me, half to himself, so he could keep himself awake. "Frackville. We'll stop there. For food. Coffee. Next exit. X marks the exit. X for . . . X for Xtian."

Ecks-chin, he said. And it wasn't a slurred syllable this time. It was my name now.

"Where are we?" I asked as he rolled the window down, flooding the car with cold air.

"Pennsylvania." He said the word like it tasted bad. "Doesn't matter, Xtian."

He snapped off his latex gloves and tossed them in the back beside me, little blue bits of bad that I immediately pushed away. Far as I could, which wasn't far, just over on the floor behind the passenger seat. Which is where he'd put the gun. The one from the night he took me.

I know now that it was an MP5K, MP for Machine Pistol, K for "Kurz" (German for "short"). Thirty-round magazine, semiautomatic. Threaded barrel for a suppressor. At just under thirteen inches, short enough to keep under a trench. A favorite of military personnel, SWAT teams, action movie stars, and Edison North.

It fascinated me. It felt like a part of what I was. But lying there in the dark, it seemed like a little forgotten nothing. He had tossed it in the back seat like an empty water bottle, one he would never use again. And it was right then that I figured it out. Edison didn't need me any more than he needed the gun, or the car, or the blanket keeping me warm. All of it was replaceable. Which is just another word for disposable. The gun had obvious utility. The car, the blanket, too.

And me? He clearly wasn't done with me yet. Hadn't left me behind to burn with strangers. He had something in mind for me. I just didn't know what that was. Not yet.

That night was not about being or becoming. It wasn't a beginning or an end. It was just one of many commas to come, a splice between one home and another.

It wouldn't be the last.

Snow Day

12/02/2010

I knew there would be snow if we came north. I knew there would be a lot more if we came to Buffalo. But I had not expected an epic blizzard after only two years. I am impressed. This storm has kept an interstate highway shut down for twelve hours and counting, but the best I have been able to pull off is about eight hours of delay, jackknifing a tractor-trailer outside Pittsburgh that one time. What is interesting is that there would be no way to know there was a storm by looking out the window; where we are, in the northwest part of the city, the ground has barely a dusting. A mile south, there is a full foot of fresh snow. The lake effect, they call it. Unpredictable when it comes to where it hits and how much damage it causes. I could take some lessons.

Impressed as I am, I really do not want to be here. I like Buffalo for her history, for the power she used to wield, but now she is nothing but grain elevators collapsing with age and neglect, the buckle of the rust belt. She gave the country two presidents and took one away. She has been bleeding population since the '60s, yet still totes the psychological weight of a quarter million lonely souls afraid to leave because there just might be someplace worse out there. Perhaps things will get better. I hope to be long gone before I have to find out.

Xtian and I are living in one of my spare nests, a gray post-war duplex on the north side of the city. I picked it for the same reason I choose anything: because it is in-between everything. The couple who live upstairs are well into their sixties and crave every little scrap of attention I am capable of throwing their way even if it happens to be only money. Although I have not been here in years, I have arranged to send them rent every month, tell them the apartment is for a business, tax reasons. Two-fifty a month, always has been. Reasonable in any economy. Why not?

It has been a long time since I sat in this room, typed at this desk, but it may as well be yesterday. Nothing has changed. Same holes in the wall, the rank odor of soot and cereal hanging in the air, the stink of a dying city that should have had the good sense to stay burned when the British put it to the torch. But then, I cannot be too critical, since I could say the same thing about Washington, DC.

One thing is different this time, of course. And she is making life difficult. Starting with the fact that she is currently nowhere to be found.

• • •

I can almost forgive him now for abducting me. I can even mostly forgive him for tormenting me with his rants and "lessons" for two years straight and being a psychotic bastard much of the time. Everyone has flaws, and at least I got something out of all of that. He taught me about politics, about people, about the way the world really worked. There was even Phys ed of a sort, lots of exercise and watching what I ate, even if he didn't follow suit. So yeah, I guess I can forgive him for all of that, at least in part.

I'll never forgive him for the uniform, though.

I couldn't go to actual school, of course. That would mean records and fingerprints and prying eyes. So we had to pretend. You'd think that would have been awesome, right? No school! Yeah. Not so much. Every morning I'd head out the door with a backpack full of random books, and a half-hour later, Edison would pick me up from 7-Eleven and we'd sneak back home.

Then he'd give me something to read while he went out and did whatever it was he did. Shopping, or stalking, or both. At three we reversed the process, and I came home from "school."

The problem was I couldn't very well pretend to go to *public* school—people in the neighborhood might notice my absence. I don't know where he got the outfit and I didn't want to know, but he got one, so he decided that I would go to Catholic school instead. If anyone ever asked, the plan was that I would pick a random name. It sounded stupid but it worked. At least, until the big snowstorm.

Neither of us were so stupid that we couldn't look out the window, see a bunch of snow, and decide that my imaginary school would be closed for a snow day. But this was one of those "perfect storms" that complicated matters. The storm had hit hardest on the south side of the city, burying entire neighborhoods and triggering school closures across the area, but our neighborhood had received just an inch or two. Edison would have checked online anyway, but I had gotten it in my head to act more grown up and take care of my own morning routine. Everything looked fine out the window so I ate breakfast, got dressed, and headed outside "to school" without bothering to check with him.

It only took a few minutes to discover my error.

The snowball caught me in the left ear about halfway to my normal pickup point. This was followed by laughter as three boys a few years older than me—twelve or thirteen at most—appeared from behind a tree.

"Where you going, dummy?" asked one of them, who I immediately named Dick.

"Where do you think?" I replied but even as I spat out the words I noticed they weren't dressed for school, didn't have backpacks or paper bag lunches. They were in fact dressed in play clothes, ripped jeans and Sabres jerseys. Sneakers and hockey sticks. No actual winter clothing, of course. Only babies wore boots and gloves.

"School's closed, dipshit," said Dick. "Snow day."

"Mine's open," I said, stupidly.

"Yeah?" he asked. "Which one?"

I stammered for a moment, then turned to leave. But someone grabbed my backpack.

"Hey—"

I don't even remember doing it—it was that hardwired. Next thing I knew, he was on the ground grabbing at his groin, and I was bringing my leg back down to catch my balance. It was a perfect shot, exactly as Edison had taught me. He was down, and I was in control of the situation. Briefly.

I forgot what to do next.

• • •

Shopping does not come naturally to me—I hate it, and I have to work at it, just like my father did after my mother got sick. He never made a list, so it was always a roll of the dice what he was going to bring home from the store. On one memorable occasion he got spaghetti sauce with onions, which I refused to eat. He never took no for an answer, poured sauce all over my noodles and said I was not leaving the table until I had cleaned my plate. In retrospect, it was foolish to think dumping it on the floor would count. And a waste of effort, since I ended up eating it off the floor anyway, sobbing as he taught me a lesson with his fists.

This pretty much sums up my childhood. Does Hallmark have a card for that?

Where was I? Oh, right. Shopping.

I usually buy groceries at two or three in the morning, when I can shop in peace, just another lonely middle-aged guy who everyone leaves alone while they stock cat food and watch for shoplifters. I still prefer that, even though the proliferation of self-checkout lines has made it easier to shop during the day without speaking to any herd animals. But the shopping list has grown recently. Xtian has been trying to make me eat healthier, so now the list contains not just the usual diet soda and frozen pizza, but things like almond milk. I am not even sure how you milk an almond. And there are too many green things, instead of my usual tan, beige, and off-white. Horrid things, weeds and leaves, fit only for herd animals, but for now I indulge her as it is improving our bond. She needs to trust me for what is to come. I do feel a bit healthier, but for some reason it just feels like prolonging the inevitable.

I had intended to take Xtian shopping with me today, so she could pick out her own evil green things, but I have no idea where she is, and I am tired of worrying about whether she has been abducted, or run away, or been found by the police. I have a shopping list. I am going shopping.

Xtian's timing is impeccable, however. I am just about to head out when Xtian comes barreling into the apartment and kicks her shoes into the corner. Dripping wet, blouse torn, tear tracks on her cheeks. Blood on her lip.

"What happened?" I ask.

She sniffles, gives me one of those looks I hate, and tells me her tale of woe. To her it is simply the worst thing in the world to have a few boys shove her into the snow, but compared to the first thoughts that ran through my head when she entered the room, this is a walk in the park. A month ago there was a story in the news about two ten-year-old boys who raped an eight-year-old girl, somewhere in London, in broad daylight. On a playground. How did society get so damaged so fast? I need to get back to work.

I am positive she is uninjured but I check anyway, more so she can learn to check herself. She is understandably reluctant, since this involves showing more of her flesh than I am yet wholly comfortable with, but that sort of thing is unavoidable. I would rather not have to deal with this at all. I appreciate privacy as much as anyone. More than.

Yet she seems fine. A few bruises on her back, one on her thigh; her blouse is worse off than she. Another tooth missing, but it was dangling by a thread anyway and the other one is coming in already. They have done her a favor, there.

"Who were they?" I ask, reaching for my coat.

"No!" she cries, stepping in front of the door. "Don't kill them! Please. I'm sorry . . ."

I had planned nothing of the sort—I just wanted to get the shopping done—but this does give me a useful piece of insight into what she assumes I am capable of. I turn and look down at the puddle of girl below me, thinking her pathetic, thinking I need to rid her of that. Yes, a lesson. She needs to learn to protect herself much better than this. The world is a dangerous place, and there are worse things than neighborhood bullies out there. There are more people like me. I am not *close* to the worst of us.

"Sorry?" I ask. "For what? What did you do wrong?"

She sniffles, confused.

"Because they said school was closed and I said mine wasn't and they said what school and I couldn't think of one and then—"

"No. I mean why did they beat you up? What did you do wrong? Tell me."

"I don't kn—"

"Yes, you do. What happened?"

"I don—"

I slap her, hard but not too, right across the face. A tap, really. She is too stunned to do anything.

"What did you do wrong?" I ask.

"I don't know," she says, confused.

I slap her again, a bit harder, on the side of her head. Her eyes tear anew.

"I don't know. I'm sorry. I'm—"

I bring my hand down again, harder. And now she stops me, near-perfect form, the way I showed her just last month in the living room. Left arm up, palm forward, her forearm pushing mine up over her head. Basic self-defense, but it's taken a long time for her to grasp even the basics, for some reason. Her legs are wrong, too, as she discovers when I sweep her to the floor. She lands hard but now she has the idea and she rolls to her feet a few seconds later. I step towards her, but she ducks under the table and pops out the other side. I can see in her eyes that this is too much a game. Not what I want, but she had her chance. Time to make my point. I shove the table into her chest, hard. She falls back and knocks her head into a chair. I think no less of her when she starts bawling. That clearly hurt.

"What did you do wrong?" I ask. I first taught her the answer to this question over two years ago. This particular lesson has been hammered home repeatedly, weekly if not daily. But it still has not penetrated, for some reason.

Regardless, she is too far gone to answer me now, so I step forward and help her up. She will have a lump, but her hair will cover it just fine. I hug her, pat her head, coo like she needs right now, and finally she stops crying. Then I lift her up, set her on the table, and look her in the eyes. She tries to look away, but I grab her chin and force her face up. She will learn harder lessons than this if I do not hammer this home right now. I do not expect her to have mastered Krav Maga or anything. This is the very basics.

"Look at me. I am twice as tall as you and I weigh almost three times as much. How do you fight me? What did I teach you? Step one. What is it, always? What? Tell me!"

She looks more scared than she has all day because she knows that now I am beyond striking, beyond pushing. This is a Lesson. And she will learn it.

"Rhymes with one."

"Run?" she says, finally.

"Yes," I say triumphantly, throwing my hands in the air. "Run. Always run. If you are outnumbered, run. If you are outsized, run. If you are out-matched, run. If you learn nothing else, learn this. *You run.* You do not slow down, or look back, or stop. Not ever. When you stop, they catch up. They eat you."

She nods. But she has not gotten it, not yet. I walk to the kitchen door and fling it open. A few stray icicles fall from the awning, shattering on the concrete steps and spraying my bare feet with fragments of cold. Despite what people say, they really are not the perfect weapon. Not even a passable one. I have tried on several occasions.

"Run," I say.

"Where?"

I try to think of something thematically appropriate.

"The funeral home," I say. There are a few but she knows the one I mean. She moves towards her shoes, but I grab her shoulder and steer her roughly through the door until she is standing in socks on the snowy steps. Crying. Good. That means she will remember.

"But—" she tries.

"I could not care less," I reply coldly. Then I slam the door in her face.

• • •

It wasn't all that cold. I mean, definitely below freezing, probably in the mid 20s Fahrenheit with the wind chill and only a few flakes drifting down. The stuff already on the ground was the problem, if there was one. A mixture of snow and slush, and me without shoes. Standing there in the snow, my feet were immediately freezing. But I knew for sure that the door was not going to open unless I did what I was told. So I did.

I ran.

I cried, too. For a few blocks. And then I realized that was accomplishing nothing. It was pointless weakness. The only reason to cry was for attention, and I wasn't getting any. And I knew I wasn't going to die. I knew because Edison had pounded it into my head with his lessons.

My core temperature would have to reach ninety-five degrees before hypothermia would set in, and things wouldn't get serious until eighty-five, at which point my brain function would be about on par with those holding public office and I probably wouldn't care anyway. Mild hypothermia would bring shivering and confusion; severe would mean blue fingers, less shivering. Heart failure, death.

I wouldn't be out here nearly long enough to worry about that, especially if I kept moving. Frostbite would be a greater concern and even that was unlikely. Digits would get red and numb, and if it was severe enough I'd get blisters, or my toes would turn black and drop off. It would take hours at least, and more likely days of exposure, to get to that point. Edison had taught me all this. He was hardly sending me out to my death. He was sending me out so I'd remember.

And I did. I remembered the cold and I remembered the pain.

And I remembered to run.

At the time, running down the slushy streets, I thought this would be the worst thing that could ever possibly happen to me. If I could just get through this, I thought, I would be able to handle anything. If I'd only known then what I was soon going to experience, what I was going to learn, what I was going to do . . .

It makes me laugh now, to think about how naïve I was that day. Afraid of snow. Of cold. There was so much more to be afraid of. Including myself.

• • •

I park here sometimes, on my own, when I need time to think. Technically they are always open, but they are usually closed. Plus, there are no cameras in the lot; no one wants to steal the dead.

AMIGONE the sign reads. I wonder. Am I?

I flip down the sun visor. The man in the mirror looks younger than he feels. Lines around the eyes. Gray hair peeking through the dye. Liver spots, whatever the fuck those are. A lot of things can be concealed forever. Age is not one of them, no matter how hard you kick and scream. But the man in the mirror is not gone. Not yet. He still has things to do. Like, perhaps, be a better teacher. Or at least more efficient.

Behind my reflected eyes I can see her coming so I start the engine and turn the heat back on. By the time she opens the door and climbs in, actual hot air is coming from the vents. Once she is inside, I put the car in gear and pull out of the lot while she puts on the dry socks and shoes I left on the dashboard. We are wordless, until I get to the Expressway.

"Where are we going?"

"Galleria," I answer. The tiny bit of Buffalo in the back of my skull wants to suffix that with "mall," but I choke it back down.

"Why?"

I almost change my mind. Almost. I am not sure if she is ready for this. But I am.

"We are going shopping for new supplies," I say. "You just graduated from fake school."

I do not want to think about what happens if she gets held back.

Venison of Sam

12/01/2011

Xtian has begged me for months to take her to Niagara Falls, which is roughly a half-hour northwest of Buffalo. It was once a true natural wonder of the world: white water, cascades, mist, probably some frolicking deer. Now the place just resembles a colder, smaller version of Las Vegas. At night, they use lights to color the water like egg dye. There are casinos everywhere. It makes me want to die. It is the perfect example of the human tendency to never leave well enough alone, and it is sadly reflective of everything society would want Xtian to be: vapid, and shallow, and pretty, and not much else.

Instead, Xtian and I have traveled an hour in the opposite direction and our destination could not be more different. It is not quite the most remote place I know of, but it will do for this. The specific name of the place escapes me. All I know is that we are somewhere between three small towns, somewhere deep in the woods, so deep we cannot hear any traffic noise. It may be the closest you can get to nothing in this area, the closest you can get to imagining what it must have been like before people ruined the world. Which ironically makes it the perfect place to whip out a shotgun or two and ruin the world a bit more. For some deer, at least.

There is no way to describe the feeling, crouched in a snowbank, back against an old nurse log, the smell of cold and pine, blast of wind teasing sweat off my neck, icy cold shotgun in hand, eyes sweeping back and forth and back again, waiting for the soft crunch of snow, breathing, breathing, breathing, snowflakes on my eyelids, breathing . . .

This sort of hunting is not like hunting people at all. That is a job; this is peaceful, blissful nothing. Or at least it would be, if I were alone.

• • •

"Do you think there are wolves?" I whispered. Bored but hopeful.

"Shhh. Yes," he said.

"If we catch one can we keep it as a pet?"

"If you'll shut up for ten minutes."

He hadn't yet told me what we were doing here; the word "hunting" had not been used. I knew it was deer season, from the hunters in orange vests. One had driven past with a big buck strapped to his hood. Edison had waved for appearances, grimacing through the entire show. But despite all that, I wasn't yet sure we were hunting anything. We'd been out in the woods almost every weekend since that weird snow day the year before, but that had mostly ended up with us tromping around in circles, sometimes shooting at targets with a .22 rifle, him teaching me to be still and quiet, me fighting that with every ounce of my being because it was so dull. After all that, part of me wanted to see blood that wasn't my own, but I wasn't getting my hopes up. It was probably just going to be another endurance test of some sort, or "let's be quiet" training.

It was harder than he made it sound, being quiet. I tried breathing like he told me. In through the nose to warm the air, out slowly through the mouth. In, out, in, out, quieter than the wind, quieter than . . .

"My face itches," I said, clawing frantically at my ski mask. After a short struggle I managed to get it off, static electricity taking my hair along for the ride. This made my head itch, too, so I dropped the mask in my lap and scratched madly with gloved hands.

Edison said nothing. I looked over, confused, and saw him staring past my left shoulder.

"Sorry," I said. He hissed in response, his universal sign for "don't move, don't speak, don't breathe if you can help it." Curiosity got the better of me though. I slowly turned my head to peek, so as to not startle whoever or whatever might be there.

He must've sensed I didn't see anything because he lowered the 12-gauge and slowly slid the frigid barrel along my face so I could sight down the gun. Sure enough, there was a deer there. No horns, no spots. A doe. I'd seen them at the zoo and even running beside the road before, but somehow this was different. More real. My heart was racing, pulse pounding, breathing coming more quickly. I was too caught up in the moment to truly notice. I only realized looking back how quickly my body had fallen into the mindset of the predator. It felt natural.

I nodded to let him know I saw and nudged the gun away with my cheek, but instead of pulling it away he brought it forward. The butt was placed in my armpit, my finger placed upon the trigger guard, and before I could say a word I was holding it by myself. It being a pump-action 870, arguably the most common shotgun in the world. I already knew how to load, clean, and disassemble it and had done so on the kitchen table. I knew that it was about forty-five inches long from end to end—nearly as tall as I was—and only weighed about eight pounds. At the time, however, it felt more like eighty, and the barrel dropped rapidly towards the snow. Edison had held it with me before, but this was the first time he'd left it all to me, so I expected him to catch it. He didn't. All he said was, "Don't drop it."

So I didn't.

• • •

I know she can lift the shotgun; despite being so thin, she regularly carts around gallons of milk and they weigh just as much. But she needs to realize that herself, which is why I offer no help. Sure enough, she struggles for a moment, but finally manages to get things pointed in more or less the right direction, more or less silently.

The trick here is not to remain absolutely still or silent, which is simply not possible unless you are dead or unconscious. But it is easier to say "be still, be silent" and work from there, rather than try and explain the concept of moving and breathing in time with the wind. She is still a little young to really grasp that sort of flow, but she needs to learn that, and more. In particular, she needs to accept what comes next as natural, as a part of becoming who she must become. She needs to be more than someone who can fire a gun. She needs to become someone who can fire a gun at a living thing. And preferably hit it.

"What should I do?" she whispers. I provide no answer. This must be her moment. Her decision. Her failure. Even though she has managed to knock down a few cans with a .22, I do not expect her to actually hit anything. In fact, I honestly do not expect her to pull the trigger.

Which is why she surprises us both when she does.

• • •

I'd had this whole sequence of events pounded into my head over the past few months, had done this countless times in practice behind safety goggles and earplugs. Killed a bunch of cans and bottles and trees. And now here, it was all over in a second, leaving nothing but the shocking realization that I'd done it.

It took a few seconds before I finally felt the blow to my shoulder, heard the crack. My ears hurt but not as much as I'd thought they would; my heart pounded, much harder than I'd imagined. Someone was saying something. Edison, telling me to *pump, come on, pump the gun and shoot again.* But either my arms weren't long enough or my hands were shaking too badly because I didn't push hard enough. I only succeeded in jamming the mechanism.

"It won't go . . . it won't go . . . I broke it." Tears came, and I couldn't even wipe them away because I was holding a gun. Barely. I could feel the barrel slipping and couldn't stop it, didn't even try, just turned and buried my head in Edison's shoulder and fell apart.

"I'm sorry, I'm sorry . . ." I don't know if I thought I was apologizing to him or myself.

Edison let me sniffle and sob, though he did at one point reach down to pick up the spent shell casing (which he pocketed) and clear the shotgun (which he then leaned against the tree). And then he grew tired of waiting, pushed me off his lap and stood, shouldering the gun.

"Let's go," he said. "We need to look for blood."

"I missed," I said. "It ran away."

"They always run away, Xtian. Wouldn't you?"

He started walking down the slope without waiting to see if I would follow. I struggled to keep up, trying to place my much smaller feet inside the holes where his feet had been but mostly wallowing in thigh-high snow. Fear kept me going, though. I was afraid he'd leave me behind.

"Tell me what you saw," he said when we reached the bottom of the gully.

"What?"

"If I shot you in the leg," he said, pointing the gun, "what would you do?"

"Cry," I said. "Fall down. Bleed and die."

"Let's assume your legs still work. You can still run. What happens?"

I shrugged. He shook his head, shut his eyes, trying to be patient.

"If you hit the deer in one of its back legs," he explained, "its back end would have fallen down before it ran away. If you hit it in the gut, it would run slowly with its back hunched up, trying to hold its insides in."

Being gut shot was a bad way to die, messy. And while a human might scream a lot and then trip over their own intestines, a deer could run for hours like that. Suffering, slowly dying.

"It did neither of those," Edison continued, "which leaves a lot of possibilities, including that you missed entirely. We need more information. Tracks, blood, hair, something."

By the time we reached the top of the hill, we were both out of breath and my knees were muddy. It felt slightly empowering to see him breathing heavily, too.

"Do you remember where it was?" he asked. "Any landmarks?"

I looked around. Everything looked the same. Snow, dirt. Pine needles. But then I saw the tree despite the forest, the one tree that looked a little out of place: a little apple tree next to a big pine. The deer had been there when I shot. I pointed, but he was already moving, had already known where to go, was just waiting for me to figure it out. Even he sounded surprised once we got there, though.

"Well, this changes things," he mumbled.

There were prints in the mud and snow. Along with small bubbles of bright red. He dipped his fingers in it, brought it up to show me. I never even thought to flinch away, was just fascinated by the sight of what I'd done.

"Lung, maybe. Air frothing out of the wound. Bright, so maybe an artery. Not a gut shot."

We searched for quite a while but didn't find anything but more blood. We followed the trail down towards a stream in the next gully. Somewhere along the way, he mumbled something about how our sitting still for a while after I shot the gun was a good thing. He never missed a chance to squeeze in a lesson or two.

"If you chase hard, a wounded animal will run harder. And farther. If you hang back, let her think she's gotten away, then she'll find a place to lie down and die. If we're lucky, she should be within, say, fifty yards or so."

She was.

• • •

I am not quite sure how Xtian will react when we actually find the body. I expect a degree of fascination, a few tears. I am not counting on vomiting.

While she is being sick, I take a moment to tag the doe in her ear, in case we get stopped. Then I stand and wait until Xtian is done retching before handing her a thermos full of lukewarm coffee to rinse out her mouth. She needs to see this next part, for a lot of reasons.

"If you decide to be sick again," I say, "do it the other way. This will be messy enough."

With that, I proceed to gut the deer. To her credit, Xtian manages to choke down any more sick, even while the doe is losing her bits. This is partly because I am keeping her distracted, explaining exactly why it is I brought her out here.

"Deer anatomy is different from human, but they have roughly the same basic body contents. Chest cavity with heart and lungs, abdominal with liver, stomach, intestines and bladder, throat with windpipe and esophagus," I say as I carefully remove them each in turn with a sharp knife. It is always good to brush up on anatomy. This is school, now.

By the time I am finished, holding the doe by its front legs to let the blood drain out, Xtian is finished, too. She sits back heavily, puts her head down, and tries to be sick again, but there is nothing left in there to come out. All things considered, she seems to have handled it about as well as I did my first real kill. Likely better. But then, I did not start with a deer.

• • •

I wasn't sick because of the blood. Not really; I was never squeamish. It was because I knew why we were out there. I had killed and now it would be easier to do again. But that's it, really. It would be wrong to say something dumb like "the little girl inside of me died that day." That's not how it works. I still played with dolls and I still liked vampire books. I still played games and chatted with distant, imaginary people I could never really know, people who knew my taste in music, my favorite shows, but didn't know my name, or where I lived, or what I was about. There was no part of me that died that day.

I'd be lying if I said I wasn't changed, though. For days, I couldn't help but stare in the mirror, looking at the strange person staring back at me from the other side. There was no breadcrumb trail to follow back to a house made of candy. I was what I was, and what I was, was *becoming*. There was no going back.

Fowl Mood

06/27/2012

At some point when I was not paying attention, Xtian grew up. She has gained several inches over the past few months, in more ways than I am comfortable with, which makes me glad her only real friends are fake online people that live states and continents away from us. They probably know more about her biology than I do, which is fine. I know more than I want to. We talked briefly about a webcam. Briefly. She got over it, just like she got over the fact that I forbade her to use the words *face* and *book* in the same sentence. I told her if she ever utters the word *sexting* I will tear her twelve-year-old tongue out.

It has taken a great deal of effort to keep track of what little I know of her inner life. I should not have to sneak into her room when she is out for a run to discover her dolls thrown in the closet, her bookshelf swiftly morphing from teen romances into something more adult. I have not censored anything, though. She is on her own, unless she asks. Fashion, too: she has dyed some of her pink clothing black—occasionally, to my dismay, with my not inexpensive dye—and has started with makeup. I have no idea where she got it; I hope not on the web, unless she was careful. Preferably somewhere involving cash, somewhere *IRL*, to use her phrase.

I do try to stay involved, to give in on little, inconsequential things, to keep her somewhat content. She wanted an iPhone, she got a burner flip-phone and an iPod instead, several generations old and untraceable. A concession to keep her quiet. The thing has been connected to her ever since—shooting, running, probably bathing. And lately, the noise from her earbuds sounds like a missile strike on a chainsaw testing facility. It cannot possibly be music.

"What is that?" I ask unkindly, as I have more often lately. She pretends she did not hear me. It took decades of gunshots and bomb blasts to permanently damage my hearing, and she seems hell bent on catching up to me after just a few months of loud music. But she is not deaf yet, except when it is convenient.

"Take those off," I say quietly, using my *now* voice. She immediately complies, letting the little white dongles dangle over the backs of her ears.

"Stop ignoring me," I say.

"I wasn't. Chill."

She then proceeds to ignore me as she turns to find our waitress. Missing in action. Service at this tiny little Greek place is slow, though not intolerably considering its size; they do not claim to be fast food, and anyway I am not in a particular rush. For Xtian though, this is an eternity of torment; she has yet to learn patience, to save her intolerance for when it counts.

She is a tween, I realize with horror as she bounces in the chair, ankles crossed, right sneaker doing all the work as her left leg churns limply along for the ride, blue jeans and dirty white socks, too loose. She spins around and her shoulder-length hair (black this month, matching mine) flips aside. As she casually reaches up to push it back where it belongs, I notice them. Well, *it*. I assume a matched pair. I say nothing immediately, because the movement is too artificial, rehearsed in the mirror. She wanted me to notice. No doubt, she noticed that I noticed.

She called; I bluff.

"Who are you listening to?" I ask, avoiding her desired line of inquiry.

"Die Antwoord," she says. "You wouldn't like it. It's not for old people."

"I might. Give me the CD when we get home."

She snorts.

"The file, whatever," I say. "Where did you get it? Amazon? Apple?"

"Pirate Bay."

"I'm calling the copyright police," I say, pretending to reach for my pocket.

"It's not stealing," she says, rolling her eyes. "It's copying. Don't be gay."

"And murder is recycling. And don't use that word."

"It doesn't even mean that any more—" she starts, losing interest as the waitress bustles out of the kitchen and dumps the food on the table, plain lamb burger and fries in front of Xtian, chicken souvlaki salad wrap in front of me.

"Thanks, Edena," says Xtian. I have no idea why she pays so much attention to name tags. Possibly because everyone she knows online is basically just one. Nicknames, handles, aliases, and avatars.

As the waitress leaves, I quickly shuffle the plates where they belong. Xtian is growing, and needs nutrition and vegetables. I am old and need blood.

"Calm down, it's not going to give you apoplectic shock."

"Eggs do that. Not chicken. Usually."

"Same thing," she says through a mouthful of lettuce and tomato. Even through the food I can hear dim sarcasm.

"Adults I can handle," I say, "but the young ones give me all the trouble." I punctuate with a bite of my lamb burger, letting the juice drip. A bit rare, even for me. She squirms, now that she has decided to be partially vegetarian. But she does not criticize my food selection like usual, just starts picking through her salad for bits of feta cheese. I can tell she wants to talk about the earrings. She just has no idea how to start. I give in and help.

• • •

"Where did you get them done?" he said, jumping right in. "The mall? With the gun?"

"I did it myself," I said. "Yolo. It was on YouTube. And the lady upstairs gave me these." I flicked my earlobes, wincing. They still hurt; even now I can't wear earrings for long.

"They're infected," he said. "Take them out. You could be allergic."

"I want a second opinion."

"Ask the waitress," he said, "because I'm not about to take you to the hospital over ears."

"Oh? What would you take me to the hospital over?"

"My dead body."

"Seriously, when's the last time you saw a doctor?"

"On my birthday."

"When was that?"

"1962."

He took a bite of his baby lamb burger. I stirred my salad and sighed.

"Fine, Ms. Vaguebook," he said. "What's wrong? Besides your ears falling off?"

"Oh, let's see," I said. "My only friends are screen names. I don't go to school. I have no life. I was abduc—"

He hissed. A few seconds later, Edena arrived to refill our drinks, rolling her eyes at me as if to say she understood. I smirked, wondering how she saw us. A short, dumpy blonde and her father, tall, dark and . . . handsome? At least interesting. Not average, like I'd originally seen him. As much as he wanted to seem ordinary, to me he was turning out to be more than that. It was like I could see the real him, even as I was grappling with what I was. Not that he was exciting, or unpredictable. Or even colorful. He was never black or white, just an everlasting gray. And that's what he wanted me to be, too. Gray was fine, except when it's all you get. Ash without any fire. I was tired of being a ghost. His shadow. I wanted to exist. I wanted to matter. And I think he was finally starting to realize that. Even if I wasn't.

I didn't want to be him. I wanted to be like him, in the sense that he was something. And he was sure of what he was. He had a definition for himself. At the time, I was just a synonym.

"There are a lot of kids your age who would kill to have a life like yours," he said when the waitress left.

"Is that what it takes?" I asked. "Killing?"

• • •

What will it take? And who will give it to her, if not me? Who does she have to look up to? She is friends with a few waitresses, but they are hardly role models. School and teachers are not an option. The lady upstairs was born before time. There are no kids her age around, and her fake online friends are probably half pedophiles, half drug addicts: it seems every time I hop in a chat room to listen in, I see them discussing either sex, music, or drugs. Same as always, I suppose. The more things change, the more they drift towards the mediocre.

I know she deserves better, but right now I have nothing else to offer. Not personally.

We finish up dinner, and the waitress comes back. She is disturbingly attentive.

"Dessert?" she asks.

Xtian cuts my "no" off at the pass and snatches up the dessert card from behind the napkins.

"What's balaclava?" she asks.

"A ski mask. Crack a book sometime," I say.

"Amygdala? That sounds good."

"Let me see that menu." I reach for it, but she pulls away.

"That's it anyway. Oh, and chocolate cake. Bleh."

"We also have *ipovrichio*," says the waitress. "It's . . . vanilla syrup on a spoon. Want one?"

"Yes!" Xtian looks like she just won the lottery. As she bounces happily, my phone vibrates in my pocket. Like most of the phones I have owned, it will only be used a single time. It has never been called before and never will be again. In theory, at least—these days, every phone gets telemarketers calling, so I take a peek at the number just to be sure. It is who I thought, so I do not answer. This is not just a phone call—it is an alarm. I have been "sleeping" since we got to Buffalo, and I have just been woken up. This is good timing. I am ready for it. I am not as sure about Xtian, but I guess now is as good a time as any to find out.

I flip the phone open.

"Speaking of vanilla," I say to Xtian as I dial a number I memorized years earlier but have never called before, "what happened to all the extract in the cupboard?"

"I put it on my cereal."

"That is disturbing. Stop doing that."

"Stop buying shit-tier cereal."

"And stay out of the alm—" I break off and hold up a hand to shush her as the line picks up.

"Hey," I say into the phone.

"Hey," they reply. The caller's voice has been modulated to obscure their identity, but I can tell from just that one syllable who it is: my fixer, Marc. No one else can pack so much into one three-letter word. Marc is tired: of work, of life. Of me, sometimes.

"You calling about dinner?" I ask. I have to be careful to use code when others can overhear. I have no idea what I am signing up for yet, but I am sure it will not involve dinner.

"You still in town?"

"Yeah," I say. We both mean Buffalo. Marc knew I left DC after the subway job.

"Come over for the Fourth. Surf and turf."

"Sure, I'm up for it," I say. I give Xtian a glance, then quickly add, "But I'm plus one."

There is a brief but noticeable pause before a one-word reply: "Who?"

"My . . ." What? I look over at Xtian. What is she? ". . . someone."

"Someone?" repeats Xtian. I stand and wander outside before she can say something I will regret.

"It'll be fine," I say into the phone. "I'll vouch for . . . them."

"Them?" asks Marc. "Or *her*?"

I do not reply. Even though the traffic outside the restaurant is somewhat loud, I imagine I can hear pacing on the other end of the phone. Scowling, perhaps.

"Fine," says Marc. "But it's *your* ass."

I am given another string of numbers—the next phone number I will be expected to use, to arrange the actual "dinner engagement"—and then the line goes dead; we are not the sort for long goodbyes. I return to the table simultaneous with Xtian's dessert, which arrives in a glass of ice water. I paid money for this? She seems happy, though, licking the spoon like a lollipop, dancing it around to test loose molars. She gives me a sly grin.

"What?" I ask at last.

"I'm your *someone*?" she asks.

"Save some of that ice for your burning ears," I reply. Although inflamed earlobes may be the least of her worries, depending on how things go a week or so from now.

The least. And possibly the last.

Proof Through The Night

07/04/2012

Things happened rather quickly after Edison got his call, just like they had in DC. There'd been a long period of nothing, followed by a brief flurry of activity leading up to the job. There wasn't much time for extra practice, or preparation, which was probably good: if I'd had time to really imagine what might be coming, I might have tried to back out.

When I'd heard we were going out on a boat for the 4th of July I expected something rather placid, since I'd always seen lakes as something peaceful and serene, but as it turned out, the experience was anything but. Boats were crammed in nearly on top of each other, at least half of them piloted by very loud people well past sobriety. If I closed my eyes, took in just the sounds and the smells—the reek of fish and grease and smoke—I could almost imagine we were in line for sandwiches and fries somewhere. Only the constant crackle of illegal fireworks leading up to the official show at dusk kept the vision from being complete.

There were two other people on the boat. Introductions had not been made, but I got the impression that whoever these two were, they were in the same line of work as Edison. I had always assumed there were other people who did what he did. Since there was an employer somewhere, there were probably other employees, right? But actually meeting them felt like looking at myself in a full-length mirror and for the first time seeing all of myself, all at once. Like I'd known all the individual bits were there, but the overall picture was just now coming together. And now I couldn't ever be unaware of it again.

Or something. Never mind.

The sixteen-footer was pretty cramped with four aboard, plus work stuff: coolers and cases and canvas bags, filled not just with beer but bullets, and binoculars, and other tools of the trade. At first I'd thought it would've been better with just me and Edison but it was always awkward when he took me somewhere without other people to pretend for. It's not that I was uncomfortable around him, but when we were alone I felt . . . exposed? With others around, there were more targets. That's what other people were, basically: targets. For conversation, mostly. But I suppose the other kind, too. Even if Edison hadn't taken me out to actually kill anyone. Not yet.

• • •

"Isn't she a bit young?" Gabe (not his real name) says. Not quietly, either, but between the fireworks and the purring engines nearby, there is no way Xtian can hear him. I shrug and glance back. She just sits quietly, reading *Fast Food Nation* with a penlight, unabashedly whispering to herself. In dark-gray jeans and navy blue sweater, she is the sole splash of any sort of color amidst a sea of gray and black, bare ankles flashing as she shifts her weight and her cuffed jeans slide away from her saturated sneakers.

"Do *they* know she's here?" he asks. "Fuck, Tom." This is the name Gabe knows me by, here in the greater Buffalo area. We have met before, years earlier. I try to forget. I never did like Gabe. Not many people do, but we needed a boat, and Gabe knows how to get things.

"I'm sure they know." This comes from Joe (also not his real name), who is lying in the bottom of the boat, mostly beneath a ratty blue tarp. Like Xtian, he is reading a book with a little penlight, but his contains no words, only columns for wind speed, elevation, and shots taken. Several other sheets have little drawings of men on them, sort of like I imagine a comic strip might look like in the early stages, raw sketches with the barest indication of storyline, a few notes in the margins suggesting what might be. Or more accurately, what soon won't be.

Joe also has a rifle. This will be relevant, soon.

"Tom's not stupid enough to do this without them knowing," Joe adds. "Is he?"

"Yes," I answer, and then, because I need to clarify which question I'm answering, I add, "They know." True, for some definitions of "they" and "know."

"Fine with me then," says Joe. And that is the end of it. As with Gabe, I have worked with Joe before, but the two of us have a professional respect for one another. The kind where we keep out of each other's way, mostly. Joe has been with the Buffalo cell for a while now, while I have moved around the country, rather than settling down and finding steady work like so many do. As steady as it gets. You stick around in one place, you increase your risks, but you also build relationships, trust. I am no one's best friend, just someone who will do almost anything on short notice. An extra pair of hands. Or two pairs, in this particular case.

"How old is she?" Gabe bleats like a lamb, reminding me of the under-cooked meal I recently recovered from; his white, shoulder-length hair completes the mental picture.

"Eighteen," I lie.

"What, in metric?" Gabe throws his hands up in exasperation. "Joe, you have no problem with a baby on board?"

"She's not a baby," replies Joe. "She looks about as old as my daughter."

"And how old is your daughter?"

"Somewhere between fuck off and mind your own fucking business," answers Joe.

Gabe turns back to me, still unconvinced.

"Is she safe?" he asks, meaning not her safety, but his own. This boat would barely slow down if she fell overboard, got turned into chunky salsa by the two overpowered Bulldogs lurking back there (though to be fair, I would probably not slow down for Gabe, either).

"Yes." Safe enough.

He shrugs and goes back to steering us through the crowd of boats, most stopped, some anchored, all of them waiting for the official show to begin. Gabe wanted to run without any lights at all, but not only would that have made maneuvering all but impossible, it would just have attracted more attention; there are police and Coast Guard out here.

I scan the area again with my binoculars, review the dais on shore once more, counting suited figures. In the corner, a helpful range finder tells me we are a thousand yards away, about where we want to be. Balance is the key; every yard closer is another three feet to get back out.

"Right here," says Joe. Joe does not have a pair of binoculars; he simply knows. Unlike the rest of us on the boat, he received the proper training, after all. Even though he has been out of the military for years, he still likes to wear black BDUs and camouflage hoodies that—while appropriate for things like this—tend to catch second glances from concerned citizens wondering if they should report him for suspicious activity. But he is very good with a rifle, which is why he is the primary shooter here; if we were fishing, Joe would be using a rod-and-reel; I would be using a net. Or explosives, burning dolphins and all. Especially the babies.

Gabe grunts and stops the motors, the relative silence suddenly deafening, leaving us with just the lap of waves and the muttering drunks and the shouts, firecrackers, and flares. Just, indeed; it makes me wonder why we are even trying to be quiet. We could be throwing grenades taped to kittens and there would be zero risk of getting caught. Kitty-kitty, bang-bang.

"Yellow high," says Gabe. "Wait for black." I roll my eyes at him speaking in code. As if anyone else can hear us. And anyway, we all know it is not quite time yet.

"No shit," says Joe, verbalizing my inner thoughts. "Tom, you got secondaries?"

Here we go.
"No," I say. "She does."

• • •

I looked up, my book forgotten. I was the only *she* here, so Edison clearly meant me, but I had thought he'd only brought me here to watch.

"Yes, you," he said.

"What the fuck," said the white-haired dude.

"Whatever," said the other guy, peeking out from underneath his tarp. "Get down here, Mathilda."

"It's Nichole," I said. My middle name, my code name. Edison and I had agreed it would be easier for me to remember.

"Whatever. Joe, Gabe, Nickie, Tom, now we're all friends. Let's do this." Joe didn't sound impressed, just pulled the tarp back to give me room. I still recall the feeling I got when I actually saw the guns unveiled, when I fully realized what was coming. What I was going to be asked to do. Joe didn't stand up and wave the barrels around, but there was enough light for everyone to finally see what was under there.

"Fuck, Joe," said Gabe. "Is that a Light Fifty?"

"It fell off the back of a truck."

Joe had an M107, which held ten rounds of .50 caliber ammunition (at five bucks a round) and could fire all of them in half as many seconds. It was quite effective out to a bit over a mile with a good scope (he had a holographic monster on top). It was also technically an anti-materiel weapon, not anti-personnel, but Joe evidently figured it was multi-purpose.

I knew all this not because he told me, but funnily enough, because I had been playing online multiplayer shooter games lately, and one of them had this gun in it.

By comparison, Edison's 700 PSS was outmatched, but only because Joe's gun was overkill. At the time, the 700 was the most widely used bolt-action rifle in the country—or so he said—and at under a thousand bucks was by comparison quite affordable. Whereas Joe had probably used his own weapon for years and doped all his shots, Edison had gotten his a few days earlier and had me practicing on it as much as possible. Fortunately, it was very accurate out of the box. Unfortunately, I'd not had any inkling that I was ever going to be using it for real.

But there was no backing out, not now, so I knelt down and crawled under the blue tarp with Joe. It smelled like aftershave and rust.

"Hello, Nikita," said Joe. "My name is Joe."

"My name is Nichole. Not N—"

"Nickie," he said, patting Edison's 700 like it was a little baby. "Have you fired this gun before, or are we being fucked with?"

I had to think about which question I was answering. Under the circumstances, I realized it was probably the same answer either way.

"Yes."

"Do you know what this is about?"

"Um, no?"

"Good, neither do I. I guess we'll find out on Wikipedia in a few years."

He moved over a few inches and patted the deck beside the rifle.

"Come on," he said, handing me some squishy orange earplugs. I took them with a slightly shaky hand, which he must have noticed.

"Just like shooting up a school," he said. "You kids do that all the time, right? Mine do."

"You have kids?" I asked.

"Yeah, but they're not super-skilled ninja assassins like you, Mattie."

"Nichole," I insisted.

"Whatever," he said.

• • •

I can hear them murmuring, barely, over Gabe's griping. With the tarp between us, she has no choice but to listen and do as she is told. There is no looking to me for escape.

"This is wrong," says Gabe. "She's a kid for god's sake."

"Nothing about this affair is for *god's sake*," I remind him.

Synchronized music, horrifyingly patriotic, begins to emerge from radios around us, and Joe pulls the tarp down. For a moment, it is quiet enough that I can hear the low buzz of the Steadicam tripods, keeping the weapons more or less pointed at their targets as the boat rolls with the waves, and then my earplugs are in and there is nothing but the motion of the water, water everywhere. Here and there. The targets are just a bunch of heads at the end of the day, and inside each is a big juicy brain, about two pounds of which is water. The human body is mostly water, in fact, roughly two-thirds. We are literally trash bags full of liquid, waiting to pop. There are a hundred thousand miles of blood vessels, connected to a fist-sized muscle pushing five liters of blood around with enough force to squirt ten yards through the air should someone put a bullet through your neck.

Ah, yes. People fascinate me. I could kill them for hours.

The fireworks start with a flash of green and red, and a moment later there is an infinite little pause somewhere between three-hundred million meters per second and three-hundred meters per second where you could imagine you heard one noise closer than the rest. I watch through the binoculars as the primary topples, just a little over a half mile away, half his head vanishing, nobody noticing, just peacefully folding up like the chair he was sitting on. I barely notice the lady behind him falling as well, the round having traveled straight through him and into her. It sucks being collateral damage.

"Confirmed," I say, but no one can hear.

There is a brief pause, then more fireworks, and somewhere amidst the noise a few more bullets are thrown at the shore, and three of the secondary targets crumple. And with that we officially have an international incident that someone, somewhere, is going to use to enact some sort of legislation or other. Go us.

I kick the tarp, and somewhere underneath Joe begins to break down his Barrett into bite-sized chunks, packing it into a very large tackle box. Fireworks are still popping overhead, unstoppable, but the crowd on shore is reacting, pointing, panicking. As expected. As desired.

We sit there for a few minutes and watch the show, and there is a mixture of applause and screams as the last cascade of white flares up and dies, and then we are left with the smell of beer and smoke. A hundred boats fire up their engines at once and head for home, oblivious, and we are just one of them, Gabe taking us casually along with the crowd back towards the marina.

They should all go that easily.

As soon as we are reasonably far away, and alone, Joe pops up from the shadows and crawls to the back of the boat, leaving Xtian alone under the tarp. Knowing it is disposable, without asking permission he tosses my broken-down rifle overboard into the fastest moving water in the world, water that winds its way past the Peace Bridge through whitewater rapids and over Niagara Falls. My gun is followed by his gloves, and this is followed by a stream of piss. Then Joe sighs and grabs a can of beer, tosses it to me before opening one for himself. I open it and sip; I hate beer, but they do not know this, and some day this lie might be useful.

"How'd we do?" asks Gabe.

"Four," I say, not bothering to mention the collateral damage. "Enough." To get paid.

"How many did she get?"

"One," says Joe, staring at me. But a slight shake of his head tells me it was "zero."

"One more than me," says Gabe. "Give that girl a beer."

Joe grabs a cold one and throws it on the tarp, not gently. It lies there, twitching slightly with the gentle motion of the girl beneath. Joe looks at me and shakes his head, and I know that somewhere behind us, gradually sinking beneath the waves, is a rifle with a full magazine. Every kill today was Joe's, and I am not sure who I hate the most for that: Joe, Xtian, or myself.

We are silent for the rest of the ride in, mostly following the current, slow speed ahead. I do not bother to look back; you can never look back. Instead I watch the shore approach, all jagged black shapes and shadows, cold angles, mathematical. I am not quite sure where we are, or where we are going, but I know one thing for sure.

One way or another, each of us will end up right where we need to be.

Cloudy Climes & Starless Skies

12/21/2012

Come on," I say. She ignores me. It is not at all easy getting her to do anything these past few months. Homework, dishes, laundry. Once she has herself a nice little corner to camp in, she never wants to move. Both virtually in her games, and here in real life, her room smelling of unwashed plates, empty soda, and her. Part of this is winter. Part of it is her age. And to a certain degree, I have myself to blame; I bought her the games, forbade her real-life friendships. And I have not exactly provided her with anything else to do. Because there is nothing.

We are "sleeping" again now, the events of July 4 well behind us and nothing new on the horizon. This situation has nothing to do with Xtian's failure to pull the trigger as requested on the job, at least not that I know of—Joe did all we needed to do, and more. I doubt anyone else even knows. Rumors *do* spread, and there are leaks despite *their* best efforts, but that is unlikely, and I am not concerned. I am used to this pattern of ebb-and-flow, plenty and famine. Months or years between targets is normal, especially after a major election. There are shifts of power high up the invisible chain of theoretical command that take time to resolve themselves. I expected quiet, at least for a year or two. It is too early to worry about any of *that*.

I do worry, though, that Xtian's failure is because of me, just as my near failure in DC on the subway was because of her. Like it or not, our fates are at the moment uncomfortably intertwined. And I do not like that her present state of lassitude reflects on me. I do not care if anyone else knows. I know. That she is dragging me down. And I do not like it one bit. She has been listening to my lessons, but not learning.

Enough with the games.

The ironic thing of course is that I am the one who introduced her to these multiplayer brain-destroyers. I had read that they were supposed to desensitize you, make you more capable of committing violent acts, that sort of thing. I had no idea if that was true, but it sounded worth a try. When I was her age, all you could ever do in a game was die, eventually, regardless of how many quarters you put in or how good you were. That seems like a good lesson to learn. But what I've learned by watching Xtian play is that all these games actually teach is that everyone is immortal. You die, you respawn with a new life. You kill another guy, he comes right back. I do not like this lesson.

"Xtian, now."

She does not respond, but her little solider onscreen does. Her fingers dance over the keyboard; the little arms obey her commands, sniper rifle always in motion, the scope ever-so-briefly outlining a digital head before vanishing once again. Somewhere in the distance that head explodes and she gains a point. Quick scoping, she calls it. Within the span of a second she reloads her gun, pulls out a combat knife, hurls it into the air, and blows another head off. Somewhere in the distance the knife hits someone in the head, instantly killing him. What will the next chapter involve? Zombies? Aliens?

I move to grab her arm, and she shifts it away to avoid my grasp. I yank the headphones off her head but she just shrugs it off and keeps going; the volume is maxed out, and I can hear tinny, pubescent voices shouting racial and homophobic slurs at one another, at her. At least until I walk over and pull the Ethernet cable out of the router. It takes a moment and then she sees the message saying her connection has been lost. She looks over at me and hurls a slur at me.

"I told you not to use that word."

"It doesn't mean that anymore."

"We are going for a walk," I say. We are also going to meet someone, but she does not need to know that. Yet, anyway.

"It's four in the morning," she complains.

"And we are both awake," I reply. But she already knows this argument is futile, is already tugging on her sneakers. We have both fallen into an unhealthy regimen, odd schedules. Up till dawn, sleeping most of the day away. No school to pretend to have, no work to prepare for. The games are not helping. Or the television. Neither of us has been out much, and we are both paying for it. Mentally and physically. I have no idea about games, but an hour of television reduces your lifespan by twenty minutes. You burn more calories while sleeping.

Shoes tied, she stands and glares at me, arms crossed. "Well?" she asks.

"Get dressed."

"I am," she says, matter-of-factly.

She most certainly is not. Not for December, not even for July. This is not navel-baring weather, and she knows it. She is doing this to annoy me. She is succeeding.

I reach into her closet, way in the back, and pull out a fuzzy sweater, throwing it at her.

"Where did this come from?" she asks, smelling it.

I take a deep breath. Losing patience.

"The outside world," I say. "Let me show you."

• • •

It was horrid out, not even cold enough to be interesting, and it was raining, a sort of irritatingly gentle mist that got in my face and hair and raised the stink off the street, tainting everything. I felt dirty and greasy and my socks were wet, as they seemed to be all the time back then. The world was ugly. And so was my mood.

"You don't seem to be enjoying yourself," he said, once he'd settled on a street to prowl.

"Jesus had a better time on the cross," I mumbled. He'd said we could go back when the birds sang, but dawn was a couple of hours away.

"I highly doubt that," he said. "You're not bleeding from the wrists."

"That's later, over the bathroom sink," I said.

What bothered me most about these "walks" was that we never went anywhere in particular, just wandered around the neighborhood, playing a game he called, "Let's see if you're paying attention." We would walk, and he would ask questions, and I would answer.

It went something like this:

"How many ways are there out of that house we just passed?"

"Front door. Back door in the enclosed porch. So two."

"No."

"Four?"

"This is not Sudoku. Five. Why?"

This took some thought. "Windows?"

"Irrelevant. Five ways out. North, south, east, west, up."

"How?"

"You just need the right tools. We're next to one fifty-seven. What number is across the street?"

"One-sixty."

"Children?"

Toys in the front yard, two cars . . . "Two."

"Describe them."

"Blonde hair, blue eyes . . . She's got six fingers on her left hand. I don't know what you mean."

"Two kids, let's say seventeen and six," he said. "A boy and a girl. Beater in the driveway, high school sticker in the window, bumper stickers scream 'male teen.' Fresh dents in the fender, tires are bald. Probably just got his license."

"And the girl?"

"I saw them with her yesterday in the store."

"It's cheating if you know the answers," I said, punching his arm.

"Cheating isn't losing," he replied. "It's efficient winning."

"Do I get a prize if I win?"

"Yes. You get some fake gratitude. 'Good girl. Such a good girl.'"

"I can't wait to tell my fake friends that—"

He held up his hand and hissed, and I shut up immediately and listened. It took me a moment, but then I heard it, too. The sound of a bird, whistling in the dark.

• • •

"Blue jay?" she guesses. At this hour, this would be improbable, especially in this area, this time of year. And anyway, the correct answer is thrush. She would know that if I had bothered to teach her the code, but it has not been a priority and I hate using it, personally.

Regardless, we are done walking.

"Get back home," I say. "Now."

I give her no time to argue; she is on her own.

I vault the nearest chain link fence and vanish into the black, then hop another fence. This takes more out of me than it should, which is why I am glad that my contact is waiting for me in the next yard, beside a house we both know is vacant, since we made it that way. I would call it a "safe house" but I really do not like that word. Nothing is ever safe.

He sees me about the same time I see him and whistles again. I repeat, and he steps half out of the deepest shadows. Neither of us are fully relaxed, hands buried inside pockets, not because it is cold outside, but because we are each holding weapons.

We stand close and speak quietly.

"Been a long time, Al," he says.

"It has," I say. So long that I have forgotten the name I used to call *him* by, or whether or not he wanted to kill me. Irrelevant—names do not matter, only that we are useful to each other. Plus, he was the only one to answer his phone when I was calling around last week.

"Was that the girl I heard about?" he asks.

"Yes," I say, wincing inwardly. So much for the threat of rumors being *unlikely*. But he has no more to say, so maybe people have not been talking as much as I feared. At least not yet.

"I appreciate you coming," I say. "It was short notice."

"And short on details."

"Is that a problem?"

He shakes his head, so I go ahead and give him the address and apartment number. It is quite refreshing not to have to speak in code. He notes that this is nearby and asks when.

"Now would be great," I say.

"Right now?" he asks. I nod. He hesitates, but ultimately just shrugs it off.

"Fine," he says. "Who is it?"

Now it's my turn to hesitate. I am unsure, now that it has come down to it. But I only pause for a moment. Because this is for the best, no matter what happens.

"You just saw her," I say.

He raises his eyebrows. Part of me is surprised too. But it makes sense. So much sense. Every lesson I have taught her has been for naught. Failure after failure. She needs a real test. A trial by fire, as it were. And that is not something I can give myself. Not yet, at least.

"Is this some kind of setup?" he asks. Stupidly, as if I would tell him if it was.

"No," I say. "It's a job. There's a little girl arriving at my home right about now, and when I get back there in a half hour, I do not want to find her there."

He takes a moment to think about this, but I think he gets the gist. Or one gist, at least.

"I don't know—"

"You owe me a favor," I remind him. "Don't forget that."

He narrows his eyes for a moment. And then he remembers when I did something for him not so unlike this. Something he simply could not do himself. Outside of normal channels, unofficial, and—as I recall—quite nasty. Something neither of us will ever mention again.

I have done a lot of favors, over the years. People owe me a lot. I like that.

He paces for a moment. I know how he feels. With a group, you are just thinning the herd. But one target, one at a time, is more like downing Old Yeller. Personal. Which is still pretty easy to do, mechanically speaking, but it stings a little. He knows this well. Which is why we will be even, after this. Some things cost more than money. This is one of them.

"You're *sure?*" he asks, finally.

"If I had any doubts, I would not have called."

But there is doubt, and more. There is a brief, faint twinge of guilt somewhere in my chest. I have felt it before, long ago, and pushed it down just as easily. This needs to happen. Xtian only has at best a fifty percent chance of a positive outcome, but I win either way. These are the types of games I prefer to play.

"Thirty minutes," he whispers. And then he is gone.

I stand there for just a moment but I am not one to wait around, so I walk the opposite direction for the corner store to buy some groceries, pulling out my phone as I walk. One more phone call to make. And then it will be out of my hands. Maybe forever.

● ● ●

It felt cruel, taking me out to see nothing, then sending me back just when things were apparently about to get interesting, but I knew better than to argue. And I'd been wanting to go home for over an hour, after all. So I just turned and ran down the street, zigzagging back the way we'd come, alternately skidding on black ice and tripping over hardened lumps of gray. By the time I reached the apartment everything from foot to knee was completely soaked and cold, and it was all I could do to fumble my key into the lock, lunge inside, and be warm.

Wet sneakers hit the wall with a thud, leaving puddles on the kitchen floor that Edison would complain about when he got home. That is, until he saw the jeans in the corner, and the wet socks beside the door, and the rest of my things, a trail of me leading towards the bathroom.

I didn't even wait for the tub to fill, just wrenched the hot water knob all the way over, then added a bit of cold so I didn't boil and slid in the moment the water was warmer than me. I ignored the hurt and by the time the tub had half-filled, I was feeling quite toasty again. I could easily have died right then and gone to heaven.

Of course, right about then is when my cell rang.

Only one person had the number for that thing, so if it was ringing, it was him, and it was something worth calling about. I turned off the water, hopped out of the tub, and grabbed a towel on my way out the door. Slipping through the dark into the oasis of light that was my bedroom, I leaped onto the bed and crawled across to the cell on my dresser. I got it on the fifth ring and flipped on my back, watching as the glow-in-the-dark stars on the ceiling charged up, powered by the unicorn lamp on my desk.

"Under your bed," said Edison, and hung up.

And then there was nothing but the slow creak of hot pipes fighting cold air. Except, I knew, it wasn't the pipes. It was footsteps on the loose floorboards in the hall.

My numb fingers dropped the cell, but I didn't see or hear it hit the floor. I was already looking for escape, realizing that the window was not an option, that it would take too long to peel off the weatherproofing plastic, pop out the screen, and climb through. The door was the only way out, and that's where the intruder was. I was vividly aware of the butterflies dancing in my stomach, and somewhere deep in my skull I could hear Edison's cold voice telling me that those were actually involuntary muscle contractions as my body diverted blood away from my stomach and towards my legs. Nothing romantic, just biology. Reaction. Wanting me to run.

They always run, Xtian. Wouldn't you?

I wanted to, I did. But my brain realized that I needed to wait, that darkness would hide me better. Even though my legs wouldn't work, my fingers managed to fumble over to the lamp switch. Then I let gravity take over and fell on the floor. Above, the glow-in-the-dark stars flickered into life, cold and green and pale. Orion. The Hunter.

I wriggled under my bed to hide, dust collecting on my damp, suddenly all-too-naked body as friction trapped my towel beside the dresser. Footsteps neared the door, and I crammed my eyes shut, too scared to cry. Just a stupid little girl hiding in a stupid little place. I tried to hold my breath, letting whoever he was breathe for me as he slowly entered the room, walking like Edison, moving like Edison. A killer, like Edison. I prayed he didn't see me, not even knowing who I was praying to, just someone, anyone. Anything.

And as if on cue, the intruder's feet moved out of view around the foot of my bed. And I was back in the restaurant, eight years old, blood on my face and blood on the floor and all I could do was stare at my hands. Run. Run. I felt dizzy as I counted to three in my head, closed my eyes, and pushed myself forward, with the intent of lunging for the door.

I never had a chance.

A thick hand grabbed my ankle from behind, sweaty palm hot and slick on my cold, shivering flesh. I must have screamed as my hands dropped out and my jaw cracked the floor, sending another loose tooth skittering into the darkness, where the tooth fairy would never, ever find it. Bleeding and in pain, I could do nothing but grab wildly, fingers finding only dust bunnies and dirty socks. And then, just as he pulled me out and into the light, I found death.

Courtesy of Edison North.

• • •

I come home to my neighbors peering out the upstairs window. I wave as if nothing is wrong, and they smile and wave back, and like everyone they go back to watching their television and ignoring me, and ignoring the world, which is how we all like it.

My door is open. In the kitchen there is water, and blood, and Xtian's clothing. In the bathroom, there is running water. And in her bedroom, there is a broken lamp, and a little pink throw rug stained bright red.

I set the groceries on the table and sit down in the darkness to collect my thoughts, decide on a course of action. Time to move, time to disappear, to find myself a new garden. This one has gone fallow, it seems.

But just then, the faucet stops running, and the bathroom door opens. I do not turn. I know exactly what is coming. I hear it in the way the killer crosses the floor softly, steps up behind me. I can feel it as the barrel of a handgun, still warm, is pressed against the back of my head, a tiny ring of black branding my neck like a kiss. I smell it in the air, rancid and bitter, pity and hatred and uncertainty. Hours stretch into minutes, minutes eternal seconds.

Through the door, I can see the glowing stars on the bedroom ceiling fade to black.

And then she drops the gun, the one I placed under the bed for her last night, and follows it down. Her knees strike the floor hard enough to hurt, and her head is briefly upon my lap. But I do not react, and she quickly sobs and slides off, limp arms drifting down my legs until she can fall no further, damp hair tangled around my ankles, cheek upon the floor.

Xtian weeps.

A Splash Quite Unnoticed

01/01/2013

The airport lot was relatively empty, so we had our pick of spots. Edison chose the third from the end, sandwiched between a rusty van and a filthy station wagon, both of indeterminate make, neither of which had apparently been moved for days. He slipped our old Chevy into park, the engine sputtering from the cold, but before it could die a natural death he put it out of its misery. I wanted the same done to me.

He leaned back heavily in the seat, hands still on the wheel. Silent.

It felt like the end of the world, sun tinting the windows pink. But even with the residual heat in the car and the sun shining down, I shivered. Feeling empty.

I felt Edison's gaze and looked away, staring at the side mirror. Objects were closer than they appeared. I was a wreck. Hair still wet from a last-minute shower, my face pale. My lips red, like I was stained with fresh kill. But the kill had been a week earlier, and the only blood on my lips then was my own, from where I'd chewed off the chapped bits.

"Xtian, we have to go," said Edison. "If you want to stay, stay. But I'm not coming back."

"Did you send him?" I asked.

"What?" He somehow managed to act surprised even though he knew what I meant.

"Did you send the man," I repeated, choking up. "To make me have to—"

He didn't reply, just stared at me for a minute. If he looked anything, it was disappointed.

"Does it matter?" he asked.

And with that, he got out of the car and slammed the door before fumbling our bags from the trunk. I thought about dying there. It would take weeks before they found me, ripe and bloated. Unless it stayed cold out or got colder. Then I might freeze, become a big block of ice. A thing of the past, without a future to worry about. It sounded tempting.

The trunk slammed. Temptation faded. What would I do if I stayed behind? Die? Get arrested? I had nothing here. No one. No money, nowhere to live. The only thing I had in the world was walking away. Daring me to follow. And he didn't even need to bribe me with ice cream this time. He knew deep down I had no choice. Whether he had tried to have me killed, or simply stood aside and let someone else take a shot at me.

Cold air slapped me in the face as I stepped out and followed him. The smell of old snow, black with grease, grabbed and refused to let go. It followed me all the way across the lot to the main terminal, slush sticking to my ankles as I dodged puddles, trailing in Edison's wake.

"San Francisco will be a good place to lie low for a while until things . . . calm down again," he was saying, to me or himself I'm not sure. "The SFPD are notoriously behind the curve when it comes to homicide. Last year over half their murders went unsolved, well below the average of other large cities. Better than fifty-fifty odds, to start with. And that's if you don't know what you're doing, if you rely on chance. Which we don't—"

I tuned out. He had been talking the whole time since it had happened and especially while we had . . . cleaned up. It was all a blur, only meaningful in retrospect. Ramming a metal rod down a barrel. Filing off a serial. Dumping bodies. Chopping off my hair, dying his. Swapping vehicles. And, of all things, moving the furniture around. I hadn't quite understood the need, since he burned the place down anyway—along with just about everything we had owned—but he'd insisted it would cover our tracks. Hiding evidence, placing objects to suggest something that never was, never would be. Then burning it all anyway. Feng Shuicide.

We couldn't stay. And we could never go back.

How could I have . . .

"Stop crying," he said, and I only then realized I was. But to hell with him. If you couldn't cry at an airport, where could you?

I studied the carpet pattern while he checked the luggage, which didn't take very long since it was very early and there was hardly anyone else using our airline (probably why he'd chosen it). Before I knew it we were nearing the security line, and I could almost sense him tense up a bit. Not that he was concerned about the TSA—far from it. I think maybe he was concerned that this would be a good opportunity for me to throw a tantrum, get separated from him, and then be forced to rat him out. The thought never crossed my mind, though. I would have incriminated myself, too. My guilt outweighed his by a lot, just then.

"Homeland insecurity," mumbled Edison as we finally approached the checkpoint.

He sounded responsible, somehow. I wondered how, before I thought to wonder if. I was beginning to get a sense of what he was doing. What *they* were doing. In DC, with the subway. On the lake. Maybe even with me, and the man trying to kill me. It was about change. Acting, to cause a desired reaction. Edison saw himself as an agent of change. For all I knew, he had been involved in 9/11, in causing all of the change that came about afterwards.

It didn't take long to get through security. Edison knew better than to have a fit, assert his rights, and have it all filmed for YouTube. He went quietly, as did I. Shoes off, jacket off, plastic bag of toiletries in the gray bin, into the scanner, arms overhead while they collect your nude photos, move on through and hope they haven't stolen anything. We didn't have a lot to lose. Besides Edison's laptop—he got real nervous when that hit the scanner—all I was carrying were a few bits of clothing and some shampoo. Everything else I had owned had died in the fire, with the sole exception of my brand new 23, fired just once, which had been disposed of in the river. Practically an arsenal down there by now. Fish mafia.

As it turned out, the only snag we hit was my shampoo; it was like point-three ounces over the limit so they confiscated it, in case it was plutonium or something.

"Give them something obvious to take, and they'll assume it's all there is," said Edison, once we were well clear of security. "Give them the illusion of power and control, and you're the one in control. Misdirection and lies."

Little did they know that for all their security, we walked among them. I imagined all the things we could do. That we had done. That I had done.

"They're not there to stop terrorists anyway," he said once we were clear of security, on our way to our gate, two hours early.

"What?" I asked.

"They have never prevented a single terrorist incident," he replied. "The TSA fails to catch fake weapons and bombs the majority of the time. But that isn't really their fault, because their job is not to prevent terror. Their job is to remind us to be terrified."

Their job, and Edison's too, I thought.

● ● ●

We ate terrible chicken fingers and fries, both tasting of freezer burn, and watched the news to see if we'd made the cut. We hadn't. We browsed the gift shop, bought a five dollar bottle of water and two puzzle books we'd never use, then walked the concourse twice. There was too much time and then suddenly too little, and before I realized it we were getting called for boarding, and it was too late. For anything. Just like before, something was ending just before it had stopped beginning. I'd always had lots of beginnings and endings, but never quite enough middles to make a story out of it. Comma, after comma, after comma.

And now a period. It felt unnatural.

Edison pulled me onwards, my left hand clutching his right in a death grip as we waited for our group number to be called, and I was suddenly afraid that if I let go I'd fall. A cold little corpse on the tarry tarmac . . . on the sticky floor of a fast food restaurant.

When it was our group's turn to board, Edison stepped forward to get in line immediately, but I stopped. I expected him to just drag me with him, but instead he stepped us out of line, sat me down next to the window, and looked me in the eye. There were six of him, so I blinked the tears away and focused on the one I knew best.

"Why did you do it?" he said, softly. Then he handed me my ticket, turned, and got back in line to board the plane. It wasn't a long line; we were the last group called, and before long, he was on board, and I was alone.

How could he just leave me? What would the flight attendants think? That he had abandoned me? Would he get in trouble?

Why did I care so much?

Numb, I turned and stared at the plane through the window, considering the past, pondering the future, seeing only my own face staring back. He had let me go. I could go. I could run, leave the airport. But to where?

Wrong question; the question was why. Why did I do it?

"You all right, sweetie?" asked an airline attendant in a sweet "unaccompanied child" voice; I guess I looked more my own age that day, maybe on account of the tears. I nodded as I read her name tag—Samantha—then turned back to the window so I could look myself in the eye. I looked for answers but saw nothing but my own reflection, breath fogging the window.

Edison had left me the gun, but I had used it. Defensively, sure. But not consciously. Instinctively. Amidst the fear there had been a spark of rage that had driven it all, made me do it before I realized I had done it. *No, you can't do this to me. I won't let you.* Nothing so clear as that, of course, but that nonetheless. And that's what frightened me the most. What I was capable of. Not because it was something I chose to do. But because it was something I was.

And now I could get on that plane and fly away, and no one would stop me. I would get away, quite literally, with murder (or something close enough to count, for me). There would be no punishment for my sin. If it was a sin at all. If it mattered at all.

I had questions. And the only answers were on that plane. With Edison.

Samantha stepped closer, no doubt growing annoyed at the delay, and I smiled at her.

"Sorry," I said. "Just saying goodbye."

I turned back to the little window, leaned forward, and kissed the girl in the glass, tasting her cold lips. Then I picked up my bag and boarded the plane.

I left Christian behind, crying in the fog.

Murder Of Crows

09/15/2013

San Francisco had the best food in the world—Asian, European, Mexican, Antarctican (is that a thing?)—yet we still ate nothing but "American beige" at diners, fast food joints, hot dog carts, pizza places, same as we could have eaten anywhere else. I don't actually think Edison liked it; I think it was to make some kind of point. Eat your own dog food or you are what you eat—something like that.

I looked down in disgust at the rectangular thing in my hand and forced myself to swallow. Wondering if this is what I was becoming.

"You wanted fish," he said.

"I wanted sushi," I said, tossing the sandwich back on its tray. Edison immediately picked it up and took a bite like he hadn't seen food in weeks. That day he kind of looked like a hungry homeless person: scruffy gray beard, lanky gray hair tipped with black, tattered jeans, and a loose sweater full of holes. I barely recognized him.

Which of course was the point. As always.

"What?" he asked, swallowing. Caught me looking at him.

"Nothing," I said, finger-painting on my food tray with ketchup.

"No, not nothing. What?"

"What do you think people see? When they look at us, I mean."

He chewed thoughtfully for a few moments, then took a drink of coffee. He winced as he sipped. Hot? Bitter? Probably both. Coffee wasn't a beverage for him; it was penance.

"Why do you care?" he asked. Not the answer I was expecting. I thought about it.

"They probably think I'm your daughter. Adopted maybe. From some foreign country in Europe. Or some place with castles. I used to be a princess. Heir to the thr—"

"Stop stalling and finish your sandwich," he said. "You are nothing but skin and bones."

"No," I insisted. "I'm ten percent bones and fifteen percent skin and fifty percent water."

I may not have been attending school—if I had, I'd have been graduating from junior high that school year—but that didn't mean he was letting me off easy. He'd gotten me a new iPad in lieu of a laptop, so there were plenty of free ebooks to pore over. There was also a grimy little thrift store around the corner from our place in the Mission District, and there I spent hundreds of dollars, a quarter at a time, on real books that smelled like basements. Only a few were trashy novels. The majority were text books: chemistry and especially biology. I now knew that babies had 300 bones, I had 206. I knew human thighbones were stronger than concrete, but it only took eight pounds of pressure to dislocate a knee. Seven pounds of pressure to rip off an ear. Et cetera. Probably not stuff I would have learned in eighth grade.

"Couldn't we be friends?" he asked as I picked at my food. "Why must it be family?"

"Because you're o— of a more advanced age than I am."

"Well, this is San Francisco," he said. "We could be co-workers. You could be my intern."

"No, *you* could be *my* intern. Boy, fetch me more coffee. Fetch. Woof."

"I suggest friends and you spin that into pets?"

"The politically correct term is animal companions. Hey, how about that?"

"Companions? That's the best you can come up with?"

"I saw a video this morning where a monkey and a dog were playing," I said as I fished for my cell. But then I remembered it was turned off and the SIM was in my pocket, because he didn't want *them* tracking us everywhere. "Never mind."

"I've seen it anyway," he said. "I'm pretty sure that monkey was trying to abduct the puppy. That's not exactly companionship *or* friendship."

"So?" I asked. "*We* get along and you abduc—"

He hissed before I went any further, but I had already stopped. Was doing math in my head.

"What's today?" I asked.

"Wednesday," he said, checking his burner phone. "The fifteenth. Why?"

"We missed it," I mumbled. "Last week was when . . . the day you . . ."

"Oh. Guess I forgot," he said. "Not much of an anniversary dinner, is it?"

For a moment it all came spilling back. I don't know why that year stung more than others, but it did. I could see the coins on the floor, feel my sticky hands, taste the blood in my hair. Then he spoke and brought me back.

"Hey, let's go," he said. "Partner?"

I looked him in the eye, blinked back tears. Yeah. It sounded right. It was better than monkey, anyway.

● ● ●

She is silent as we walk to our car, a blue Honda this month. Blue is currently her favorite color. She remains silent as she squirms herself cross-legged into the front. No socks, backless canvas sneakers on the floor, tight blue jeans that match the tips of her three black pigtails, a blue halter top hanging loosely from her thin frame. Ninety pounds. More a child than I sometimes pretend. Hardly malnourished but wren-like and light for thirteen, though not her height—five-one, barely, last time we checked. It concerns me she might not be eating enough. Which is ironic, since I tried to kill her last year.

Of course, neither do I want her to drift too far in the other direction. It is no secret that childhood obesity rates started to skyrocket the same year

Happy Meals came out. A third of kids get a quarter of their vegetables as french fries, ten percent of their calories from soft drinks. A third of America eats fast food every day. Fifteen percent serve it, or will, at least until the robot uprising. Not that any of this matters since she never eats a full meal when we go out.

Xtian turns towards me as I start the car, but I can tell she is not looking at me; I can see the focus in her eyes shift as she stares at, not through, the window, watching the scene behind her head from within the reflection behind my head. Children inside the restaurant, laughing behind the golden arches on the window. She wants friends. Or thinks she does. I know better.

The distant look on her face makes me second-guess myself. The truth of the matter is I had not forgotten what today was. I had plans for tonight. Special plans, made a few weeks ago, that involved a few calls to some people I have not talked to in a while. I had planned to acquaint her with one of the San Francisco Bay Area cells. I want to get us both back in the loop, where we can be involved again. Her glance at the children playing makes me wonder, though. Is that what she wants? To be a child? To play, to go home and eat ice cream and take a bath and read one of her books? And if so, is that what I should let her be?

No, I decide. I should not let that happen. That would be a waste. Of her. And me.

And so I turn the car left instead of right, as we leave the parking lot. She can tell almost immediately we are not heading for home since I get on 101, but she says nothing until we are on the Bay Bridge, just past Treasure Island. Only then does she ask where we are going.

"To meet some . . ." What?

"Friends?" she asks.

"No," I say without hesitation. "Not even close."

• • •

Even the bad part of town has a bad part. The sort of place where bars don't check IDs because they sell them inside, where police don't go because they're outgunned. We drove past that neighborhood and stopped at a sports bar instead. I found it hard to believe that anyone who worked with Edison would be caught dead there. From the ridiculous bird clock over the bar that sang every hour, to the Raiders memorabilia on the walls, to the jukebox with a horrid selection, it seemed to me the last place people like Edison would meet. Of course, this made it perfect.

Also they had bar trivia. Not the kind for extroverts, with the goofy guy on a mic and people spilling beer on slips of paper, but the kind where you played on a touchscreen against people you couldn't see in other bars around the country. Trivia for sociopaths.

Question 9, Category Food Facts: "Which nut has a poisonous shell?"

"Cashews," I said. But Abe (surname unknown) tapped "Almonds" and we lost the round.

"Shit!" he yelled, pounding his fist on the table. Abe was one of. . .us? It had surprised me he was black—even more than being surprised that Edison had brought me here not on a whim, but to meet more of his colleagues—but I immediately buried the thought, thinking it racist to presume only white men could serial kill. Abe was big and bald and looked like he could rip your head off with tweezers, if he could avoid crushing the tweezers.

"It's almonds!" he complained. "This game is fucked up."

"No," I said, "Cyanide just tastes like almonds. Supposedly. Cashews have a poisonous shell."

Question 10, Category Pop Culture: "Which film featured the hit Aerosmith song, 'I Don't Want to Miss a Thing'?"

"*Armageddon*," I said.

This time Abe listened, but still threw a fit when I was proven right "What the fuck? Were you even born when that movie came out?"

Edison had forbidden me to discuss things like my age or actual name, of course, so I was stuck for a moment. Fortunately Josh (real name undisclosed) jumped in to defend my honor.

"A better question is how *you* know that movie, Abe," he said, "since there are no black guys—"

"Michael Clarke Duncan, mother fucker," said Abe, ignoring the racist assumption from the white guy—apparently this was just how he and Josh got along. "*Green Mile*?"

"He was in *Armageddon*?"

"He was one of the main characters. How do you not remember?"

"I guess I'm color blind," said Josh, shrugging.

Josh and Abe were both dressed in brand new dark-blue jeans, dark-colored T-shirts, and gray hoodies, slightly different shades but the same styles, like they had bought each other Old Navy gift cards last Christmas. The resemblance ended there; Josh was thinner, hairier, and taller than Abe, with a pleasant, fuzzy sort of smile hidden beneath a short-cropped beard. Nice, and thus a sure bet he had someone's limbs in his freezer. I liked him anyway. I couldn't help but wonder if he was like the team hacker or something. Like a league of super villains.

"The best thing about *Armageddon*," said Josh, not content to drop the issue, "is the part with the space madness." His voice dripped sarcasm. "Sometimes astronauts just *go crazy*."

"It's true," said a man at the door. "I heard that John Glenn ate four guys and they covered it up." When he stepped around the corner my heart dropped into my stomach. It was Joe from Buffalo. From the night on the lake. Joe who knew what I hadn't done. He looked like he had just stepped out of my memory; not a single detail had changed.

He walked straight over to the table and sat down next to Josh, across from me and Abe. I did my best to ignore him, but he decided to be a dick and stare right at me, grinning.

"You know each other?" asked Abe, unnecessarily loudly.

"Yeah," said Joe, too casually. "You could say that. Isn't that right, Nickie?" I felt my face get red. Thankfully I had given these guys the same alias I'd used in Buffalo.

When we'd arrived, Edison had immediately preoccupied himself with a man named Nick (actual name a secret), who had thus far ignored me to a degree bordering on suspicious. I had pegged him as a leader of some sort, and if nothing else would have, *he* cemented in my head the certainty that this visit had been arranged in advance, at a place they treated as some kind of office. He was kind of a dick—with his hipster glasses and slicked-back hair, but what mattered more was that he screamed business, of the wrong sort. Well-dressed, though. If he'd gotten a gift card from Josh, he'd thrown it out and gone to Men's Wearhouse instead.

When Joe said this, however, Nick's studious avoidance of me evaporated. Even though he and Edison were standing by the pool table, a fair distance away from our booth, it was quiet enough in the place that he must have heard or seen what was going on. And I was suddenly the focus of his attention. If I'd learned nothing else from Edison, I knew this was bad.

● ● ●

"What is he doing here?" I ask. Joe is the last person I expected to see here, and he happens to be the only one who can undo some of the half-truths I have been spinning about Xtian. Nick was of course *very* interested in why I had brought her here without telling him. We had talked about nothing else the entire time, which was growing tiresome.

"He was invited," Nick says, eyes locked on Xtian. "Unlike her."

For a moment I expect that one of us is about to kill the other, which seems inevitable, really, given enough time. But instead of starting something I will have to finish, he just says, "I know him, but I don't know her, and I don't like not knowing people, Edward." This latter being one of the names he knows me by. I prefer variations on a theme with my aliases.

"So get to know her." I sweep my arm invitingly. Far better he talk to her directly, before Joe gets a chance to muck things up. "All yours."

"Yes," he says. "Yes, she is."

I wave for Joe to come visit with me, hoping to peel him away from the situation until I can get a better idea what the hell is happening, but he just smiles and peruses the drink menu as Nick slides into the booth beside him. I wish him luck, there—the wait staff has been off their game tonight. Probably for the best. I could squeeze in beside Abe, but instead I casually drift over and lurk off to one side just in case I need to kill everyone. Joe first, I think. Then Nick.

"About time we got introduced," says Nick. "I see you apparently already know Joe."

Thankfully he is not talking down to her, no attempt to mask anything or treat her differently because she is a girl. She probably finds this refreshing but I find it disconcerting.

"Apparently," she says. Josh, unrealistically preoccupied with his phone, smirks.

"How did you two meet?" Nick asks, looking between her and Joe.

"If you don't already know," she says, "then you're not supposed to."

Nick does not look happy about the response, but really, it is just about the best one she could have come up with. Regional cells are almost always separated. What happens in Buffalo stays in Buffalo, and so on. People sometimes move—floaters like myself—but information does not move, and regardless of the exceptions, Joe does *not* fucking move. He's operated in Western New York and southern Ontario for well over a decade. My own presence here is questionable, but Joe *absolutely* should not be here.

"Edward said you're his partner," Nick says. Xtian does not respond, so he adds "I asked you a question."

"Actually, you didn't," says Xtian. "You made a statement."

Nick smiles, and then viper-quick, reaches across the table with his right hand, grabbing Xtian by her chin. No one else moves. Protocol is to come to the table unarmed, so I know he is not planning to shoot her. He is simply establishing the pecking order.

"Please take your hand off my face," she says. A bit rattled, I can tell, but playing it cool.

"You're very polite for someone in your position," says Nick.

"You're very impolite for someone with a gun aimed at his balls," she replies.

For the first time, I realize she has her hands under the table, and I remember that she had her 3032 when we left the apartment this morning. And we have not been home yet to ditch it.

Abe laughs. On anyone else it would seem wrong, but for him it is a genuine, deep Santa Claus sort of laugh. A scary, homicidal sort of Santa, but honest nevertheless. About the only honest thing in his head. I do not know him that well, but I know he has some deep, dark secrets. He hides them very well, though.

"Little girl, you get a free soda for that," he says, rising, ignoring the danger.

"It's pop," says Joe. Abe ignores him and asks Xtian what she wants.

"Vanilla Coke, please," she says in that little baby doll voice I am growing to dislike. Her hands are still under the table, her eyes still locked on Nick's.

"How dare you," says Nick, letting her face go to lean back in his chair. But he is talking to me. "How dare you bring her here, to this table, with a weapon?"

"Slipped my mind," I say. "You know I never carry."

"A clean shirt, of all things," he adds. What Xtian would call a "noob."

"She ain't clean," says Joe. Nick waves him off, and Joe shuts up. I begin to wonder if maybe Joe knows more about what happened in Buffalo than what went down on the boat.

"Come on, Nick," says Abe. "I'll get your next one, too."

Nick glares at Abe, but Abe makes it clear he wants to talk about something, and the two of them head off to the bar together. Possibly to plot our deaths. You never can tell. They would not be the only two imagining murder scenarios right now, that much is for sure.

"Gun," I say, sliding into Abe's former spot, beside Xtian. "Now."

She sticks out her tongue and then disappears below the table for a moment before reappearing beside me. I am the only one who notices when she slips the gun into my hand while crawling under the table. Then, like nothing happened, she is skipping off to the jukebox.

"How much you want for her?" asks Josh, fiddling with the trivia game while I break the gun down in my lap, then slip the pieces into my coat pockets.

"Not ripe enough yet. Or is she . . . Edward?" Joe cocks his head at me, trying to goad me into a reaction. I clearly note the emphasis on the name, telling me plainly that he was discarding the "Tom" he knew me by previously. I mentally file this away under "inevitable." I am not worried about it. I know things about him, too. Not just the things he tells everyone, either; I know which of those things are true.

"She's as old as your daughter," I say, picking one of them. "So you tell me."

This is about as close as I am comfortable getting to the sort of vile insinuation he just tried, and to his credit he gets it, holding up a hand in feigned submission. I raise an eyebrow at him since no one is watching, and he nods. The unspoken agreement: we will both drop this, whatever it is, at least for now. Good on him. Nobody has to die. At least not tonight.

• • •

Nick and Abe got back to the booth about the same time I did, and somehow we all fit inside, one big unhappy dysfunctional family. Almost immediately, people started talking weird. It took me a few seconds to figure out that it was the same sort of code they'd been using on the boat, back in Buffalo. Here, of course, it made more sense to be sneaky. We were in public.

"When are we meeting next?" asked Edison. Since it didn't seem like we were quite done here yet, I suspected immediately that there was more to it than paying the bill, and I was right.

"After graduation," said Nick. Then, oddly, he repeated himself. "After graduation."

"You're still in school?" I asked, and immediately got four and a half dirty looks.

"Shut up, little girl," said Nick. "Go update your Tumblr."

Beside me, Edison gave a little shake of the head, so I just wrapped my lips around my straw and kept quiet.

"That's a long way off," said Edison, turning back to Nick.

"And?"

"Just saying, it's odd." Edison looked around the table, and there were some shrugs, but apparently no one else had a problem with whatever they were discussing, so he dropped it and they moved on. I tried to keep up, as best I could under the circumstances, but the majority of what followed meant nothing to me at all. At the time it sounded like five guys discussing a vacation or something. And I guess maybe that's what it was. A hunting trip.

"Decide on a place yet?" asked Josh.

"Local," said Nick. "No back roads. Straight shot up an interstate wherever we go."

"Overnight stay?" asked Edison.

Nick shook his head.

"Just a day trip. Joe will be in charge of bringing a packed lunch."

Joe began to hum the Oscar Mayer song. Everyone pretended not to notice.

"Casual attire, of course," said Nick. Groans around the table.

"Isn't Canadian currency made out of tree bark?" asked Joe. Nick shot him a dirty look.

"Isn't American currency made out of the skins of natives?" asked Abe, who I would later learn was from Vancouver originally. Relevant to nothing, of course.

"That and broken treaties," said Josh.

The table went quiet as Nick pulled out a disposable burner flip phone like they all seemed to use. He dialed, listened, and then spoke rapidly in what was either French or Japanese before returning to English, for our benefit.

"Yeah, that flight out of Quebec isn't working for me." He listened, then asked "Athens?"

"I like gyros," said Josh.

"In Germany it's pronounced like 'Oreos,' did you know that?" asked Joe.

No one cared. However, everyone seemed happy with whatever had just been decided, so Nick said "do it" into the cell and then closed it.

"Three-hundred," he said, without further context.

"And how are we splitting the check?" asked Josh. I suspected he wasn't talking about our bar tab.

"Looks like six," said Nick, surveying the booth. For another ten minutes, they argued over numbers, with eyes continually coming back to me. Ultimately it seemed like they settled on whatever "three-fifty" meant. It felt like unnecessary obfuscation. No one else was listening, were they? I tuned out, figured I'd be told what mattered, and forgot most of it almost immediately.

But I remembered the end part.

"I think we're all settled," said Joe. "Except for the time. We got a rough estimate?"

In the corner, the jukebox spat out the last few chords of some old song about murder, then went silent.

Nick considered, watching the screens over the bar. "Blackbird," he said.

• • •

Nick leaves soon after with Joe, and in the less oppressive atmosphere I decide to let Xtian socialize, catch up on current events with the men she will soon be working with. If nothing else, she can grow accustomed to the superficial insults and false camaraderie, all masking a deep distrust that is more important for her to learn than the coded language. Everyone is a colleague, and a rival. Everything, all of it, is a falsehood. Masks beneath masks, layers of an onion. Most of the things we know about each other are lies.

After more mindless conversation and a few drinks, Josh and Xtian head off to play nine-ball for a while as I catch up on lies with Abe. I try to drop some hints about Joe, but if he knows any more about that situation, he is not sharing: there is nothing in him tonight but the same millimeter-thin gilding of emptiness, diet cola on an empty stomach. Lacking substance.

"Did you see?" he asks. "Gold is down another seven-fifty. Good time to buy."

"You work for Rupert Murdoch?"

"Maybe I just think, you know, society is about to collapse."

"Should be investing in lead then," I mutter.

Abe gestures vaguely towards the bar. Televisions are showing highlights of the Seahawks trouncing the 49ers, at that moment, but I get his point. News. Terror. Politics. ISIS is suddenly everywhere, even though they have been around for years. Amazing what a marketing campaign will get you. A new kind of destruction—and distraction—every month.

"It's all coming down," he says. "Slowly maybe, but it's coming. And whoever has the money when it's all over is gonna be in charge."

Abe goes on like this for a while, me nodding along, but thankfully before he can start talking about the earth being flat, Xtian walks over with Josh and asks if we can leave.

"The Ladies' room here is ghetto," she says, "and Josh says the Men's is worse."

"I wouldn't touch a toilet in this place with Abe's dick," says Josh.

"You come near my dick and I'll cut it off," replies Abe, brandishing a spoon.

"We have a bridge to cross," I say, ignoring the banter. "Can you hold it?"

"My kidneys are about to blow," says Xtian.

"Shame," says Josh. "Kidneys are worth five grand a piece."

We wander outside to find a bush or something, but there is nothing around but cars, so we head for mine. On the way, Xtian asks what was going on with the Oreos. It takes me a minute to figure out what she is talking about.

"Oy-rows," I say, enunciating. "They were being goofy. They meant Euros. European currency. That's how we're getting paid."

"Oh!" she says. "Okay, but what was the graduation thing?"

"After graduation," I said. "A.G. It means three."

"Why'd he say it twice then?"

"Because he needed to say it twice. Three, three. March third."

"What's A.G. have to do with three?"

"I'll tell you later," I say. "I thought you had to pee?"

She goes behind our car as I sit inside, door open, listening to the old engine mutter. I know how it feels, and I am twenty years its elder. My leg throbs, my neck is stiff, my shoulder hurts, and that is just an appetizer. Pain is nothing new, of course. I can trace my entire life history back along a trail of endless pains and aches. My earliest memory is breaking my arm at age six, and it has been all downhill from there. But there is more of it, lately. Pain.

And as if to punctuate my thought, the car chooses that moment to stall, and for a moment, through the silence, I can hear a warm sizzle on the cold concrete. I catch Xtian's eye in the rear view mirror as she stands and zips herself up, blue denim shrouding pink cotton. Unafraid. I can no longer cover her scent with my own; she has marked her territory, and I will not be the one to try and challenge her for it.

I will leave that to the others.

First-Person Shooter

12/15/2013

Xtian sits on her left leg. Her right swings like a metronome, keeping time to the song in her head, mumbled lyrics dripping off her lips and into her salad, which sits uneaten but for a few unlucky croutons. I stare off into the distance and stuff a pinch of congealed cheese fries into my mouth. Not very healthy, but they will do, considering that there is practically nothing else on the menu here I can eat without dying. Even their mayonnaise comes with a side of mayo.

She sighs, swishes her straw around in her Diet Coke, and glares at me as we both listen to the cacophony around us: video games, thudding bass, the gooselike burble of the slightly inebriated masses, screeches of sweat-reeking children like chalkboards dragged across a bed of severed fingernails. Beer and video games. What lunatic thought this up?

"Eat your food," I say. "Are you thirteen or three?"

"Whatev . . . Dad."

"Do not call me that," I whisper intensely. This line of conversation annoys me more than all this waiting. Three more months until our job? Intolerable.

"Why not? Dad. Daddy."

"They do not need their assumptions reinforced," I say. "They can believe what they like, but the less they know, the better. What d—" The waitress arrives with another drink, Xtian's fourth, and another basket of breadsticks, so I change the subject immediately, mid-sentence.

"—id you get on that math test?"

Xtian grabs a breadstick before the waitress has set it down and gnaws on it, thoughtfully, ignoring the bowlful of lukewarm marinara sauce that came with, perhaps wisely.

"Thank you, Melissa," she says. The waitress gives her a dirty look, the same sort I imagine she will give later when she realizes we have no intention of leaving a tip. I wave the woman away from my half-empty glass of ice water and she flees. I will never understand the incessant refilling. There is a drought in California.

"Can we go soon?" asks Xtian. I know how she feels; I am sorely tempted to take the place out. It falls well within my standard criteria for mass murder: mid-sized, enclosed, lots of people (why are they not at home playing their own games for free?), the sort of thing that nets you a high fatality-to-casualty ratio. Often you want more walking wounded, but there comes a time when you just want to smoke as many herring as you can.

Of course, that would make it difficult for Xtian to practice.

"You wanted in. This is in. So quit playing around and go play." I slide her a game card.

"Oh no," she says, picking it up. "It has your fingerprints on it now."

"That would only matter if someone had a known print to compare it to," I say as she sprinkles pepper on the card, trying to locate a thumbprint. "Now stop stalling. We are not going until you use that up."

"Why can't we just do the real thing?" she whines. "The range is cheaper."

"They will get suspicious if we visit the range every day and stay there for five hours at a time. Here, evidently, they encourage that," I say. "Plus, you are far less likely to draw attention to yourself here, surrounded by the other filthy little children."

"You're filthy," she says and kicks me in the shin. I move my foot to kick her back, but she is already on her feet and gone by the time my boot meets the booth. Signs of improvement.

• • •

I was glad to be rid of him. Though dressed entirely appropriately for the place—jeans, Sharks sweatshirt, sneakers—he stuck out like an infected thumb. His foul attitude seeped out from the bottoms of his legs and left a trail of awful behind him. I knew he could barely stand being there, but there was method and that meant risking a bit of madness. If he'd stabbed a waitress, though, we might have had to call it an early night.

Edison believed anyone could master any art if they took things step-by-step, went slow, and practiced regularly. I think his theory was originally intended for violin students, so its application to other fields (such as killing people) was probably questionable. He insisted that I stop messing around with handguns and focus on the rifle, considering my failure back in Buffalo. I should be good at it, he said. I had more "slow twitch" capability, making me more precise while men had more "fast twitch" muscles, or something of that sort. I half-believed him.

We both thought the range was more entertaining (and certainly more real), but as Edison had said this place was more "age-appropriate" and would suit us fine. Age-appropriate. Meh. I wasn't even sure what that meant anymore. I could have passed for eighteen with the right makeup, the right hair. I could probably have ordered a beer if I tried. What was it going to take for him to stop treating me like a child? Another year? Another murder?

I angrily swiped my plastic game card through the slot and the machine duly deducted several credits, asking me if I wanted to play the computer or go head-to-head with another player, a boy apparently about my age. If that other player had been Edison, it would have been a no-brainer, but on this occasion it was someone I didn't know. Oh well. No time like the present to practice killing bystanders, I thought. Why not start with a child?

• • •

The sweep takes me just a few minutes, but I learn enough to know that it is relatively safe. No one obvious, no suits, no uniforms, save for a few scant security goons, flunked out of college, most of them at the front door watching the kids line up to wait their turn. Just looking at them, smelling them, listening to them, makes me want to go get some volatile chemicals from the convenience store. Perhaps later.

I easily spot Xtian by her two long bleach-blonde pigtails; clearly those will have to go, as they are too distinctive. She has attracted a small crowd of onlookers, mostly boys, her age and—disturbingly—older. Her clothing itself does not warrant the attention—a muted gray-green shirt that matches her scuffed sneakers (no socks, ever, lately), tucked into faded jeans—so much as the fit of it does. Even from a distance I can see not only that she is on the scrawny side, but that she has at least two good reasons for attracting male attention, even if she has not yet figured that out yet. Probably she has. It is not something we discuss.

I wander right through the middle of the crowd and stand directly behind her, watching her moves, blocking their view. There are a few snarky comments, but nothing worthy of a quick death. Slow, perhaps.

"This is what you get for quick scoping all the time," I say.

"The sight's all goofy," she says as the sniper from the other side of the machine takes her out. He crows and peers around the machine as she curses.

"Ooh, she's gettin' salty," he says. Smartass little pubescent fast-twitcher, most likely to be involved in a school shooting before graduation as one of the victims. Perhaps I will enroll Xtian in school after all—so she can thin the herd.

We have at least another hour of this. I hope I make it.

"Give me room," she says, elbow intruding my thigh as she digs into the right pocket of her jeans for the game card. She slides it through the slot, and the machine counts down, and ten seconds later he has scored a hit on her. She should be better at this, but I decide to give her the benefit of the doubt and blame the prop rifle. Still, there are things she can improve.

"No. Don't use the scope right away," I say. "Back away, look at the whole screen. Watch where he is, predict where he will be. Then go there and wait for him to come to you."

Ten seconds later she nails him with a headshot. She then proceeds to kill him four more times in a row. Cheating now, of course. The game has a limited number of entry points, and she has died often enough now that she has the pattern memorized. All she needed was one hit, and now the rest is inevitable. However, I do not point this out to her for three reasons. First, my hatred of her opponent. Second, her ability to detect patterns and exploit them is a skill in itself and worthy of attention. And finally, because she is learning the proper mindset for this sort of thing, whether she knows it or not.

Humans are creatures of instinct and habit. They do something over and over, it becomes second-nature. Reflex. This is especially true with violence, which is why my view of these games has evolved since Buffalo. I even read that now they make soldiers play games like this because it makes them less hesitant on the battlefield. It makes better killers. Xtian does not necessarily share this view, but she is not naïve. She knows this is why we are here. And why we are not hunting, instead. Hunting is all about thinking. You sit still for eight hours and fire a gun once, then drag a dead thing back to your car. What she needs to do is stop thinking and just act, especially among distractions.

For now, practice is finished. Her opponent gives up.

"Wanna try Skee-ball?" he asks. Xtian looks at me expectantly, but I just shrug. Rolling balls up a ramp to earn fistfuls of paper tickets you can trade in for fistfuls of nothing. Mindless amusement, sound and fury signifying nothing but a plastic whistle and a rubber ball fit for dogs. But as long as we are here she is theoretically learning. Watching people, crowd movements, learning that people like to cluster around food, excitement, and exits.

Wordlessly she runs off, not waiting to see if I will follow. I do not. Instead, I slide my own card into the slot of the sniper game and prepare to play the machine, just to see if it is really as "goofy" as she claimed. I am stymied when a request for head-to-head combat comes up. When I do not immediately respond to the game request, someone leans around the machine—another filthy lamb, older and pimplier than the last one.

I accept the request and lift up the prop rifle, wishing it were real.

"Bet you can't kill me before I kill you," he says.

"How much?" I ask.

• • •

Skee-ball was a bust; some kid had watched a YouTube video about how to clean them out of tickets and they needed to be refilled. Someone was going home with a metric ton of plastic whistles. Instead, my new friend Denny and I migrated back into the hallway that led to the restrooms where it was quieter. He had said he wanted to talk, but it didn't take long for him to "coax" me into the unisex "family buffet" style restroom. The one for people with babies, and also apparently for making out, if I was reading the signs right (the signs mainly being how paired-off teens kept filing in and out of the room). Initially, at least, Denny was more interested in getting his iPhone positioned at just the right angle on the countertop than he was in me. I hadn't made this easy for him since I'd immediately sat down between the two sinks. He'd have preferred me on the floor, no doubt.

"Whatcha doin'?" I asked, legs swinging as if I had no idea what was going down. I'd been sizing him up since we came in here. He had a few inches, a few years, and about fifty pounds on me, but it was mostly flab. Not the sort of person I would let push me into a snow bank, much less whatever he had planned.

"Just a selfie," he said. He came a few steps closer, putting his hand on my leg. I admired the confidence, but not much else. "So, uh, you're pretty hot, y'know? I bet you're a real freak."

Well, I never.

"You like that?" he asked, taking a glance at his iPhone to make sure it still had us both in frame. He slid his hand up further. At least he wasn't wasting time.

"I'd like to put something in your mouth," he said.

I was pretty sure I'd watched this same video a few weeks ago on one of the PornyTube sites. Time to change the script.

"You know what I'd like?" I said.

I took his other hand, placed it on my other thigh, and smiled. Then I yanked his head down into the edge of the counter, splitting his face open right above his nose. He blubbered for a moment and pulled back, which was perfect. I added momentum by pushing off against his chest with both legs. He tumbled back into the stall opposite us and hit the toilet with his lower back.

"What the fuck?" he said. "What's wrong with you?"

"With me?" I replied, grabbing his iPhone, verifying it was recording. It was. I held it up to show him. "Where were you gonna post this? Facebook?"

"Nowhere," he said. He slid up onto the toilet, legs too wobbly to stand, blood running down his face. "Gimme that, you crazy bitch."

"Not yet," I said, hopping off the counter, watching him through the cell camera now. He finally stood and took a step towards me. Which is when I pulled my 3032 from the small of my back and pointed it at him. The safety was still on, but he didn't know that.

"Why, hello there, Mister Tomcat," I said. "Say hello to Denny."

I never knew people pissing themselves was a real thing until then.

"I'm-I'm-I'm sorry . . ." he blubbered. "Please. I'm so, so sorry."

"Shut up, Dennis," I said. "Shut up and get on your knees."

He silently complied as I scrolled through files on his iPhone, confirming what I'd already figured out. I was number five or six just tonight. And there were more than that. How was he not in jail? Then again, how was I not in jail? Fair enough.

"What was it you said before?" I asked, considering the barrel of my gun. "'I'd like to put something in your mouth'?"

• • •

Xtian comes back strangely flushed and, thankfully, hungry from whatever exertion she has been engaged in. She doesn't even sit down, just digs into my second order of cheese fries, congealed though they might be. She will be sick later, in the car. And I will make her clean it up.

"Hey," she says. "We should maybe go." She's a little nervous about something. I should not pry; if I need to know, she will tell me. But I press for information anyway.

"You break up with your new boyfriend already?"

She brushes it off, not taking the obvious bait.

"I haven't seen him in a while," she says, too quickly.

"You finish off that game card?" I ask.

"Yeah," she says.

"Let me see it."

"Can we just go?" she asks. "Please?"

Please? Who is this girl, and what did she do with Xtian? But I can see by the look in her eyes that she means it, that she really wants to be out of here, and I cannot disagree with that. So we immediately head out the front door and begin the long walk across the parking lot to where I parked. She checks over her shoulder a couple of times. But no one is following us.

"So what did you kids do?" I ask as I unlock the car, "Did you win any tickets?"

She doesn't respond, just gets inside and slouches down in the passenger seat. I double check the lot before I get in myself, but there really is no one else around.

"You don't want to talk about it?" I ask as I start the car. She says nothing, but when I don't put the car in gear, she looks over at me.

"What's wrong?" she asks.

I gesture towards her lap with my head.

"Not moving till you ditch that SIM," I say. She has herself an iPhone, by the telltale outline in her pocket, so she can't just pull the battery.

"I already did," she says. "Want to see?"

I shake my head and pull out of our spot, heading towards the highway. I am not quite sure what she learned tonight, but she clearly learned something. And that is progress.

Field Trip

03/03/2014

We are atop a peculiarity of geography, a steep and sudden hill at the end of a long stretch of highway with eighty-five-mile-an-hour traffic heading towards us for ten long seconds, just yards before a curve and a dip in the road and an exit that—at this hour—is eternally, perpetually backed up with traffic. Eighty-five to zero in less time than it takes to reach down for your Frappuccino, to turn and yell at the kids, to text "LOL." It is a miracle humanity has evolved to drive at these speeds, a further miracle people do not die here by the score every day.

Today some will.

It is a bit before rush hour peaks, a long half hour before the sun crests the hills across the highway. The latest boom here in Silicon Valley is, as we watch, sending a bunch of millennials off to a twelve-hour work day so they can afford the next thousand-dollar car payment or the ass raping they know as a mortgage. Sheep, lining up to be eaten by wolves, and one of them isn't even going to make it to dinner, thanks to us. In the back of my head, I keep mulling over the strangeness of this job—planned six months ago, yet relying on a specific person being in a specific place at a specific time. It seems too . . . well, specific. But then I have no specific reason to second-guess the logistics of it, and at any rate I have other things on my mind.

Joe is lying in the grass beside Xtian, the blanket beneath them spattered with dark fluids, still preferable, albeit barely, to the grass beneath us, wet with morning dew and animal waste. Xtian has her eye to the scope, and Joe sees twice as much, half as magnified, with a pair of binoculars glued to the same patch of freeway, an eighth of a mile away and straight ahead.

This time, this arrangement is Joe's doing. He is supposed to be the trigger man, being the most seasoned among us at this sort of thing. And, as far as Nick knows, he is still the one who is going to do the dirty work today. It was only when we got here a few hours ago that he decided to change things up, suggested—nay, insisted—that Xtian be the one to do it. She looked at me. I shrugged. She agreed. We had been practicing, after all, so she can shoot while Joe spots. That leaves me as a lookout, and Josh to work the phones and drive the car on the way out.

And so here we are, four killers and . . . a cannon, basically.

"What the fuck, Joe? Where did you get a Payload Rifle?" Anti-Material Payload Rifle, AMPR for short. An XM109, to be precise. Nothing Joe should have. Nor anyone else.

"Let's call it 'military surplus' and leave it at that."

All of us are in theoretical camouflage, a balance between "matches terrain on a hillside overlooking a major highway" and "blends into a crowd once we are no longer on said hill." Of us all, Xtian is unintentionally the best camouflaged, in dirty white sneakers, blue jeans, a dark green sweatshirt with a faded unicorn on the front. Not only will she be totally inconspicuous afterward, but she blends in with the landscape fairly well, so much so that I almost lose her in the mist still clinging to the hills when I look away for a moment.

"Is this a fifty?" asks Xtian admiringly. Caliber, she means.

"No," says Joe. "It's a twenty-five." Millimeter, he means.

"Is that like half as powerful?"

"No," says Joe. "This is Common Core math."

This is a good trial run for her, all things considered; at this distance, there is very little movement of an oncoming target for about a hundred meters, with a clean, straight-on, please-shoot-me presentation. Everything is accounted for: weather, the make and model of the car, the deflection expected from shooting through glass. Everything should go fine. Especially since Joe's AMPR has a fancy targeting system and everything. She could miss and still hit.

I do not know what I will do if she fails again like she did in Buffalo. Like Joe knows she did. I wonder maybe if that is why he has her shooting. Maybe he expects to get some perverse thrill out of her screwing up a second time.

"So you guys work together a lot?" she asks.

"No," says Joe. I say it at almost the same time, somewhat louder than him.

"Normally people stay in their own regional cell," I add. "This is highly unusual." I give Joe a dirty look at the back of his head, wondering if he can feel my glare.

"Well, I guess we're all rule breakers here, aren't we?" he says without looking at me.

"I never followed them in the first place," I spit back. He should not be here, I keep thinking. And then I think, well, neither should I. Or Xtian. My gut says something is brewing. My brain says I am being a hypocrite. By my own argument I should still be in DC.

Perhaps we all have our own reasons for running away from places.

"Hey, Josh," says Joe, filling time with nonsense, "I tell you my wife and I got turned down for adopting that Siamese cat? I told them 'Fuck you and your cross-eyed retarded cat.'"

"Why'd they turn you down?" asks Josh. He can banter far better than I can.

"They wanted a home with other pets," says Joe. "I tried to argue that my children were close enough."

"You *really* have kids?" asks Xtian, turning her head to peer over at him through a veil of shoulder-length blonde hair. Today, it is streaked with blue, like moldy cheese. I cannot tell if she remembers Joe mentioning his kids before or not. She could be making idle chatter or possibly pushing back at Joe since he messed with her at our meet-and-greet a few months ago.

"Two," he says, rolling off the blanket and into a crouch with one smooth movement. "But they didn't want to come out and play. Too busy watching cartoons like *normal* children."

Ah, there we go. Joe playing the long game with his insult. He tries too hard sometimes.

"You do not raise a capable, confident adult by letting the television babysit," I say.

"No," says Josh. "I guess you teach them how to kill."

Touché.

● ● ●

We'd been awake since before dawn and lying prone for the past two hours, yet no one had bothered to tell me exactly what we were going to be shooting at. I didn't care if I had to kill everyone on the freeway at this point, if it meant we could go home. I wanted a shower.

"Punch and pie?" asked Joe. He looked at Josh, who was suddenly on a brand new cell. There was a mumbled, very brief conversation, presumably with the rest of the team. Then Josh pulled the battery out of the phone, held up five fingers, and said, "Yellow."

"What's that mean?" I asked. Edison still hadn't gone through the whole code with me.

"Yellow means five," said Joe, showing me his own palm, calloused and filthy.

"No, that's not wh—"

"Last year six thousand people checked into emergency rooms with pillow-related injuries," said Edison. "That's how safe people are in their homes. Watching their cartoons." Evidently he was not done talking about the earlier issue, still trying to one-up Joe somehow.

"Clearly a lack of funds for pillow safety education," said Joe. "I was reading—"

"You can read?" asked Josh.

"*Hooked On Phonics* worked for me. I read a study that said those most likely to become teachers are those with the lowest averages in their classes. All the smart ones take other jobs. So each generation is taught by dumber teachers, creating dumber students."

"That is not an education problem," said Edison. "It is a cultural problem. If you blame one thing, blame the Internet. The average person has an attention span of about eight—"

Josh's second cell rang, once. He looked at the display and nodded to Joe and me. The first call, from our first spotter a few miles up the road. Nick, maybe? I had no idea.

"—seconds," finished Edison.

"What was that?" asked Joe. "I wasn't paying attention." He lay down beside me, reached around to correct my positioning, hand on my waist.

"Remember what I told you," he said. "Try not to miss the first shot, but if you do miss, just aim downstream and hit whatever you can. With how fast traffic's going, close might be enough to take him out if you cause a pileup."

"'Kay," I said. My hands shook. What if I failed again? What if—

"Should we get her a laser sight?" asked Josh, sarcastically. As if it could help at that distance.

"You know," said Joe, "I once bought a handgun with a laser sight on it. There was a warning on it about not pointing it at people's eyes."

Josh's third and final cell rang. Probably the second spotter. Abe? Josh made a noise like "Mmhmm" and nodded at Joe.

"Silver Beamer, Oregon plates, center lane, thirty seconds," said Josh out loud. Then he nodded at Edison, and the two of them jogged down the hill behind us to get the car ready. No discussion of who the target was or why he needed to die.

A girl had a gun. And that was that.

"Well," said Joe, "Let's see how much you've grown."

• • •

Three minutes later, Joe tosses his blanket-wrapped cannon in the trunk and he and Xtian climb in the car. Josh loops around the hill and back to 280, the long way around just to be sure, and we head south. There is no traffic for a long few minutes, and it makes me a bit nervous when we first hear sirens, but nothing comes of it. We get away cleanly.

"What now?" asks Josh.

I catch Xtian's eye in the side mirror. She looks numb. Whatever happened up there has affected her, somehow. Made her feel, when she did not want to. I used to get that way. Used to. No way out but through.

"South," I say. "Punch and pie." It is as good as anything, right now.

• • •

They had made breakfast reservations while we were on the hill in the middle of a job. It left me speechless, although I did wonder exactly what I had expected from a bunch of ruthless killers. Of which I was evidently one, now. Gooble-gobble. One of us. We accept her.

When we were seated, which was quickly, they got their pie. Joe got cherry. Josh got apple. Edison got something called olallieberry. Everyone got coffee; there was no punch. I wasn't hungry, and the reek of cooked eggs in the air turned my stomach over and over. It was a wonder Edison didn't drop dead. Evidently the pie was safe enough, or else he was feeling suicidal.

Joe and Josh took their time, but Edison's pie was gone in five bites. He lingered over the coffee, though, stirring.

"Reminds me of Waffle House," said Joe. "Haven't been since I got back from Saudi Arabia."

"What were you doing there?" asked Josh.

"Eating waffles?"

"You went to Saudi Arabia for waffles?"

"No," said Joe. "Texas. Saudi Arabia only has MeccaDonald's."

I squirmed. Josh and Joe were oblivious, but Edison noticed. He finished stirring and tapped coffee off his spoon. He narrowed his eyes at me. I looked away.

"Was that racist?" asked Joe. "I can't tell any more. Edward, enlighten us with some of your wisdom. Please. Expound upon the evils of religion, race, and fast food."

"Religion is a value meal," Edison said, taking up the challenge and pretending he hadn't just been mocked. "Judaism is your regular size; Catholicism is the value-sized version, all the basic stuff plus a side of guilt; and Islam is super-sized. Hinduism is tacos instead of burgers. Same ingredients, different delivery mechanism."

"Taco places serve beef though," said Josh, waving for the waitress.

"That ain't beef," said Joe, a sour look on his face. "Ain't no cow even breathed on it. And did you ever notice they have like a hundred items on the menu and they're all the same five ingredients? What's five factorial?"

"Hundred twenty," said Josh.

I hated them. Hated Joe for existing. Hated Josh for trying to be funny. Hated them all for not caring. Hated myself most of all. Not because I had failed again. But because I hadn't.

"MeccaDonald's is the place with the big golden cube, right?" asked Josh.

"The Kaaba," said Edison. He looked at me, but I looked right past him, glued to the screen over the bar, showing the fiery traffic pileup on 280. I felt the blood drain from my face.

"I always wondered what's inside that thing," said Josh.

"It's filled with candy," said Joe. Josh spit out his water. Edison shot them both a dirty look.

And right about then is when the helicopter camera panned over the school bus.

Eighty-five to zero. Blood and metal and flames. My skin rippled. I suddenly had to leave the booth, had to be empty. I shoved at Joe, somehow made it out, fell on my ass halfway to the ladies room but luckily made it into a stall before I threw up in my hair. They let me stay in there for a half hour, and then they sent a waitress named Cindie in for me.

She smelled like hash browns.

• • •

She sobs all the way back from Pescadero but is better by the time we get home, or at least quieter, the worst of it seemingly muffled by the fog that grows denser as we near and then enter the city limits. Or so I think; we are not two steps inside the apartment when she runs to the bathroom. I think about going in but I hear the shower start, and so I leave her alone and crash in bed to consider the damage. Aside from the primary, who was confirmed dead in the pileup, there are an additional twelve dead and twenty-seven injured.

Mostly children.

It was accidental, of course. Secondary. Collateral damage. Random. But it is, in the end, not just part of the job. It is the job. Kill one guy, nobody cares. Kill a million, too many to fathom. Knock down a couple tall buildings, kill a few dozen or a few thousand, right in the sweet spot . . . That is just real enough to matter. That changes things. And change is the goal. Terror begets change, action begets reaction.

What did this change? Not for us to know, or at least not for us to care. Perhaps the man was important. Perhaps he mattered. Or perhaps it would matter because he did not, because he was anyone, because anyone is anyone, and it could happen to anyone. Unknown. Only one thing is certain: for a certain group of kids, it was a field trip they will never forget, and for the ones who were in the back few rows of that bus, the ones who saw the car as careened out of control towards them . . . it was a day they would never remember.

The shower stops, and a flush of the toilet carries some more bad away. Then Xtian turns off the bathroom light. My brain is just cycling back to thinking about the primary target, and about why it took so long to plan this job out, when Xtian comes into my room unannounced and sits on the floor beside the bed. Feigning sleep, I allow her to take my left hand, which she clutches to her shoulder like a security blanket. After a while, she lets go and curls up in the pile of clothes beside the bed like a cat, shuddering in the cold until she falls asleep, no doubt dreaming awful.

She is still there in the morning.

Under Pressure

04/01/2014

It has only been a month since the job, but it has felt much longer this time. We were paid well enough that we could go anywhere, but there is no pressing need to burn everything to ash and run this time, so we have not. Perhaps this is why Xtian has not moved on, either. I have left her alone, though—some problems you need to figure out on your own, especially if you are the only one who sees a problem. She considers the bus incident a tragedy. I see it as a good start.

She is in her bedroom moping when one of the phones rings. Nick. I immediately sense that the "something wrong" I have felt since we got to San Francisco is about to get even more wrong, that the second shoe is about to drop. I usually go about eighteen months between jobs. Nick should not be calling this soon. Nor should anyone. This does not stop me from answering, however. I like working. And I do not have that many more years in me to wait around.

"I've got a dinner invite open," says Nick.

"I'm available," I reply. "But—"

"It's not for you," he says.

I walk into the bedroom. Xtian is sitting by the window, staring at anime on her iPad, dressed for bed in the middle of the day in my clothing, shirt and boxers. I throw the phone to her. More at, really. It hits her in the leg and lands on the carpet and for a moment she stares at it like a used tissue. I leave the room without bothering to see if she picks it up. Her problem, now.

Ten minutes later she comes out, dressed somewhat more appropriately in her own clothing. Torn denim shorts, dark long-sleeved shirt all stretched out past her fingertips, sneakers without socks again. Blonde-and-blue hair now done up in sloppy braids. A shade closer to normalcy.

"Can you drive me?" she asks.

"Where?"

"He didn't say."

"He did. What did he say?"

"Cruise. Pier." She furrows her brow, trying to remember. "Meadow . . . something."

"Lark."

"Meadowlark. Yeah."

"Do you know what that means yet?" I ask.

She shakes her head.

"I will tell you on the way," I say.

• • •

And he did. Sort of. Finally.

"You know what a one-time pad is?" he asked as soon as we were driving.

"Yeah but I use tampons," I said, goading him. He hated when I brought that stuff up. Even in the depths of depression I still liked to try and get a rise out of him.

He was quiet for a few seconds, then continued on as if he hadn't heard me.

"Passwords. You ever forget one? What did you do?"

"Used the recovery question."

"Right. What color is our neighbor's cat?"

"Orange."

"What if I asked you that two years ago? When we had a different neighbor."

"Uh . . . black?"

"Contextual cipher. Same question, different answers, both true. We can have the exact same conversation in thirty different cars, on thirty different trips, and it will have a completely distinct meaning if we refer to a shared context. So later, if I ever refer to Buffalo, that sets a new context, and then if we talk about cats, we might be discussing something black."

"What if there's more? Than two people. Like—"

"Like at the bar," he said. "Then we refer to something we *all* know. A common context."

He accelerated and veered right to escape a line of traffic, then dodged left into an open parking space, seemingly at random. The gull that had been occupying the spot gave him the evil eye and flew off, dropping half a cheeseburger on the windshield.

"It's bird names isn't it?" I said, remembering past conversations. "Meadowlark, Blackbird."

"Yes," he said. "But context changes. It can mean directions, or colors, or—"

"Numbers. Three three. March third." He nodded. "But what's the common context?"

"It's time," he said, tapping on the digital clock in the dashboard. "Time to go meet Nick. We'll finish this later."

• • •

Nick only keeps us waiting at the end of the wharf for a few minutes before he shows, dressed in—as far as I can tell—the exact same outfit as the last time we saw him. Alone, but only apparently. He knows better.

There are no formalities, no greetings; not even words to begin with. Nick just looks Xtian up and down, as if sizing her up. She looks to me, but I have no idea what this is about.

"How many people know about you?" he asks at last, nodding at Xtian as if it is not obvious who he means. "Joe, apparently. Abe, Josh. Who else?"

Xtian and I look at each other. She shrugs as I do some quick mental arithmetic.

"Eight, possibly," I answer. It is probably more than that, but eight sounds plausible. I am practically a nobody, and she is less than. Still, Nick frowns. Too many, I can tell.

"There's only a couple from before," says Xtian.

"From Buffalo?" he asks, and she nods. I wonder what he knows. About Buffalo, about DC, too. But he does not press, just tugs on his lower lip, considering whether or not this is going to be a problem. Perhaps overacting a bit for her benefit.

"Fine," he says at last, looking around to confirm that we are more-or-less alone here on the wharf. He ends his sweep with an extra-long look at me and clears his throat.

"She's just going to tell me whatever you tell her," I say, reluctant to leave. He is a pissy little upstart full of machinations, and I do not owe him any favors, nor any amount of trust.

"That's her problem, not mine," he says. "Leave us alone."

"Don't come crying to me if she tries to shoot you again," I say as I leave.

"I'll risk it," he says.

Risk her, he means.

• • •

Nick took me aside—no Edison, now—and spoke of tools, opportunities, and unknowns. And then he explained what he wanted from me now, and what would be involved, what I would have to do. And then I said yes. Simple as that. No codes or anything, thankfully. I wouldn't have known what to say if he'd asked me if I wanted to be paid in Purple Martins.

Edison was nowhere to be seen after Nick left, but frankly I was glad for a moment of solitude. I stood there on the wharf for a while, even as it started raining, just listening to the gulls scream and watching the waves churn, angry and uneasy. I tried following them out to the horizon, imagining where this was all going. All I could see were clouds, black and ugly and wet.

Why are you doing this? I asked myself. I've asked myself that a lot, since. And I suppose there were a lot of answers, all overlapping. Part of it was that I actually did want to be a part of what was going on. It was what I knew, it was my world, and now that I was actually involved I wasn't content to just take a backseat. Part of me also wanted to prove—to Edison, and myself—how capable I was. Partners were co-equal. I needed to step up and pull my weight.

Really, though, the main reason underneath it all was compensation. Not the monetary sort—the psychological kind. When I'd killed in Buffalo, there'd been a reason for it. But when I'd pulled the trigger on that hill, that was all me. There was no excusing that—I had made a choice. And I'd been punishing myself for it, wondering what sort of monster I'd become.

Doing this thing for Nick, it was *different*. It was a chance to move on. Not far, really. But maybe far enough. I'd only know when I got there. And if it wasn't enough, then I could move a bit farther. As far as I needed to go. I couldn't game myself out of this, or read myself out of it, or sulk myself out of it. Maybe this would do the trick. I had no better idea.

I guess I was also looking for another form of compensation, too. The kind that involved making amends. Whether I hoped to repay the people I'd killed, or myself, I wasn't sure, but either way, in a sense I was using myself as payment. My version of cutting, maybe. This was my life now, and I wasn't going to be up on a hill like a coward shooting at cars. I was going to be in harm's way. And whatever happened at that point was going to be what I deserved.

I stood there in the rain for a while, and then walked off to find Edison. He wasn't far.

• • •

We are surrounded by seafood, of course—this part of Santa Cruz is wall-to-wall oysters and crab—but I am not in the mood for anything that comes inside a shell, so we head down the boardwalk, past the souvenir shops, past the reek of fish and salt, until I catch a familiar odor.

"Pizza?" I ask. She shrugs. Good enough.

We push inside the building, a gigantic airplane hangar of a place with one entire wall given over to an enormous painted volcano, spewing neon dots of lava over and over, waiting for virgin sacrifices. There are plenty of them, too. The place is filled with shrieking children playing games, the rattle of air hockey, and the clatter of empty water glasses. I immediately have regrets, but the odds of a mass murder will diminish once I get some food in me.

Xtian peers at the menu, seemingly disinterested, or at least distracted by her thoughts.

"I feel we should get something with pig," she manages, just as our server wanders up.

"We have a great Hawai'ian pizza," says the waitress, emphasizing the apostrophe. I am not in the mood to argue so I nod and wave her off as if she is a leper, unclean.

"Tell me what he said," I say to Xtian, once we are alone. "Or don't. It's up to you."

She considers, but not for long, and tells me a tale of something that quite remarkably makes a lot of sense. She needs to get into a house, plant an electronic bug, then get out. No one needs to die. The house will be occupied, but there are dozens of ways to work around that, and the plan they seem to have settled on is perfect for her, almost too perfect. This is like Joe for long work, since he is best with a sniper rifle. Or me for noise and chaos, when bombs and chemicals are called for. This is not a job I would ever have been offered, not something I would ever have even known of, because I am not right for it. Not everything *they* do is about killing, just everything that I do.

Xtian is the right tool for this particular job. The only tool for this job. And that is what concerns me, in all of this. Not that Nick chose her for this, but that he thought it up because she came along. I delivered him a hammer and he found something to nail.

At least this explains why this job came together so quickly. At least, I hope it does.

"Are you over being depressed?" I ask, when the pizza arrives and she perks up. She has no immediate answer, just takes a slice, sniffs at it, and then starts picking the ham off.

"I thought you wanted . . . you know what, never mind."

"How do you deal with this stuff?" she asks, once her slice is ham-free.

"Pork? I eat it like a human being," I say. She throws a piece of it at me. And I eat it.

"You know what I mean," she says, nibbling her slice. And I do. She means the jobs. The work we do. I am sure I felt like she does now, once, but that does not matter. She needs to find her own way to cope. To not care. To learn that you cannot bury skeletons beneath other skeletons, no matter how small they are. You have to learn to leave them behind. Let them burn.

"Step one," I say. She looks up. "You feel you have a problem and you are powerless to do anything about it."

She chews on a piece of pineapple long enough to suck out the juice, then spits yellow thread onto her plate, shoves it around with her fork like a priest reading entrails.

"What's step two?" she asks.

"Believing a higher power can help you."

She furrows her brow. "Is this some sort of cult thing?"

"Addiction," I say. "Twelve steps." Then, considering, "Yeah, I guess it is."

"So I'm addicted to what? You?"

"You're addicted to second-guessing. To doubt. You did something last month, and you regret it. You did something else back in Buffalo, and you wonder if it was the right thing. There were plenty of times where you could have said no, but you said yes. Now you're questioning what might have been. Why you made those choices. If you can live up to them. Am I close?"

She shrugs.

"This world is like an ocean, Xtian. You can stay on the shore and dream about the horizon, but once you wade out into the surf, get out past the breakers, there is no coming back. Doubt is pointless. You swim or you drown. You got dumped in the middle of the ocean before knowing whether or not you could even float. But it doesn't matter. You learn to swim by swimming. Not by wondering if you can."

What I do not add is that if she stops swimming now, she drowns. But I think it goes without saying.

• • •

The ride back somehow seemed longer than it was on the way out. No music, no radio. Just the windshield wipers doing their thing, trying to encourage conversation, back and forth, back and forth. But none was forthcoming. Edison left me to my thoughts. My doubts and regrets.

He looked like a dad, I thought, watching him drive. Dad jeans and a dad shirt and dad shoes and a dad haircut and just a shade of goatee, black bleeding gray around the edges. The perfect dad, if not for the killing thing. What would I have to do for someone like him to ground me? Date girls? Rob a store? Shoot a cop? Shoot him? Was everything okay to him?

"What?" he asked, noticing my stare.

"What do you think about all this?" I asked. "What would you do?"

He thought about that for a few minutes before answering.

"I think it's strange this is so soon after the last job. Strange that the last job was planned so far ahead. Very strange that Joe showed up here. And a bit too convenient that you're so perfect for this job. Something's not right. Things aren't adding up. I would have turned it down."

"Oh," I said. After a moment, I added "So, should I call Nick back and say I won't do it?"

Edison chuckled.

"That's not how it works," he said. "You missed that chance. You're committed now."

"What if I did, though?"

"*They* need a tool for a job. You are the tool they chose. And when tools stop working, they get replaced. No one keeps a broken hammer. They dispose of it."

I looked away, watched the past fade in the mirror for a while.

"So what should I do then," I asked.

"Your job," he said. Simple as that.

Tag Along

05/04/2014

Of course, she has to do it alone, Nick says. It is stupid of me to even ask. Bad enough I know this much, that I am here, helping prepare. I will not be allowed within a mile of the actual place. A few blocks away from here, she will hop on a Muni bus and from that point she is completely on her own. I am still not comfortable with this, as there are too many questions and unknowns, but I think that this is more a problem with me than with anything else. When I am on a solo job, no one else knows where I am at any given time. It is foolish to think otherwise about this job.

Nick goes so far as to suggest we try to remove any distinguishing birth-marks but I quash that idea. We have no scalpel.

"Fine," he says. "Let's get her dressed."

This is met with some fuss, but ultimately she comes out of the motel bathroom wearing the outfit Nick has procured, handing me her old clothes, backpack, and iPad. Not her gun, though. She is keeping that, just in case. Nick does not need to know.

"Where did you get a Girl Scout uniform?" Xtian asks.

"Same place I got the cookies," he says.

She does a little spin, skirt flaring, newly-dyed brown ponytail fluttering in the air. Her saddle-shoed foot catches the ominous green box, and no doubt several of the cookies inside are now crumbled, but hopefully not whatever listening device is in there. For it to remain unnoticed, it will have to be something very thin and flat, adhered to the inside of the box itself. At first I imagined it might be one of the cookies, but that would be rather stupid since it would get eaten.

Nick picks up the box and stuffs it into her arms before she can kick it again. There are several other boxes in a satchel she will carry, but the green box is the one that matters.

"You knock, or ring the bell," he says. "Whichever. And when he comes to the door . . ."

"I try to sell him cookies and make up a reason to get inside."

Nick nods. "Then once you're inside you leave the box. Try to conceal it somewhere but if you can't, just leave it wherever. Then get out. Get to the bus stop and get on a 71, or anything going downtown. Ride for twenty minutes, then get off and call for a pickup."

"Get off anywhere?"

"Anywhere," says Nick, patience evaporating, hand on the door knob. "You decide."

"You mean improvise."

"Yes," says Nick. "Improvise."

And off they go, not so much as a goodbye.

All grown up.

• • •

Several hours pass, and I find myself under a bridge near 380 with Joe and Josh, inside Joe's Taurus, all of us dressed in matching Giants sweatshirts, different shades of denim jeans, sneakers, light coats just heavy enough to hide a gun apiece. Just some ordinary guys thinking about baseball who do not consent to a search, officer.

I do not know why we are here specifically, other than that it is far enough away from where Xtian is to make sure I was not going to follow her and ruin things. As if I needed to be watched, babysat. As if I would have been seen, even if I had a mind to counter orders.

That said, I am curious, so I find myself fiddling around with Xtian's iPad in the back seat as we wait. She is not very good with passwords and has failed to use Private mode on her browser too—very sloppy—so it is easy enough to check her Google history. She was checking out the Street View of a particular house in the Sunset District. Not nearly as deep a search as I like to, though, so I hit a few real estate sale sites, still convinced that something is not right about this arrangement. Even if it is already too late to do anything about it.

The car is heavy with the odor of breakfast sandwich egg. I feel as if I might be sick.

"Bullshit," says Joe from the passenger seat. Josh is driving, since he is a native and knows the area better. "Utter bullshit. Bush knew. Lots of people knew. 9/11 was allowed to happen, regardless of who it was that did it."

"The Saudis?" asks Josh.

"Or whoever," says Joe. "Who knows? *They* got Trapwire, *they* know. Something that big happens, someone has to *let* it happen. Like Pearl Harbor. They got an ulterior motive."

"Which they? Our they or their they?"

The others in my line of work bullshit like this all the time, but none of us have any idea who pulls our strings. I am the only one who does not care. At least, not about 9/11. I am finding it really interesting, however, that the house Xtian has been sent to was sold *very* recently.

"Waste of a plane," I say, pretending to contribute as I try to look up property records. "Planes. Could have been put to much better use."

"Oh, like you'd know what the fuck to do with a plane when you had it," says Joe. "Uh, okay, this is my plane now and, uh, I say . . . smoking's allowed. Extra peanuts for economy.'"

"They could have at least hit a target that mattered," says Josh. "What did they accomplish? Nothing. Got some new real estate and a nice insurance payout."

"Started a pretty good war," says Joe, tapping the back of his head. He smiles. "Court of public opinion."

"Wait," says Josh. "Which war are we talking about?"

"Exactly," says Joe. "Exactly."

No one speaks for a bit. They listen to the radio, Morning Edition talking about Sudanese unrest. I browse the Internet, running semi-random searches for things that might connect these dots I am seeing. News articles. Traffic accidents. Then Joe's phone buzzes. Text message.

"One of my kids . . ." says Joe, perhaps a bit too quickly, fiddling with his phone for a second. Something lights up in the back of my head but I am not sure what it is yet. Before I can even think to ask, Joe pulls out his wallet and starts to flip through photographs, showing Josh, nominally by way of killing time. No way of knowing if they are his real kids or came with the wallet. You can buy some attractive families at Target.

"Joe junior is eleven," says Joe. "And Casey is fourteen now."

"Is she still in Scouts?"

"Yeah," says Joe. Slight hesitation.

"I missed my window for the cookies, didn't I?" asks Josh.

And then my 27 is at the back of Joe's head, barrel right next to where he keeps the bullet he got in Afghanistan. Josh's eyes go wide, but Joe is remarkably calm. And no doubt starting to realize it was a bad idea to keep me in the back seat.

"Thought you said you didn't usually carry, Edward," he says.

"I did say that," I say.

I swear I can feel the bullet shift beside his spine as I press the barrel in. I know I am right. I am just not sure yet exactly what I am right about. You get to be my age you have to trust your gut instincts more and more. Neurons take their sweet time. Driving like old people.

"Something on your mind?" asks Joe, calmly. He tries to catch my eye in the mirror but misses the angle, only sees himself.

"Yeah. I'm wondering why you and Nick just sent Xt— Nichole . . . to a house that used to be owned by the guy she shot back in March."

"What?" asks Josh.

"Wasn't hard to pick his name out of the news article," I say. "He was the only one older than twelve that died."

"And . . . it's . . . his house?" As confused as he is right now, Josh wisely keeps his hands on the steering wheel. He is not supposed to know anything, but then technically neither am I. And we are already past "fuck it."

"Yeah. But he sold it two weeks *after* he died. Or maybe . . . Doesn't matter." My head is throbbing. This sounds insane. And that's why I know something is wrong. "That's where . . . she is now, selling cookies door-to-door. The only girl in the country doing that today."

Josh turns his head towards Joe and raises an eyebrow. Joe just stares straight ahead.

"Your daughter know you borrowed one of her uniforms?" I ask Joe.

"I don't understand," says Josh.

Neither do I, yet. But I'm going to, before this day is through. One way or another.

"Out, now," I say, prodding Joe with the barrel of the gun. I want to just do it right there, but we will need the car and I do not want to drive with the stink. I keep the handgun framed by his back the entire time, hidden from any traffic that might pass by, unlikely as that seems. He kneels without my asking, does not struggle as I take his gun and throw it in the back of the car. I also collect his phone, look back through recent messages, but he has already deleted the logs. I hurl it at the ground. It bounces, rather than shatters. That used to be so much more impressive.

"Ed—" Josh tries, but I wave him off, moving to get a better angle, where I can keep both of them in sight at once, just in case. This brings me around in front of Joe. He shakes his head.

"You should be thanking me," Joe says. I want to laugh and cry.

"Should I?"

"Nick wanted to use *you*," he says. "I was the one who suggested her instead. Someone unknown, from outside the area. Expendable."

"For what?"

"I have no idea," he says. "Honestly, I don't. Something big. Sowing chaos. Infiltrating other groups. Cell leaders, fixers maybe. I think he's just getting started."

Joe telling me all this is not surprising. It's nothing to do with disloyalty and everything to do with apathy. He knows he's going to die, so he may as well rid himself of the baggage. This is why we work in isolated cells; it minimizes what you know, what you can damage on the way out. Even the most talkative bird can only ever crack one shell. Which reminds me . . .

"Why are *you* here, anyway?" I ask.

"I was called, I came," says Joe. "It's called having friends, not that you'd know anything about that. We met in Iraq, when I got recruited."

"Bullshit. Nick's never served a day in his life."

"I never said he was military."

I press my hand against my temple to try and rub away my growing headache. This is getting me nowhere. But maybe that's where I have always been headed.

"You never thought to ask why Nick was doing this?" I ask.

"Fuck no," replies Joe. "I got paid. You'll get paid, unless you fuck yourself here. It's just business, Ed. Don't treat it as something personal."

"How the *fuck* is this not personal?"

He stares me in the eye. I really hope Josh isn't sneaking up behind me right now because I'll be damned if I break eye contact first.

"It *is* personal for you," he says. "The point is it *shouldn't* be. And you know that. You fucked this up for yourself. I don't play bring-your-daughter-to-work-day like you do."

"No, you brought someone else's d—" Someone else's what?

Someone else's someone.

"I did you a favor," he continues. "Both of you. I got Nick someone for his job, and I got rid of a problem you wouldn't admit you had. Two birds, one stone."

"You missed a bird," I reply coldly.

"Know the difference between us?" he asks. "I have something you don't. Ambition."

"Yeah? Well, I have something you don't."

"What's that?"

"A gun."

After I give the bullet in Joe's head a partner, I consider doing Josh, too but I need him to drive, and I need him to help me put the body in the trunk, and frankly I need the company. My hands are shaking, and I'm not sure it is adrenaline.

• • •

The Sunset District is not far on paper, but everywhere takes an hour in this city. By the time we arrive, I am bouncing off the car door, but Josh takes his time and parks around the corner from the place. I am not thinking clearly and would not have done this myself.

Once we're at the address though, and Josh's sanity is no longer holding me back, I lunge through the unlocked front door, not caring who might see us. No time to think. Thinking would make me question what I was doing. This is all about momentum right now. If you are moving, you know where you are going, and if you know where you are going then you are at least making progress. Of a sort.

Inside, it is clear right away that whatever is going to happen has already happened. There are two bodies. One more than I expected. And I am far too late, I think, because I did not stop this. I do not want to think about it, but it plays out in my head. Inexorable.

• • •

There are children around when she gets to the door, about her age, and this makes her nervous. They are watching her from across the street. Staring. It is cool and cloudy out, but she is sweating. This uniform itches. Something is not right. But she has no idea about cookie-selling season. She does not know that she needs to run.

Instead, she knocks and waits. A few seconds later, a man answers the door. His beard reminds her of Josh, for some reason. His feet are bare.

"Yeah?" he asks.

"Hi," she says. "I'm selling cookies—"

"Sure," he says. "Come on in."

She hesitates. It was not supposed to be this easy, especially since normally a girl like her wouldn't go inside, wouldn't be alone. But he is already turning, leaving her to come in of her own accord, or not. Run, she thinks. But she has a job to do. She does not want to screw it up.

"No shoes in the house, please," he says, tapping a pair of boots with his toe. There are multiple pairs of shoes there. It seems ordinary enough so she heads inside, kicking her own shoes off next to the pile.

"Head on into the kitchen," says the man, gesturing with his thumb. "I'll get my wallet."

"Can I use your bathroom?" she asks. One of the excuses she had planned to use, even though it is no longer needed. She bounces a bit to really sell it.

"End of the hall," he says.

"Thanks," she says, skidding in stocking feet as she rushes to the last door and shuts it behind her. And realizes as she does that it was not a lie; she really does have to go. While she's in the bathroom, she looks for somewhere to stash the box, maybe on top of the mirror or under the sink, but realizes how obvious a green box would be in there. It will have to be in the kitchen.

Still, something is wrong, so she sneaks out of the bathroom without flushing, trying not to make noise. She can hear the man muttering somewhere. She creeps closer, and she is nearly to the doorway when she hears something he says, on the phone with Nick maybe, or to someone else in the room. Something about a girl selling cookies. About keeping her there. Or maybe she hears the bird clock over the fireplace chirp the hour. And she realizes exactly what kind of place she is in. What kind of people these are.

Whatever it is, it is *there* that she sets the box of cookies on the floor—the box still lying there now—and *there* that I imagine she pulls the 29 out of her waistband, thumbing the safety off. Glad she listened to me about the gun, maybe hoping she can get out without having to use it. But as she steps past the living room she peers inside and sees that the man is not alone. She hesitates, but her delay is countered somewhat by the fact that they are not expecting to see a mint-flavored girl holding a gun, and so they hesitate as well. She fires. Wildly, perhaps, but accurately enough. She gets the first one in the chest, a certain kill, and the second one in the neck, so he dies slower. And then . . .

• • •

And then, I have no idea. Perhaps it went nothing like that. Certainly they knew right away it was no longer cookie-selling season. Probably Nick told them to watch for her. I do not know. This is a game of seconds, and I am late. Mistakes. Too many mistakes. All I know for sure is there are two dead bodies here, and neither of them is hers, and she is gone. And I might think she got away clean, might, except her shoes are still here, right where she kicked them off beside the door, maybe twenty feet from the useless green box of cookies.

I call Nick's number. The only one I know. No answer. No surprise.

Of course there is no identification on the bodies, no evidence in the house, nothing to indicate anything. In the whole of the place there is no single clue to their identity. Save, of course, the bird clock over the fireplace. A bullet has smashed it, broken it forever, frozen it on 9:01 AM forever. Just after the Red-Winged Blackbird sang its hourly song. It is ridiculous, a movie thing, some Hollywood nonsense contrivance. And yet there it is, undeniable.

"Now we know when it happened," says Josh, needlessly.

And we know who was involved. The clock could be a coincidence, but I refuse to believe that. It cannot be, not with everything else. This house belonged to a cell, and Nick had Xtian go there under false pretenses. The clock is not random; it is a shared context to hide conversations, everywhere we might need to discuss business.

We?

No. *Them.* It always was *them*, and always will be. Especially after this.

Two minutes later we are on the road. Ten more and we hit 280, and then time becomes meaningless and we fly past SFO and are halfway to SJC and Josh asks me where we go now, and I tell him to just drive, as I try again and again to call Nick. Pointlessly. Whoever, wherever, they are hours ahead of us. Eventually light goes dark, and we find ourselves no closer to nowhere. And nowhere is safe, now. Besides, we need to get rid of erstwhile Joe, in the trunk with his collection of artillery. Getting pulled over right now would be ludicrously entertaining.

"Where should I go? Ed?"

I have no answer. I know nothing. I am useless. Impotent.

"Edward?"

"Why are you here?" I snap. I have to attack something. Have to hurt something else. "I never did anything for you. I barely know you. Why are you still here?"

He is quiet for a moment, fingers tapping idly on the steering wheel in time to the dotted white lines flying past.

"I believe in right and wrong," he says at last. It sounds memorized, like a story he has been reading himself for a while now. "And I believe at the end of the day what we do is right. I know you don't give a shit, but I do, and I believe that the ends justify our means. But this shit? I don't know what's going on here, but I know what fucked up looks like, and this is fucked up. And it's wrong. So that's why. Because I won't be part of anything wrong."

And there is a pause, and then, partly for my benefit, but mostly for his own, he adds:

"Not again."

I turn away, watch the mile markers fly past, connecting the dots, past to future. And it is not true that I know nothing. I know Nick is involved, and he is meddling with things he should not. Even with what little I know this is bigger than I imagined. For all I know it involves the entire organization, top to bottom. Pieces are shifting on the board, and pawns are going to fall before this is through. And I can come to only one inevitable conclusion: Xtian is dead.

And where does that leave me? Nowhere. And with what? Nothing, and less.

Nothing but a body in the trunk, and a broken clock on the back seat, and—in my lap—an empty pair of shoes that smell of a girl I once knew.

Once upon a time.

Ever After

05/07/2014

These men, Xtian," I told her more than once. "You have no idea what they are capable of."

The last time, she looked at me and smiled. "I think I do," she said. And I guess she did, eventually. Three days ago. If she had not quite figured it out before then, she knew before the end exactly how terrible people can be. People like me.

I am not the best at what I do, but neither am I the worst of what we are. Those I work with stand for nothing and will stand for almost anything—no morals, no compunctions, no ideologies in the way. Murderers, arsonists, tax evaders, rapists, serial killers, child molesters, car bombers, suicidal antisocial bastards. We will do anything we are paid to do, whether that involves killing or arson or mere terror, whether we target one man or twenty, or twenty thousand. Whatever it takes, and for whatever reason, as long as the money is good, and sometimes even when it is not. This is why *they* use us. We can do anything that needs doing, and we will. And when they are done with us, we are easily disposable. Lunatics and lone wolves. Conspiracy theorists and psychopaths.

According to some calculations, one percent of everyone is what might be considered a psychopath. Seventy million people, worldwide. Lawyers, politicians, serial killers. These are the people I introduced her to. Let her work with. Yes, let. I was complicit. I let her. I could have refused, could have taken her away, could have . . . what? Left it all behind? For what?

For a girl?

I could not have done that, walked away to be something I am not. But there are things I could have done. Warned her sooner. Refused to let her go alone. Paid more attention to what was going on. There were signs I missed, or ignored. Signs I am seeing now, as I sit here and run it all through my head again, trying to decide what to do with myself now. Where I might go. Who I might go with. These were easy questions when Xtian was around. I got used to having someone around. Now there is no one, and I need to get used to being alone again.

I hope she is dead. It feels odd to write that, but I do. I think it is proba-bly better if she is. Because if she is not dead, I can imagine what is going to happen to her. All too vividly. Things that have happened to me, in the past. And worse. Which is why when we arrived in California, the first thing I did was show her how to kill herself.

Priorities.

• • •

I remember it like it was two days ago. She was wearing a white shirt bought at the thrift store, well-stretched out at the sleeves and waist, hanging loose over dark blue jeans and all the way down to her thumb pads, tips of her fingers visible, unbroken, unpolished nails, which she tapped on the desk specifically to annoy me.

"Why do I need to know how to kill myself?" she asked.

"In case something bad happens," I said. "In case I get caught. Or you get caught."

"They won't catch us though," she said. "They only get the bad guys."

"What are we then?"

"*Worse* guys."

We ran down the list together. Guns, of course, came up. Quick and painless if done right, neither if you flinch. Hanging, short and long nooses, benefits of each. Carbon monoxide or pure nitrogen, if you can get it, but it is fairly complicated. Slit wrists are simpler—"down the river, not across the stream" and warm water. Messy and slow, but certain if you do it right.

"I saw this girl at the mall who cut herself on her thighs," she said.

"That is not suicide," I replied. "That is just California."

And I remember it like it was two hours ago. Her bell-bottom jeans had torn embroidery around the hems and underneath them she was barefoot inside sensible brown shoes with heavy black buckles, and she kicked me and smiled.

What she liked best were the poisons, of course, perhaps because it was so like cooking, creation and destruction all at once, a little Hindu goddess. Aspirin, iron supplements—plenty of things to overdose on if you want to suffer on the way out. If not, insulin, or codeine, or hydrocodone, but you need a lot. All of these benefitting from a vodka chaser.

"But you are not old enough to drink," I said.

And I remember it like it was two minutes ago. She raised her hand and her sleeve slid back and she showed me her middle finger, delicate and perfect, her first knuckle bearing some silly piece of costume jewelry from a gumball machine, yellow plastic the color of her hair, the color of chlorine. How she always smelled to me.

Household chemicals. Bleach and vinegar for chlorine gas, bleach and ammonia for hydrazine. Painful. Malathion, warfarin, painful and bloody. Antifreeze and OJ. Or one of nature's own concoctions: digitalis, white oleander, hemlock, belladonna, nightshade, mushrooms, ricin. So many ways the world is trying to kill off humanity. Possibly it knows something.

"But how would *you* do it?" she asked.

Her tablet buzzed, and she turned to fetch it, leaning over the chair, and the three inches that separated her top from her bottom turned into five, and at the small of her back was a soft down, like a baby bird. She had been seeming older every day, but suddenly she was just a little girl again.

"Gun to the head," I said. I always have one around even if I opt not to carry it everywhere. "If not that, then cyanide. Pricey, but certain and quick if you're in kind of a hurry. I keep some of that around too."

"And if you weren't in a rush?" she asked.

"Distilled nicotine," I said. "Takes a while to make, but four or five drops means a permanent coma in about thirty seconds. Lovely stuff. By the way, never smoke. It is very bad for you."

"Everything is bad for me," she pouted. "Even you."

"Especially me," I said.

• • •

I realize my right hand is trembling, but this is not a surprise as it has been clenched around a gun as I have stared at this screen, pecking out words with one finger, remembering, trying not to remember, thinking about going back to read what I have written of her, to help bring part of her back, here and now. But no. That would be a betrayal, and I will not betray history, not for this.

Strange, that thinking about her dead makes me think about all those ways to do herself in, if such an occasion as this should arise. Stranger still, that thinking on this should result in me holding a gun to my head. Not the first time, of course. During my lengthy absence from work, there were several nights I did much the same. But those times, it was purely selfish. A theoretical escape from a pointless existence. This is different.

I am just not sure why.

I'm not sorry. I know that. And I have not cried. I can, when it is convenient. I am physically capable. I can pretend to care but I cannot really care. At least not usually. Knowing that makes me *want* to cry sometimes, but that is nothing but a vicious cycle of rinse and repeat. An Ouroboros of self-loathing and depression that takes me back to a place I never thought I would be again, a place I have not been in almost six years. Not since I found a little egg in a store and took her back to my nest to . . . to what? Hatch? Or scramble?

And there it is again. I feel something deep inside, hatching, unfolding black wings. Small, but present. Something has changed. I am not sure what it is, but it hurts. Is it guilt? Responsibility? Regret? Is that the same as sorry?

And the phone rings, is ringing, has been ringing, I realize, for long minutes now, four rings and then silence and then four more, over and over. I listen to it for a while, a song in four/four time, a lullaby, and for a moment I cannot decide: gun, or phone?

There is ample time for both, I think.

Left first.

"Ed? It's Josh. I found them."

A cascade of thoughts run through my head like a slot machine. They line up cherries.

"Ed?"

"Tell me," I say.

And he does. Josh tells me where, and who, and how. He leaves *when* up to me.

I tell him I will call him back. Then I hang up.

My hand is no longer trembling as I put my handgun down, and push back my chair, and stand, and begin to gather things. Things for killing. Because *when* is soon. Only because it cannot be right now.

I cannot bring you back, Xtian. But I can send some people with you. They are not the best company, but they will have to do. Compensation.

I get dressed in near-blacks and grab my coat and stuff my pockets full of everything I need. Laptop and weapons in a messenger bag, more weapons in my coat, and what remains of my cash wherever I can fit it. The rest will burn. I will not be coming back. And it feels good to be moving, good to be doing. This is right. This is proper. It is time to move, time to move on.

Time to stretch my wings.

Apoptosis

05/08/2014

It is raining, which helps, along with the ocean crashing. Noise and cover: the freedom to make small, inevitable mistakes without them becoming fatal. Not that I expect to survive this. I would not mind surviving, but as the song goes, we get what we need, not what we want.

This is fine. I need this.

"You ready?" asks Josh.

I look down the hill across the old naval base, long abandoned and turned into an imitation of a residential community, probably owned by some Spooky PAC no one will ever know the name of. Most of the homes are empty, but a few are occupied by government workers and at least one— our target—by employees of another organization entirely. Everything is painted a uniform institutional pink, the sort of color they used to use in schools and prisons to calm the inmates. Even the barbed wire around the place has been painted blunt under the same pink paint, someone's idea of a joke.

I am not laughing.

"Ready?" he asks again. "Ed—"

"Yes," I say. "Let's just do this."

"Let's just."

Their defenses are nonexistent or apparently so. Despite the fence and security systems, the front gate stands wide open, daring anyone, everyone, to just wander on in, and although there are cameras, they are not connected to anything, mere props. Security theater. At least out here. Nearer the house, they have more cameras. Thermal. Likely some fancy sonics. But it is a fairly large house with fairly large blind spots, especially by the kitchen and garage. The trees and bushes—while giving them cover from the highway—also make an approach fairly simple, if you know where you are going. And especially if you do not have to worry about getting out.

I scan the house one more time. There are probably four of them inside. Perhaps five, but I have only seen four, and they only have the one car. Not enough to keep watch indefinitely. Even they need sleep. But not me. It has taken twelve hours to prepare, two more to get here, and in that time Josh has slept. I have not, not since. I am more awake than I have ever been. More alive. I am fully and completely here, in this moment. In this now.

It feels like enlightenment.

It feels like right.

I look at Josh, hold out my hand. He gives me the keys to the Mercury, then hefts Joe's old M107 and spits a gob of chewing gum off into the rain. Then he holds out his other hand, waits. I take it, glove in glove.

"We're going to die, you know," he says.

"I know," I say. "But not first."

He nods, pumps my hand twice, then melts into shadow. I hear him sigh, faintly, through the rain, and then he turns and is gone. He is, of course, right. This is death. Death for us all. Not just for us, but for this entire cell, and perhaps others adjacent. This is not supposed to happen. Operational security demands that cells never learn of each other. Compartmentalization, they call it. Everything goes through channels. But Nick has changed that with this power play of his. He has disrupted the state of things, and everyone will pay for it. Starting with him.

Of course, the thing is, this scheme of his probably works under most scenarios, precisely because of who he used. Bring her in, let her hands get dirty and take out your opposition, then take her out, and step into the vacuum. His only mistake was using her. Because she was not his to use. She was mine.

I run a hand up and over my face, pushing rain-soaked hair back across my head. The other hand is through the open window, reaching in past the driver; he does not complain, on account of being dead. He learned the hard way why you never pick up hitchhikers after midnight. I slide the key into the ignition, and my hand lingers there for a moment. Rain wets the door, the steering wheel.

• • •

"Can I drive?" she asked me, not long after we got to San Francisco. Passenger window open, her feet dangling outside, front seat misted by rain drifting in. She did not seem to notice. We were cruising around on 280, not too far from where she would eventually commit infanticide. But that was just a future imperfect at the time.

"Can you?" I asked.

"May I?"

I pulled over at the next rest stop and got out. She slid across the seat, ankle catching on the gear shift momentarily, one of her laces coming untied in the process. She let it dangle as I clambered in the opposite side and shut the door. The imperfection annoyed me; not that it existed, but that I could not fix it.

She started the engine, and then sat there, hands on the steering wheel. Seconds passed.

"Is there a problem?" I asked.

She looked at me and smiled.

"I don't know where we're going," she said.

• • •

Down, I think. We're going down. Together.

I turn the key. There is a spark, and flame and noise, and smoke in the rain. Then I shift the car into drive and let gravity take over. Headlights bounce and bob, and the front door of the house opens and one of them steps out, raising a hand and a gun. But the car does not stop, will not stop. The man shouts, and as he takes aim at the windshield there is a noise and what is left of him falls to the ground. If nothing else goes right then at least Josh has given us first blood. The car drives onward and hits the front of the house at about four miles an hour, a few feet from the door, not nearly hard or fast enough to cause any structural damage, not even enough to break the front window. But that was never the point.

Two more of them come out the front door and they fill the car with fury: the windows smash and the nameless driver collapses against the steering wheel, drawing more of their fire. Josh and I had disagreed on this part, briefly. He wanted to tie the guy's shoelaces to the accelerator, let the car build up speed and send it through the wall and into their kitchen. I talked him out of it. The object was not to destroy the car or the building. It was to destroy the people inside. Infrastructure is hard. People are soft. Either you get inside, or you get them outside. Why try to crack the shell when they will do it for you?

The two guards keep low profiles, duck and cover, communicate well. One checks on his friend. Former friend. The other stays low as he moves cautiously around to the driver's side of the car, opens the door, and closes the circuit.

The explosion sends him into a nearby tree, the concussion taking out the rest of the glass in the car and some of the house.

This part, Josh and I had agreed on.

Now the clock is ticking. And calls are being made, and the nearest police are just minutes away. I step from the shadows, pocket my earplugs and let the sound of the rain fill my head once again. I open my trench and pull out my MP5K, then move towards the back of the house, because that's where they'll be coming out now, if at all. Josh will have to be trusted to clean up the front. I only hope he stays somewhat on target, because what he's using can shoot right through the entire house.

I'm not one for guns, as I've said before, but they have their place. Given more time, more warning, more materials, I'd have gladly gone with another plan, something safer, something where I'd be far, far away when it all went off and scattered ashes in my wake. Something with more bombs, more chemicals, and less risk. I've seen over half a century this year, and my body is well aware of this. But we do what we can with what we have, and right now I've little in me but hate, and blood.

Guns will have to suffice.

I can hear Josh firing as I near the back door—not just to kill the two out there but to drive the rest out the back. And sure enough, one pops out, and I give him two steps and then open up, fully automatic. I swear I can hear each individual bullet—*crack crack crack*—watch each one spin across the way like a little black bird finding its home. It seems like slow motion, like a dissection, as the shred of bullets disrupts his vascular system, the hydrostatic shock stretching and compressing vital organs, his nerves trying desperately to communicate with his brain fast enough to respond. For several seconds he operates on remote control, finger twitching and spraying a few rounds roughly in my direction, but there's more *not me* than *me* to hit, and he hits only not.

And that's four.

I give it a full minute, as long as I can, before deciding that if there's a fifth, he's not coming out. Which means I have to go in. And I throw away the MP5K and pull the 870 from under my coat as I step over the body of the one I brought down. Parts of him—of all of them—will live for up to a day. The corneas, for instance. And I think that perhaps, somehow, they might have to watch each other slowly die for the rest of the night, and this seems just.

I step towards the back door and slip in the mud, stumble sideways. And this saves me, because there is a sudden flare and a crunch. I know I'm not dead because I can feel the pressure tear my ears open and there is no more sound, and I am bleeding from a dozen tiny cuts and my ears and my nose, tiny bits of shrapnel with me forever now, for however long that is. But it does not hurt, because I don't have time for that. I step forward and the fifth is there, and his handgun is yelling at me but I cannot hear a thing. My vest takes two rounds and my arm takes one and then it hurts, but not enough to matter. I raise my shotgun and squeeze something and his insides go out as he falls back into the bedroom. I fire again.

And again.

And again.

And it's only when I am reloading that I notice this fifth man was Nick, and this is what I came here for, this act of vengeance. I feel cheated somehow, having not realized it before. Cheated that it came and went without my knowing it. So I fire one last time, for Xtian.

There.

I lower the shotgun and scan the room. The world spins and pain crashes down, and the details hammer themselves home, bright graffiti on white walls. The room is saturated in red, from the haze before my eyes, from my trench stained and growing darker as I bleed. Nick is dead, they are all dead, and there is a girl on the bed, and there is a girl on the bed, and there is a girl on the bed, and she is broken, so broken, pink and red and unmoving. And she is Xtian.

I drop the shotgun.

She is tied, hands behind her back, face mashed into a pillow, and her back is black and blue from neck to thighs. There is red, some of it her own, and there is more, but I cannot look, just knock over the electrodes and knives and pliers, knock it all aside and grab a blanket and wrap her limp body inside because I do not want to see what is left. I try to lift her but my arm is not working right, so instead I just drag her by a cold broken ankle through the living room and towards the garage, because I will not leave her here. Because she is mine.

Although I cannot hear it, I can see through the haze and the tears that the goddamned television has stayed on this entire time. Nothing has survived in here but this and me, and I am having doubts about the latter. I want to laugh and cry and scream. Instead, I find the remote and after a moment of blue uncertainty, Nickelodeon comes on, and I imagine Xtian watching it in my living room, laughing, happy to be alive.

And I can think of no better thing. And no worse thing.

There is movement to my left, and I drop Xtian to the floor and pull out a random handgun and turn and aim, peripheral vision driving it all. Josh enters through the front door. He drops his rifle and pulls his balaclava off his head.

Whoa, whoa, it's me, he mouths, and I cannot hear the words through the ringing in my dead ears but I can read his lips, his expression. I give him a moment, just long enough so he knows this was not reflexive, that this was not accidental. That this was, in fact, necessary.

And then I pull the trigger, and tie off a loose end.

In the garage, I find keys in the ignition of a black Saturn, and after the briefest of moments on the cold ground, Xtian's body goes in the trunk, because I cannot bear to look at that in the rear view mirror. I rest her head atop my messenger bag and drape my bloody coat over her face, then lie the shotgun alongside her, closing the trunk just as the garage door slides open, and I feel like something rising from a tomb, biblical. Death behind, and who knows what before me. Whatever Nick was trying to start, I just ended it, along with whatever plans might have been brewing here in this dead cell. Dead by my hands, murder-suicide of a sort because there is going to be a large price to pay. At least one semi-involved party has survived all this—Abe—along with I don't know how many others who were not here tonight. I don't know who was involved with what, but that won't matter. Word will get out, and when it does, I will be to blame for all of it.

I am going to be cut off, probably completely, and perhaps forever. There will be no more jobs but those I find for myself. No more money but what I already have. No more secret nests but the ones I make myself. No one to trust, now, except myself. But somehow rather than depress me, all of this just renews my desire to live. To spite them.

It is time to fly, and I am flying far and fast. Farther and faster than ever before. Goodbye, goodbye California.

Although time is short, I pause for just a moment as I slide into the driver's seat, aches both old and new making their presence known. I turn back like Orpheus, considering the cans of gasoline in the garage, the fertilizer in the other room. Normally I would burn it, burn it all and leave nothing but ash, but instead I decide to simply leave it. Some things cannot be scrubbed away, only covered up, and that is not my job.

Not any more.

SEA

Clean Slate

08/15/16

It is sometimes hard to imagine that it has been over two years now since everything fell apart. I have of course done plenty to stitch myself up even with so many missing pieces—I am nothing if not a survivor—but lately I am realizing that some holes can never be filled, some wounds never healed. I want this *thing* to scab over, to scar and fade and be done with, but instead it festers and hurts. Infected. This will last, this new thing, and I had better get used to it.

I am still in Seattle, still in the Ballard neighborhood, still living in the only hovel of mine that *they* did not know about. Seattle is as commercial and urban as things come—there are at least four coffee shops, including two Starbucks, within a block of where I sit—yet somehow there is a sense of escape here. The friendly reek of fish and oil off the pier, the cry of seagulls from above, looking out for me. Safe. Still a city, still horrifying me with the sheer number of other beings around, breathing, moving, sweating. But it feels different, tastes different. Here I can occasionally see nothing but trees, can wander down to the beach and look out across the Sound and imagine I am alone.

I could have been alone in Portland too, and that would have been the easier option. It was in the way of Seattle, after all. And there were several hours that first night when I thought of staying there, of sinking some roots, trying to get back in, to see how far the damage had gone. I had places I could stay, there. Theoretical jobs. But *they* knew Portland. It was too risky. And seeing Xtian ruined . . . changed my mind.

To think that I brought her in, and in the end, she brought me out.

The end—could that be true? Is it over? Or just me?

The smell here reminds me of my youth. We had a boat, for a while, and the month before my mother died, we went fishing on the lake. On the way back in, we saw a wallet in the water, and my father fished it out with a net and found a few hundred dollars inside. A lot of money, back then; my father had been out of work, like I am now. He said we should just keep the cash, but my mother insisted the proper thing to do was to return in the wallet, so we got in the truck and drove for two hours to the address on the license. My father knocked on the door, and went inside, and two minutes later he came back to the truck and threw four dollars on the front seat; this was the reward for returning a wallet full of cash.

I suppose the moral of the story could be that kindness is its own reward, but what I take away from that whole thing is that sometimes doing the right thing is the wrong thing to do.

And I wonder a lot lately, if I have made the same mistake.

• • •

I walk down to the Fremont neighborhood and select another café to lurk at. Not in a hurry, and I do not think I can tolerate the bus. Or afford it. This is what I do these days—walk from coffee shop to coffee shop, sometimes buying something, sometimes not. Writing. Wasting time. Looking for opportunities. Like the one that jumps upon me here almost immediately.

I hear her before I see her, or perhaps I feel her first, a subtle shift in air pressure as she sits at the table beside mine with a rustle of shopping bags and a grunt. I sneak a glance at her reflection in the window: mid-forties, leopard-print coat, more makeup than a clown college. I want to turn away but I cannot help but stare as she fastidiously wipes off her fork, knife, and spoon with a napkin, then inspects her glass for smudges and viral contagion. Then she pulls out her purse and pops open a little bottle of hand sanitizer and rids her hands of all but zero-point-one percent of what is bad with the world.

I would remember none of this if not for the fact that she then—thoroughly disinfected—proceeds to pull out two filthy things: a phone, and a cigarette, both of which she sticks in her face as she walks to the corner, beyond the magic railings and No Smoking Within 25 Feet signs. The irony of it all sticks with me, how selective she is about her pollutants—so much so that I almost do not notice she has left her shopping bags behind at the table. My initial reaction is instinctive—concern, since I have personal experience with abandoning packages in public areas. But she does not seem the type to bomb a coffee shop in the middle of the day, so I push concern aside and move on to my second reaction, which is to tuck my laptop under my arm, grab her bags, and walk away as fast as my legs will take me.

This is what I have been reduced to: shoplifting, petty thievery. What have I become?

• • •

Before I even think to sift through the bags, I head all the way up to Greenwood, an hour walk, straight to the diner I frequent several times a week. Sometimes more. This is further than I need to go, but it is familiar terrain, and I am hungry, and I know I can order just about anything here without accidentally ingesting something full of egg. They even know to do the coleslaw without mayo, which is practically a miracle.

I get the usual—burger and fries—and down it all before I dive into the woman's bags like a vulture tucking into a pile of entrails. And of course, just as I do my peripheral vision is suddenly full of waitress. I look up, caught, but she just smiles as she places the check on the table. Waitresses do not care: it is not their job to care, just to provide service with the illusion of concern, just like their name tags provide an illusion of identity. Hers says "Edith."

She looks around to see if anyone else is watching, but the place is empty—no other customers, and the manager is out back smoking up with the cook. This is that sort of place. She blows a strand of hair out of her face and sits down across from me, taking a sip of my water.

"Get anything good?" she asks. For all anyone knows, they are my bags, and I bought whatever is inside. But she knows better. She knows I stole this. And she does not care.

"Cigarettes and vodka," I say to her after taking inventory of the bags. No receipts, sadly, so I won't be returning anything for cash. "Some underwear, some ungodly heels, and a bible."

"Will it fit me?" she asks.

"The bible? No. Religion is for sad little people who cannot accept that they are not special or immortal. It gives them an imaginary afterlife to look forward to. You and I know better. Don't we, *Edith*?"

She gives a thin, half-hearted smile, almost a grimace. But before she can reply she spots her manager coming out of the back room and slides out of the booth, dusting off her black-and-white uniform. So dull, so ordinary. She is better than this. We both are.

"I should go," I say, throwing money on the table. Exact change, since I know exactly how much this costs, and there is no sense tipping her. One of the quarters decides to make a run for it, and rolls onto the floor. Edith crouches down and smacks her hand on the quarter, ragged black skirt high up her thigh. She looks up at me.

"Heads or tails?" I ask.

And for a moment, the façade of Edith is gone, and I see her not as she appears to the world, a costumed lie of eighteen, coated in a veneer of makeup and waitress. Nor do I see her as her sixteen-year-old self, somehow both fragile and invulnerable at once. Instead, I see her as she was, eight years old, scrabbling around on the floor of a filthy fast food restaurant, smelling of grease and bleach. And I wonder how things might be different if . . .

If.

And then the moment is gone. Xtian smiles and palms the coin without looking.

"Pick me up at nine," she says. And then she is Edith again, and she walks off to put most of the money in the register, and I walk out the door with a bag full of stolen underwear.

This is how we live now. And it makes me want to die.

• • •

I wander the streets for a while longer, but ultimately I get bored and decide to wait in the car, which is parked around the corner from the diner. I sit in the driver's seat and listen to the radio ramble about Wikileaks and DNC emails, but I turn it off when they start repeating themselves and sit there in silence, wondering if *they* were involved, somehow. I write, some, as Xtian has encouraged me to do, but mostly I think, which is dangerous.

Two hours later, Xtian turns the corner and strolls down the sidewalk, and as I start the engine I can see her not-looking everywhere, absorbing everything around her. The lights, the shadows, the people across the street, watching, noticing everything and fearing only that worth fearing. Confident. Perhaps too. She starts walking over to the driver's side, but I reach over and open the passenger door, and she changes course.

She stops, sighs, and leans down to look inside.

"You promised," she says.

"Just get in," I say. "I changed my mind." It is safe enough for her to drive during the day—she has to learn—but I do not want to risk her driving at night, lest we get pulled over. She can deal. We have far bigger things to fight about.

"Maybe I'll just walk," she says, all the while scanning the street over the top of the Sonata. Always wary now. I am pleased, even if she only learned this the hard way.

"Get in the car, Xtian," I say. We are both irritated from a long day amongst the masses.

"I'm driving or I'm walking," she says.

She's doing neither. I reach over and grab her by the arm, maybe a bit more roughly than I need to. She slaps my hand away, but gets inside, and immediately the car smells of french fries and burnt coffee. I angrily hit the gas before she can get her seat belt on.

"What the fuck is wrong with you tonight?" she says.

"You," I say, before I realize it. I do not really mean it—we are both tired and cranky, and we have both been bickering over nonsense for months now, the stress of everything weighing on us—but I say it anyway. And I know that it is in some way true.

"Fine," she says. "Then let me out."

I ignore her, and a moment goes by, after which she says "Let me out, or I'll jump."

She puts her hand on the door handle and gives me a funny look of defiance. I laugh. I haven't laughed in a long time, and it comes out all wrong. She screws up her face, half horrified, half amused, and I pull the car over to the side of the road, because the laughter is making it hard to drive. There are tears in my eyes, then, and I realize that they are not all the happy sort.

"What?" she asks.

She gets no answer, because my laughter has turned into sobs, deep and painful and shocking. Eight years come spilling out and I feel old, and broken, and wrong, just wrong. Weak. And all of it is her fault. And all of it is my fault. And there is nothing I can do to change any of that. I can cry, as it turns out.

Change. That is what this is about. Where this comes from.

"What?" she asks again, more quietly.

"Why don't you leave?" I ask.

Her hand is still on the door, but she does not open it. Just watches me, watching her. Silent, too silent.

"Well, if you give me half a second, I will," she says. I shake my head.

"Not now," I say. "I mean ever."

We sit there for a few minutes, listening to the sound of the engine idling, and then she removes her name tag and throws it on the dash, putting

Edith away for the night. I put the car in gear, and pull into traffic, forgetting I have cried, wondering if it was real, hoping it was not.

We are halfway home before she says, quietly, "Because I need you."

But I wonder if she has it backwards.

Chalk Outlines

09/08/16

Of all the places we ever lived—Virginia, New York, California—I liked Seattle best. Ironically, I'm pretty sure the weather was the reason. It seemed to be overcast and gloomy most of the time we were there, but that matched our mood perfectly. It wasn't depressing; it was like a big fluffy gray blanket to commiserate with. It felt like home, more than anywhere else we'd been.

For our eighth anniversary together I baked us a cake. Before Edison could ask what it was for, I showed him the calendar. We were quiet for a few moments, not quite sure which emotion was most appropriate. Eight years, I thought, counting candles I hadn't bothered to light. Half my life so far. And considering the way things had gone, it might end up being half my life, in total.

"It's got no eggs," I said, cutting him a slice. "I found the recipe on the web. It's vegan. It's got seitan in it, so it's evil, just like us."

We each took a bite and looked at each other. Then the horrid thing went in the compost bin, and we went out for ice cream. Just like always.

• • •

We drive past the Fremont troll—a big stone tourist trap beneath a bridge that people love to suicide off of—and head through Wallingford at a glacial pace, traffic at its worst still better than San Francisco's best. The slower pace Xtian is driving at suits me fine. She was practicing a bit in San Francisco before events went askew, so she could probably handle going a bit faster, but to be honest I prefer when things are creeping along. No one looks twice at us; we are invisible. Young girl and an older man in a car, obviously someone learning to drive, nothing more to it. It is a story they know, and the best way to lie is to tell the truth, mostly. The best liars almost never get caught in a lie because they are not lying most of the time—only when it counts.

Granted, there are things we have to lie about. Names, ages, addresses. In the past it would have been trivial to get such things, but I have to be more creative these days since my connections are gone, since there are no jobs, just this parasitic lifestyle we have adopted. Fortunately those are easier lies. Names, for example: with a death certificate you can get a birth certificate and now you have a name. You get that and some fake address labels and you have a library card. With that you can get a state ID card, and from there you can get anything if you have a bit of cash. Name change, licenses. A bank account, with a borrowed Social Security number. Fifteen minutes on trash night nets enough credit card applications to wallpaper a bedroom, and it's not even messy thanks to mandatory recycling. Six weeks and a few hundred dollars, you can start a whole new life. Not a great one, but serviceable.

Making it feel new is another story. It is easy to fall into old patterns. Get lost in the past, like Xtian is so often these days. Caught in a labyrinth of memories, a dead monster in the middle, and (I hope) ample string to find her way back out. I want to pull on the string, snap it taut, give her a chalk line to follow back to what was, and is, but I do not want to pull too hard, because something bloody and soft might come out along with it. So I do not pull at all. I got her into this, but she will have to get herself out, slowly and painfully, fingernails and teeth left behind in the cracks. Literally—she left a few of each in California. Dental work is expensive but not out of reach. And the nails have grown back. They will never be quite right again, but then, nothing ever is as it once was.

"Speed it up a little," I say for what must be the ninth time. "You are going to get pulled over for driving too slow."

"I'm going with the fl—"

"Meadow," I say, using *their* clock code out of old habit, even now that it no longer matters, in a time and place we could easily have made up our own or used "check your six." She looks in the rear view mirror, spots the cruiser, and as practiced, pulls over into the next driveway as if it was our destination, letting him pass. Just in case. I am sure we are being followed. I am just not sure who is doing the following. Or when they are doing it. Or where they plan to strike. So until we know, we try to act like everything is normal. Gather information. Prepare. And then, when it all comes down—and it will—we will do like always. We will run.

• • •

Run. Always run. Good advice, but it hadn't done me much good back in San Francisco.

Edison had gotten it mostly right, when he imagined it. There wasn't as much hesitation as he'd envisioned—I got in right away, pretended to use the bathroom—and I didn't hear the clock chirp, I saw it as I walked in the front door. I actually thought about going out the bathroom window, but it was too small and I would have made too much noise, so I decided to try and sneak out the front door. I was halfway down the hall when I heard the guy say "we'll keep her here." And that's when I ditched the box, pulled out the gun, and ran for it. A lot of things happened very quickly at that point, and I'm not sure if I was too slow, or they were too fast. Either way, it was the same result: me on the floor, my left leg burning. It was only when they grabbed me, broke my wrist, and threw me in the corner, that I realized I'd been shot. Like, with a gun.

My first thought was, *So this is what it feels like to be shot.*

And my second thought was, *How is it possible—having been with Edison all these years—that this is my first time?*

My third thought was along the lines of *How did they do more damage to me in six seconds than Edison managed in six years?* but it was interrupted when Nick walked in the room. No doubt recognition pasted itself all over my face, but Nick had his poker face down, I give him that. He stared at me like he'd never seen me before, surveyed the small bit of carnage I'd caused, and shook his head.

"I told you to be careful," he said. For one second I thought he was talking to me. Then I realized I'd been unconscious for a while, probably from shock. Not only had the light changed, but everything else had as well. The room, the whole house was different. I was somewhere else, and a lot of time had elapsed. My leg was bandaged, too. I couldn't see it, but I could feel it. They wanted me alive. I was sure of that much. I wasn't sure if that was a good thing or not.

Someone was talking to me. I looked up, into Nick's eyes.

"Who sent you?" he said. His eyes narrowed. *I dare you*, they said. *I dare you to tell.* He had a gun in his hand. Mine. I opened my mouth, and I saw his finger tense on the trigger. No, that way lay death. Not a good thing, I decided. Not yet. So I improvised: I spat in his face. It's not as easy as they make it look in the movies, but I managed anyway.

He smiled.

It wasn't long before I regretted not ending it right then. There was no way out, no path that didn't lead to death at the end. And every path involved pain.

The first few hours were the worst. Probably because that's when they were the most creative, but also because that's when I was the most aware. Thoughts of suicide drifted freely through my head—of guns and cyanide and nicotine, for all the good it did me, since I had none of that right now. That ended right about nightfall—the conscious part, I mean—when Nick took a turn "interrogating" me.

"Who sent you?" he said, speaking somewhat louder than necessary, in what was almost a stage voice. "Who sent you to kill David?" This, I was learning, was one of the two men I had shot and killed. Nick was improvising, turning an attempt to bug a house into an assassination. David was, I surmised, someone of importance, seeing as nobody was mentioning the other guy. How important, I wasn't sure. Probably as important as Nick, who I increasingly saw as some sort of middle-manager trying to climb a ladder. Which, it occurred to me, was probably why I was where I was, and why Nick was where he was, pretending he hadn't sent me in the first place.

I felt like a tool, and remembered that this was because that was all I was: a tool. I had done the job, too. Just not the one I thought I was doing. And this was the reward. This was what I got for all those useless arcade tickets. My plastic whistle.

Nick reached under my chin and stared me in a blurry eye; the other was clotted shut. I tried to turn my head to compensate, center his face, but he pinched my sore cheeks together and twisted my neck back around, painfully.

"Who sent you?" he repeated. The corner of his mouth twitched, just a tiny bit. Weakness? I decided I had nothing to lose but myself, and that—that was gone a long time ago. I smiled.

"You did," I said.

It was the last thing I remember saying and the only truth I ever gave them.

They hurt me a lot, but most of the time I spent alone, crying my throat raw. They'd hurt me, and then leave me, almost like they weren't sure what to do with me, probably because Nick was still working out exactly how to finish whatever story he was telling. Sometimes they'd hurt me too much and I'd pass out, and whatever happened then I thankfully don't remember. But they seemed to be trying to keep me awake, babbling, on the edge of sanity. I said a lot of things to stop them from hurting me. But that didn't work too well, because with some of them it wasn't about information, or lies. It was just bad men doing bad things.

But I knew someone worse than them.

I knew someone worse.

I knew someone worse.

I kept chanting it in my head, whenever I was conscious. It kept me company.

I knew someone worse.

"She'll break," someone said. But I had already been broken by someone else, years before. Anything they did to me at that point was redundant.

• • •

"Brakes," I say, for the third time. We stop with a squeal, front tires in the crosswalk, and I immediately check all the mirrors for police; unnecessary paranoia. None are visible now. And at any rate she has her learner's permit on her, which is a good excuse for novice mistakes. We also have an intermediate license and a regular driver's license in various pockets and places about the car, depending on which story we need to tell. I would rather not have to tell any, however. As she can tell that from my glare.

The light turns green, and she hits the gas too hard, jerking us forward. I am about to tell her to just turn us around and head home, but then I realize with some surprise that we are already at our destination, so I have her pull down a side street to parallel park. It only takes her four tries. Again, she manages to figure it out right before I tell her to give up and try something else. Perhaps there is a lesson in that for both of us.

The ice cream shop on the corner has four dozen flavors, but Xtian gets vanilla in a paper cup. With toppings, but always vanilla. Even though she no longer is. Perhaps an attempt to hold on to what she once was. As if deep down in there, there is an eight-year-old nugget of *once*, wrapped in layer upon layer of time, like a pearl around sand, an irritating little piece of old wreathed in polish. A bird in a gilded cage, wings clipped, door wide open.

I scan the menu. It looks healthy, considering this is an ice cream shop. Too healthy.

"I need something without eggs," I say.

"We have ten all-natural non-dairy, soy-based varieties to choose from," says the horrid blonde girl behind the counter. "All completely animal-safe," she adds. *And completely flavorless*, I do not add. Instead, I order orange sherbet and hope for the best; sometimes it has eggs, but this place seems safe. If I am wrong, well . . . I am due for a painful death. Overdue.

Once we have our cones, we leave to walk around the block, because I am done dealing with humanity. We are at the far side of the block when I notice that Xtian has stopped, is staring at the sidewalk. I turn and see a hopscotch grid. She asks what it is.

"You have no idea what hopscotch is?" I ask.

"I've led a sheltered life."

I squat down and trace the lines, try to remember the rules. I have never played, just watched. And that was a lifetime ago.

"You throw a stone and you have to hop to it, with one or two feet—" I break off, wondering what I must look like, babbling like an old man in a gray thrift store suit, my waistline probably too high. Gray hair, gray eyes. I feel for a moment as if I am falling apart right there. A scarecrow disintegrating in the wind.

"Probably easier to do than talk about," I say. Like many things.

"Well then, show me," she says, idly trailing an outstretched hand through a rosemary bush nearby, bringing it to her nose delicately.

"You really want me to show you?" I ask, struggling against gravity. And there is chalk on my hands, chalk in my mouth from the heartburn tablet I have just taken.

"Yes," she says. "Teach me, oh master."

I do not remember the rules, but then I am used to making up my own. She will never know the difference. I look around. No one is watching. I do not know why it matters, but it does.

I pick up a stone.

• • •

To Edison's credit, he really tried to be ordinary. Tried to fake it until he made it, to mangle the old saying. He hated it, but he tried to be something of a father, or at least a better partner. At least some of the time he was doing it for me, but mostly I think it was for himself. He was trying to put his past behind him, trying to forget and failing. And like Nick, I think he was trying to spin his own lie. To convince himself that what he'd done was for the best. Maybe to convince me, too.

He put on a good face, but I saw through it. I knew something was nagging at him, beneath the surface, and occasionally it would erupt. He was second-guessing himself. He was wondering if he should have let me die. And sometimes I wondered too.

Between the time Edison took me out of Nick's place, and the time he noticed I was alive, I must have woken up at least a few times. But if I did, that moment is lost now, along with so many other things. But I do remember the final time. The first time, in many ways.

There was darkness, then light. Red. A metallic slam, like a coffin lid. The trunk. And then a lifting in the pit of my stomach as he picked me up. I opened my eyes, and the world spun. For a moment I probably thought I was back in the restaurant. There was blood in my mouth, in my hair. Scabs opened, painfully, everywhere. My hands clenched tight, but there were no coins to drop this time. Everything was gone. Long ago.

"Da—" I mumbled. Or maybe it was more like "Ungh—" I can't decide which is more poetic.

Edison quickly shifted me off of his shoulder and cradled me in his arms. I looked up into his eyes. And he looked into mine.

"Well," he said, impassive. "This changes things."

There were trees and a shovel and a hole, but all that was forgotten as he walked briskly around the side of the car and laid me down in back. After that there was just movement, no way to tell time or place. Eventually we arrived somewhere bright, somewhere with other cars, and he picked me up and carried me in, and I was surprised to discover there were no nurses or doctors, no bright lights, no smell of hospital. I looked around as he set me on the bed and shut the motel room door, and then I remembered who I was with, and I was surprised I had been surprised. Where else would I be but alone with him? Where else could he take me, except nowhere? Nowhere.

He called who he could, called in favors, reminded people of all he'd done—and he had done quite a lot—and strange, quiet people came and took care of me. And over the next few months, I recovered. As much as I could. There were some things I wasn't getting back.

I knew then and I know now that what happened to me was not at all important any more. I was no longer the person those things had happened to. The past couldn't hurt me if I didn't let it. All that mattered was this: I survived, and because I survived, I got. . . Stronger? Maybe, but more than that. It wasn't any coming-of-age bullshit—that's a terrible myth. Becoming is a process, just like aging and just as unavoidable. But it added to me. It made me more *me*.

How can I regret that?

Sinking Feeling

11/05/16

The bouncer looks Xtian up and down, and I immediately regret giving in to her on this, no matter how stir crazy the two of us have been these past months. He checks her license three times, looking for some sign that it is a fake. It is as real as any piece of plastic—the record that it is based on is the fake, and he has no way of knowing that, especially since with the way she is dressed and made up tonight she looks far older than I am comfortable with. He could turn her away, regardless. Both of us. All of us. This is his prerogative, his small shred of power in this world. But he does not care. We are not trouble.

Yet, at least.

She skitters past and heads downstairs without waiting for me. I step up in line and reach for my wallet, but the bouncer declines to check my ID. Old man. Right, I get it.

The club is packed wall to wall with black and blue, half the crowd decked out in the latest fashion trends—which oddly resembles something from my youth—and the other half opting instead for the jeans and T-shirt route. There is lots of plaid, of course. This is Seattle.

At least several of the females in the room are less dressed than Xtian is, and another several seem to be younger than she is, all of which is good;

I would rather she fall into some middle ground than be an extreme. The sheep are packed shoulder to shoulder, and the reek of unwashed crevices sours my nose. It is too hot, too crowded.

The opening act is already onstage, which means not only is it impossible to see anyone clearly (Xtian is probably the only one in the crowd *not* holding an iThing up over her head to record the event), but it is also nigh-impossible to hear anything. Conversation is out, unless you happen to be standing right on top of someone. Which is tempting, but I do not want to get blood on my shoes.

I sneak a glance over my shoulder and get my back to the bar as quickly as possible, snagging a stool. A good spot, right under a vent, an oasis of cool in a sea of swelter.

I order a Diet Coke from the guy behind the bar and turn to look for Xtian. Instead, a woman nearby catches my eye and thinks I am looking at her. She is far too old for this place. Like me. I unconsciously raise an eyebrow, noting as I do that hers seem artificial, painted on. She smiles and looks me up and down. I find this disturbing and turn away. Instead, out of the corner of my eye, I can see her move closer. I sense this will be painful.

• • •

She's beautiful, I thought, watching her dance. Not Edison's new beau, but a different woman, all in brown. Brown leather over a dark brown calf-length skirt, slit up to her thighs with black electrical tape over her stockings, some sort of loose fishnet weave in a pattern I'd never seen. I wanted them. I wanted her boots, too, brown and leather and ankle-height, showing off her perfect video game calves. And her arms: wrapped in brown, fingerless gloves that matched her curly brown hair. She moved and twisted like a snake, powerful and confident, with little flashes of her bare belly emerging from under the brown scales. Fearless.

Could I be that? Like that? Unafraid, free? I stared and stared. And just then she turned and for a moment we locked eyes, and I immediately got self-conscious and turned to look for Edison. Because of course I did. He was talking to a vampiress at the bar as she applied a fresh coat of lipstick using the back of a cigarette lighter as a mirror. No doubt he loathed her vanity. I could see the disgust in his eyes.

I headed over, not sure if I was saving him from her, or vice versa. Edison just barely acknowledged me as I walked up and listened.

"No, I'm not voting on Tuesday," he yelled, competing with the music.

"What? Why not?" the woman shouted back.

"It's a pointless gesture. I'm opposed to anything where people act in unison and think they're making some sort of point, whether it's pulling a lever or waving their hands or chanting to some invisible sky person. Prayer, the Sieg Heil pledge—"

"Pledge?" she asked, not smart enough to just drop it.

"The one of allegiance, yes. Indoctrinating children before they have a chance to decide for themselves? Civic baptism. A four-year-old does not know what 'one nation under god, indivisible' means, but you make him say it every day and he gets brainwashed. Listen to a song every day and it gets stuck in your head. It's just . . . crowd control, at best."

The bartender, who had also been listening, rolled his eyes and moved away to wipe something with a sodden rag as the woman finally began to realize she'd picked the wrong guy.

"Whatcha talking bout?" I asked, too loudly, the music cutting out just then as the opening act left the stage to mild applause. The woman turned and looked at me, surprised I had crept up.

"Hypocrisy," said Edison. "Empty motions without meaning, done only for the benefit of the others who are doing it for the benefit of others. Like Halloween masks and flag pins. A shell of makeup with no substance underneath. Lies built upon lies. It's all just misdirection. Like this pointless FBI investigation . . ."

As he continued on, the woman looked at me, then at Edison. I don't know if she saw an insane old man and his daughter or some businessman with a high-paid, underage escort, but in either case, she curled up her lip and with a look of disgust walked away. Mission accomplished.

• • •

Xtian smiles as she mounts the barstool, pulls her left leg up and lays her head on her knee. Her dark skirt slides up her leg, and I catch an unfortunate glimpse of upper thigh. The sort of thing that should make me feel suddenly and awkwardly young, but here, now, only serves to remind me how old I really am. I look away and I wonder if she does this intentionally to make me look away. A way of controlling me.

There is a shift around us, then, the house music filling in a gap. People begin to move about in different patterns. The bar becomes more crowded. Yet we do not give up our seats. There is still ice in my glass. I am still a customer.

"Old girlfriend of yours?" asks Xtian.

"No," I say, not biting.

She stares past my left shoulder, watching some girl in brown leather dance with the mirror. The woman moves like a sheet flapping in the wind, fluid then crisp. Xtian has a look in her eyes but I do not know how to read it. Does she need a mother figure? A sister? A friend? Is she gay? How would I handle that? Probably better than some other alternatives, I suppose. There are books. I could read them. I assume there is some correlation with abuse at a young age. Perhaps something to do with the lack of a strong father figure. I wonder if I count.

No.

"Did you ever have a girlfriend?" she asks.

"Once," I say, regretting it immediately.

"What was she like?"

"She asked too many questions and I killed her," I say.

Xtian sticks her tongue out at me and is quiet for a while.

"She was blonde," I say after a while, unprompted. "Pale. Wispy and terse."

"Can you speak like a human instead of a thesaurus for a change?"

"Brief. Ephemeral. Transient. It did not last long. We were young, and it was school, and it quickly moved from foolish pseudo-romance to tentative, awkward friendship. Every moment of it felt artificial and forced, and from there it was a quick, steep downhill slide to acquaintance, the sort of lingering thing that hangs on for years after you part ways and everyone thinks they will stay in touch but they never do."

"So in English, you broke up?"

"It was broken from the start; there was nothing more to break."

I sip at my Diet Coke, trying to avoid remembering, failing.

"What was it like?" she asks.

"Dating?"

"No," she says. "High school."

The lights begin to dim, and the air conditioning kicks on overhead.

"I never said it was *high* school," I reply.

She wrinkles her lip in a half-smirk, perhaps knowingly.

"All school is fascist karaoke," I say quickly, to avoid further questions. "Forced to perform on stage, recite someone else's words. Be happy I did not waste your time."

"And on that note," she says, standing.

"Something I said?"

"Something I drank. I gotta pee."

The lights go out, and she goes with them. And just before it goes dark, I catch a glimpse of the cow lady, heading for the bathroom, too. I have no reason to think it, but I suddenly feel like something is terribly wrong, like something terrible is about to happen here. Sometimes the terrible is because of me, and sometimes it is in spite of me. In either case, it is a certainty.

• • •

Entering the bathroom was like walking into a ball of cotton, the music from the main room muffled, replaced by a dull thud within the walls, vibrating pipes and my guts. It was pretty nasty inside: mirror smudged with what I hoped was lipstick, the toilet seat askew, a puddle of something unidentifiable on the floor. I decided to risk it. Nature called. I was just getting started when the music swelled and faded, followed by the sound of boots on the filthy floor, heading my way. By the time I realized the stall had no latch it was too late. The door was yanked open, and the lady in brown suddenly had a better view of certain parts of me than I did.

"Oops," she said. Someone truly embarrassed would have turned away, but she smiled and asked, "Mind if I join you?" It took me a full five seconds of awkward silence to realize she was kidding. By which point she had already worked to address my ignorance.

"Sorry. Bad joke," she said, shutting the door and heading for the mirror to groom. Her heels clacked on the floor, tic tac toe, as she paced, danced to the beat through the walls. I wasn't nearly done, but there was no way my shy bladder was going to cooperate any further, so I flushed the toilet and rushed out of the stall, immediately slipping in something I hoped was water but was probably not, and falling right on my ass.

"Hey, you alright?" asked the woman. I don't know what she thought—that I was in danger, that I had an abusive boyfriend, that I couldn't pee while she was in the same room—but whatever it was, I sensed it was genuine.

She smiled. And then she reached out a strange hand, a beautiful, graceful, kind hand.

• • •

"Hey," I say, covering the distance in three steps.

The woman turns, hand dropping away from Xtian's face, or maybe throat. I cannot tell and I do not care. She is not expecting it when I land a fist beneath her left ear, a perfect brachial strike, hard enough to knock her feet out from under her on the slick floor. Her cheek strikes the porcelain and something cracks that is not the sink, and she falls heavily and does not move any more. There is some amount of blood.

Xtian is frozen. I kneel before her, calmly.

"You alright?" I ask.

She glares at me. Angry?

"Why did you do that?" she shouts, shoving me away. "What did she do?"

"She was . . ." But was she? In retrospect, probably not. No threat at all.

Oh well. Spilled milk.

"She wasn't doing anything," Xtian says, standing. "She was being nice. What the fuck!"

"Nice is a fantasy," I say. "Everyone is after something."

"I'm not going anywhere with you ever again."

"Xtian . . ."

She pushes again, trying to run past me, and it happens. It just happens.

• • •

He had hit me before, of course. Training. Punched, tripped, hurt. Attempted to kill. Left for dead. Left to be tortured. He had killed in front of me, had made me kill, had done horrible things. But all of that was somehow in that single moment acceptable. It was a collective nothing compared to that shocking slap across my cheek.

Tag, I was it.

I stumbled backward, tripped over the brown lady and nearly fell but caught myself at the last moment, lowered my center of gravity and fell to my knees instead. It hurt like hell, but I was damned if I was going to show it just then. He had crossed a line. I stood back up and, without taking my eyes off of him, walked straight towards the door, daring him to stop me. Wisely, he stood aside, and I kept right on walking, straight out into the too-cool night air. Wanting distance between me and him, between me and her. But especially him.

He caught up with me two blocks away.

"Xtian," he said, voice neutral. I was anything but.

"God damn you," I said turning to face him.

"What?" he said, looking confused.

"Why can't we be just normal, just, like normal people. Just leave all that shit behind. No, you had to ruin it. You are a fucking ruiner. You ruined my life."

He reached out, but I backed away. By the look on his face I could tell that to him this was just one more day, that the woman he'd killed was just another bit of trash, and her death didn't mean a thing to anyone, not really. Why did one person matter when he'd killed thousands? What did one day matter? Why did I care?

And which was worse: that I cared, or that I could understand not caring?

"Xtian . . ."

"And that. Stop. It's Christian. Stop. Stop saying it like that. It's a fake shitty name."

"You are fake. We're fake. It's all name tags and credit card numbers and mirrors, Xtian."

"Well I don't want to be Xtian anymore. Or Edith. Or—" I had forgotten who I was supposed to be that night, stammering as I clawed around my pockets for the fake ID.

"Or Patrice. Patrice? What the fuck." I flung the ID towards a trash bin, nearly made it.

"I didn't tell you to be a nobody waitress at a nowhere diner," he said. "You chose that."

Both of us quieted for a moment as some random passers-by passed by. In the distance, we could just barely hear sirens. I started walking again, in a random direction, and he followed after as I yelled back at him, choking back tears.

"How has any of this been a choice? You took me and you broke me and you made me and now I *choose* to sit here and smile while you spit the world down my throat?"

"I never forced you to swallow."

"Go to hell," I yelled, knowing as I did that it was meaningless, because we had been there already, and come back. And where did that leave us?

We were about to find out.

I turned and started to walk back towards the club, and saw him stiffen as if to . . . to what? Hit me again? But it was a bluff, or a feint.

Instead of stopping me, he just stepped to one side, and laid a hand on my shoulder.

"Xtian . . ."

"Let me go," I said, shaking him off. Wondering if he would.

He did.

Dead Pressed

01/21/2017

While the country has been busy figuring out what the hell happened in the election two months ago, I have been busy thinking about what happened in the club. Thinking of how, even after all we have done together, that it was one more nobody that made the difference for her. One feather on the wrong side of the scale. Why does this one stick with me? It was just one more person, one more day. There are so many more things that have happened to us that could have tipped the balance. But it was this. This one, stupid, pointless inconsequence.

I should not even dwell on it. She has probably forgotten. Perhaps it is just my brain trying to keep itself alive. Focusing on recent events, replaying them over and over, because my long-term memory is fading and failing. The days blend together, the weeks puree until everything is one unimportant gray clump of time. It would be easy to just let it happen. Lie back in the easy chair, turn on the television, and let it all blur together into reruns.

But I am not content. There are things happening, important, insane things, and I am not part of them. Everything about this insane presidential election. This pipe dream of a wall along the Mexican border. The Russians allegedly being involved. All of it hammering home day after day how broken society is. Globally, but especially nationally. Fundamentalists are having conniptions about trans people in the wrong bathroom, but no one blinks an eye when two dozen horny football players gangbang an underage sex-abuse victim in a high school lavatory.

This is to say nothing of the literal circus the TSA has become to calm the masses tired of standing in three-hour lines. Clowns and miniature horses? Marching bands. It makes me wonder why there has not been an attack on American soil like in Brussels, or Istanbul. All those victims all lined up . . .

"You wish," she said, when I mentioned this. And I do. And I know her intent was to wound when she said it. To point out that it was just that, a wish and nothing more. Reminding me that I threw everything away to come here with her. That there will be no second chance for me. And she is right. There will not be. Not as long as we stay here, stagnant.

I have done this before, of course, in Portland—not this most recent pit stop, but the last time, before DC, before Xtian, before all of this. But then, it was not by choice. *They* fired me, basically, sent me so far underground that I had nearly forgotten myself. And I coped then, in a fashion. I did without certain things, had to adapt. To change. Not so different from where we are now. Nor so far away. The main difference is that this time is voluntary. I got us into this. And the "us" is the second difference. Back then, I was alone. Dealing with anything is easier when you are alone. No matter what you decide, the vote is always unanimous. And no matter how terrible the outcome, it is always easy to find the person responsible.

This? This should be easy, too. Me at home, lounging in a chair watching television. She at work at her diner, earning a paycheck. Ordinary. Simple. But it is not. It is anything but.

This is as complicated as it gets.

• • •

"Well, are you sure you love him?"

I shook my head and shrugged as Delia watched me put grounds in the coffee maker. Our own little Women's March, just the two of us. Sans marching. I wanted to be out in the streets, but I couldn't afford to miss a shift, and wasn't sure Delia cared. She seemed more concerned with my plight, and I regretted bringing Edison up again. We'd had the conversation during a few shifts already, and although her questions changed, my answers remained the same.

"No, I'm not sure," was all I could say. It was easier than the complicated truth. Especially considering the disaster a few months ago. We hadn't talked much since then. But did that mean things had gotten better, or were they still stuck on terrible?

Did I love him? Maybe. If nothing else, probably yes, in the same way as I might love a dog, or a car, or (god help me) a job. Which is to say that all those things really mostly suck, but it's easy to find yourself overlooking the suck if it's all you have. It's not so bad, you say. The muffler's fallen off, but it will still get me around. It pukes all over the sofa, but it'll keep me warm at night. At least I get paid. Comfortable chains, gilded cages.

"Then just leave him." Delia waved her hand like she was shooing away a fly. She seemed so confident about relationships, even though she couldn't operate the coffeemaker. If only she knew what my life was really like. That she'd started work just a few days after Christmas seemed like the perfect present, considering that Edison hadn't bothered, never did. Delia and I were like a sitcom together. She was the ditzy blonde and I was the sociopath who'd seen too much.

"I can't leave," I said. I didn't know where I'd go.

"Are you sure? Maybe he'd just let you go." She reached for her hidden cigs behind the shake machine. She was about to offer me one when the bells over the door jangled, and a man walked in, just an ordinary guy, jeans and a T-shirt, flannel tied around his waist, sneakers. No one you'd look at twice. Except I did. It was how he carried himself. The little almost invisible sidelong glances, the way he took the room in. He didn't need a suit; he *was* the suit. He sat down with an easy confidence, back straight in the corner booth, didn't even reach for a menu, just sat there waiting. And it was then I was sure it was a costume, and that he was trouble, although I wasn't sure for who.

I turned to ask Delia if she'd grab the table, but she was already out back feeding her addiction, and there was no choice. As if there would have been. He looked over at me, slow, and smiled. Genuine, it seemed. Seemed. I slid a knife under my notepad, dropped it in my apron, and grabbed the half-empty pot of steaming hot coffee. All smiles and sugar, I flounced over.

"Coffee?" I asked.

"Two cups."

"Waiting for someone to join you?" I asked as I inverted two mugs, filled them.

"Yes," he said. "Christian."

I dropped my pen. Not accidentally.

"Excuse me?" I said, kneeling down. Right hand reached for the pen, left slipped into my apron. A soft sound stopped me, the brush of metal against denim, and I looked up under the table and saw the gun peeking out from beneath the flannel, not pointed at me, but close enough to count. I slowly put my hands out to either side, palms down, and looked up at him. He smiled, and it was a nice smile, if no longer genuine.

"I just want to talk," he said. "For now."

I looked up at him, ran the odds. Fifty-fifty. Maybe a little better. Chance.

"Cream and sugar?" I asked, standing up slowly, unthreateningly.

He shook his head.

"Black."

Of course.

"Sit down," he said. "You're off the clock."

Black. The clock. Code? One of *them*? Not necessarily. They were just words. Maybe he was government? Hell, for all I knew, *they* and the government were the same. Edison had never been clear on that. Regardless, it was obvious that whoever they were, I didn't want to screw around. They had the place surrounded, or at least there were enough of them to convince not just the customers but the staff to leave in a hurry. That we were alone, so quickly, made an impression. It also convinced me that one way or another, what I had was over. I couldn't very well just come back to work. Seattle was done. Well done.

I can't say it felt all bad to realize that. I was ready to move on. Edison seemed to thrive on drama and conflict, seeing it even where it didn't need to exist. He liked chaos. For me, this wasn't a sign that it was time to go out, guns blazing, fires burning. It was just time to go.

The man sipped his coffee, winced at the heat as he looked me up and down. I focused on my coffee, alternately adding more cream and more sugar, postponing the inevitable. Plus it kept my hands from shaking. Not fear, per se, but adrenaline. I felt like a caged bird, beating itself against the bars. The cat waiting patiently nearby.

"The license," he said, setting his cup down, folding his hands. "How we found you. Patrice, I think it was? Incident in a club back in November, lost license. Fake name, but we pulled real fingerprints off of it. He's not in the system, but you've been there since kindergarten."

Stupid stupid stupid . . .

"Stupid, they said. A mistake. But you're not a stupid girl. Are you?"

I didn't answer; I was starting to wonder.

"You wanted to be found. To be rescued."

"Did I now?"

"You know who we are," he said, all but confirming my theory, or perhaps just trying to push me down a false narrative. Either way, I wasn't going to just let it go at that.

"Enlighten me," I said. "Who exactly are you?"

"Please. You know how this works. My name doesn't matter. Especially since if you're lucky, you and I will never cross paths again."

"Well then who do you work for? For all I know you're an ISIS sympathizer."

He rolled his eyes but humored me nevertheless.

"I'm a strand of the same web you and he are part of. That you pretend to be part of. I just happen to be somewhat closer to the center of it all. Close enough to see more of what's going on. More than you. More than him, maybe. Certainly, enough of it to be able to find both of you."

"And vague enough to avoid the question."

"Use your imagination. You knew . . . Nick, I think you knew him as? I'm higher up the food chain than him. You know what he could do? You can imagine what I can do. What we can do. We bury the messes. Control the chaos. And when it becomes necessary, tie off loose ends."

I kept up a good, calm front, leaned back.

"Well if you're here to kill me, you need to speed it up, because the dinner rush is coming."

There were violent thoughts in his head, I could tell. I'd seen the eyes enough. But he held it down, just sighed away the moment. Listening? Was that an earpiece? Edison said those were just a good way to get an ear infection.

"I'm not here to kill you," he said. "Quite the contrary. I'm here to set you free."

I ignored the obvious fact that those two things were not entirely contrary and shrugged, surprised at how genuine it felt to not care. Was I not free? I could leave whenever I wanted, couldn't I? There was a twinge in there somewhere, a flutter. Maybe it was the coffee. I added another sugar, as if that was going to help, swirled coffee around in my cup as if reading tea leaves. Could you predict the future with coffee grounds, I wondered? Folger's new age crystals?

"You don't care?" he asked.

"I'm waiting for the other shoe," I said. "The part where you want something from me."

He smiled.

"See? Smart girl. I told them."

"Just get to the point," I said. "You want me to kill someone? Maybe blow up a bus full of kids?" It came out so quickly, so smoothly, that it startled me. I guessed I had gotten over that. Probably Nick had something to do with that. There were worse things that could happen to children than what I did. I learned that firsthand.

I should have known it was none of that. I should have known what it was. It still surprised me to hear him say it.

"We want him."

• • •

I died for the first time when I was sixteen. My father died at the same time. The key difference being that he was in the bottom of a shallow pit with a bloody hole in his face, and I was up top with a shovel in my hand. He was going to die anyway, and not because of me; the hole in his face was a self-administered remedy when he knew *they* were coming, knew he had messed up for the last time. The other hole—the pit—was mine. I buried him, let the dirt cover his fish noises. He would have died anyway, if not in a hospital then by their hands, when they finished the torture, but technically I killed him—and myself at the same time. The only thing I felt at the time was amazement that I had not done it sooner.

After it was done, and I had ransacked the house for money and what-not, I had the whole world before me. Powerful with options, knowing that no matter what I did, where I turned, it would be into the unknown. No name, no family, no attachments, nothing except me and a backpack full of (I thought) unmarked twenties and tens, the final remnants of my former life now buried in a smoldering pit behind the house. I could become anything. I could buy anything.

And the first thing I did with the money was to go see *Alien* in theaters. I remember rooting out loud for the alien because the crew were so stupid, let themselves get picked off. Whose fault was it? It was the space miners who ignored common sense, set off a bomb that blew up in their faces and their guts. All the alien did was try to survive, follow its instincts, try to find a worthy host. Kill or be killed. Survive, breed. You cannot set a fire and then ask it to play nice.

The rest of the cash I frittered away on random things. Now, of course, I have a healthier respect for money. Especially since right now we need more of it. I cannot pay the bills with stolen underwear, and Xtian cannot support us on part-time diner earnings, no matter what arbitrary number they assign to the minimum wage. I cannot stand to see her doing that job. Waitressing is like whoring, service for cash, and she is better than that.

Both of us are.

So it is time to die. Time to kill off who we are, to move on, to start anew somewhere else. It will not help the money situation per se, but it cannot hurt. We can move somewhere cheaper. Somewhere east, or south. Maybe somewhere either of us has never been. I have done it many times. She has done it thrice with me. We can do it again. Moving is easier than stasis as long as you ride the wind.

And perhaps that is the mistake I made. With her. I could have walked away the night I killed Nick and sealed my fate. Could have gone anywhere, and started fresh. But I went back for a peek. I fought inertia, and I looked in the hole, when I should have been filling it in. And here we are. We. Stuck in the same cage.

There is no other choice, now. We are changing. What we have is not working. I cannot let it chain us down. The club, this limbo we find ourselves in. The woman in brown, whatever her name was, she does not matter. The past does not matter. All that matters is what can be done in the present, to change the future.

I could let Xtian decide. I cannot see what harm it could do. She has trusted me all these years. Perhaps it is time to return the favor and trust her. I owe her that much.

• • •

"Dead pressed," said my new worst friend. He waited for a reaction, but I just gave him a blank stare and sipped lukewarm coffee. Too sweet.

"You know what that is?" he asked at last.

"Yes," I said. When you put an explosive under pressure, so much that it can't be detonated on its own. In order for it to explode, it needs a detonating agent. I didn't say this; I figured it wasn't a vocabulary lesson. He wasn't Edison.

"It's you. He's kept you down so long, put so much pressure on you that you wound up here, can't do shit for yourself. Paying his bills. Feeding him. And for what?"

He was right, and I hated that. He could have been reading my mind over the past few months. I had been complaining about the exact same things to Delia earlier.

"But forget him for a moment or forever," he said. "Consider what *you* want. A normal life. A family. Safety. A nice house. Kids. Whatever. You can go back to where you belong, and he can never get to you again. You can be whichever you that you want. Simple as that."

I wasn't sure it was him talking at that point, not entirely convinced it wasn't something inside me, trying to talk me off the ledge. Which way off, I wasn't sure.

"Pick an identity. Christian, Edith, Nichole, Alice, whatever. Fucking . . . Lindsay Lohan. I don't care. Pick a country. Anything you like. Find your family if you want. If you still consider them family. Run away. Whatever. You don't matter to anyone after today."

"I matter to—" I started. Maybe unconvinced. Maybe finally realizing the truth.

"Listen." He tented his hands, trying to play patient. "I know your story. Not everyone does—you hid pretty well. But I took the time to find you. So I know. And I don't much care, frankly. It's trite. Like some fucking Internet fanfic, 'Mary Jane Melodrama and the Killer with a Heart of Gold.' You bore me. You're not unique. You're not important."

"Then why would you let me live?" I ask.

And with that, he seemed to turn off, ran out of script.

"Why let anyone live?" he asked, dismissively.

"Yeah. Why?"

He shook his head as if talking to a child. I guess he was.

"No one wants to kill everyone in the world," he said. "That would be pretty fucking pointless. We only do what needs doing. You want to round off in the spreadsheet, you need to lose a few after the decimal point. Everyone has a potential value, for a limited amount of time. And you have about three minutes to decide whether or not to help us out."

"And if I don't help . . ." It wasn't really a question. He let the ellipsis hang there for a few seconds as he reached for my coffee mug, now abandoned, swirled the dregs around and watched the coffee whirlpool. Poison, damn it. Why did I always get the good ideas when it was too late?

"We can let you live, because you don't know as much as you think you know. You think you're special, important, but you're not, except for this one thing. For what you can do, right now. You can't hurt us. But Christian . . ."

And there it was at last: the safety was off. Finger on the trigger. Squeezing.

"We can hurt you," he said.

Bang.

It was the eyes, I think, that hammered it home. They say when someone dies the light goes out of their eyes, and the light had been gone from his for a while. They were cold, burnt-out, dead deer eyes. Nick's eyes. Black holes. And they sucked up the last of my hope.

My cell vibrated. A text.

"Is it him?" he asked. Of course it was.

"What's it say?"

"He wants to meet for dinner."

I felt sick as I said the words. Could hardly believe they'd come so easily. But maybe that was how to do this. Quick and easy, gulp it down. Throw up later. Fall off the ledge and pray for a haystack without needles.

"Well that's convenient." Words wet, like a hot tongue in my ear. "When?"

I hesitated, but not long enough to ever feel good about it. Ever.

"Thirty minutes," I said.

He smiled. "Tell him yes."

Second thoughts chased each other around my skull, stirring up memories of what Edison had done. Pain. Fear. Danger. Attempted murder. It was a solid argument. It seemed so easy. But then, why couldn't it be? Why hadn't I done it before?

Was it fear, before that moment? Or was it only fear now?

"Are you going to kill him?" I asked.

Dark, cold eyes, black-in-white-in-black, like a hungry bird of prey.

"No," he said.

I pretended it was true.

Back

01/22/2017

Darkness. Smell of alcohol. My ears are ringing, like after a gunshot, but this is not that. This is drugs. I have been drugged, and I am coming out of it, or going into it, or—if they know what they're doing—I am right in the middle of it. It takes a while to focus my thoughts, but as the fuzziness fades, I start to hear other sounds. Mouth noises. What are they called. Words.

"Hello, Thomas."

I look around, see dark. Blindfold? No, my eyes are bruised shut. Try to move. To speak.

"Ask your question—" I manage with a foggy tongue. Saliva runs down my chin. At least I think that is what it is. I cannot tell.

"I just did," the voice replies.

I try to get a sense of time and space, but everything loops back in a dizzy circle. Who knows me as Thomas? I feel like I am falling forever, sideways.

"Did I answer?" I manage.

"No. Not yet."

I force a smile and . . .

• • •

. . . I am sixteen again. Even though I was ignorant of the world I knew better than to be surprised about them picking me up so quickly. I had not covered my tracks, did not know what I was doing, had not developed the instincts. My father's money was easy to follow, and I was even easier to tail. So when *they* got me, threw me in a van, and drove me off to who knew where, I was not at all shocked. Scared, but not shocked. I think part of me wanted them to find me. Dared them to. After all, what was the worst they could do to me? Kill me?

Yeah, I was naïve back then, too.

"Where is your father?"

"I have nothing to say to you," I said. "I have rights."

He smiled. And then he showed me that I was wrong about rights. I guess I expected it, having been hit by my father for much the same attitude, but I did not expect it to hurt quite so bad. This man was remarkably good at causing a large amount of pain very rapidly and with very little obvious effort. Better than my father, even.

That first day, they tortured me for an hour or so. I thought that was bad enough, but then they gave me a break to think about it, and came back a few hours later. It went on like that for three entire days, alternate waves of pain and isolation, tied to a chair the entire time without food or water, until I started hallucinating. And that was when the *real* torture began . . .

• • •

. . . or ended. I cannot be sure. Am I here or there? Then or now? My arms tingle, from where they either started or stopped pumping drugs into me. My mouth is dry, my eyes even more so. I force them open, painfully, and look around. Most of what was inside of me is now apparently soaked into the towels beneath my bare feet, although the lack of a strong odor means either I have not wet myself or they have been cleaning up. I am naked, but that tells me nothing. If I could feel my chin for stubble . . . but I cannot, since I am handcuffed to the chair. Savages.

There is no blood anywhere I can see. I suppose that much is good. I try to lift parts of myself up to check for damage and pain, and I feel a lot of the latter, signifying a lot of the former. Hands hurt, knuckles raw. Both arms are likely broken. Humerus in each, is my guess. Likely a shoulder dislocation, too, possibly an elbow. There is an IV in my left arm, and I wonder if they have been dripping me painkillers. I hope not, because if I am on something now and it hurts this bad, I cannot fathom what this is going to feel like when it wears off.

I try to remember a time when it was this bad, but I have never let it get to this point, especially not that first time. I told them everything I knew so they would stop hurting me. I assumed, back then, they wanted something my father had known, like maybe where he had gotten so much money. I had no idea, so I just told them everything I could think of. At the time, I thought it was stupid and weak of me to spill my guts about everything just because they had withheld food and water for a few days. But what was stupid—in retrospect—was holding out that long. Nothing I had to say was of any consequence any longer. My father would have been useful, but he was dead. You could not get information out of a dead man.

This is why I am certain I have not given up any information *now*. I am alive because I still have value. I still know something they do not. That gives me some time to work with.

I take a few deep breaths, try to focus as the drugs distill out of my bloodstream. I am not in a basement, not at a black site, but in a motel room, a fifty-dollar-a-night sort of operation in the sort of place that does not really mind a few screams from next door, or an extra stain on the carpet afterward. Probably not government, then. At least not openly. Government-trained, though? That much is possible. The lack of torture tells me that they are at least current on technique. Sometime between Abu Ghraib and Gitmo someone figured out that when you torture people all they really tell you is what you want to hear. Waste of time.

The arms: that was probably not torture. Possibly accidental, perhaps a spiral fracture as they were dragging me around, after they'd clubbed me in the back of the head and choked me out in the diner. Everything looks clean, but of course it could be a lot worse than it looks: spiral could take months to heal. Nowadays, they barely even cast you for these sorts of breaks, just sling it and send you home with drugs. Lots and lots of drugs.

Unlike torture, drugs do work, especially with hypnosis, which has been all the rage these past few years despite the stigma. You cannot hypnotize an unwilling subject, make him do or say things he normally would not, but add some drugs, some abuse, and now you can. They know what parts of the brain do what, now, can slip in behind and get inside, make you trust them, and then before you know it you are saying things you did not intend to say.

Yes, you can lie on drugs, under any interrogation, which is why they did not call it truth serum, not even back in my youth, except in movies. It is only *partly* truth serum. It is up to the interrogator to sift fact from fiction, and here I am guessing they have more than an outline; they have a first draft, and now it is not really about finding out the story, but editing out the fiction with their big red pens, removing extra commas, fixing run-on sentences. Occasionally, editing the edits, unsure. Stet.

I wonder what I might have told them so far. I wonder if it was true. Memory is faulty, and I have been half-conscious through most of this. I wonder if the lies I have been telling myself have become so ingrained that it is what I spat back at them under the influence. Mostly though, I wonder if I can get something to eat. The drugs are really wearing off now, and with a better sense of time and place, my stomach has decided to remind me it exists.

Through the window curtain, I can just make out what looks like a man and woman, dressed like tourists, jeans and T-shirts from SeaTac, goofy hats. Second floor, looks like. I can hear planes. I yell in a mostly not angry sort of way, and someone arrives after a few seconds, not from outside, but rather stepping in through the door that joins this room to the next one over.

"Problem?" asks the man. A professional, I can tell immediately.

"I need food," I say. "You want me to talk, feed me." Like some sort of trained bird.

The man walks over and removes my handcuffs before helping me stumble over to the bed. I am still dizzy, and the pain is excruciating. Knee, ankle. Sprains, tears. Bruises. While this happens, I tell him what I want, and he checks his phone to see what might be in walking distance. Once he tells me, I give him my order, from memory. For a moment he looks at me, as if to question how I know the menu so well, but he does not, just writes the order down on the back of a receipt, then takes a twenty out of his wallet and slides both of them under the outside door, knocking twice. Through the curtain I see the woman walk over, then disappear again. The door never opens. Definitely professionals. Or at least professional enough.

The guy walks back over and seats himself facing me.

"How do you feel, Thomas?" he asks, removing the IV needle from my arm. I barely notice, too busy immediately parsing that name, trying to figure out who uses it. But at this point it is completely moot. Everything I knew blew up many months ago.

"Jesus had a better time on the cross," I say. The closest I will let myself get to mentioning Xtian here: quoting something she said to me once. I will not drag her into this. If they know about her, if they have her, I will find out eventually anyway.

"Sorry about the arms," he says. "I can get you some morphine."

"Fentanyl?" I ask. I consider saying no outright, but I am not a sadist. Nor do I want the needle stuck back in me if I can help it.

"We have Oxy," he says. I consider, then nod, and he goes rifling around in the room. "I've only got tens. How many you want?"

"A few. What do you want from me?"

"Everything you know," he says, filling a plastic cup with tepid water.

"Like how to cook rice?"

"Sure. Why not? We have a lot of time."

After he feeds me a few Oxycodone, he helps me into a button-down shirt, loose shorts and sandals—are we going somewhere, or is this an effort to help me keep my modesty?—then helps get my arms slung. This confirms my shoulder theory. Tears run down my face. Humiliating, far more than the nudity was, but not as much as trying to choke it back would be.

We talk a bit, but it is casual, pointless. I am in too much pain, too hungry and dizzy and everything to cooperate. By the time he is finished, and I am somewhat recovered, there is a knock on the door. For a moment I wonder if they plan to feed me fries under the door, but he just walks over, unlocks it, and swings it halfway open.

"There was a line," says a female voice. He does not reply, just snatches the bag, shuts the door, and locks it again. I get the feeling that door is not opening again unless someone dies.

He walks over to the bed, drops the bag, and stares at me. I shrug to make my point, though it sends pain burning up both arms. He sighs, but since he is playing good cop today, he sits down and dumps out the bag to feed me my burger and fries . . .

• • •

. . . which is what I remember most about that first week with *them*, as they dragged a much younger me around between low-end hotels and high-end motels, chasing every lead my stream of information led them to. Most of it dead ends, but certainly some of it got them something. I knew little about what my father had been involved with, but from what I was seeing now, I had a pretty good idea. Through it all, they spared every expense. Every place we slept was a dive, and every meal was fast food. I swear the stuff set up home in my taste buds, crowding out everything else.

Then one morning, just like nothing, I woke up in an Ashland motel and they were gone. I had told them everything they wanted to know, we had finally come full circle back to where my family had once lived, and my utility to them had been expended.

Or so I thought at the time. Something about me must have intrigued them. Maybe my willingness to cooperate, or my eagerness to learn, or the fact that I really did not seem to care what was going to happen to anyone my information led them to. Whatever the case, when I got out of bed there was a twenty-dollar bill next to the phone, folded into a rectangle so the serial number was just about the only thing visible. Thinking this relevant, I memorized it, then broke the twenty on breakfast at the place across the street: a muffin sandwich with egg and cheese, and a black coffee, after which I became violently ill. At the time I blamed the coffee . . .

• • •

. . . although now, I am well aware of my limitations and always order appropriately. I look around at what is spilled on the bed and grow concerned. Is it what I ordered? I do not eat at this particular place *that* often, but the wrapper looks different. I was still under the influence when I ordered, and this place likes to slather mayo on everything. But what can I say? Nothing. *They* do not know about this limitation of mine. I have made sure of that. Everyone who does is dead, save one. I cannot give that away, cannot afford to give them that leverage, now.

I try to taste it as he crams the burger in my mouth but I can never tell. Mayo does not taste like anything to me, just bland sticky sandwich glue. Was there any on there? I start to sweat. Is this how I go? Now that would be ironic. Or would it? I forget the definition.

"Okay," he says. "Let's start with everything you know about cells."

For the next few minutes, I rattle it all off. About Nick, about everybody. I start with DC and the subway, and then jump ahead to Buffalo and the job on the lake, where Joe came into the picture. I talk about San Francisco, and what I have assumed about Nick's plot. This is where he gets particularly interested in what I have to say, which does not surprise me.

Whoever this guy is, he does not write anything down; no doubt this is being recorded. Next room over, probably. Shotgun mic, cameras. This place was prepared ahead of time. This was planned, months before.

"You know what Nick was up to?" he asks. I do not, not for sure, but I tell him what I pieced together. That Nick's first job for us was a hit on someone else within the organization. That a new cell moved into the dead guy's house within a few weeks, and Nick sent a patsy in there and then betrayed them. That he captured and then tortured that person for information they did not have. Then I showed up and spoiled the party.

"Who was it?" he asks. "Who did Nick betray?"

"I knew him as Josh," I say. "He was dead when I got there."

There's a moment of silence, then, and I wonder what he already knows. Certainly he knows that Xtian exists—they were at the diner. But it is possible all they knew is that I often went there for dinner. For all I know, she got away. For all I know, she is dead. But it matters not, either way. They can torture me all they like, but I will not drag her into this mess. And I certainly will not tell them about how I found her, broken and—

My throat begins to itch.

"What was Nick up to?" he asks. And this is a question that I, too, would like answered. I tell him the truth: I have no idea. And I find myself parroting Joe's last words to me, which sickens me. But the guy had a point.

"It was just business," I say. "Just a job."

"Any guesses?" he asks.

My guts churn, but I swallow hard and keep talking. I give him my theory, which is unsatisfying but is probably true: that whatever Nick was trying to do, it wouldn't make a difference. This organization (if it can be called that) is set up so everyone operates within distinct cells, with big thick walls, independent operators, plausible deniability. Everything is autonomous and separate. You can be in two cells, or three, or more, consecutively, just never simultaneously. No overlap. And you never try to move up the food chain, never touch other cells. You do that, you get cell death. Suicide or murder, depending on your point of view. A problem that solves itself. Damage control.

Nick broke the rules I tell him, and Nick paid for it. With his life.

What I do not say is that I think this guy interrogating me wants me to help him do the same thing. To build upon the fallen foundation of Nick's would-be empire. If they were just another ordinary cell, they would know better than to be asking these questions. But that just tells me what they are not, not what they are. They might be some new cell that does not yet know any better, or they could be that theoretical brain behind everything trying to regain control of an experiment gone wrong. The *they* behind the *them*. Could be Hezbollah for all I know. FBI. CIA. Sinn Fein. Al-Qaeda. Doctors Without Borders.

But even as I try to puzzle it out, I realize that it is all pointless. I have never cared, and caring now will not make one shred of difference. Regardless of who they are or what they are about, I already know what is going to happen. I can feel it in my guts, in my throat, in my buzzing head. The room spins, my ears ringing, my vision dimming, and not from drugs.

At least, I think, I will not be dying on a toilet . . .

• • •

. . . which is where teenage me spent most of that morning, back after *they* had discarded me like a used paper bag. While I was in the restaurant bathroom being ill from eating eggs, I had plenty of time to occupy myself with numbers and letters, scratching out graffiti on the wall of the bathroom stall. The individual digits from the serial number on the twenty they had left me. It had to be meaningful, but I needed to figure out how. Eight numbers and two letters . . .

"Can I help you, son?" asked the manager after about an hour, knocking on the stall. I took the hint and left, then crossed the street, bought a pack of gum and picked up the public phone. I no longer remember the entire number, but I recall it started with B, followed by the numbers zero and two. On a telephone keypad, it made a lot more sense: 202, the Washington, DC area code. I dialed the rest, seven more digits, and then waited. And waited. The phone rang and rang, and I thought for a moment I had misdialed, or maybe gotten the wrong idea entirely. But then an answering machine picked up. It beeped immediately, without a prompt.

"Hello," I said tentatively. "I got this number from a twenty doll—"

Someone picked up the receiver on the other end.

"Where are you?" said a voice, heavily distorted.

"Ashland. Pennsylv—"

"Get to DC and then call again. Not before." Click. Immediate dial tone.

I could have gone anywhere, done anything. They—whoever they were, whoever my father had been working for, or against—were done with me. But for some reason, I was not done with them. These were powerful people, doing powerful things, like putting phone numbers onto actual currency. I had nothing tying me down. No obligations. All I had was an invitation.

So I took it. I got to DC, and I called the number back.

And that is how it began . . .

• • •

. . . and this is how it ends? I can't help but wonder as the cramps hit me hard. I hide it as long as I can, but then there is one that is just a bit too much, pain cresting above pain. And it chokes the words from my throat and doubles me over, erases the ache in my arms, makes me feel whole again for a moment, like Humpty Dumpty, falling off the wall. Inexorable.

Someone says something. I try to answer, but my throat is past itching and into swelling. Time ceases to have meaning. It takes everything I have just to breathe. Out of the corner of my eye, I can see him knocking on the door, yelling at it. Back and forth. Then, finally, he opens it and the woman come in after him. Shapes and shadows and echoes.

". . . drugs maybe . . ."

". . . how much . . ."

I'm in and out, ears ringing, vision dimming. Heart pounding. It's never been this bad, but then that's how it works; each time is worse, until it gets so bad that it kills you.

". . . could we . . ."

My head hits the pillow, lands on a bunch of napkins and loose fries. With nothing else to do, I find myself counting them like some sort of vampire, deducing nothing as my vision fades out. Sherlock Dracula, done in not by garlic, nor any criminal mastermind, but by mayonnaise.

There's a rush of white noise. And then there is darkness.

And then.

Flock Theory

01/22/2017

The last words we spoke to each other were meant to be lies.

"When will you be home?" he had asked, wandering into the kitchen as I pulled on my work shoes. I ignored him, passive-aggressively untied and retied the same lace.

"Seven," I said, picking a random number. "I might work late because I love my job so much."

I realized he was putting on a coat, and this was turning into a race to see who left the house first. I decided to let him win and went for the same lace a third time.

"I am going out," he said, as if it wasn't obvious.

"Going to look for a job?" I asked. I expected one of his long silences in response to my sarcasm, but he jumped right in.

"You want me to work in a diner, too? Maybe I can get a fast food job. Put on a blue collar and a name tag and a hair net. Is that what you want from me?"

"It's apparently good enough for me," I mumbled.

"No," he said, hearing me. "It's not."

He grabbed a stupid-looking fedora from the coat rack that he'd never worn before—never would again—and jammed it crookedly on his head.

He turned and considered himself in the mirror beside the door. He looked ridiculous.

"How do I look?" he asked.

"Handsome, as always," I said.

He nodded, stepped into the hallway, then paused.

"I promise," he said over his shoulder. "Things are going to change."

And then he was gone.

In the end, after it was all done in the diner, all I had to show for my betrayal was an envelope stuffed with what looked like a thousand in mixed bills; a slap in my face, harder than Edison's best. Was that what I was worth, or all that Edison was worth? It may as well have been three dollars in dimes.

Then—just before I walked out forever—the man had pulled a folded twenty from his own pocket, placed it on the table, and slid it across with his index finger, smirking. A tip? I jammed it in my pocket without looking, without thinking to be insulted, then ran out to the alley and got into the Sonata, shaking like something was after me. I suddenly remembered something Edison had said, years ago. A lifetime ago.

"When will I be grown up?" I had asked. He thought about that for a moment.

"You think a thousand dollars is a lot of money, right?"

I had nodded. It was. Very, very much.

"Well, when you stop thinking that. That will be when."

I sat in the car for a half hour, rolling that thought around in my brain as I breathed rancid fumes from the grease bin behind the diner, waiting for something. But there was nothing, not even a sound to indicate what was happening in there. Maybe he knew it was a trap. Maybe he knew I had betrayed him. Maybe I could save him.

I flipped open my burner and scrolled through the list for Edison's latest number, stored under "Pizza." Then I sat there, just staring at it, until the screen darkened. He'd probably turned his cell off. Would it matter? Maybe the attempt would matter? What if I called, and *they* answered?

None of it mattered. Before I could decide, a black van drove past the far end of the alley. *Them*, I knew immediately. Without thinking I dropped the cell on the seat, started the car, and followed. I don't know why. Instinct? Denial? Maybe just morbid curiosity. I hung back like he'd shown me, tried to remain a block away, a turn behind, cars between us. I trailed like a coward for half an hour as we went south on 5. At last the van got off in SeaTac and pulled into a fast food lot a bit north of the airport. I kept going past the lot but got stuck at the light on the corner, and just as it turned red someone got out of the van. A man. Scary big, dark like a bruise. He just stood right there and looked at me. It wasn't angry or threatening. It was just a look, maybe pity, maybe disappointment that I still didn't get it. He looked at me until the light turned green, until I knew: it was over.

I drove home crying, trying to distract myself with crazy plans. I could have done anything at all, everything. I wanted all of it and none of it. Every time my mind whirled round like a roulette wheel, slowing, near deciding, the little ball of guilt inside me would skip out of line and toss everything back into disarray.

I knew I'd have to make a decision soon, but when I got home, I didn't feel like I needed to be in any particular hurry. If *they* had wanted me dead, I'd be dead already. So I had time to plan. To think. Hours, at least. Maybe a day or two. Almost too much time.

I did what I'd done back in DC when he'd left me alone: I cleaned. Probably on a subconscious level because he would have, though he would have used fire and I didn't want to disturb the neighbors. My head swam, like there was ammonia in the bleach, but it was nothing so lethal. And maybe it was an hour, maybe a day, but ultimately there was nothing left to clean but myself. I angrily kicked my jeans into a ball, stripped down, and plunged into the shower so hard I cracked my shin on the soap dish. I turned the water on and stood there naked under the cold, numbing my skin to a shiver until finally the hot caught up and burned it all away. Guilt, rage, sadness, despair, all dripped off and bled down the drain. Sorry for myself, I knew.

Tears are for the survivors, not the victims.

When the water went cold again, when the wrinkles on my hands felt as if they'd drop right off, when I had run out of tears, I finally gave up and collapsed in the tub, turning the water off. Sat there listening to the shower head drip, to the squeal of my bare feet against the pockmarked tub, listened to the water heater banging on the pipes because it was empty, and alone, and it had nothing to do but start all over again like me.

It was almost time to fly.

• • •

The last time he'd mentioned flying, we were at some rinky-dink pumpkin patch I'd dragged him to, an hour north of Seattle and halfway to nowhere. Halloween eve, two weeks before the club. Most of the pumpkins were gone. Most of the few that remained were rotted out, green and black, as if smashing themselves preemptively. But it meant there were fewer people about and that meant we could maybe try for normalcy, which I was still convinced was an option.

"Flock theory," he said, pointing at the blackbirds, wheeling about madly in the air over the corn maze, black and black and then a whisper of red like blood.

"A flock?" I asked. "I thought it was a murder."

"Murder of crows," he said. "Flock of blackbirds."

"Murmuration of starlings," I said. "Unkindness of ravens."

He looked at me strangely.

"Animal Planet," I said.

We watched the birds for a while longer while I played with my cell, one of those brief windows when he allowed me a device manufactured in the current decade.

"Birds in the air, herring in a current, whatever," he said, right back onto his earlier train of thought. "Each member of the group knows where to go, how to react, all based on countless small independent decisions. Instinct. Any one of them might make a subtle change that affects the rest. No way to tell who is leading because no one is leading. Each one has a tiny piece of a tiny piece of a bigger picture that no individual is ever completely aware of."

"Anonymous," I whispered.

"Order in the chaos, all self-organized. You take one out, the flock remains."

"Cloud." I showed him my screen. "Google says it's 'cloud of black-birds.' Like the Internet."

"To destroy the fl— *the cloud,* you have to dig deeper, disrupt the system. Deceive it, throw up plate glass windows and mirrors, lay down poison and plastic, and let them do themselves in. Make things unnatural, unpredictable. Then each individual has to react separately, and it does, and that shatters them. No cohesion, no flock. No cloud." He paused, then added, somewhat randomly, "If the magnetic poles shift, all the birds will die. They will have no idea which way home is."

I thought he was lying. Animal Planet hadn't said anything about that.

"Point is," he said with a pedantic tone, "if they ever come for us, that is how they will do it. Something unexpected. Something we cannot possibly adjust to."

"Maybe they won't come," I said. "Maybe we got away."

"No," he said.

"How do you know?" I asked.

He pointed. The blackbirds continued to loop back and forth on invisible currents, unceasing. Definitely cloudy, I thought.

"How do they know?"

We sat in silence for a moment. It was getting a bit chilly, so I decided to test his theory, and impulsively moved a bit closer to him, resting my head on his shoulder before he could react. That lasted about ten seconds, and then he grew uncomfortable and stood up. A single strand of my hair clung to his jacket like desperation. A small victory.

"We should go," he said. "Before it gets too late." And then he walked to the car, leaving me alone to watch the birds, trying to find a pattern in the pointless current, the sudden reaction to something unseen. Wondering, maybe, if it was already too late. I waited until I heard the door slam before I got up, and then I took my time picking through half-rotten pumpkins, knowing he was watching, irritated with my passive aggression.

That night, I tried carving mine into a frowny-faced Edison, but I screwed it up and did a vampire instead. Same thing, I figured. I tried toasting some seeds but set the smoke alarm off. He didn't carve his at all, just let it rot from the inside out, until we threw them both into the compost bin on Election Day. Like the election itself, it was quite a mess, but I didn't see any way to avoid that. Some things are just messy.

• • •

I was done with memories, by the end of the day. With cleaning, too. I had even dyed my hair, using up the last of his black, since that's something he would have done. All that remained was packing, so I got to it. I thought it would be harder. Our things had never merged, barely touched, my things in my room, his in his, the rest of it just shared nothings we'd picked up along the way to nowhere. Everything I really cared about fit in one small backpack: a few meager books, some clothes, and my laptop. I had plenty of room for more, so I pushed open the door to his room, slowly, as if I expected him to be in there, asleep. More than once I'd crept in there, stood at the foot of the bed, watching him. He liked to think he was a light sleeper, but he never woke up.

There wasn't much. There never had been. I drifted over to his decades-old laptop, which was still on, warm. It was mine now, I supposed. The fan disagreed, buzzing angrily as I sat down and fingered the track pad, gingerly, just enough to light up the screen, bring up the password prompt. Was he inside here, somewhere? As if it mattered. None of us is what we were; we are what we are now. Moving targets.

Reverently, I closed the laptop, unplugged it and wrapped the cord around, strangling it shut before swapping it out for my own. There was no way I could leave it behind, too.

I considered the envelope in the other room. Full of tens and twenties I knew I could never spend. Counterfeit, traceable, something. There was no way they'd let me get away clean. Whoever they were. I thought the more I knew, the more I'd understand, but it was the opposite. The more pieces I added to the picture, the cloudier it got. Full of whys and hows and ifs.

I took the money with me anyway. Just in case.

Then I took some weapons, each wrapped in pieces of his clothing, half of them still containing price tags, never worn. A few other things, some loose change, some random IDs and cards, some pills and extracts and tinctures, needles and vials, medicine things, suicide things, things that were dangerous, anything I wouldn't want the next door kids finding. Dumped it all in my faded pink backpack, slung it on my shoulder, considering the weight. I looked around his room for something more, but there was nothing else to take. It was like he'd never been there, like he'd never been. I half wondered if he had.

Dizzy, I went to the bathroom and splashed my face with cold water, shut my eyes, and counted. On ten, I grabbed my things and walked out the door forever.

I was on autopilot for the next hour. Somehow I got the car loaded and got inside, started it and drove off towards nowhere, numb and unfeeling. For some reason, I migrated south, airport-wards. At first I thought I was trying to escape somehow. As if I stood a chance of that. With no ticket and a bag full of guns and drugs, I'd end up in a small room with a large man wearing a rubber glove. If I was lucky.

Regardless, I found myself taking the SeaTac exit, found myself back in the parking lot of that same fast food restaurant I'd last seen him at. Or at least, the van they'd had him in. I don't know why I did it. Maybe to be close to him, one last time? Or maybe I was just hungry. Regardless, I managed to steal a parking spot near the door, grabbed the backpack just in case some kids decided the car looked ripe for the taking, and went inside before I reconsidered. Rather than feel strange to be alone, I felt comfortable somehow as I took my place in line, scanning the menu. For the first time, I could choose anything I wanted. Anything at all.

I had nearly made up my mind when Delia walked in.

Delia from the diner, the new girl, the oh-so-convenient new arrival, so eager to work long hours overlapping with my own. The helpful ride home, the shoulder to cry on, the confidant. Delia the romantic, always trying to find out more about my relationship, yet so, so vague about her own. The girl who always seemed just a bit too old, a bit too confident, a fact I'd overlooked because I never played at my age either. I had been played, for months.

She queued up two people behind me, didn't seem to notice me for the crowd. No surprise, really. I'd always been in uniform, always worn my hair up, high and tight. That day it was down, loose on my shoulders like a cloak, left to dry after I'd dyed it and trimmed my bangs. Every time she glanced away I snuck a peek and built a story. She had a list along with her money. Her brow was sweaty and she was winded. She looked extremely irritated. If nothing else, that was proof she had been in Edison's presence recently. He must be close.

It was not necessarily logical, but it was intuitive. This is where they'd been the day before, right after they took him. The van wasn't outside that I could see, so she must have walked here. She was one of *them*, and they must be shacked up nearby. A hotel, maybe—I didn't see any through the window, but I swore I'd driven past one to get here, just a block or two away. There were other explanations, but none that fit so easily. All that remained was to act.

Or not.

So maybe Edison was close. So what? Wasn't this my chance to get away, throw away the past, and flee screaming into the future? Wasn't it a chance to get out of the cage? A chance to decide what I wanted to do on my own, for myself and no one else? To fly free and clear?

But then I considered the rest of the story, the bits that Delia couldn't tell me. Chances were probably very good that they were doing to Edison what Nick and crew had done to me back in San Francisco. What they would probably still be doing, for all I knew, if Edison hadn't . . .

I hated him, I did. But not all of me hated all of him. There was a spark of empathy, deep down. I could let it die, turn to cold ashes. Or I could blow on it and make it flare up again.

The crowd parted. The space before me cleared. The boy behind the counter faked a smile, waving me forward. And suddenly everything was crystal clear, and I stopped worrying about decisions yet to come. I stopped thinking and started acting, went where the current wanted to take me. It didn't need to make sense because there was nothing to decide.

It had already been decided.

"Can I take your order, ma'am?"

Aww, he called me ma'am. How quaint.

"Yes, thank you . . . Matthew. How are you today?"

He seemed a bit taken aback, maybe expecting me to be rude. Really though I was just stalling, trying to piece things together. What exactly was I hoping to do?

"I'm fine. Can I . . . What can I get you?"

"I . . . I have a special request, Matthew. By the way, I'm E— Christian."

I unslung the backpack from my shoulder, reached between nested drugs and guns and underwear, and pulled out the envelope. I placed it on the counter in front of us and fished a twenty from inside to pay with.

"Matthew," I said, speaking low but fast. "I'm going to say this once, and you'll have one chance to say yes. Got it?"

I smiled and winked and everything was fine. He nodded. I opened the envelope a bit, just enough for him to peek, not so much that the people in line behind me could see. Camera? Maybe, but that wouldn't matter.

"This is a thousand dollars and it's yours, if you do me a favor. I want to . . . prank someone. You won't get in trouble, and you'll be a thousand richer. No taxes, no questions. Yes or no?"

"Is this going on YouTube?"

"Let's say yes. Are you in or out?"

He hesitated. I could tell he needed the cash. Or maybe just wanted to be a celebrity. I pulled the envelope back a bit, and he put his hand on top. I let go, and the envelope disappeared into his back pocket, so smoothly I would have sworn he'd done it before. The whole time I was talking, smiling for the cameras. Just a nice girl flirting with the boy behind the counter.

"Good. Now listen. There's a woman in line behind me, two back. No matter what she orders, I want you to give her my order instead. She gets in another line, you make sure she gets my order. If she doesn't, I will tell your manager you stole the money. Is that clear?"

He looked as if it was not but he nodded, and I placed the order. He punched it in and went back to his script: "Will there be anything else today?"

Was this cruelty or compassion? Maybe both? Or just instinct? I had no idea.

"A small vanilla cone. Just for me."

Matthew nodded, rang it up and gave me the total. The twenty covered the bill and then some, so he fed me a bunch of change. I scooped the lot of it into the backpack, zipped it up and reslung it, pulling the strap tight. Just in case. Then he headed over to make my cone, looked back from the soft serve machine.

"Nuts?" he asked. I smiled.

"Yes, Matthew," I said. "Prolly."

There was no way this was going to work. Whatever this was.

• • •

I ate my cone while I waited, and it was nearly gone when Delia at last came out the door, bag in hand. She darted across 99, not even bothering to wait for the light, which was good because she was focused on dodging cars and didn't see me at all as I strolled to the curb, pressed the button, and patiently waited for the little white man to tell me it was safe to cross. From afar, I watched her walk down the street, then turn into a motel parking lot. So close, this whole time.

Traffic slowed and stopped. Someone ran the light, proving the little white walking man wrong, and the traffic camera flashed, reminding me that someone had this all on tape. Everything is recorded somewhere, Edison used to say. The trick is not to avoid being seen, the trick is to avoid being remembered. But despite his warning, I couldn't imagine anyone was watching as I darted across the street, hair blown wildly behind me. As

I reached the other side, I took an elastic from my wrist and tied my hair into a tail. Reconsidered. Wrapped it in a bun, high and tight and out of the way, like it was when I was at work.

Because, I realized, I was.

Heart pounding, I turned into the motel lot like I belonged there, all the while scanning the balconies. There. Second floor, room 212, Delia beside a guy with a newspaper who was leaning against the rail, casual as anything. Instinct told me she was going to turn, was going to see me and ruin everything all to hell, so without thinking I drifted right into the lobby.

The bell rang overhead, and the manager smiled at me even though he was helping someone else at the time. It was like the circus had come to town and handed out chocolate-covered kittens. He wasn't in a particular hurry, which was good, because I needed to take my time with this. Figure out a plan. So I stood there patiently, alternately watching him and peeking up at Delia, until it was my turn. Delia disappeared from view just as he waved me over.

"Hi, I need a room," I said. "Do you have anything upstairs? I'd feel safer."

He nodded and checked his records as I scanned for cameras. There was only one in the lobby, moving slowly back and forth. I caught the rhythm and timed my movements to make sure my face was turned away. Probably failing, but I felt clever.

"202," he said, turning around to grab the key.

"Is 210 available?" I asked, fiddling with my shoe, twisting my sock around the right way. Not time yet. Draw it out. "It's closer to the stairs."

He shrugged and turned back to the screen, typed some more. I took the opportunity to kneel down, take my gun out of the backpack, and stow it in my jeans. When I came back up he was looking at me, but I didn't think he noticed what I'd grabbed. I hoped he didn't, for his sake.

"Sorry, it's booked. Best I can do is 216. Bit further, but I can help you if—"

"That'll be fine. Thanks."

I handed over one of Edison's cards, now glad I'd bothered to take them.

"Michael?" he asked. "Odd name for a girl."

"Yeah," I said, showing him the matching ID. "My father wanted a boy."

• • •

When I came out of the office, the door to room 212 was unguarded. I was too far away to hear anything, but I imagined it would take some significant chaos to make them slip up like that. Which was, in the end, what I'd been hoping for. I skipped every other step on the way up and reached behind into my waistband for my EMP, still not really understanding exactly what it was I hoped to accomplish here. But before I could pull the gun out, someone emerged from the door, and I spun away and pretended to be very interested in the wall. It was very clearly the same guy who drove the van away from the diner, but somehow with my new wardrobe, newly blackened hair scattered in my face, he failed to sense I was anyone worth attention. Was too preoccupied running down the stairs, maybe to get the van ready for some unexpected occurrence.

I didn't even really have to think about what happened next, just spun around and swept the back of his legs out, sending him tumbling. It was sloppy and stupid, and it stood no chance of doing anything remotely useful, but then it did, and he fell forwards, cracked his head against one of the concrete steps, then tumbled several more down and stopped moving. At least for a moment.

There was no time to linger; as soon as I heard skull hit stone, I had my EMP in hand. The door should have been locked, or at least closed, and it should have been one of those fancy key-card locks, triple-reinforced with the deadbolt thrown and the privacy bar secured, but it was not, it was open, so I just stepped in without thinking and went with the flow. I was in a zone.

If they had been prepared, if chaos had not slowed their reactions, if they had not been just then starting to lift Edison off of the bed, I would have been dead.

But as it stood, Chaos was on my side. And she was in a mood.

Edison was quickly abandoned, but he'd done his part and there was no way they'd be able to get weapons drawn in time. Even before he'd bounced back onto the bed, I was firing, somewhat wildly. More than a few bullets hit the wall, but enough of them hit home to count: two in the chest of one, at least one in the other's leg. I quickly moved around the bed and put another bullet in the head of the larger target, who I recognized then as the guy from the diner who'd paid me off. I already knew the other one was Delia, and I knew now she was dangerous, but since she was busy clutching her bleeding thigh and screaming, I gave her enough time to recognize me back. As her eyes widened, I gave her a smile, then took hers away forever.

I was sure the two of them were dead, at that point, but I still wasn't sure about Edison. I knew what he'd eaten would do bad things to him, I just wasn't sure how fast it would happen. He could have been dead already, although I figured if that were true, they probably wouldn't have been in such a hurry to move him. They'd clearly wanted him alive.

Did I?

I suppose I did. At least, part of me did. That little glowing ember, now brought back to life. Before I realized what I was doing, I'd pulled a yellow EpiPen out of my backpack, bit off the cap and jammed the needle into his left thigh, holding it in place for far longer than the recommended ten seconds. He didn't react. Throwing caution to the wind, I immediately pulled out another, repeating the process in his right leg. Still nothing.

"Come on," I said, ears ringing, head swimming. "Don't tell me I did this for nothing."

Why had I done it, though? I'd hoped he would die, ten minutes earlier.

Whatever, I thought. That was then, this is now.

I was reaching for the last syringe, the Benadryl, when he moaned. Eyes caught mine. Recognition. He looked at me, the pen, me. As you wish. I stuck him again, this time in the arm. He didn't even react, didn't even register the pain at this point, he was so far beyond. Just shut his eyes tight. When they opened, I had the backpack slung and was reaching for him.

"Can you walk?" I asked. Edison shook his head. Either he couldn't talk, or he couldn't hear me—his ears were more sensitive than my own and all he probably heard was his tinnitus, all that gunfire in an enclosed space—so I just tugged on his arm to get him to stand. I had just gotten him leaning on my shoulder when he suddenly spun and fell, taking us both to the floor as the guy I'd dumped down the stairs appeared in the door and fired, missing us both. Crushed beneath Edison, I watched heavy boots cross the floor, the guy evidently reluctant to shoot through the bed, perhaps for fear of hitting Edison. He stumbled sideways, too focused on holding his bleeding, broken face to avoid Delia's body, and it was then that I got him twice, in the belly and in his leg, and he went down hard, gun forgotten. Maybe realizing he was already dead, he looked straight at me, black-and-blue stare following the barrel of my gun, down my arm, past my shoulder, into my cold, pitiless eyes. Nick's eyes.

I gave him my last round. Least I could do.

Somehow we made it down the back stairs and out to the parking lot before the police and/or ambulance arrived out front. And they would be arriving soon—someone had pulled a fire alarm at some point during the mayhem. No doubt there was a trail of bloody prints to follow us by, but I didn't stop to look back, lest one of us turn to salt and crumble away, just focused on finding the van, figuring they wouldn't have had time to change vehicles yet. And they hadn't—the van was parked right next to the street, angled for a quick getaway.

It only took a minute to limp across the lot with Edison on my shoulder, but it felt like the longest minute of my life, perhaps second only to the agonizing amount of time it took to lean him against the side of the van while I slid the side door open. It was all he could do to collapse in the back, limbs twisted in ways that were obviously wrong. I didn't have time to dwell on his injuries, though, just shoved his legs inside along with the backpack and then slid the door shut.

Only when I was in the driver's seat, with the van running, did I think to set my gun down, idly wondering if anyone in the motel or the adjacent buildings had noticed any of this. Any kids. I tried to feel bad but came up empty. If nothing else, maybe someone would have an actually interesting story to post on their Facebook wall, for once. Maybe I could be a meme for a day.

We were on the highway and headed north before it occurred to me that it was over. From the moment Delia had walked into the restaurant to right now, it couldn't have been more than thirty minutes. Including commercials. And only now that it was over was I really starting to ask myself what it all meant.

I twisted the mirror around to peer at Edison. Beads of sweat, tears, and more ran down his face, and I could tell he was in serious pain, serious harm. But then, I'd survived an eight-hundred mile trip in a fucking trunk, so he could suck it up a little longer. At least, I thought so.

"Will you die?" I asked. "From the mayo?"

"No," he croaked. "Worst's past." Then, after a moment, he asked, "Why?"

I thought about it for a moment. But the longer I thought, the harder it was going to be to answer. So I just went with what I had.

"I didn't want you to suffer," I said. Not like I had suffered. "I thought it would kill you."

It was probably only half the truth, at best, but somehow, this seemed to comfort him. He settled back and shut his eyes. I bent the mirror back the other way to watch for police, but they did not materialize, so I turned onto 90, and we flew east, ran towards the rest of our lives. We rode in silence for a while, and after a while Edison started snoring, so I thought it was better to just leave him that way, dreaming of commas and fragments and run-ons. Unfinished sentences.

"It'll be okay," I heard myself say. "We'll be okay. Everything will be okay from now on."

But that, like most things that came after, was a lie.

Behind me, Edison slept.

Before me, the night sky yawned.

I never looked back.

Riptide

07/04/2017

It has taken me six months to recover. Though that word is inaccurate at best, because there has not been and will not be a total recovery from this, not without hospitalization. But it is too late for that now. I am entirely broken, here and hereafter.

Despite clipped wings we have flown far. Settling here, there, a week, a month, never longer. Just enough to find money and medicine, steal or buy or barter. But I am running out of repaid favors, had already nearly run out in Seattle, and I need to save what very little remains for when there are no options. And as for Xtian, she is now one of the few I have ever owed. I have already asked too much, and she has given freely: fed me, bathed me, cleaned me while both arms were still in painful slings. She has seen all of me. I suppose that makes us even.

This is the first I have written since things went wrong, the first my arms do not ache me to tears when I try to type. I could dull the pain, but there has been pain before and there will be more to come and this is nothing more than one pain among many. What pains me most of all is how much has happened in the past year that I was not a part of, things I have experienced only vicariously through the television: Baghdad, Orlando, Dallas, Atlanta. But strangely, I have no desire to comment on those things. Xtian's foolish online friends can take care of speculating, for all the good it will do them. I have more immediate concerns. More personal.

It is warm in Columbus, nearly too, but I do not dislike it as much as other places, mostly because I do not know it enough yet to do so. I sit here writing on the front porch, and it feels always just on the edge of being safe, a restful sleep I can never quite fall into. All around, fireworks pop and sizzle, and I find myself flinching, looking over my shoulder. Surprises. The unknown. That is what surrounds me now. I only know that I can trust Xtian. At least for now.

She is working in another restaurant, stagnating herself, though now she dresses better and the food is not fast. She waits on others, like she does on me, and I hate that she does it for them, and especially for me. Perhaps what she does comes naturally for her. Serving, feeding, cleaning when necessary, doting in exchange for . . . what? Tips, from them. And from me? What does she get from me? What did she ever? I have asked.

"I need you," she always says. "And now you need me."

And though this is perhaps true, it seems to me that need is a horrid foundation, one that must necessarily crumble and fail. Need is taking, and one can only take until the other is empty and gone, and then all that is left is a Giving Stump. Both are empty, and neither can provide. Which is why this country, no matter what course it chooses, is doomed. This world, this society built upon taking, raping each other, the earth, upon cereal commercials and superficiality, musical greeting cards, and twenty-four ounce steaks.

And as if to reassure me that all is lost, my neighbor chooses this moment to wander over and invite himself up onto the porch. One day I shall kill him, but today my shoulder hurts, and again I have heartburn.

• • •

When I arrived home from work that day, sweaty and awful, our neighbor was in the swing, Edison in the lounge leaning forward as he always did, never content to relax. Maybe not able, not even in this perfect disguise, graying and soft and harmless, looking just like the man beside him.

The neighbors had all assumed from the start that Edison was my father, I older than I looked and he younger than he felt. So I came up with a story about a car accident, how my mother was killed and he was left crushed inside and out. Said never to mention it, as he was post-traumatic—which was more true than they probably thought—and they agreed. I don't think he ever knew. He was the only one who never knew what he was to them. Weak and broken.

Work, too, was a lie, though not as big as that one. False ID, a few other fibs where needed, but overall it at least felt honest to be working, and I needed honest things in my life, especially then. When Edison could talk again he asked me what had happened, and I—wrapping his arms in bandages, watching him choke back pain—couldn't quite gather up the courage to tell the truth about how his capture, his torture, was my fault. The lies came freely, and then less freely but more necessarily, until removing one lie and replacing it with truth would have toppled everything. I suspect I learned that lesson not from Edison, but from my parents, long before. What I remember of them is just hazy, unreliable eight-year-old fuzziness, but I'm sure that most of what they said to each other was lies. Small ones and big, purposeful lies and lies of omission. They survived not in spite of but because of their lies.

Even memories are lies, every one; each time you recall something, you're not remembering the thing, you're remembering the last time you remembered. Lie built upon lie. But I know my parents were real, that their lies were real, that I am real, that all of this was real, not because of my memories, but because of my emotions. My feelings. That's how I know things are true. Chemicals don't lie; they only burn, and scar. Quick, and deep and forever.

Of course, these were Xtian thoughts. Dinah, the friendly stock character waitress, bedraggled and dizzy with tip money, did not dwell on such things. So I just waved at Edison and the neighbor, shut the car door and flounced towards the porch, white blouse open a bit too far. Itchy black skirt I longed to peel off. Bare legs, stockings in the glove compartment. Edison hated it. Which is why I did it. One of us needed to be the antagonist in the relationship.

"You're early," he said, biting back further commentary.

I nodded, made sure there was no hidden meaning in what he was saying, no code that said "Run, you fool, they're inside the house." He nodded back, subtly.

"Half-day," I said. "For the Fourth."

"How'd ya do today?" asked Mister Neighbor.

"Hundred," I said, a small lie not far from truth (the best kind, Edison would say for the eighth or the eightieth time). "Not too ugly for a holiday."

There was more small talk, punctuated by the constant crackle of fireworks, but I stopped caring and went on autopilot about the same time Edison rolled his eyes at me. We went on about nothing for a further five minutes or so, and then I said we had to figure out dinner and peeled the neighbor off the porch. Edison waited until he was out of earshot before spewing venom.

"One day," said Edison, "I will inflict upon him such agony."

"He's just being nice," I said. "Not hurting anyone."

"All the more reason for picking up his slack. A hundred?"

I reached down to help him, but he shook me off and lifted himself up, hiding his own hurt. Either he was genuinely getting better, or more likely, getting better at burying the pain.

"We didn't do so bad," I said.

We? Me.

"That's four . . . and twenty, I think, total for the weekend. All of it tax-free."

"When have we ever paid taxes, Xtian?"

"Shhh. They'll hear you."

"With that much we can each have our own chicken pot pie tonight, instead of splitting one. It's the American dream."

I shrugged, and he paused at the door, noting that I had not budged. "You have a better idea?" he asked.

· · ·

We go to the usual place, so I get the usual things, though I will suffer for it later. My stomach is not what it once was, not without many pills. But the rest works, and the food tastes like it should, false and salty and sweet, and it almost makes me forget. Almost. Children scream nonstop in the background, reminding me yet again that the world is a horrid place full of horrid people who deserve to be removed from it so that there is more room for me. And her.

"Tomorrow," I say, "I am coming back here to give them a reason to cry."

"Someone's feeling better," she says. Diet Coke for dinner. Does she ever ingest calories? Not in front of me lately. Perhaps at work, when she can, crumbs on the floor, leftovers. Grass, perhaps. I push some fries towards her, and she ignores them, just vacuums at the empty at the bottom of her cup. It seems I should speak, as if this would be where I put a lesson, but I wonder instead if there is any more to teach, and more importantly if there is any more she will allow herself to learn. I pick at the remnants of my food until she is done chewing her ice.

"Ready?" she asks. We walk three long blocks to the car, too cool giving way to too hot, nothing just right. Then down an alley and two extra turns, just because we are being careful nowadays. When she pulls out of the parking lot, she turns left instead of right, away from the house. Wrong.

"Where are we going?" I ask.

She just smiles. The worst sort of answer.

· · ·

It was a long way to the lake, hours, but we got there before dark, which was lucky for us because the boat deposit had been paid in advance and was nonrefundable. He didn't want to get on at first, but it didn't take much. I promised to keep us out of Pennsylvania waters. Besides, we had nowhere else to be, nothing else to do, and this was better than watching the news spew fear and hate, or driving aimless circles around 270, playing spot the tourist. And this had a purpose.

I lifted the box from the trunk, carried it into the boat, set it down, almost daring him to ask. Nothing. Maybe he knew it was not a fishing rod, which was why he refused to look, just stared across the lake, watched the fireworks redden the waves. I steered towards the gore, turned off the engine and let the current take us where it wanted. There were surprisingly few people on the lake, and we didn't have to worry about running into a drunken boater.

I lifted the top off the case, leaned the barrel on the edge. Now he couldn't ignore it.

"Where did you get that?" he asked. He didn't comment on the fact, but it was a model 700 rifle, almost identical to the one we'd been using out on this very same lake, five years earlier.

"Online," I said. "Don't worry, I was careful."

I expected him to press further, but instead he got straight to the point: "Why are we here?"

"I'm trying to help you," I said. And maybe I believed I was.

"Help me what?"

"Get back what you lost."

"What I lost."

And he looked me right in the eyes, and I was immediately and completely convinced that he knew I had betrayed him. And I would tell him the truth, all of it. And I would leap overboard and play at Ophelia. And I would kill him. And I would kill myself. And I would wither under his gaze and dissolve into nothing. And the stars would fall and angels would cry blood. And.

But the moment passed, and he did not know and would not. It didn't make me feel better. I wanted him to know but I couldn't be the agent. Instead, I pulled the rifle from the box and held it out for him. He still refused to take it, so I loaded it and set it on the seat beside him.

"Go on, shoot. No one will hear it over the fireworks."

"This is not going to accomplish anything," he said. Not angry, more amused. "You think this will fix me? Like butter on a bee sting. A folk remedy, something you can cure like hiccups."

"Ten bald men," I said, unable to help myself as I imagined Edison bald, old. Doddering and senile, a cartoon character.

"You cannot wives' tale this away, Xtian. There is nothing to cure."

"Nothing to cure," I asked, "or nothing curable?"

"Just nothing."

"Come on. It'll make you feel better. When's the last time you killed someone?"

"Ask me again in three seconds," he said. I smirked and began counting.

On two, he picked up the rifle, spun it towards my head, and fired.

• • •

The shot is aimed generally landwards, but there is more to miss than hit out there considering the light crowd—although you never know. Of course the only purpose here is to not hit her. It was not so long ago that I did quite the opposite, intentionally put her in harm's way and thought her dead, after she was tested and found wanting. That time, it ended with the gun to my head, her victorious after failure. This echo of events seems appropriate, somehow.

"You were right," I say. "That did help."

I hold the gun out to her, giving her a turn. She ignores me.

"Take it," I say. "Maybe you'll do better."

This is a poor attempt at dark humor—*go on, see if you can hit me.* But she takes it the wrong way, I think, assumes that I am referring to her failure back in Buffalo. And maybe I am.

"Fuck you," she says softly. So I toss the rifle into the lake.

"That was three weeks of tips," she says angrily. The atmosphere seems to change. There has been something brewing for a while, but suddenly things get a little darker and stormier.

"Get a better job then," I say. "What you do is slavery. You may as well pick cotton."

"While the master sits on the porch, drinks lemonade and reaps the benefits."

"I did not ask for this. And I do not think you want it, either."

The fireworks are all but over, leaving naught but stars and shadows against the night sky, and she could be anyone, and I anyone to her. But I know this is not true. We could not be anyone but what we are, could not be anywhere but here. This is as sure as gravity, as sure as a train wreck and just as messy. It will get messier still, before it is over. And it will be over, eventually. That much has been certain since the moment I picked her up nine years smaller. It was the goal, in fact. She is old enough now to ask the right questions. And answer them.

She turns and looks at me—I can feel her eyes burn in the darkness—and something ends as she does so. Something releases. And I feel suddenly that we have been rising all this time and now we have crested the hill and are falling. This is where *becoming* becomes *became*, where potential becomes kinetic. This is where guts churn and stomachs turn inside out. But I feel strangely calm. Because though we both know something is coming, only I am sure of how it will end. This is a bullet in a gun, and it wants to come out, hit or miss.

I wonder if either one of us will survive.

● ● ●

I watched him watch me for a long time, wondering what he wondered. It seemed like something needed saying, but I wasn't sure what that was at the time.

What're you thinking?

Hell no. I didn't care what he thought, just then. I wondered, rather, if he knew how I felt about him. Really felt. Love, hate, all of it. Especially love though. The Greeks had four words for love, and I had no idea which one fit, but it was there: real, chemical, inevitable. You spend enough time with someone and your molecules blend. You become part of each other. It seemed like it should be obvious, though it maybe wasn't, or at least would not be to most people. Would he be surprised? Probably not. To him it would have been inevitable and impossible, both at once. And he would have laughed at my words and ruined my soul.

The thought made me consider the truth again. Not because I wanted to come clean, to beg forgiveness and reconcile. I wanted to wield the truth like a knife, to tear him apart and hurt him like he'd hurt me. But what stopped me from doing that was the thought, dim but persistent, that this was what he wanted, to see me dirty, to show me how horrid I had become. As bad as him. Maybe worse than him.

Yes, he wanted me to say something, anything. Wanted it so badly I could see it on him like a scab, waiting to be picked off. Like a blister aching for a pin. He wanted a lunge so he could riposte. And so I said nothing, did nothing. I just slid over to the wheel of the boat, started the motor, and took us back in. We rode in silence the entire way. At the time, I thought it was victory. Now I'm not so sure it wasn't cowardice instead.

The shore loomed ahead like the edge of the world. It felt like the future was shrinking, like there was not much time left. For something. For anything. But all there was, then, was not yet. Not yet.

It was well after midnight when we got to shore, the entire boat ride back in silence. Silence would keep on filling us up for some time, to over-flowing. It followed us to the car, broken only by the doors slamming in tandem, the purr of the motor, the chatter of the radio. And then, despite the noise, our personal silence accompanied us home.

Nesting Instinct

05/28/2018

The next year or so in Columbus was uncomfortable. Not much changed on the surface: I went to work and made money while Edison stayed home, watched TV, and—when he was up for it—wandered aimlessly, as far north as the Ohio State campus and as far south as downtown. We walked together, sometimes, but mostly he did it by himself while I was at work. Or claimed to.

It all seemed curiously normal, which I thought was probably driving him crazy. Crazier, rather. After all, it had been well over a year since Seattle, and all he'd done was stew and feel old and older. He said he had nothing to do, so I told him to write, so he said he had nothing to write about, no one to rant about. Except me, I supposed. He needed a change of scenery. We both did.

The zoo seemed a good enough idea. I was shocked we hadn't been there yet—it was one of those things you forget to do when you live somewhere. I thought it would be good for us both, to see something else in a cage. There was a risk that he'd flip out and start massacring whiny children by the penguin exhibit, but I was willing to take that chance. It might be entertaining, if only to find out how discerning penguins were about what they ate.

It was hot as hell when we arrived, and it still took five minutes to coax him out of the car.

"It's a million degrees out," I said. "I'll be arrested for animal cruelty."

"Crack a window," he grumbled.

"Can we just please pretend to be a couple of average, normal socio-paths today?"

"We need to pretend?"

"'Zactly."

I climbed out and waited. Two minutes later, he finally got out, too. Global warming one, Edison North zero. He squinted in the sunlight as he gazed around the parking lot. Needed glasses, or surgery, refused both. Which was fine. We could afford neither.

"This is that big room with the blue ceiling I've been telling you about." I pointed skywards, imagining the cold up there. Outer space was closer than Cleveland.

There were a lot of cars, and I hoped for everyone's sake that most of them were there for the water park, because neither of us wanted to deal with an overcrowded zoo. For a moment I imagined Edison in swim trunks, flailing about as he flew down a waterslide. It was impossible to envision without also giving him an imaginary shotgun.

"How will we find the car?" He had a point there; we always drove vehicles that looked as ordinary as possible. There were probably dozens of vehicles of identical make, model, year, and color in the lot. One of them probably shared our license plate, knowing Edison.

"We're parked next to the van full of enriched uranium," I said.

He turned and peered through the window, as if to prove my accusation. "Language tapes . . . a big red bundle of dynamite that says 'BOMB' on the side . . . a seven page letter from the leader of ISIS . . ."

"They still a thing?" I asked. I had been avoiding the news, mostly for his sake. Every time I brought it up he got a look on his face like he was missing out.

"Who knows? Every time you see something on the morning news about a van full of evidence, you can pretty much assume it was invented.

And by that evening they will have found a badly manipulated image of two Arabic guys in turbans planting dynamite in a puppy factory. Pay no attention to the man behind the curtain."

"Are you going to rant, or can we go in and get something to drink?" I wiped my face.

"Why choose?" he replied.

• • •

We are in line for half an hour and I want to murder her, them, myself, not necessarily in that order. Whose idea was it to come on Memorial Day weekend? We are not even inside the actual zoo and already amongst animals—tweens and teens and millennials and . . . I do not even care to discern. They are just one solid mass of foul. The way they move and sound and smell. This is the future. This is what is to come. I did not murder nearly enough when I had the chance.

I instinctively back away, though not so far back as to lose our place in line.

"Xtian, apologize for your generation, please."

"*You* broke us."

"Not enough."

My skin crawls and itches, old scars slipping back into awareness. Why did I agree to this? And which of us, in the end, decided this? I recall thinking this might be worth trying, and I know she believes that this . . . normalcy might work for us and has thought this for a very long time. But how can she not see? This is wrong. For us, for anyone. This cannot work.

She has forgotten what happened, every time things have seemed to settle down. In San Francisco. In Seattle. Perhaps she needs a reminder.

We reach the window. A uniformed nothing person inside the air-conditioned booth watches us drip with sweat, takes her time finishing out the last order. A full minute passes before she deigns to speak with us. Perhaps Xtian senses this, for she steps in front of me and deals with the transaction, lest I end our outing prematurely with violence.

"One adult, one child," she peeps, age-shifting now that it is convenient to be young, rather than aching to be older. If she knew what ache was in store, she would do this more. Though I do not approve of the clothing, the too-short skirt and the too-tight top with "Peaches" on the front and "Cream" behind. If nothing else, if nothing more, she looks like her peers, and once again I feel a growing desire to kill that part of society away.

She looks back to me, as if seeking approval, and I fake a smile. Yes, honey, you go ahead and order the tickets. The clerk is convinced, or more likely does not really care, does not get paid enough. We get our tickets and step through the gates. *Lasciate agni*, et cetera.

"What first?" she asks, unfolding a map of the zoo, which suddenly looks more immense than my legs were prepared for. I choose something nearby, and enclosed, quite at random.

"Ooh, ice cream."

Before I can argue, she snatches the map away and skips off. I follow but only because that way lie fewer child beasts.

• • •

Edison got some sort of rainbow-colored theoretically eggless concoction that looked like what you scrape out of the freezer when you're defrosting it. I got something called Blueberry Sunrise, which turned out to basically be blue corn syrup.

Had I ever tasted real blueberries?

"I could get a job here," I said. "We could come to the zoo for free every weekend, and I could get discount ice cream-like product. Megyn said they're hiring."

"What is it with you and serving people?"

"Do what you know." I shrugged. "This is what I know."

"You know a great deal more than this. Working for tips is—"

"Not working? Yeah, my tips paid for this ice cream . . . replica. And our tickets. And gas."

"And now you are penniless and have to beg for more tips. Welcome to the machine."

"Yeah, having money is bad," I said, voice dripping with sarcasm.

"Money is not the evil," he said. "Society is. I thought you had learned that by now."

"Look at us and our first world problems. Our apartment only has four walls. We only have three laptops. I'm so depressed, I don't know how I'm going to live another day without slicing my wrists open with a box cutter. And I don't even own a box cutter. What ever will I do?"

"You can get a box of fifty at Home Depot. Here, my treat."

He reached towards the back pocket of his jeans, and I smirked, imagining for a moment he was going for one of those old people change purses, stuffed with silver dollars. I immediately felt guilty for the thought.

"Fifty seems redundant. You only need six to take down an airplane."

"Not even," he said.

"Oh? What's it take?"

"I will show you someday."

"Promises."

• • •

The zoo has one section for each continent on earth, and walking around between them is about as tiring as walking to each of the actual in turn. We make it through North America and halfway through Asia before, wheezing, I find my knees are about to give and my head hurts. Most of what is wrong with me only starts hurting if I exert myself doing something stupid, and this?

This is stupid.

"Come on," she says. "Elephants."

I do not want to see elephants unless they are being electrocuted. I am in bitter pain, with worse coming if I am not careful. The back of her neck is already sunburned and I fear for my own. I sit heavily on a bench fortuitously located beneath a particularly shady tree. A fountain nearby sprays cool, tainted water into my face, and I welcome it. Eventually she comes over and sits down next to me, concerned or feigning it.

"You 'kay?" she asks.

"Yes," I say. "Go, explore. I will wait here and suffer alone."

"No, I'll sit with you. I need a rest, too."

"I do not need your pity."

"I'll pity you," she says. "I'm gonna pity you so hard."

When I do not react, she sighs and gets serious.

"I just want to help you. You helped me, so why won't you—"

I try to laugh, but it comes out hoarse and broken. When I stop coughing, I spit out, "How have I helped you?"

She has no ready answer.

"Let me get you something to drink," she says and runs off to fetch.

This should have ended. I should end this.

I look around, and see no one else alone, save for desperate zoo staff sweeping up peanutty detritus from the sticky ground. Alone in the crowd.

I could leave, I realize.

I could run. Well, walk quickly, at least. For a short distance. I would not get far, but far enough to hide until she left. And then I could be alone again. That would be safer, for both of us. She could be happy waitressing and I could . . . do something else.

But what would I do? And since when have I ever made a decision based on how safe it was? When have I ever run from something that meant me no harm?

Before I can come to any conclusions, she returns with a neon orange cup, carrot-shaped with eyes. "Stay Healthy," it says on the side, mocking me. "Get Five Servings a Day!" If they mean the Diet Coke inside, I do.

"No straws?" I ask, sipping from the side.

"I know. I'm disappointed, too. I wanted to feed them to the monkeys."

We sit for a while, me drinking. She says nothing else, suddenly distant. Has no doubt done some thinking while gone. But I am done thinking for the day.

"Come on," I say, standing, with some great amount of pain. "I want to go home."

Home. The word tastes wrong on my palate. Sour and salty. Unhealthy. Stale baking soda smell. Home is no longer where my fridge is kept, where I am alone. The fridge we have is hers, bought with her money. Home is now the opposite of alone. Home pins you down with an illusion of security and comfort, an iron maiden with a security deposit. Is that what she wants? What she thinks I want?

The point is moot, as the car breaks down three miles from the zoo.

For the moment, no one is going anywhere, least of all home.

• • •

"Sorry," I said as the car rolled to a stop. "I didn't do it."

"And yet you apologize," he said.

He popped the hood, and we looked inside. It was beyond our capacity to repair at that point, if at all. It appeared to need several quarts of everything.

"Bus? Uber?" I pulled out my cell phone but he shook his head.

"I know this sounds strange, but I really do not feel like killing anyone just now."

We looked around for options. That left a divey motel that reminded me of where Edison had been held, and a nicer place with a restaurant attached. Fine dining? Not quite, but still somehow appropriate. Too much so, maybe.

• • •

I order an adequate if pricey burger, while she ingests some sort of pale-yellow vegan monstrosity. She also drinks, perhaps to see if I will stop her. Why would I? In Ohio, at eighteen she can legally drink in the company of a father or guardian, and I am close enough as far as the wait staff is concerned. So she drinks. And by the time we are done eating she is in no condition to walk very far, and I am out of patience. She has not had much, just some sort of bright red alco-pop, but she is a lightweight in every sense of the word. A tolerance for alcohol is something you must build up and then maintain. Much like murder—it has been years since I have committed one. I have lost the taste of blood.

I make the decision to check us in, even though it is a bit expensive. The girl behind the hotel desk does not even raise an eyebrow; I suspect I am not the first middle-aged man to check in with a young girl. I find this more disturbing than anything so far today.

Of course, once we get to our room, the air-conditioning is not doing its job, but at this point if I have to go back down to the lobby there is going to be blood, so I drop Xtian on the bed, dive into a cold shower, and come out searching for my heartburn medication, staving off an ulcer for one more night. I am ready for a fitful, painful sleep.

The room is stifling and hot, and she is sitting on the opposite side of the bed facing the futon, which is where I intend to sleep. It is only when I pass by her that I notice she is wearing nothing but her shirt and left sock, the mate just hitting the floor as the cushions welcome me with a squeak. This in itself would not concern me. It should, but it would not. No, what makes it different is her smile. It is like something Cheshire as she rolls her head, stretching her neck. Unfolding. Eat me, drink me. Thirty minutes ago I was her father. Now I am anything but. Or perhaps I still am. Which is even worse.

As much as I feared this would happen some day, I never let myself think about it long enough to prepare a response. I should run. Always run. But I do not.

"No, Xtian."

"Why not?" she asks, standing.

"You're too . . . you're not—"

"I'm old enough," she says. "I can be the first legal thing you've ever done."

She walks slowly forward, every movement seemingly exaggerated for my benefit. Tense, a band ready to snap. I recoil.

"No."

She frowns, moves past me to the curtains as if it was her plan all along, drawing them closed before (futilely) turning the air-conditioning up, which accomplishes nothing except making the fan louder. Close enough for me to smell her sweat, reeking beneath fading deodorant. Literally repulsive. And then she turns off the light and moves back to the bed. Each time, as she passes, I find myself drawing away, into myself, avoiding even the slightest contact, for fear it will trigger something destructive. Something final.

And at last she sits back down on the bed, and though it is dark and my eyes have not yet adjusted, I can see her skew her head and look at me like a cat watches a bird.

"It's like you're afraid to touch me," she says.

"I am," I reply. A minute passes, then she stands and walks toward me again, hands out.

"No."

"Just stand up."

She grabs my hands and pulls me up, and then she wraps her arms around me. I close my eyes and let her, my own arms hovering slightly above her shoulders, unsure what to do with them. I was a child the last time someone hugged me, half her current age, a bit older than she was when I took her. At least a minute passes. Possibly forever. But eventually, I take her shoulders and push the hug away, push her back to the bed and turn away.

"Do you love me?" she asks.

I don't respond.

She sits heavily on the bed and removes her shirt, which she tosses in my direction. It lands on the air-conditioning vent, which does not make much difference one way or the other.

The bed squeaks. I screw my eyes shut and pretend to stare out the window through the crack in the curtains. Nothing moves, not even the air. I feel as if I'm suffocating.

"Hey," she says.

No.

"No," I say.

"You don't like me?" she asks.

"I don't like *this* you," I reply.

A sock hits me in the back of the head, drapes itself over my shoulder. I shake it loose like an insect, a serpent. A disease.

"It can't be worse than my last time," she says. "Funny. Last time was the first time, too."

I want her to shut up. I do not want to envision what might have happened to her, or for her to remember what actually did. But she keeps going. I block it out, take myself somewhere else for a while. I only turn from the window and face her once she is quiet again. She is lying on the bed, head hanging loose from the side as she stares at me upside-down. My eyes have adjusted, and I can see what I already knew. This is not the first time I have seen her naked, but it is the first I have seen her nude. Exposed.

"Come here," she says.

"No." It feels wrong to be even this close. Unhealthy.

"Why don't you love me?"

I don't answer. Not the first time, nor the third. Eventually she stops talking and starts breathing more or less rhythmically, and I move to the futon and collapse.

It is not a matter of "don't." It is a matter of "can't."

I do not sleep.

● ● ●

I woke up what I guessed was quite a few hours later with a terrible headache and a crick in my neck, the sun in my eyes and the sheet draped over my body. He had moved to the couch and sat there judging me. Crumpled fast food bag on the floor, smell of bacon and hash browns. He'd gone for breakfast, hadn't bothered to get any for me.

The TV was on, muted. Cat food commercial.

"Do I need to say sorry?" I asked.

"If you don't remember," he said after a tense moment, "then I suppose not."

I rolled over to ease the pain in my neck, awkwardly twisting myself in the sheets to the point where it became uncomfortable. In the end I just kicked them loose into a ball and curled up, arms around my legs, goose bumps up and down my arms despite the growing heat. I wondered exactly what I'd said. I supposed the lies were still safe or else I'd probably be dead, or he gone, or both. Which meant—

"No," he said as I jerked my head around, question on my lips.

After a moment, he added, "But not for your lack of trying."

"Well, shit."

I got dressed in silence as he stared out the window, at the window. At anything that wasn't me.

"Well, I suppose it can't get worse than this," I said, dropping onto the bed to pull on shoes.

"It can always get worse."

I thought about that for a second. And decided he was right. I had been through much worse.

Only when I was fully dressed again would he look at me, staring in silence. Not judging, just evaluating. Or re-evaluating. It was, in many ways, the closest we'd ever been, and I think somehow, right then and there, we finally knew where we stood: on opposite sides of a canyon, tethered by a length of rope. We were connected, yes, but we could never be closer than we were at that moment. Not unless one of us jumped and dragged the other one down with them.

After that, we were both ready to be gone.

"I wish I could be like you," I said as we walked down the long hall in dense, carpeted silence. To fill a sudden, obscene absence of words. "You like being alone. I don't. I need you. I need to take care of you and be taken care of. I need to matter."

"You need to matter to yourself."

"How?" I asked.

He thought about that for a few moments. It was only after we reached the elevator two right turns later that he answered. As the elevator opened, he got inside, turned around, and put a hand out to stop me. And as the doors closed in my face, he said one word.

"Practice."

He was gone by the time I got downstairs.

I found my own way home.

String Theory

08/15/2018

Summer flew past before I knew it. We talked, we fought. I baked cakes. He tried to teach me things; I tried to ignore him. He spent a lot of time like a slug on the couch, and I spent a lot of time at work and made some money and got a raise. I went out. I had fun, such as it was. I suppose I "practiced." It all felt hollow, a dress rehearsal for a canceled show. But I did it anyway, learned the lines, and became one with the part. We got good at pretending things were okay.

It seems impossible to think that two people could coexist under such circumstances for that long, much less their entire lives. But I guess it's really easy to bury the bad stuff for the sake of convenience. It builds up and gets compressed. And then it's just a matter of waiting for a trigger.

That day, the trigger came innocently enough, shortly after my shift started.

"Someone here," said my manager. "Says he wants you."

"Old?" This was how I described Edison. It was how he looked lately. That and defeated. Although I got the impression that maybe he was putting on a bit, in both respects.

"No. One of *them*."

For just a moment my stomach flipped. Somewhere inside I conjured up an image of the diner in Seattle, the hotel incident, but of course it couldn't be any of them. I'd seen them dead and then some. And then I remembered that my boss was simply a racist bastard. It was hard to comprehend being like that. I'm color-blind as long as green's involved. A tip's a tip.

"Keep it short," he said. "And where is your—"

I ignored the rest, put him behind a swinging door, and strolled out like he was nothing. Because he was. I winked at the busboy and popped on over to table six by way of three, then slid into the booth opposite my new customer while he still had his face buried in the menu. Before I said a word, I grabbed a purple crayon from the tray and started etching my name into the paper tablecloth, writing upside-down like they made us learn.

"Hello there. My name is Dinah, and I'll be—"

Abe.

My gun was in a little holster at the small of my back; he had one under a napkin on the table. From the look on his face as he lowered the menu, I got the impression he wasn't here for trivia night.

"Hello, Dinah. What are your specials today?"

"Chicken parmesan," I mumbled.

"That's it?"

"Sorry. We're not very special today."

"Oh," he said. "But you are."

• • •

"Fights are never won defensively," I say. "You win by attacking. And there is always a weak point. Everything has a vulnerability. A soft spot."

"Like a baby head."

I glare at her, but that has no effect any more. Especially not when she is getting dressed for work. For some reason this involves every room of the house at once. I do my best to track her with my voice and not my eyes as she rushes between rooms, snagging her work blouse from the couch, already pulling a T-shirt off. I would call this a game that I refuse to play but it is past a game; at this point it is just a lonely chess set in the living room, abandoned halfway through at a convenient, difficult check point. I wonder who is black and who red. I wonder who is winning.

"There is always a thread to pull, however slender," I say. "You follow that thread, you pull the string, the puppet moves; you yank the thread, the cloak unravels, and there you will find your weak point, the staple holding the string. You find that, you yank it."

"I'll yank your string," she says, "if you ask nicely."

"I sense you are not interested in discussion right now."

"Discussion?" She walks into the kitchen brushing her teeth, spits a mouthful of toothpaste into the sink. "This is a monologue. You just want me to nod my head and smile."

"Smiling is optional."

"Good," she says, "I can save two minutes a day by not brushing."

For a moment I watch her collect the things she always takes with her: her apron full of work, her phone, one of her guns (the P3AT, it looks like), and I think how I can barely hold any of those things now without pain. I sigh and stare at my bent hands on the table, tree roots struggling to find purchase in sand. Other things are healed, but my hands will never be right again. Age, damage, soft things and hard. Bones and nerves, tendons and ligaments.

"You pull the string," I say, collecting my thoughts, "and sometimes it goes from there, like a ripcord. Pull, result. Action, reaction. But sometimes the string is long and tangled."

"You now have ten seconds remaining," she says, wandering back in with her blouse thankfully buttoned now. She plops herself on the floor to pull on shoes.

"Sometimes you pull, and you get more than you expected. The sweater unravels, but it turns out to be woven into something bigger, longer. Something connected. Everythi—"

"Time's up," she says, dancing to her feet to grab some yogurt from the fridge. Then she is out the door, with not so much as goodbye. She may as well have patted my bald spot on the way out.

"Everything is connected to something else," I say to nothing, no one.

I stew for a few moments, then wander into the living room to get angry at the television, watching for signs of *them* at work, listening to the world fall apart almost as fast as me. Sit on something the wrong way, feel a sharp pain and even worse. The local news comes on and gives me ideas. Some foolish, impossible, but some reasonable, for certain definitions of reason. I make mental notes. I look for strings and fontanelles. I weigh options. I squirm and try to find comfort, but the pain will not abate, so I stand, and feel better having done it. I look down and see the cause of my pain is, perhaps not surprisingly, her. Or rather, something of hers, that she should not have left without. I should take it to her, I decide.

I grab my own things from the table: guns, and sharp things. More slowly than she did, minutes ago, proving my point. I need to keep working out, try to undo some of what injury and middle age have wrought. Middle? More likely near the end. If I am lucky. Nature designed us to copulate at fifteen. To die by thirty. And what am I now, nearly twice that?

I was not supposed to live this long. No one is.

• • •

How did Abe find us? Wasn't he dead? No, that was the other guy. What was his name? Josh? What was happening? Too many questions, no answers. I tented my hands, stayed calm. If *they* wanted me dead, I would be dead. Get into character. Put up a front. Gather information.

"Where is he?" asked Abe, confirming my suspicion. Not me at all, then.

"Home. Listen, Abe, I'd love to catch up, but let me lay this on the line: my manager is a white supremacist prick with a triple K. If he catches me sitting here yammering he's gonna come over. And if he does that, then one of us is going to kill him, and odds are it'll be me. So for now let's pretend like you're a customer and I'm a waitress named Dinah."

He chewed on that for a moment, and I thought I might die. But no.

"Fine," he said. "But first put it on the table."

Damn it. I reached back, grabbed my gun, and slid it across behind the menu.

"Not what I meant, but thanks. Now give me your phone." I slid it over, and he picked it up in both hands, leaving the menu to hide the weapons.

"He won't answer."

"Yes, he will," he said. "Go get me a beer."

I smiled like they taught us on day one, pulled out my pad, and scribbled down an order. Maybe I could kill him with the pen. Yeah, sure.

"How about some artichoke dip?"

"Don't push your luck," he said, idly sifting through my phone. It wouldn't take long. There was only one number under recent calls. "And don't fuck around. Stay in the room."

"Yes sir, right away, sir." On my way to the bar, I scanned the room as casually as I could, trying to find them. He wouldn't have come alone. One by the door, maybe. One at the bar. Probably one in the bathroom, one by the back door. Enough to matter. Still, I played it out like a champ, every fake smile and smooth move crisp as I stepped behind the bar, tore the top sheet off my notepad and slapped it down on the counter, making damn sure Samuel saw it.

"I require a pint of your finest bitter, my good man," I said. "And a Vanilla Coke."

Read it. Read the fucking slip, Sam. But no, instead he reached for a pint glass—he didn't need to read the order. We only had the one on tap. Change of plans. I pushed past him and grabbed another glass, hot from the dishwasher. Too hot, almost. I dropped it straight into my apron, juggling it around between nervous hands. Heart thumping faster, fingers itching.

"What are you doing?" he said.

"I'll get the beer. You do the Coke. I don't know where the vanilla stuff is." And read the goddamn fucking slip of paper, you idiot. I looked over to see if Abe was watching. No. He was too busy with my cell. I could totally spit in his beer if I wanted.

Fuck you, Abe, see how you like this.

"What's wrong with you?" Sam asked, moving off to concoct my potion while I topped off the beer. "You're acting weird."

"Your face is weird," I said, too preoccupied for anything more clever.

By the time Sam returned with my Coke, I was already gone with the beer, dancing between tables, leaving him to puzzle out the meaning of the abandoned beverage and the slip of paper that he needed to read. I presented the glass to Abe with a flourish and quickly sat down, watching bubbles dance down the side of the glass as I whipped out my pad and pen, *tap tap tap.*

"No, I didn't spit in it," I said, trying to push, keep him off balance. "Maybe. Guess you'd better drink it fast. That way you can't tell. So, business. Are you here to negotiate a peace treaty?"

"Nothing to do with you," he said, rolling the glass between his hands. "Unless you involve yourself. I'm just here for Edward."

It took me a second to remember that this was how Abe knew Edison.

"He's a popular guy. People keep inviting him to dinner."

"You have no idea," he said, menacing. And as he sipped his bitter beer, I shot a glance back at the bar, saw Sam on his cell covertly dialing the number I wrote on the slip, hoping my threes didn't look too much like eights.

• • •

It always feels good to be moving, going somewhere. Even if it is only to visit her at work. I think movement is the key. I need to be moving, getting more exercise, taking the air as they used to say. I have been doing more of it, in various ways, while she works. Something to do with my time because sitting in the house all day—as she thinks I do—is too stifling, like a too-tight, too-warm sweater. Uncomfortably comfortable.

We are in the same sweater, too. She seems content, perhaps even happy, but it feels wrong. Dangerous. On the surface things are calm, but it cannot last. We live in a crumbling, burning house of cards. A slow burn, granted, but building strength. She wants something from this . . . partnership that I cannot offer, and in her perfect image of us I think I am on the bottom, and she is on the top. Not that it matters, because it will kill us both, one way or the other, unless something changes. And she does not seem inclined to change.

Once she looked at me with fear, or awe, or respect. Now there is only pity, though she denies it. I am the bird with the broken wing, and she has me in her little shoebox and tends to me. The child never wishes the bird well. Healthy things fly away: you let them go, and if they were yours, they come back, or whatever bullshit that is. Healthy things fly away forever. Sick things come back. Broken things never leave. And I am broken.

I stop and rest near a bus stop, leaning heavily on the post. Knees aching but enjoying the pain, somehow. Pain is change. Pain is becoming. Pain means you are alive. Lack of pain is death. Is that what she wants? Painless, stagnant death?

I imagine her, for a moment, lying still in that hole I dug outside Portland. Would I be better off with her dead? Would she? She would have never been at the diner, and they would never have tracked her there, and I could be doing so much more. Images from the television return to haunt me, ideas that are not quite so ridiculous, plans, actions, worthwhile things that are more than this nothing I am. Than we are. Things I could be doing, instead of nothing. Changes I could be making. Getting back to what was.

Being change, instead of being changed.

I told her to practice, to learn to be alone, but I should have done that instead of watching myself rot and wither. I cannot end like this. I have little future left; I may as well borrow from the past while I still can. How long has it taken me to get this far? How old and broken am I, really? I reach for my phone to check the time and realize that I am apparently very much of both. For I have forgotten to take it with me, again.

• • •

Sam shrugged and pocketed his cell. Shit. No answer? What now? *Impro-vise.* Yeah, shut the fuck up, Nick. I'd been doing nothing but.

"Know how we found you?" Abe asked as I wrote four-letter words on my order pad.

"License? Fingerprints?" I asked, admiring my fingertips. "I should file these off."

"Edward's pills," he said. "One too many favors called in, not enough money, a few loose lips. I imagine you know all about that, though, right?"

I ignored the obviously crass innuendo as he chuckled and took his first big sip of bitter brew. It'd been months since Edison called in the last of his favors, to get medical help in the wake of our flight from Seattle. If that was really it, it had taken them quite a while to catch us. What had taken so long? And why was it Abe? He wasn't in Seattle, he was in San Francisco with . . .

"Nick," I said. "This is about Nick, isn't it?"

He laughed as he hit the Call button on my phone, then set it down to take a sip of beer.

"Nick thought he saw the big picture," he said. "But he only saw a small piece. He was just a pawn. Like the rest of them. Edward did me a huge favor when—"

"Us."

"Hmm?" he said, sipping. Frowning, watching the phone call go unan-swered.

"You said 'the rest of *them*,'" I said. "Don't you mean 'the rest of *us*'?"

"Oh, I was including you in there, don't worry. You're just a pawn, too."

He smiled, and I finally understood what he was getting at.

"Them, not you," I said. "You were what? Nick's boss? Handler? What-ever it's called?"

"Fixer," he said, almost having to choke the word out. "Is what you mean. But no, it's different. Nick was the fixer. He arranged the crew. I set him up with the work. Him and others."

"So why are you here? I thought everything was supposed to stay nice and separated."

"Yeah, well, things are different now." He angrily shoved the phone at me. "Call him."

"You think he can tell who dialed?" I toyed with the phone. "Maybe he's not even home."

"Well you better find him, because if he's not here in twenty minutes I'm breaking your fingers."

"Didn't do enough damage to me last time?"

He looked confused for a moment as he fiddled with his collar, but then it dawned on him what I meant: what had been done to me in San Francisco, after I'd been set up.

"That was Nick," he said. "Not me. I wasn't part of that."

"Oh, come on. Maybe you weren't there in person, but you knew what was going on. You set up all the jobs, right? I don't know why I had to be involved in your grand scheme, but—"

"You really wanna know what it was all about?" Abe asked, coughing. "Bec—"

"No. You know what, fuck it. I don't care. Shit happens. 'Cause of shitty people like you."

"Fine, enough chit-chat then," he growled. "Where the fuck is Edison?"

I leaned in conspiratorially, the better to see his reddening face.

"Answer my question, and I'll answer yours," I stage-whispered.

"What?" he asked, his face betraying a sudden, suspicious concern.

"Does it really taste like almonds?"

And at that point he'd had just about enough, and he tried to do something, but there was nothing for him to do but collapse across the table, twitching, clawing, heart seizing, exploding like fireworks. Perfect timing, really. But that was the end of perfect, because this couldn't not be noticed. People began rubbernecking and across the room. It was suddenly clear who *they* were, because they were on their feet and reaching into holsters. I lifted the menu and took a gun in each hand and as bystanders panicked, I slid under the table to collect what few thoughts I had.

Improvise. Right. What did I have that they didn't? What was my advantage? Where was the string to pull? What was nearby? Crayons. Olive oil. A corpse. Not much. Back to basics then.

Run. Always run.

I looked for exits, ways out. It was a math problem. Trajectories and angles, physical and otherwise. Back door? Two guys, methodically headed this way. Front door? Edison.

Edison?

• • •

I take the first one down about three seconds in. He never sees me, is facing the other way, and since he's pushing in and everyone else is trying to get out, I make a bold assumption that he's one of the bad guys—yeah, I know, perspective. I step right up behind and, really quite easily, no strength required, I push him off balance and bury his face in a stone planter. That's probably enough, all things considered, but just to be sure I pull out my 941 and water the plants red. I am disappointed when they turn out to be plastic.

Before anything else can change meaningfully, I find another likely target and fire a few rounds his way, the first two hitting bystanders but the last taking my target in the neck, I think. It's very hard to tell: panic increases, if that's possible, but this is what I want, just what we need. There are more of *them* than there are of *us* only if you leave out the sheep. With them on our team, albeit unwillingly, the odds are in our favor. I shoot at a few more, mostly intentionally missing and as hoped and expected, some turn and ridiculously move back into the fray.

I'm sorely tempted to just say fuck it and make this a party, but I restrain myself and save the ammo. They have heard the shots now—all of them, however many that is—and they go down low and so do I. Through the chaos and the tinnitus, I hear shots from across the room, Xtian's P3AT. And I think, for just a moment, that we have them right where we want them, and then I wonder about that word, "we."

The crowd thins, too much, too fast. And this is suddenly and completely not my thing, not my element. This does not work, guns blazing into a mostly empty room full of armed killers, this in fact is quite the opposite of *work*; it is guaranteed permanent unemployment. This is not even how they fight wars any more. This is stupidity. When I did this with Josh, I expected to die and nearly did. This time around, I'm really not looking forward to it.

I fall to my knees and get behind the planter and reload and look for a way out. Run.

But then there are two more shots, followed by silence.

I crawl to the corner of the planter and look, watch as Xtian walks across the room, gun in hand. And the last of them, mortal already and bloody besides, is scrabbling towards the kitchen. He pulls himself up and barely has time to turn to face her before she puts the gun up to his face and ends him, cold, face unblinking as he spatters and fades. Just like that.

She sees me, reloads, stepping over and on and through bodies, moving like liquid glass, and I stand and meet her gaze, incredulous.

"What're you doing here?" she asks loudly, voice almost inaudible through the ringing in my ears, and in response I just reach in my pocket and toss it on the ground, something small, insignificant, something sharp and now bent. Like so much is.

"You forgot your name tag," I say.

• • •

We didn't have time to burn down the restaurant like he wanted, barely had enough to get out the back and sneak through the park, ditching the guns beneath a footbridge in the goose-shit pond. We took the extra-long way home to make sure we weren't followed, even with him limping and gasping, and by the time we got back after dark both of us were exhausted. We put the news on immediately, and of course the restaurant was the top story, but they didn't even have our pictures up yet, probably in great part because the security cameras in the restaurant were just for show and had never worked. It would take a while for the police to find us, anyway. It's not like I'd used my real name and address.

Edison was most upset about the cyanide, which I found amusing. He did, too, after a few moments. I told him I was just taking his long-ago advice to heart. I'd planned on having to drink it myself, one day. I wasn't ever going through what Nick had put me through again.

"How long have you been carrying that around?" he asked as I carefully rinsed out the little vial of not-almond extract at the kitchen sink, idly thinking about all the marzipan-scented fish I was killing somewhere at the far end of the pipe.

"Since Seattle," I said. From when I'd packed up his things, assuming he was gone forever.

"You take it to work with you?"

"Took, yes." Work was past tense, now. Among other things.

"How many of my things do you have that I don't know about?"

"Noth— get out of there!"

I chased him into my room, which he playfully ransacked with nervous energy, and I think we laughed, though now it's hard to remember that part. It all ended with us laying there on the same bed for what seemed like hours, watching the ceiling, imagining little green stars, maybe, as I told him what little Abe had told me, and Edison tried to piece together a plot out of it.

I realized as he rambled that something felt inside-out. Some invisible string between us had snapped, and we were no longer tethered, to each other or anything else. Our whole life had been either him rescuing me, or me rescuing him, or one of us trying to get the other killed. What had happened in the restaurant was different. It was just two people in the same place doing the same thing. Two equal partners. And I wasn't sure Edison could handle working with someone who didn't need him. Someone he didn't need.

"What's happening here?" I asked. "It feels different."

"Something is brewing," he said, speaking with an energy he hadn't had in a very long time. "Some sort of power struggle. Realignment. Today,

Abe, here. Joe and Nick out west. Whoever that was in Seattle. Everyone has an agenda. It's starting to make sense."

"Is it?"

"I think they're all jockeying for position, taking what they can grab," he said, ignoring my question. "And there's lots to grab. Presidential last year, now mid-terms in November. I wonder who's left. Someone's head is missing, somewhere, and everyone is playing king of the hill. And with that game, there's only one guy on top at the end of the day."

"Or girl," I said. But I suspected he was picturing himself on a throne made of skulls.

"It's political. Like it was, before it wasn't. Someone is trying to take charge, trying to clean things up so they can start the engine again. This is why it feels different. Because it is different. Something is changing. And there will be carnage. I wish I knew more. Wish I was still in . . ."

I nodded and listened as he went on and on. And when he at last fell asleep, I got up and made some tea and watched some "fake news" as I cut and dyed my hair and began packing, because we were going to have to run.

I thought about Abe and Nick and wondered if someone had been helped by their deaths, or hindered. I thought about what was going on in the world, the elections, the wars, the social change. I thought about how deep this rabbit hole might go, and—if I ever fell in—how much it might hurt if I hit the bottom. Mostly, though, I thought hard about how Edison hadn't answered my question. When I'd asked about what was happening, I wasn't wondering about *them*.

I was wondering about us.

Threshold

08/16/2018

The lights flicker and die, something far off and electrical failing. Hopefully, wherever Xtian is shopping still has power. It is bad enough we have put off running for almost an entire day. I am fairly certain there are no more of *them* lingering nearby—or at least no more of Abe's crew—and we have covered our tracks. But we have nosy neighbors, and at some point someone is going to ask about the girl from the restaurant, and the old man she ran away with, and things will get back to us. We need to be gone by the end of the day. Weather notwithstanding.

One forgets thunderstorms on the west coast, they come so infrequently. Here in the east—at least this summer—they have come more readily, and unexpectedly. Sun at noon, rain by six, muggy all night. Any by itself might be tolerable, but in sequence they become something greater than the sum of its parts, something that sets me on edge and makes my skin crawl.

But weather is the least of my problems.

Has it been ten years? Nearly so. How many things thrown away, decisions altered, chances wasted, offers ignored, opportunities lost, bones broken. All because of a single decision I still cannot explain after all this time. She has guessed at it many times over the years: because I was lonely, because I wanted a child, because I pitied her. Because, because, because. At the time

I imagined it was because I saw something of myself in her, and still do, possibly more so now than ever, since last night, since I watched her emerge and become the very thing I always wanted her to be, the very thing I feared most. Feared, because it meant it was over.

Though it pains me to use this analogy because I hate that plaque and want to beat someone over the head with it every time I see one, she has at times held my hand and walked beside me, and at other times I have carried her, and lately she me. We have never been closer, more alike, than right now. We are both stagnant. Wasted. And perhaps that is why I am most able to do this, right now.

I stare at the dark television set for a while, then wander the apartment. Change into blacks, pull on hard boots, walk outside to feel the wind in my hair. Feel strong, for a change. I've healed more than I thought, and I'm certainly stronger than Xtian suspects. Just like she turned out to be stronger than I thought. There are things that will never be the same—my arms are always going to ache—but most of what matters is in order. I am well enough to fly.

I stand motionless on the threshold for a while, idly flipping the useless kitchen light switch on and off, watching rain sluice down off the corner of the roof, etching a long, deep gouge in the mud, excavating worms. As the long minutes go by, I cannot help thinking it into a grave. Whose, though? It does not matter, I think. In the end there is no difference. It is all force, from somewhere. Liquid, gaseous, kinetic, electric, emotional. Just some forces we cannot see, irresistible though they are. At least, until they meet immovable objects.

• • •

"I'm back," I said to the blackness as I entered, arms full of bags, wondering briefly and too late if this was more of *them*. I set my burden down, pulling the 92FS from the small of my back as I flipped the light switch, but the only one in the house was Edison, who immediately came in with an LED flashlight he'd just screwed the head onto. No longer necessary since the power was clearly working just fine now.

"Where have you been?" he asked.

"Kroger."

I set my gun on the table beside his, peeled off my wet blouse and tossed it in the sink, then switched on the TV out of habit.

"I told you to get supplies," he said. "Not groceries."

"Road food," I said, wriggling out of my jeans, leaving them where they lie. Changing one last time on the way out of town. If we were setting fire to the place on the way out anyway, no sense cleaning up. I stepped forward to get dry clothing, leaving a trail of water through the kitchen, and he shifted himself to the opposite side of the table, said something.

"Clif bars, sunflower seeds, bottled water, jerky for you. The not-spicy kind. And I got ice cream from UDF, but we have to eat that now. What did you say?"

"I said you need to leave," he repeated.

That was obvious, I thought. But something about the tone brought me back out of the bedroom in red underthings and bare feet like Robin the Girl Wonder. I resisted the urge to put my hands on my hips and strike a pose. For once, he didn't look away, caught my eye and kept it.

"What?"

"You. Are leaving. Now."

"Well, obviously—"

"Without me."

I was speechless for a second, but it didn't take very long to realize what he meant.

"Just—"

"Just like that, yes."

"Okay. Well, I don't want to."

"You have no say in the matter."

"The hell I don't."

"We can't keep this up," he said, gesturing with both hands. Talking faster, more intensely as he went. "They'll keep coming. This won't end. Not now, not with this, not especially after what just happened. There are things happening. Big things, things you can't even see. It's got layers of obfuscation, nothing in the middle but noth—"

He was starting to sound like a conspiracy theorist, becoming incoherent.

"Slow down and—" I tried.

"No. No! That's the thing we can't do. That's when they get us. When we stop. I don't want to go out like this, them coming in the front door some day, me in my easy chair. Not in a retirement home, or a wheelchair, or a hospital bed. And not a pathetic victim, a . . . wage slave, a welfare leech, a useless nothing. I don't want what I've become. We."

"So you kicking me out will fix that?"

"Yes. Perhaps. Not my problem."

"Oh, isn't it? And where the fuck would I go?"

In response, he reached over to the kitchen table and picked up a yellowed piece of heavily-folded paper, held it out to me. I didn't move.

"What is that?"

"Take it." And when I still didn't move, he balled the paper in his fist and threw it at me. I let it hit me in the stomach and fall to the floor. "Or don't. I don't care anymore."

"Did you ever?"

He didn't answer, turned away. I gave in, knelt down and grabbed the paper, uncrumpled it as I squatted and stared at a scribble of numbers. Ten digits and nine, ten digits and nine, over and over again, row after row. Each sequence was spaced out, three and three and four, then five and four. All but one of the rows was scribbled into oblivion in different shades of blue ink but the one at the bottom was in black, clear and recent. Ten digits and nine digits.

Phone number and zip code.

"What is this?" I demanded.

"Your father," he said. "It's your father."

• • •

She stares at the paper for a long while, then at me. Takes it in one hand and half-crumbles it into her fist. I think of the coins, the coins.

"This is my father's number."

"As far as I know. Been a few months since I checked."

"A few months?"

Weeks, possibly. I let the statement stand, though.

"How long have you been doing this?" she demands.

"It doesn't—"

"It does."

"Since the day I took you."

She goes quiet, then. Very quiet. Rocks forward and to one side, sitting on the kitchen floor, filthy with whatnot. We have never bothered to clean it.

"You kept the receipt," she says. I say nothing as she pushes herself across the floor until her back is to the wall. She stares me in the eye. I want to look away, but I dare not. "You kept the fucking receipt. In case you ever wanted to take me back. You were never sure."

"Yes. No."

"Why didn't you ever tell me?" Now, a tear, perhaps several. "Give me a choice."

"You wouldn't have used it." I shrug.

"Bullshit. All those times? When you asked me why I wouldn't leave. You know why? It was because I had nowhere else to go. You were all I had. All I knew. Know. You wanted to just be rid of me in the gutter."

"You know everything I know. Everything that matters, anyway. You will eat them alive. That last man, you killed without a thought. No hesitation. With that, you can do anything you want. Just not with me."

Quiet, long and hard. The rain picks up outside. Tears on the roof, making up for the scarcity in here.

"This is for both our goods," I say. "Either way I lose. This way I lose less."

"You need me."

"I do not. Needed, once perhaps. Not now."

She shakes her head. None of this should come as any surprise, but she does not want to hear it. I have a hard time believing any of it is actually getting through right now. It might be for naught.

"So that's all I am, then," she says. "Past tense."

"Or future imperfect. Simply not present."

She looks up. "Oh, I'm not present?"

She stands, unfolds like a crane and steps too close, and for the first time I realize we are the same height, see eye to eye, and she standing in socks, white at the ankles, black with grime underneath. Two sides to everything.

"Tell me you never loved me," she says.

"I never loved you."

She steps even closer, face next to mine now.

"I don't believe you," she says.

I don't move as she leans in, then, grabs my face and kisses me on the lips. Our first. It's not a polite kiss. When she moves away, nails gently raking down my cheek, I reach out and slap her in the jaw.

It's not a polite slap, either.

• • •

I wanted to hurt him back, tell him I lied, tell him I gave him up in Seattle, throw it in his face. Maybe even to prove to him that we could live with a lie, had been, and that it was not so bad. We could keep playing pretend until gradually it felt real and then was real. But I couldn't do it.

"So it's over," I said.

"It was over ten years ago, Xtian. We ended before we began. Me most of all. Look at me. Look at what I've become."

"So keep becoming. Change. Why end this now? We have time."

"No one has time," he said. "Time has us."

"You're just a coward," I said. "A fucking coward, afraid of change. Death afraid of dying."

"You're one to talk."

"Oh, I'm afraid? No. I just prefer what I know, here, to the shit out there. You know why the caged bird sings? It's safer in the fucking cage."

"You're afraid."

"And you're afraid of me staying."

"Then I guess we have the same problem. You."

I didn't want to do this. I was tired. Exhausted and mindless. I wanted to be in the car, listening to the radio as he rambled on about whatnot and nonsense, bare feet out the window stung by rain. I didn't want to leave. I didn't want to fight. I just wanted to sleep. To wake up and have this all be back to what it was, a day ago, a year ago. Ten years ago, even.

I collapsed into the chair opposite him, elbow on the table supporting my soggy head. Not defeated; disgusted.

"Look at us," he said, trying to talk me off of a ledge. Or maybe over the edge. "You really want this? This is mediocre and mundane. We're both better than this. Not both. Each. And you'll be better off without m—"

"Oh my god. Stop. Just stop. Listen to yourself. I don't need your . . . emotional . . . fucking cupcakes. Stop with the clichés and be real for once."

"I've nothing to give, real or otherwise. I'm done giving."

"Oh, sure. And you've been so generous these past few years. You really expect to live long without me, huh? It's me that cleaned you when you had broken arms. Me that helped you in and out of the tub when you couldn't stand without crying. And it was me that did all the work yesterday while you were hiding behind a fucking planter like a child."

I immediately regretted it. All of it. And then, almost immediately thereafter, I regretted regretting it. Some things just need to be said.

Especially truth.

• • •

And she has it right, exactly. I cannot be a doting grandfather, she crawling about the floor in diapers, and neither can I be the one in diapers. I will not be old, ruined with arthritis and tinnitus. Or Alzheimer's, Xtian tacking up signs around the house to help me remember: "Do not leave the water running. Do not leave the toilet seat up. Wipe yourself after you go. Do not wipe yourself on the laundry."

This must end here. For both our goods. The broken scarecrow gets his brain back, and the little girl flies home. The fucking end.

"I will give you a choice," I say, coldly.

She folds her arms on the table, collapses her head atop them, then looks up at me across the crumb-filthy wood. I step forward and shove my 941 across the table; it does a slow, lazy half-turn and strikes her in the right forearm as I pull her own gun towards me.

"What are you doing?" Head off the table.

"We are going to end this right now. One way or another. I will not live like this. So either you pick up that gun and end me, or I will end you."

She looks anything but confused. Disappointed, perhaps. Or resigned.

"You coward," she whispers.

"Call it what you want. Whatever word you use, it is absolutely preferable to the slow, lingering gut wound we have been living."

"Is that what I am? A gut shot?"

"Yes. You are a festering wound that will not clot. A tragedy that will never fucking end."

"You bastard," she says. "I should have let you die in Seattle."

"You should have. You have every reason in the world to pull that trigger. I tried to kill you. Nearly buried you alive. Took you away from everything you had. Put you in the hands of people who . . . I did it. It was by my hand. So many reasons for you to kill me. But only one matters right now: I do not regret any of it. I would do it all again. All of it."

And the next part hurts, it hurts to say, hurts to think, and it hurts me that it hurts, because I do not want to feel it. But it has to be said, because sometimes things just need to be said.

"I would let them take you, and hold you down, and ruin you. All over again."

Her face is a porcelain mask, but I can feel a shift nevertheless, electric.

"You would," she says, and it is not a question.

I nod, take a half-step back away from the gun, and drop my hands to my sides. "And I will do this, too. So if you will not end this, I will end it for you."

And my fingers ache, my wrist, my elbow, from my efforts the other day, from Seattle, from before even that. And somewhere deep inside, something not made of bone likewise hurts. Because I know that everything I have said is true.

I reach for the gun, and the moment I do, the very moment my aching bones stir into action, the microsecond the electrochemical reactions reach my muscles, she is no longer here and now, she is ancient and deadly and eternal, she is *kaishakunin*, second to the dishonored samurai, and she does not wait for the sword in the belly, the pain and anguish, she does not react to the motion, or the action. She reacts to the intent, the will. She knows me.

Before my hand can even clear the table, rise above my waist, she reaches out and in one unbroken, inevitable motion picks up the gun, aims at my head, and pulls the trigger.

I do not flinch.

Neither does she.

Chiburi

08/17/2018

Just after midnight, now. Nearly time for me to go. For both of us. She is cradling her knees in the living room, staring out the window. Short black hair, shorter and blacker than ever before, still wet from the shower. Wearing her tan chamois jacket over a black velvet top descending towards slit blue skirt atop black fishnets rammed into ankle boots. Everything locked together, like armor. She is motionless, but for a single finger stroking the trigger guard of the gun in her hand—her own, now. Wondering, perhaps, if she should pull that trigger, too. After all, she knows *that* gun is loaded. There is no point, though. And she knows that, too.

It is finished.

For a moment, I wonder if this could have gone any other way. I consider the different paths we might have walked, going all the way back to the beginning. But there is no point second-guessing. From the moment I took her, we were always standing on the brink of something from which there was no return. From the moment it began, it was ending. We were always falling.

Where will she go now? I only know where she came from, where she might have been if not for me. I have not kept close tabs on them, but I have seen enough to know that they have not fared well, and they would only have taken her down with them. If nothing else I gave her a decade to learn how to fly. If it had been them who pushed her from the nest, she would just be a fallen nestling, a broken, useless thing. Perhaps married young, like her parents, to raise her own as they raised her, teaching them dogma not worth teaching dogs. Mother, and wife, and broken. Falling on doorknobs and slipping in the parking lot, consoled by television, romance novels, fake friends who twitter and yammer about nothings. Computer games and diabetes.

She would be ordinary, the only thing she never was with me. The only thing she can now never be. Not after this. I have cared for her and carried her, broken her and mended her, killed her and brought her back—and she did the same for me. And why? Because something must be done. The world moves—it is a horrid treadmill—and we must move, too, or die. It is cruel, and so must we be. But victim or predator, we are always moving, and moving targets are hard to make out. Hard to understand. Her biggest mistake was trying to hold on to what could not be; mine was in letting her try.

I do not end here. For me this is a new start. But this part of me, this we: this ends.

But now I am just stalling. Time to move.

I have already gathered the things I will take with me, did that while she was out, once I had decided. Weapons, money. What pills remain. Identification. Four sorts, here; more in a box two hours away, one of the few caches I have left to draw on. The keys to the car. Nothing more. Nothing. I will leave the rest behind.

I will leave these chronicles.

I will finish this final entry, and close this laptop, and I will step into the kitchen, and walk past the fallen groceries, past the melted ice cream, and out the door. I will busy myself with plans, with somethings, with actions. Things are brewing, and I wish to be steeped in them. Perhaps I will attempt to reconcile with *them*. From every action there come opportunities, and perhaps they will recognize that. And if not, then I will act alone, as I so often have, doing what I can to rid this world of what corrupts it—the unwashed, uncouth masses.

There are things to break and I must break them, before I am too broken to do so.

Enough about me. This ends with her.

From the moment I saw Xtian, I recognized something of myself in her. Now it seems clear what that was. "The lion is alone, and so am I." We were both alone, from the start. Two individuals, never a couple of anything. Perhaps we were partners, but we were never equals, and I think partners must be that, at least. No, we were companions, even though I so immediately discarded that when she suggested it. We were animal companions. Two birds in the same flock. Or cloud. Going the same way, with the same penultimate destination in mind. And as is ever the case with companions, they become erstwhile, and it is time to sign yearbooks and say goodbyes and move on to ultimates, alone. We cannot be a pack of two. We were both designed to be alone. I hope she figures that out.

Before I leave, I will turn one last time to see her, to remember her then, a huddled little blackbird, curled on the rug. And I will watch her in silence and I will wonder again why I took her in the first place. Why, if I knew she was meant to be alone, did I not leave her alone. Perhaps instead of yet one more suffix on the same question, there will instead be a final answer.

And if not? Then at least there is this: that for a time, I walked with a girl named Christian, and she with me, and we were not alone.

And that mattered.

• • •

The slam of the door punctuated a very long sentence. Ten to life. Minimum time served. I wished for a moment there were final words, a whimper to follow the bang, but it would have been pointless. From the moment I'd pulled the trigger it was over. We both knew it. There were no more words, no more arguments. There was just utter exhaustion and disgust, and finality. I felt like a ghost, cold and gray and empty, left to haunt a barren house not my own. No fear, no sadness. Just absence. There were no more lessons; there was nothing to do now but hit the ground or fly. It was time to be in motion, to be elsewhere. This place was through with me, and I with it.

Only one question: where to?

My eyes drifted to the balled-up paper on the kitchen floor. I reached down and grabbed it, pondered. And then put it into my pocket.

No, not that. Not yet.

So, fine. What then?

I could easily have killed myself with possibility. Without him, there was no direction. Had I grown up and gone to school and done as I was told and listened to my elders like a good girl, I would have all of that. Not my own, entirely, but it would be something. It would be a thread to follow through the maze, a decision made for me. It was how everyone else did it and it seemed unfair I could not be led, too.

I wondered at this as I packed the things I would spare from the fire: all of my guns, some of my clothes, what money I'd been saving, the laptop—I could almost understand him leaving me, but why would he leave *that*? More importantly, where would I go? Certainly not west, not with the memories, and not with the chaos we'd wrought. Maybe close by. North or east. Places I had been. Lived in. Familiarity, and comfort of a sort. Fewer decisions to make, fewer unknowns. I could take the time to get used to acting on my own. Build up my world slowly, one molecule at a time. One cell.

"Practice," he had said. Practice being alone. Had I been with him long enough to do this alone?

Yes, I thought. Yes.

Was it fate that sent Delia my way that day? Was it free will that pushed me to take him back? Was anything in my hands, ever?

Yes, this once. Because in the end, it was me who chose to pull the trigger, me who was willing to end him. It was the choice that made all the difference, not the outcome. The outcome, after all, was assured. He'd seen to that. When I picked up his gun and pulled the trigger, I had no idea it was unloaded. I'll always wonder if he knew that, too.

And I'll always wonder if it would have made any difference.

Reverse Migration

09/01/2018

Of course I looked for him anyway. How could I not? A piece of me had fallen off and walked away. Phantom limb syndrome in its most extreme form. I knew he was gone, that it had ended by my hand. But though my mind was sure, my heart had to catch up. Muscles have memories. We fool ourselves far better than we fool others.

Since Edison's final gift to me was taking the car, my first problem was transportation. I spent a good chunk of my savings on an extremely used Camry born the same year as me, the first thing I saw on Craigslist that didn't sound like a lemon. It was easier than I thought it would be, just gave the guy a wad of cash and took the title since he had no idea what "notarized signature" meant. I assured him the paperwork would all be on its way to the DMV next week, you bet. But the only thing on its way within a week was me, flinging myself desperately away and hoping I would catch something before I hit the ground.

First was Buffalo, by way of Pittsburgh. I stopped three times, gas and bio breaks, but never ate, barely drank, drove the whole way with the radio off for some reason. Not enjoying the silence, but thinking it somehow necessary. And when at last I got into the city, I circled at least three times, trying to decide where to land. Like a ball in a roulette wheel, numbers and colors. 90, 190, 290, 33, 198, over and over. Until I picked a target and just went for it.

I hit the old neighborhood first, parked a few blocks away from where we'd lived, then wandered aimlessly. All the homes were occupied, and there were plenty of cars on the streets, but it seemed lifeless on some deeper level, as if it had died long ago and still hadn't realized it.

There was nothing there for me, so I moved on and drove to the few places I remembered well. The places we got ice cream. The Galleria. Anchor Bar. The Greek place where he got sick on bloody lamb. So much of what we did in Buffalo, what I remembered, revolved around food. Had we been avoiding conversation by filling our mouths? Or had he been fattening me up for the kill? I lingered for a while, sat on the small patio and watched cars trickle by while swarthy Greek men conversed in short sleeve shirts. Eating, and talking business, like we had. Secrets.

I ordered dessert from Noël, and as I waited, I dared to pull the laptop out, hesitating, wanting to keep hope inside. I'd kept it charged since leaving Columbus, waiting for the day I'd get the courage to look. It argued like a cranky old man, but eventually spun up and asked me for a password. I tried a few and failed. Just as I was about to give up, to call it futile, I smelled it. Faint, but definitely there. I moved closer, sniffed at the keyboard, startling some neighboring diners. And yes, there it was, unmistakable.

V - A - N - I - L - L - A

I read somewhere once that Thomas Edison breathed his dying breath into a glass vial, and Henry Ford (the car guy) locked it away in a safe, thinking he had captured the great inventor's soul. I can see the theoretical value for Ford, but what was the upside for Edison? In a best case scenario, his immortal soul was now trapped for all time. The only thing I can figure is that he felt it was holding him back, that leaving it behind would let the rest of him move on, unburdened. Wherever it was he thought he was going to end up.

I'll never know if that's why *my* Edison left his laptop behind, but what I found on it certainly looked a lot like what I imagined his soul might look like.

His desktop was a mess of shortcuts, horrid and scattered, some layered four or five deep. The trash was full and beyond, and though my brain itched to click "Empty," I resisted. Many folders, many files, some going back way before I was born, if I was reading the time stamps right. Back into dates that didn't make sense, dates that ended with eighty-threes and -fours. Meaningless, old people dates, file extensions I didn't recognize. Chaos. That was fine. I could work with chaos. She was my friend.

The first thing I looked for and found was a file dated September 8, 2008—the day he'd taken me. I opened it immediately, but I'd only gotten a few words in before I immediately closed it again, rubbing away the goose bumps. I made an alias to the file and stuck it in the corner of the desktop so I could find it again later. I needed something more relevant to where I was. Something from Buffalo.

• • •

091412.rtf

She again wants school. I cannot and will not tolerate that. It is enough that the television has tainted her mind with prayers and slogans, history according to someone. She does not need any help learning wrong. I can teach her right.

It seems hard to believe four years have passed since we met, since I took her out of her old life and gave her a new one, a chance at something better. Or perhaps worse; I have no idea. Four months and six days today, and she is already not what she was, yet neither what she needs to be.

What that is, I cannot say.

Would I make her into me? No. One is enough. Large events shaped me, pieces blasted off like Rushmore, creation in destruction. Rather, I have taken to this with a more delicate hand, shaving pieces here and there, slowly revealing what lies beneath. It is tempting to throw her into the fire, to see what happens. It might destroy her, or it might do what I have been unable to do. Push her out of the nest. And if she should fall? What would that mean for me? It is tempting to think nothing at all. But true?

Perhaps it is worth the effort. The events of the Fourth continue to resound in unexpected ways. The border is still locked down, for one, and (at least supposedly) authorities are still on the hunt for the perpetrators, or so they claim. It seems a bit too obvious to me. Certainly no one important was taken out; I know their names from the news reports, and how little they were. But there has been a clear impact: trucks backed up across the bridges nearly to the county line, passports out and security checks, on both sides of the border. This must have been their goal. Fear is an excellent motivator.

Perhaps I should keep that in mind for Xtian.

• • •

Fear as motivation. That entry of his was three months before he put me in a kill-or-be-killed situation in our apartment. It was interesting, reading into his inner thoughts at a time when a younger me had very little idea what was going on. But there weren't any great insights to be had; all it did was confirm what I'd already figured out, that he hadn't had any better idea what was going on than I had. I wasn't going to find him in Buffalo. I had to keep looking.

I tolerated the city for about a week while I decided where to go next, most of it spent in squalor near the airport. It seemed wrong to splurge, like I didn't deserve that yet. I finally broke down and bought a map, and it served as a bedspread for half that time as I read through his chronicles, sometimes adding my own words where his own seemed insufficient. Looking for clues, talking to myself. Planning. Forward from here was California, but there was no way he would go there. And going backward? What would that get me? A convoluted out-of-the-way trip out to Syracuse, down through Scranton to Harrisburg, back to DC, where it began for us.

It seemed the better option. Or at least, the least worst.

So I drove back east, the way we'd come a decade earlier, trying to find the same rest stops and failing, many of them now gone, others lost to shoddy memory. I got lost in Rochester and stopped for food. I poked around the laptop some more, feeling more and more confident, less like an invader. It was mine now, wasn't it? Beyond the initial password, none of it was protected, which I guess made sense. Everything here was past and gone. He only ever wrote about what he was doing immediately after doing it. There were no concrete future plans, nothing anyone could stop. If he had ever encrypted it before, he had decrypted it before he left. Possibly that last day, as I stared out the window while he spread vanilla extract on the keys. Maybe smirking.

Still, it felt like there was something for me to uncover. Some way to find him. I wasn't even sure why I was bothering, but I couldn't have been more curious if a box of old love letters had fallen on my head while digging through his closet. There were pieces of him everywhere, and so much I didn't know. Things he never talked about, feelings he never expressed.

I was still convinced I might find him, too. Something deep down wanting to track him down, change his mind. So I followed the breadcrumb trail.

I jumped back, way before he'd met me, all the way to the beginning. His beginning.

• • •

070483.DO

DRINKING IS OVERRATED. HAD TO. WOULDVE
SEEMED OUT OF PLACE HERE AND MY JOB IS
NOT TO STAND OUT. MY FAULT FOR COMING
DURING SOME ANNIVERSARY TODO AT HOTEL.
FAKED INTEREST. SICKENS ME. MAY STAY
A FEW MORE DAYS BEFORE 17927 AGAIN.
COULD BE WORSE. COULD BE AFGHANISTAN.

070583.DO

STILL IN SUNBURY. SHOULD BE GONE, BUT
NOT TODAY. HEADACHE. SHOULD KNOW BETTER

THAN TO WRITE THIS. FIXER SAID THIS IS
ONLY FOR SENDING UPDATES. THAT SEEMS A
WASTE. ITS MY MEWS SO HOW WILL THEY
KNOW? I CAN USE IT FOR NOTES. IMPORTANT
REMINDERS TO MYSELF. NUM 1. NEVER DRINK
NUM 2. NEVER TRUST ANYONE. ESP. WOMEN.

090883.DO
FINISHED MY FIRST JOB TODAY. KILLED
SOMEONE. NOT THE FIRST TIME OF COURSE.
DAD WAS FIRST. BUT HE WAS DYING AND
THEY WERE COMING AFTER HIM. THAT WAS
MERCY. THIS WAS WORK. OF COURSE I DO
NOT KNOW WHY THEY WANTED THIS MAN DEAD
OR WHAT THIS ACCOMPLISHES. NOT MY JOB
TO CARE, ONLY TO GET PAID. WHAT I DID
NOT EXPECT IS THAT I WOULD LIKE IT.

• • •

It kept up like that for some time, spelling gradually improving, along with everything else, as far as I could tell. But I kept coming up empty handed, missing some piece of the puzzle. The devil was hiding in the details, and there were just too many details. I shoved the laptop away, frustrated. I needed something to go on, some place to go. A week in Rochester was wearing on me, and even if I was slumming it, motel life was depleting my funds rapidly.

My eyes drifted towards my backpack, imagining the crumpled yellow ball of paper inside, tempted. My version of the apple in the garden. An easy way out. Just a few numbers and . . .

Numbers. I grabbed the laptop, scrolled back. There. Command-F. "17927." Return.

• • •

061585.DOC

They are not thrilled I have to relocate. They like having someone nearby to handle disposals. But they cannot really do anything about that now. Govt is buying everyone out of 17927 and it would be foolish not to take the cash and get out of here. It suddenly seems more urgent and I wonder what it was they dropped here recently that they want all of us gone, or digging up. I hear talk of shale and thorium. Some guy named Llewellyn. No idea. Regardless, I expected they would want me nearby but that is not the plan. Too many risk factors, suddenly. Understandable, sensical. Got a new number, and a new fixer, name of Craig. In the morning, I fly to El Salv. Craig has something for me to do there. First time out of country, first time flying. Hope I survive.

103192.doc

First time on the new laptop. Powerbook 180. I think it will do. Sick of swapping and at any rate this is going to be it for a long while, now that things have taken a shift. Govt declared eminent domain on 17927. Related? No clue. But if you wanted to hide something forever, that would be the way to do it. Either that, or dig it up. Things are quiet up top. Got everyone nervous, apparently. Craig says things are in the works, big things. Not sure what, exactly. I have heard NYC mentioned. And February. Nothing I will be anywhere near, nothing any of us will be close to. Except those of us who will be. Hope I am one.

031593.doc

Things have been confused, more so than normal. The WTC bombing threw everyone for a loop. Craig vanished. I wonder if they're shutting it all down, burying things like they did in 17927. Been in now what . . . thirteen years. Active nine of that. Now nothing? I wonder how much of this is political, if this goes all the way to the top, and how much a new regime changes things. I wonder, briefly, who I am really working for. Or, at least, who I was. For now it seems I work for myself. At least until they find me, or I find them.

I have a few places to run to, but no plans. A few contacts, but nobody I really like, some of whom feel the same about me. I did manage to reach one of my old 17927 connections. The conversation was brief. Stay out of the way. Keep your head down. Money is your problem. Someone will find you. Eventually. Then just a dial tone. Another burned phone.

Freedom sounds great, until you have it. Then what? No idea where to go now. Centralia? I wonder if anyone still lives there. As much as I hate Pennsylvania, maybe visiting home will inspire me. If nothing else I can look for some new places to hide a body.

• • •

When I first arrived in Centralia, PA, it immediately felt like something Edison had had a hand in, immense yet surreptitious. I couldn't help imagining that it had been he who had lit the slow-burning fuse that slowly ate up everything from below. The hidden and unseen and smoldering mine fire that had gotten the town legally wiped off the map.

I had to park a mile away and walk there, past the heaps of dirt, fragments of fence. I didn't have maps of the fire, couldn't see how it crept below, stretching out like cancer. I could only imagine it was everywhere I walked, waiting for the right moment to reach up and crack open the earth beneath my feet. The number 17927—the town's old postal code, rescinded by the post office over a decade ago—was painted, carved, taped on everything, but at that point there was little left. If you didn't know there was once a town here, you might not realize it ever was. Just funny graffiti. Almost every building gone, most minor avenues covered in brush, quick-growing trees converting the area to forest. Erasure.

It was foolish to be there, of course. Not just because of the dangers, the things the signs warned of as I wandered through the trees, imagining houses, children, him. More because there was obviously nothing there to be found. It was a graveyard, a place where secrets went to die. Whatever it was that got buried there, it was gone. Like he was gone.

Some things, when you dig them up, they try to pull you in.

I walked back to the car, disappointed in myself. He'd come back here once, but not recently enough to help. A false lead. Where else had he gone? Back somewhere in New York?

Open laptop, Command-F.

• • •

091101.doc

Nothing to watch on television. Same shit about New York on every channel. Makes me wonder what they really have going on, with a distraction this big. Could be anything, with the whole world looking one way. Banks, perhaps. Whatever it is, *they* are involved. Otherwise, why would Marc have called me just last night, after five years of nothing? No details on a job yet, but maybe soon—going to try to connect me with a different cell in Buffalo. I can only imagine what the job might be, there. Do not really care. Work is work.

Laptop is dying. Maybe I will get a PowerBook. Worthwhile investment—if I might be working again, soon, I might have more to say to myself. And this is all that keeps me sane. Note to future self: that was a joke. You are *not* sane.

Not bad timing, anyway. I need to go shopping anyway. Marc says I need to pick up a new clock. Something about birds. Whatever.

• • •

"Come on, you bastard," I said aloud, "give me something I can actually use."

I read through the last entry again. Marc? Who was Marc? Command-F returned hundreds of results. I opened a few at random, scanning through the text for something more relevant to my current interests. And found it, at last, in the most obvious of places.

Not at the beginning of my story, but just before, in the prologue.

• • •

043008.docx

I get the call in the middle of the night. I would complain about being woken from a sound sleep, but I have not slept soundly in months. And I cannot ignore this one. It is the first call I have gotten on this particular phone, and of course the last one I ever will.

"Tom." I recognize the voice immediately, though it has been years since I last heard it, angry, accusing. Five years? Six? I am surprised, uncertain, but immediately willing to listen, no matter what the words. One syllable is all it takes to get my blood flowing, anticipation or something similar. Finally.

"Marc?"

"How you been? Still on the west coast? How's the job market?" Marc, never one for small talk, dropping immediately into code. Thinly veiled, but appropriate, considering the state of the economy. The best kind of lie.

"Not great."

"You want to come to DC? Got some work, maybe." Interesting. Bush one was barely out the door last time I had a job there.

"You still working, uh, at that same place?" I ask.

"Yeah. Same shitty office. Come on out and interview. Dress up, bring your fancy briefcase. The Black one. We can ride the Metro down to the Mall."

"Yeah," I say, decoding. Briefcase bomb, September, subway. "Sounds good."

"Great. Just, Tom, you gotta promise me something."

"Yeah?"

"Don't blow this like last time."

And silence.

Unsure, again. Hateful uncertainty. It worries me a bit, the timing, this no doubt being political somehow. And why me? I have done some good work over the past few years, but nothing I can take credit for—even if I wanted to. Am I expendable? Stupid thought. Of course I am. And perhaps that is reason enough.

How can I refuse? I have been west for too long. Grown soft like old flannel. I have fallen into deadly patterns in hibernation, lazy, sleepy. Have stopped caring enough to try and change things. Perhaps this will be good for me. Get the fire going again, make things happen. Things that need to happen . . .

I think about it for the rest of the night, write out the pros and cons on index cards and paper towels, and come up with more cons by far. But it is really all a waste of time. I do not need to think about this. This is inexorable. This is inevitable. This is already happened. I have been waiting for this moment to arrive, and it has arrived, and though my body has not yet caught up, I have already decided. My mind is already out the door and flying east, into a growing fire.

Behind me, nothing but ashes and black.

Edison North

09/14/2018

On my way back to where it began I missed an exit and wound up in my old neighborhood. I knew my family was not there anymore, but it wasn't true until I saw it with my own eyes, saw the strange children on the front lawn, vinyl siding slapped over peeling paint, a new roof, all of it in different colors. I wondered how long they waited. How long they looked for me. Probably not very long.

The park where I'd spent so much time as a child had grown in all the wrong ways, new landscaping, a new fence where I used to be able to cut through the neighbor's yard. I took off my shoes, wandered through fresh-cut grass, trying to make a connection. Walked barefoot on blue moss beside what used to be the playground. Nothing was recognizable, myself most of all. I wasn't the same *me* anymore.

Maybe that's why I never thought to look harder for my family. They weren't mine any more. And I wasn't theirs.

I left and took surface streets from there, sick of the traffic on 66. Why had he taken that Metro job? Why had they given it to him? DC needed all the mass transit it could get. Or maybe that was the reason; shut that down, shut everything down. Gridlock. And somewhere in the midst of that, something else, something small, but meaningful. What? I had no idea. Would never know. Wondered if anyone alive knew. Besides him.

One person, at least. Whoever hired him for that job, whoever had arranged for him to be in town that day, had pulled the strings to place him in my path.

• • •

It felt strange to be in the restaurant again, as if my presence corrupted the memory. But of course memory was no match for reality anyway. Remodeling had been done. New construction, new menus, more parking. Streets had been widened. There were new shadows. Larger trees and more of them. It felt wrong but still familiar, in an uncanny way. It seemed to fit the fact that I'd taken my time, had avoided the anniversary by about a week. It was all a near miss. Close, but not quite the same as it had been. Like me.

I forced myself to go through the motions, as if this would somehow help me find him again. Parked in the same spot he had—back behind the dumpster, facing the next street over—walked back the way we'd come, through the glass door and into the lobby. It was still early afternoon, and there was no sign of a crowd, so I walked right up to the counter and ordered a medium Diet Coke, big enough to give me time to think. The cashier was twice my age, the sort I'd normally expect to be running the place. Economy's a bitch.

"Do you want a large? It's only twenty cents more."

"N—" I started to say, a kneejerk reaction to his upselling. But it occurred to me that I might be a while, and the more I had to drink the longer I'd be a customer.

"Yes, thank you, Willem," I said.

"Do you want anything else?"

I sighed. A million responses went through my head, a thousand reactions, some over. "No. Thank you."

I tried to remember which booth Edison had sat in, then realized I hadn't seen him sitting, and picked one quite at random, a corner near the door. It seemed like where he would be—everything visible, no one behind him. Safe, for him. Not for anyone else.

And then I sat and waited. Waited for . . . I didn't know what. A feeling? Ghosts? Whatever it was I expected, I was disappointed. There was not going to be a revelation, a chill down my spine. Had I come all this way for nothing? Was this—this nothing—what I needed? There had to be more. So I brought out the laptop, woke it up, and checked to see if the store had an open wireless network available. I was surprised to find that there were two.

I chose the one named "17927."

There wasn't much to see. One single network connection, one damned login window that would not accept the stored username and password no matter how many times I tried. I blamed the computer, I tried rebooting, I tried changing network settings, I tried everything I could think of with a laptop running an obsolete operating system.

I looked for clues. Whose network was this? Why had the laptop connected to it before? Who was in DC? Marc? Was he still around? Was this his? Where was he located? Nearby, if it was wireless. But what was nearby? A few restaurants, a supermarket. There were some tall buildings and an apartment complex several blocks away, but it was way too much ground to cover. And the moment I moved from this corner of the restaurant, "17927" went away. Whatever it was, it was intended for just this place. Just this booth.

I needed to talk to Marc. He, of all people, would know where to find Edison. He might not tell, but I had to ask. And so I sat like a fool, typing in no end of different usernames and passwords, connecting and ditching. I tried the obvious—Edison, Thomas, Vanilla—along with every bit of code I'd heard Edison, or Abe, or Nick, or any of them speak. Then I got creative and vulgar. Then I got a hotel room and slept, and came back the next day for three meals, two hours at a time, and pretended I was writing the great American novel when in fact all I was typing was this irrelevance in-between his recollections.

The best I could hope for was that someone was logging this mess. That they would notice my failure, and come find me. I was right.

It took three days.

• • •

"You can stop now," said a voice. I peeked over the laptop as a woman slid into the booth opposite me. A bit younger than Edison, graying through the blonde at her temples. Dressed smartly but not overly so, business casual a bit heavy on the casual. Honest eyes, deceitful lashes. Tray full of burger and fries with which she knocked my empty salad container aside, plastic fork skittering to the floor.

"Every time you do that, I get a text message," she said, voice as crisp and thin as her fries. "Do you have any idea how much that costs on a pre-paid phone?"

"Sorry," I said, though I wasn't. She glared as I shut the screen to conserve what little battery I had left, then started peeling open condiment packets, lots of them. Long, delicate fingers, fingernails just long enough to be feminine, not quite long enough to make me itch with unease and try to bite them down.

"I had to shut off my cell. That was quite inconvenient." She pointed at me with a cluster of fries, dipped them in ketchup and crammed them in her mouth all in one go. Chewed, swallowed, spoke. "And you know, once would have been enough. Really. One time. I still would have come. I leave town for three days. Three days. And . . ." She shook her head, took a long sip of her drink, wiped her mouth with a napkin, and suddenly appeared to get over it all, smirking.

"I'm amazed that relic is still running," she said as I turned the laptop over in my hands and finally set it down on the table. "Tom got sick of chasing upgrades, said he'd only replace something when it broke or died."

The way she looked at me, it was clear this also included me.

"You're . . . ?" I asked, somewhat bewildered.

She took a large bite of burger, immediately wiping her mouth. Fastidious. She waited until she was done chewing before answering. Polite, too.

"Marcella," she said crisply, emphasizing the soft c that couldn't possibly come across in a text file without a cedilla attached.

"Ed— Tom's fixer," I said, using the name she'd used. She didn't react to the slip-up.

"Former. But yes. Kind of ironic though, when you say it like that. Tom is unfixable."

"I'm C— Nichole."

"I know all your names. We don't need an introduction. We already met. Not that you would remember. You were asleep."

But, suddenly, I did . . .

• • •

Half-awake. Words. Shouting.

"Didn't I say not to do anything stupid? Didn't I? Why is she still here?"

A shrug. Shadows under the door.

"Why not?"

"Did you kill her parents?"

"No. They weren't there." A long pause, then: "I'll figure it out."

"Get rid of her."

"There's nothing stopping her from leaving."

"Isn't there. Why hasn't she left already?"

"Maybe she doesn't want to. When she leaves it'll be her choice."

"Well, you be sure and let me know when that happens." Movement, pacing back and forth. Angry. "I am so sick of cleaning up your messes. What is this now, the third time? This is not why I woke you up. This is not part of the job."

"I—"

"I swear to god, Tom. The office will recover, but if you fuck up this job because of a fucking child, I will fucking end you. I will end all that you are."

"And what exactly am I?"

A pause for thought, not nearly lengthy enough.

"An asshole."

• • •

"This was your office," I said. "This is *the office.*"

"*An* office," she said. "Sort of. Not that Tom had any respect for it."

I looked around the lobby, needlessly. It was all new, but it was all the same. I think that was part of the reason Edison had been so fond of places like this. Familiarity.

"Technically, the stuff that matters is a mile away and several stories up, but there's nothing there but a desk, a server, a fax machine, and directional wifi. Pointed here, and a half-dozen other places nearby: coffee shop, library, park bench. It's a hundred square feet of empty behind a locked door. We don't use it much anymore. It's obsolete, like that thing."

No wonder he never worried about the cameras here. It was safe. And suddenly I got a much better sense of how deep this thing went. The conspiracy sites liked to talk about how some secret agency controlled every single camera in the country. Maybe it was true. And maybe, just maybe, if you have the ability to see everything, you can also decide when to look the other way.

"I'd forgotten about this place, frankly," she said, eyes narrowing as she conjured up an unpleasant memory. Sour gaze. "He got in touch with me, I guess it was the day he left Columbus? A lot's happened since then, most of it not in his favor. He thought things got bad after SFO . . ."

"What did he say?"

"Not much. Mostly he talked about how you sold him out in Seattle."

He knew.

It was like an ice pick in my chest. All along, he knew what I had done. And yet he went along with it, watched me stumble over my lies, for years. I hated him for it, hated myself for lying, for not knowing better, for not assuming he'd see through it. I wanted to be dead, ten years ago, dead on the floor of this restaurant, by his hand.

"He did?" I managed to croak.

She nodded as if we were discussing the weather.

"He told me everything. How you gave him up, how they took him to the motel and tortured him, for fun or for information, he wasn't really clear on that. Or who they were."

"Do you know who they were?"

"Yes," she said. Period. She maintained eye contact with me as she reached for a french fry and bit it in half. Clearly that was the end of *that* line of inquiry.

"I guess you don't want to talk about that sort of stuff here," I said.

"They don't care," she said, waving her hand towards the counter as if brushing away a fly. "They don't know to care. Morons. Some of them don't even know what went down here ten years ago, and there's a memorial plaque on the wall."

I hadn't noticed it when I came in, and decided I would continue not noticing; I had no desire to see who was deceased. I was sure I'd known some of them.

"Doesn't matter anyway. They'll all be replaced by robots and kiosks in another year or two." She took a moment to polish off her burger, sip, and then continued. "Point is, he didn't want anyone getting the wrong ideas, coming after the wrong person, especially after that San Francisco debacle. He wanted me to know who did it."

I casually reached across and took one of her fries. My other hand was rummaging about under the table for my new handgun.

"And then he told me that he was solely responsible."

What?

"Told me he pulled some fucking James Bourne shit, murdered his way free. Got home, found you hiding in the closet, chewed you out, made you lick his wounds for a while and then cut you loose. Then he asked me if I believed his story."

"And do you?"

"Not a word."

Here we go. Lean back, calm, nice and easy . . .

"But I don't care. So what he told me is what I told *them*. So it's good as true and no one is going to come after you, at least for now. You can put the gun away."

I debated for a moment as she finished the last of her fries, neatly licking the final traces of salt off her fingers. She seemed very confident. Were there snipers somewhere? Maybe I could . . .

"You could," she said, reading my thoughts, sizing up the distance between us. "But it would be pointless, and unlike the last time, the cameras in this place are in working order. Besides, I have no intention of hurting you. Quite the contrary. I have something for you."

Intrigued, I returned the LCP to its intimate resting place and sat back. "What is it?" I asked.

She shook her head as she finished off the last of her drink with a slurp and rattle.

"I'll tell you outside," she said. "I need a cigarette."

She cleaned up our table as I packed up the laptop, and then we wandered outside to the parking lot so she could partake. She offered me one, but I declined.

"I would never have guessed you smoked," I said.

"Only when I eat this shit. Gets rid of the taste."

An awkward silence reigned for a few minutes. I'd never smoked with someone before. Were you supposed to interrupt their smoking? Was the smoking the point?

"Okay, here's the deal," she said. "If he taught you *half* of what he knew, I can use you."

"Use me for what?"

"Tom was exceptionally good at making messes. As far as I can tell, you're pretty good at cleaning them up. I can use someone like that. There are a lot of messes to deal with right now."

"Like what?"

"It doesn't matter," she said. Puff of smoke. "You work, you get paid."

"You're telling me I should work for you without knowing why I'm doing it?"

"He would have."

"And as you just pointed out, I am not him."

She thought about that for a second as she took a drag.

"There are three reasons to take a job," she said. "Any job. First reason is you're good at it. You're good at farming, you farm. Second is if you get something out of it. Money. Enjoyment. Fulfillment. Whatever."

She paused, then, seemed to struggle to find words to wrap her third category around. "Bird flu. Comes and goes. It came back big, a couple years ago. The vaccine killed a few thousand people, worldwide, but it maybe saved millions. Was it worth distributing, knowing people would die because of it?"

I shrugged. Edison had said much this same thing before, numerous times, and in not so many words. I wondered if there was an employee handbook.

"Nothing changes until there's reason for it to," she went on. "There are small losses, but a catastrophe might be averted. Vaccine hits before the epidemic, immune response prevents catastrophe. If not, you get a New York. London. Madrid. Moscow."

She turned her cell on to check the time. Frowned.

"Anyway, that's the third reason. Sometimes there are things that need doing, things no one else is going to do. Garbage men. Taxi drivers."

"And who decides that? The Abes of the world?"

"What exactly do you know about him?" she asked, narrowing her eyes.

"Only what he told me." This time it was my turn to end a line of questioning.

"*They* decide," she said, returning to her point. She gestured upwards to indicate people higher up the food chain. "They find reasons to act. We act. Other people react."

"Yeah, I get that. But *they* are . . . who? There has to be someone in charge, right?"

There was a short silence as she either prepared a lie or tried to sort out some complicated truth. My mind skimmed Edison's chronicles to determine if I already knew. Edison's father, the government. False flags.

Northwoods. Centralia, Oklahoma, Waco. MKUltra. New regimes and broken cells. Apart from the pieces I was part of, any of it could have been fiction. I needed truth.

"You remember that shit with the ninety-nine percent a few years ago?" she asked. "How one percent of the population holds most of the wealth and power?"

I nodded.

"Their aim was off, by a few factors of ten. Try more like point zero zero zero zero zero zero one percent." She counted on her fingers, maybe missed a zero, maybe added one extra. "Maybe a thousand out of seven billion. But despite what the nuts say, there's no New World Order. There's nothing new about it, and certainly nothing orderly. It's too fucking big to manage."

"So the all-seeing eye doesn't exist."

"Oh it exists. Anyone who can is recording everything they can get their hands on, and anyone who can afford it is buying it all up and poring through it. There's more than one reason Congress keeps doing away with Internet privacy laws. But there's no conspiracy. It's been going on forever. Only difference now is efficiency. There's so much more you can do when you can see everything. There are patterns in that data, if you look hard enough. Eddies in the water that for all I know might be predicting who's going to be at war a century from now. And there are people who have a vested interest in that war. That theoretical war."

"Then whoever that is, they're the ones in control."

"No. What I'm saying is that who is in control, whether anyone is in control at all, is irrelevant. There are people with money and people with power and people with information, and when you put those together you can make things happen. But to try and define that as some sort of control is idiocy. There are people making decisions, yes. There are people who decide to make decisions based on those decisions. And so on, eventually it gets to us. To me. Then I call someone I can trust to get the job done. Or, god help me, someone like Tom. But to call that control? To figure out who's in charge? It's pointless."

"Shit happens."

"Exactly," she said, stubbing out her cigarette on the curb and pocketing the butt. "And you're either the one it's happening to, or the one making it happen. Which would you rather be?"

She offered to walk me to my car, and I accepted. I didn't plan on driving this one for very much longer anyway, so it didn't matter if she could ID it.

"So, you don't know where he is?" I tried, hating myself for bringing him up again. I knew she wouldn't answer, but I wanted to keep her talking, feeding on crumbs, anything she was willing to give.

"No," she said. "It was two weeks ago. He's vanished. And even if he wanted to be found, with everything he's done, there's no coming back."

"There's nothing you could do for him?"

"There's nothing I *would* do. I won't miss him a bit. He was just a co-worker and a bad one at that. He was useful because he was willing to do anything, but that made him dangerous. Bad for everyone around him, present company included. He ruined everyone he came across."

With one exception, I thought. I had made it this far mostly *in spite of* Edison. But at least some of what I was, was *because* of him. And I didn't feel ruined. I felt . . . whole. Entire.

"So that's it," said Marc. "You're on your own now, Christian or Nichole or Edith or whatever. You want in, you call. I'll arrange it from there."

With that, she reached into a pocket and handed me a crisp twenty, already folded in half, and held it so that her fingernail emphasized the serial number. Counterfeit or real? Who else was involved? The Treasury Department? The IRS? I tucked it in my pocket, next to the balled-up scrap Edison had left me. These were my two choices now, each with some appeal, neither one ideal. Maybe I could flip a coin to decide, after Marc had gone. It was hard to believe she was part of a plot to manipulate world events. She smelled of nicotine and soap, smiled, laughed, ate french fries. She seemed nice. Normal.

Long, awkward pause. Say goodbye, Christian.

"I wonder," I said instead, "how things would have gone if it had been you in the restaurant that day, instead of him."

"That's easy," she said. "You would have been the first one I shot."

And then she smiled and walked back towards "the office." Stopped after ten steps, just at the door, and turned like a duelist.

"One last thing," she said, barely audible over the traffic, the wind.

"What?"

"He left a message for you, if you ever showed up here. A bit odd, but . . . he said when you pull out of here, watch that right hand turn. Carefully."

After that she was just gone, as if she never was. Nevertheless, the cryptic instruction rolled around in my head as I pulled out of the lot and onto the side street. And as I waited at the intersection just like we had ten years ago, I remembered him doing the same thing I was doing: watching, carefully looking both ways. Left and right.

Left, no traffic, street light, telephone pole.

Right, fire hydrant, mailbox, street sign . . .

• • •

After we've gotten ice cream at the mall, he puts the car in gear and swings out towards the street, cutting across empty spaces, the shush of water as we pass through puddles. When we reach the street, he stops to wait for traffic to clear, and peeks in the mirror to watch me watching him. Waiting for him. He lowers his eyes, closes them, as if searching for an answer.

And he suddenly remembers the street sign beside the restaurant, the one he's seen dozens of times, the one we'd driven past as we escaped: N. EDISON.

"Edison North," he says, feeling it out as he says it. "My name is Edison North."

And he is, for a while.

For me.

Acknowledgments

It's easy to pinpoint when I started writing *Blackbird*: July 6, 1999. It's less easy to say when it was done; it was a long journey with many starts and stops, and it involved a lot of people who contributed to *Blackbird*'s evolution in some small way, whether they are aware of it or not.

Thanks of course to my agent Chris and the people at Victoria Sanders & Associates, my editor Chelsey and the folks at Skyhorse Publishing, and my original copy editor Jennifer. People like them do a lot, but their most important job is letting you know when something is done growing, and when it needs to hang out in the nest a bit longer. Until it's ready to fly.

Thanks as well to all the superfans who've followed *Blackbird* on its long journey and suffered through early drafts, including Aaron, Ana, Brian, Colin, Dan, Danielle, Dustin, Erin, Felix, Frack, Jason, Jerry, Jessica, Joshua, Kimberly, Leon, Melissa, Mercedes, Mike, Milly, Rachelynn, Renee, Ryan, Sean, Su-Anna, both Nicks, both Wills, and the rest.

Special and/or oddly specific thanks go to: Calisa, for the box cutters; Ean, for documenting the moment *Blackbird* was born; Gosu, for giving Xtian a voice; Jestyr, who helped get this entire journey started; Juge, for the stars on the ceiling; Kenshiro, for the MANPADs and his advice on keeping it real; Melinika, for the bird clock; and Rois, for the map font. You all deserve thanks for a lot more than that, but those things in particular helped shape this novel.

I would also like to thank: Drew Curtis of Fark.com for helping publicize *Blackbird* in its fledgling online serial days; the people of the #fark IRC channel, Iconoclast MUD, and Writer's Block Discord server; my parents, for always being my biggest supporters; and especially my wife, for putting up with me throughout most of this process.

To all of them, and all of you: the next one won't take nearly as long.